# MUSIC TO MY SORROW

# MUSIC TO MY SORROW

## Mercedes Lackey
### and
## Rosemary Edghill

MUSIC TO MY SORROW

A Baen Books Original

Baen Publishing Enterprises
P.O. Box 1403
Riverdale, NY 10471
www.baen.com

ISBN-13: 978-1-4165-0917-2
ISBN-10: 1-4165-0917-8

Cover art by Jeff Easley

First printing, December 2005

Library of Congress Cataloging-in-Publication Data

Lackey, Mercedes.
  Music to my sorrow / Mercedes Lackey and Rosemary Edghill.
      p. cm.
  "A Baen Books original"--T.p. verso.
  ISBN-13: 978-1-4165-0917-2
  ISBN-10: 1-4165-0917-8
  1. Banyon, Eric (Fictitious character)--Fiction. 2. Parent and child--Fiction. 3. New York (N.Y.)--Fiction. 4. Evangelists--Fiction. 5. Musicians--Fiction. 6. Brothers--Fiction. 7. Wizards--Fiction. I. Edghill, Rosemary. II. Title.

  PS3562.A246M87 2006
  813'.54--dc22

                                    2005025956

Distributed by Simon & Schuster
1230 Avenue of the Americas
New York, NY 10020

Production & design by Windhaven Press, Auburn, NH (www.windhaven.com)
Printed in the United States of America

10   9   8   7   6   5   4   3   2   1

*To Brenda Schonhaut and "Molly"*

# Contents

*The moon's my constant mistress*
*And the lonely owl my marrow*
*The flaming drake and the night crow make*
*Me music to my sorrow*

—Tom O' Bedlam's Song

# PROLOGUE:
## SHUT OUT THE LIGHT

*Another day, another stupid office.* Devon Mesier was a veteran of offices, of waiting rooms. They all had the same happy-happy magazines, the advertisement flyers for this or that pill to cure depression, anxiety, ADHD, ADD, and every other clinical name that shrinks had thought up to slap onto kids who didn't come up to their families' standards of appropriate behavior. He almost wished his parents would try pills on him for a change. If he didn't like what the pills did to him, he could always throw them up; one of the bulimic chicks at the last concentration camp had taught him how to throw up at will, 'cause a good way to get a "camp counselor" off you was to projectile vomit on him. And if you started throwing up, they tended to get nervous and stick you in what passed for an infirmary and leave you alone.

He was fifteen, and long before he'd gotten anywhere near "troubled teenhood" he'd seen more of shrinks' offices than a clinical psychologist four times his current age. He'd been through every kind of "give in and submit" camp, therapy, program, and counseling there was, and by now he knew they came in two kinds: the kind that put the broken kids back together, and the kind that tried to break kids that weren't broken.

1

Devon wasn't broken, and he didn't intend to break.

He didn't know *why* he and his parents had been on a collision course ever since he could remember. It wasn't that he had a deep-seated hunger to set kittens on fire, or any of the more terrible things he'd found out that other kids did once they'd started putting him into those programs and groups calculated to turn him into a Good Little Robot. But . . .

He asked questions. He always had, ever since he'd been a little kid. He'd wanted to know "why," and how people knew what they knew. Dad said that made him "insubordinate." He'd gone and looked the word up in the dictionary, and said he wasn't. Dad had refused to discuss it. Mom had (as always!) taken Dad's side. Devon had yelled. He'd been sent to his room. He'd gone out the window. He'd only been gone a few hours and a few blocks before a policeman had brought him back, and Dad had been even more furious.

He guessed he'd been seven, then. Things had never gotten any better. One of the few psychologists Devon met that he'd actually liked had told him his only problem was that he was twelve—which meant he was subject to whatever his parents determined was "best" for him, too bright for his own good—which meant he didn't just accept things passively, and didn't suffer fools gladly—which meant that when things didn't make sense to him he was always flapping his mouth about it. Unfortunately, in Devon's opinion, the world was full of fools. That headshrinker hadn't lasted long, not past the first "parent conference." Evidently the man didn't tell the 'rents what they wanted to hear.

*But I can outwait them,* Devon told himself grimly. Sometimes he wished he could stop fighting with his father, but he was damned if he was going to back down first. And he was double-damned if he was going to turn himself into the mindless drone his father wanted! Particularly this time.

While he'd been getting himself kicked out of the latest *Stalag* (for cheating—although he hadn't been; if there had been any copying going on, it was some of the others cribbing from *his* papers) apparently Mom had gotten Religion. He hadn't been home from Arizona a week before the behind-his-back phone calls started again—this time to something called Christian Family Intervention, which sounded pretty depressing—and then, as usual, Mom cancelled all her house showings for the afternoon and Dad came home from the office early and the three of them got into the Lexus to drive off somewhere.

Of course they didn't tell him where. It wasn't as if anyone in the Mesier family *talked* to anyone else. Certainly not to him. He was just supposed to do as he was told—or better yet, figure out what he was supposed to do and say by some sort of telepathy.

Screw that.

They didn't want *him*—they wanted their idea of him, which was something else completely—and they didn't want to let him go his own road, either. So by now Devon figured he didn't owe them very much at all.

To his vague surprise, their destination was Atlantic City, only a couple of hours away. Not a place Devon would have thought of as a hotbed of Christian family values. Casinos and Miss America. Right.

They didn't go anywhere near the Boardwalk, where most of the casinos were, and the rest of the city was pretty thud. He'd almost decided they weren't stopping in Atlantic City at all when they pulled off into a business park on the outskirts of the city that said it was the location of—get this—The Heavenly Grace Cathedral and Casino. There didn't seem to be anything else here.

Cathedral *and* Casino. The sign made him tilt his head to the side like a dog hearing something weird. What next? Synagogue and cathouse? What kind of Christian yahoos built themselves casinos? Holy Dice-Rollers? Maybe his parents had finally gone crazy. Maybe he could become a ward of the state.

They parked around the side of the building—to Devon's great disappointment, since he would have loved to spend more time inspecting the front of the building, with its three-story-high light-up cross that looked like it was made of LEDs, which was excellent—and went in through a perfectly normal-looking door marked "Heavenly Grace Ministries." Devon's spirits sank. He hated preaching, whatever flavor it came in, and it looked like he was in for some gold-plated holy-rolling here, and no dice involved.

But inside it was a perfectly normal office building—they weren't even playing hymns on the Muzak—and when they'd taken the elevator to their floor and found the waiting room of Christian Family Intervention, it looked like every other "family counselor's" waiting room he'd ever been in, aside from the fact that they were the only ones there. They'd barely sat down—Mom looking like she was going for a job interview, Dad looking like he was the one going to be doing the interviewing, when an inner door opened.

Devon distrusted the man who stood just on the threshold on sight. There was just something too perfectly *appropriate* about him: distinguished, graying, kindly, tweedy . . . he would have been the perfect headmaster for an American version of Hogwarts.

In Devon's experience, *nobody* was that perfect. So he was the worst sort of counselor, shrink, whatever. He was an actor. He didn't care about why the 'rents had brought Devon here, and he especially didn't care about Devon. He cared about money, and the 'rents were the ones holding the checkbook.

Something else occurred to Devon then, something one of the other inmates of the last labor-camp had told him.

*Look out for the religious places. Nobody has to be certified in those, and they can get away with anything they want as long as they don't actually kill you.*

"Won't you come in?" the man said. "I'm Director Cowan, the head of Christian Family Intervention."

"Ours is a special program," Director Cowan was saying a few moments later, when the three of them were seated in his office. Devon was disgusted to see that it, too, was perfect—a little Christian (that was to be expected) but not scarily so; comfy chairs and dignified books. He'd seen offices exactly like it a thousand times before. "Normally—as our name implies—we are an intervention program, for cases in which a child is actively at risk in a hostile and dangerous environment—but Sarah—may I call you Sarah?—has eloquently convinced me that young Devon is indeed actively at risk, as much as any of the poor young souls we pluck from the streets."

Devon glowered. His father shifted uncomfortably at the mention of "poor young souls" and Devon smirked inwardly. Good! Let him suffer! It hadn't been *Devon's* idea to come here and get his soul saved.

"All I want is a little peace in the house," Mrs. Mesier said, sounding as if she were going for the Best Actress Award.

*You've got that every time you and Dad pack me off to another boarding school,* Devon thought with deadly accuracy. *But that's not really "all" you want.*

"And you, young Devon, what do you want?" Director Cowan asked, smiling at him.

"What do you care?" Devon asked.

"Keep a civil tongue in your head!" his father snapped. "And answer the question!"

Devon smiled his sweetest smile. "Never to have to answer meaningless questions like that again."

"*Devon—*" his father began, his face darkening. Director Cowan held up a hand.

"No, Matthew—I hope I can call you Matthew—it's a fair answer. One of the things we see a lot of here at Christian Family Intervention is what I like to call 'Therapy Fatigue.' Many of the children who come to us have been failed many times before by the system, and they're understandably wary of it. In fact, I'd say that Devon's is a healthy response. It gives me hope for his healing."

"You can help him?" Mom said, just as if he were some kind of leper with six months to live. Good going, Mom. That Oscar was almost in the bag. *I'd like to thank the members of the Academy . . .*

Director Cowan's smile got even wider, and now he was dripping kindliness from every pore. Another five minutes, and Devon figured he'd have diabetes from all the sweetness. "I'm certain of it, Sarah. Now, if you'll just leave Devon here with me, we can start the evaluation process. My receptionist will assist you with the financial arrangements."

So they were dumping him here, right now, didn't even pack him a bag. Typical. And now that they'd fobbed him off on another expensive problem-solver, they couldn't wait to get out of here fast enough. Probably going to hit a couple of the casinos on the way home. Devon fought back a pang of fear. As soon as they were safely out of the way, these guys were probably going to load him onto a bus and take him off to a reeducation camp somewhere: bad food and bargain-basement brainwashing techniques. He guessed it was time to try his patented jailbreak routine again, because this didn't look like anything he wanted to spend time with.

The door closed behind his parents.

Director Cowan leaned back in his chair. "It's the same old thing, isn't it?" he said, as if to himself. "Two people who never should have met—let alone married—decide, for inexplicable reasons, to produce a child—and then are utterly stunned when the child becomes a *person*, with a will and opinions of its own. Woe to that ill-assorted family if that child's opinions don't march with theirs. What to do? They can't send it back. They can't very well sell it—alas. The only available course of action left is to crush all resistance, which works better in some cases than in others. It doesn't seem to have worked at all well with you, my fine young halfling."

Devon stared at Director Cowan, worried now in an entirely different way. He knew honesty when he heard it, and in his experience the only times people were honest with you was either when they had nothing to lose—and Cowan had a lot to lose—or when they didn't think there was going to be any comeback.

"Still," Director Cowan said, sitting up, "there's profit to be made from other people's pain, as well as enjoyment to be taken."

Devon got to his feet and began to back slowly toward the door.

"Oh, go ahead," the director said airily, not moving from where he sat. "It's locked, but do try it. And scream if you like—the room's warded. But as I was saying—and why not, since you won't remember any of this?—when we return you to your parents after a suitable interval, you'll be everything they ever dreamed of: docile, submissive, eager to please. Not a spark of rebellion left in you. Not a spark of much of anything, frankly, but *they* won't notice, because they will have gotten exactly what they want, a child-shaped Neopet. And you won't remember. It's horribly painful, of course, and quite terrifying, but—" he actually shrugged "—we must have our fun, you know."

Devon had reached the door. It *was* locked.

He didn't waste time screaming. The last seven years had taught him that much. He looked for a weapon.

All he found was the books on the shelves, but he picked them up and threw them anyway. In his experience, if you made adults angry enough, they made mistakes.

But Director Cowan simply laughed, and raised his hand. The books stopped in midair.

"Innovative, bold, and clever," he said admiringly. He shook his head. "But . . . promised, and it does not do to disappoint them. Stupid they are, but always hungry, and with a long memory if they are cheated. Were things otherwise, little halfling, I'd find them other food, and ask my master to craft a changeling to return to your parents in your place . . . but time is short. It is time to embrace your fate."

He gestured again, rising to his feet. The books dropped to the carpet with a dull thud.

And Director Cowan . . . wasn't there anymore.

There was still someone standing behind the desk. Only now instead of a kindly headmaster type, it was . . .

*An elf.*

Devon stared, feeling the bottom drop out of his world. Flowing silver hair, eyes that showed green even from the far side of the room, long pointed ears. The tweed jacket was gone, replaced by a velvet jacket with a high collar. It even wore gloves—no, gauntlets.

Unhurriedly, it moved around the desk and came toward Devon. Devon didn't move. He felt a profound despair settle over him like a coat made of lead, rendering him unable to move. Either he'd just gone deeply and completely insane, or the fundamental nature of reality was completely different from what he had always believed it to be.

And either way, there were two things he still knew for sure.

He was completely at this thing's mercy.

And it didn't like him.

Worse, it didn't like him in a completely dispassionate, impersonal way. As if he was an inconvenience that was easily dealt with, and didn't need to be considered for more than a split second.

Toirealach O'Caomhain clasped the young human's arm just above the elbow, savoring the shock and despair that radiated from him. These were the sweets that went with the tedious work among the groundlings. Alas that the greater feast was reserved for another, but so long as his liege-lord played this deep game among the mortals, Toirealach was bound to aid him in it.

As he pulled Devon toward the other door in his office, the boy roused from his stunned stupor and began to struggle, but the human had not been born who could prevail against Sidhe strength. And the creature was, after all, a mere child. Toirealach easily bore him through the door.

The room beyond was devoid of all the artful camouflage and distraction of the office. Walls, ceiling, and floor alike were grey—dull grey to mortal eyes, Toirealach supposed, though to Sidhe eyes they glittered with the feeding pen's containment spells, and the spells that would time the opening and the closing of the *peu de porte* that led to the pocket Domain in which the Shadows were penned. It was a place Toirealach himself never hoped to visit: he was no Magus Major, to command and constrain them. They fed upon magic itself, and upon those things similar to it: passion, creativity, will. Something like a Bard, or any Gifted mortal, those they sucked dry, leaving a husk in a state of stupor that would soon fade and die. The master never accepted children with Talent; it was too dangerous for now. Perhaps later, when they did not need to fear repercussions from parents.

If the Shadows fed lightly on a mortal without the Gift, they would leave behind a docile slave . . . but there was no light feeding when their victim was one of the Sidhe. Then, their feedings ended only in a quick and agonizing death.

Toirealach shuddered faintly.

But what they did to the unGifted mortals, now . . . there was a market for that, just as he had told young Devon. So many parents did not want a real child, only a simulacrum of one that would obey every order. His master had no use for mortal coin, of course, but providing such a useful service gave Prince Gabrevys influence here in the World Above.

And influence was power.

He flung the wildly struggling boy away from him, taking care to stun, but not hurt him. The Shadows preferred their meal alive and fighting.

Before the boy could get to his feet, Toirealach slipped out the way he had come.

Devon landed hard, all the breath knocked out of him. For a moment he lay on the floor, gasping and choking as he struggled to breathe.

Finally he sat up.

Grey room, dimly lit. The floor and the walls felt . . . rubbery. He got to his feet, struggling to breathe evenly.

*Hallucinogens.* Tentatively, he tried the explanation for what he'd just seen. They could have sprayed them into the air, or . . .

He stopped. He'd heard a chime, very faint.

The air was glowing.

An oval of light had appeared against the grey wall. It was the same shade of purple as an ultraviolet light, but it shimmered and swirled like smoke.

And something was coming out of it.

Devon didn't know what was coming out of the light, because the moment he saw movement, a completely irrational panic hit him between the eyes like a mallet. He didn't care what was coming at him. All that mattered was that it terrified him with a fear that was impossible to fight, and all he wanted to do was get away.

But there was nowhere to go.

He ran into a corner. He tried to claw through the wall, tears running down his face. He'd been wrong. He *would* break. He'd do anything his parents wanted, if they'd just come back and take him out of this room before whatever was coming out of the light touched him.

But they didn't. They wouldn't. They'd left him here, and what-ever they'd left him with was going to destroy any semblance of *him* and leave behind a soulless husk. He knew it; he knew it with his deepest instincts, without anyone having to tell him. That one fear-fogged glance had been enough to tell him. He tried to bury himself in the wall.

Something touched him, and he screamed.

And he went on screaming for a very long time.

First from fear.

Then from pain.

By the time the chime sounded for a second time, and the *peu de porte* opened again to draw the Shadows away, Devon had finally stopped screaming, because by that point, he was beyond noticing or caring.

One week later—as arranged—Mr. and Mrs. Mesier returned to the offices of Christian Family Intervention.

Devon was waiting for them in Director Cowan's office. He'd been told they'd be coming today, and how to behave. That wasn't a problem. Devon liked following orders. Following orders made him feel secure, and Devon liked to feel secure. Not having orders to follow made him uncomfortable, like being hungry or thirsty.

When they came in, Devon got politely to his feet. He knew his father liked that. It showed proper respect.

"Father. Mother." He smiled, just as Cowan had told him to do. He was supposed to be glad to see his parents. He hoped they were glad to see him, because that would mean they would take him away. Cowan had told him there would be lots of orders to follow if they did.

"Devon." His father sounded cautious. That made Devon feel uncomfortable. He was supposed to show his father that every-thing was going to be all right now. "How are you?"

He remembered the speech he was supposed to make perfectly well. "I'm fine, sir. I feel much better now. Mr. Cowan explained a lot of things to me. I'm sorry I disappointed you all these years, both of you. I'll try to do better in the future."

His mother burst into tears. That wasn't supposed to happen and it made Devon uncomfortable, almost as uncomfortable as not having orders, but he wasn't sure what to do. No one had told him she would do something like this. His little speech was supposed to please her.

"Go to her, lad," Director Cowan said quietly. "Show your mother how much you love her." And Devon went over and put his arms around his mother.

"Mom," he said. "Everything is going to be fine, now."

Everything was going to be fine. As long as his parents were happy everything would be fine. Director Cowan had said so. He looked up at his father, simulating an expectant expression.

"Can we go home now, Dad? I'm going to be just what you want from now on. I'll never disappoint you again."

# CHAPTER 1:
## NEW YORK CITY SERENADE

*This is not spring,* Eric Banyon thought grumpily, looking around at the grey sky and the patches of dirty ice that still lingered in sheltered areas around the edges of buildings here on the Upper East Side. *I have seen spring, and this is not it.* Even though spring's official beginning was a week and more away, it was March, and in Southern California it was already T-shirt weather.

And Underhill, snow was purely for decoration.

But he was neither in California nor Underhill. He was in Manhattan, and it had been a long, bitter, *wet* winter, one that seemed to intend to hang on long past the time when any polite season would have known it was no longer wanted.

He'd graduated Juilliard at the semester break in February—either ahead of or behind his class, depending on how you looked at it—but he'd been considering a number of possibilities for what to do with his shiny new degree since late last year, and he'd decided on this one.

He wasn't sure whether you'd call it "paying back," "paying forward," or just staying out of trouble. It wasn't as if he *needed* to work in any financial sense—kenned gold from Elfhame Mist-hold took care of that, and even if it hadn't, all he had to do was hint to Ria that he wanted paying gigs and he'd be doing society weddings and political banquets every night and day of the week, and for big fat fees. But Eric knew he sure didn't want to waste that degree on becoming a live and expensive version of Muzak—and he also doubted he'd be comfortable just sitting around in front of the TV all day—or even for more than the length of the average movie. He hadn't come back into the World Above from a very comfortable life Underhill just to turn into a slacker. Yes, his initial reason for coming back into the World Above had been to finish what he'd started—primarily his degree—and he'd done that. And it wasn't enough, not anymore, not when he knew what a mess the world was in. He needed to be doing something. Doing good, in fact.

He was pretty sure this counted, in a small way. And it left him free for the big things that came up from time to time.

Although on days like this—raw, cold, windy, and almost-but-not-quite raining—he really wished he didn't have to make house calls.

He trudged along with his head down against the weather until he sensed an indefinable change in his surroundings, looked up, found he'd reached the address he was heading for, and went in, nodding to the doorman. Since he'd started his new gig before he'd graduated, Esai passed him with a smile and a nod: Eric was a familiar face here.

He stopped at the front desk to give his name and destination, and waited while they called and checked—both his ID, and whether he was expected. A dearth of uninvited and unexpected guests was only one of the many things people like the Tienhovens paid for the stunning service charges of a building like this.

Vicki, the incredibly discreet *au pair,* greeted him at the door and led him into the music room. Vicki was of the sort described as "a treasure"—so polite, so polished, so flawlessly invisible that Eric would have suspected an import from Stepford if he hadn't caught Vicki and her charge—and sometimes Vicki and her employer—miming the occasional wordless comment in "woman-speak" behind his back. Sometimes at his expense. He didn't mind;

it made him feel better to know that she wasn't some cowed little thing, trapped in the walls of this gilded cage, subdued into the "appropriate" image.

Belinda Tienhoven, Eric's real reason for being here, was waiting for him eagerly, her flute already assembled, blonde hair pulled back in a ponytail with a plaid bow that matched her school-uniform skirt. It was bizarre to think that here in Manhattan, where rent for an efficiency the size of an Underhill closet was so high that most people had roommates, there were people who had the money to spend to have rooms devoted only to music.

Then again, where on earth would you put that monster hi-fi set out of the fifties that was Ian Tienhoven's pride and joy, except a room devoted only to music? For crying out loud, the thing was the size of a van! It had *tubes,* tubes the size of mustard-jars, for chrissake! Eric was half afraid to go near it. He kept expecting Ian to rise up out of the middle of it, hair on end, shouting, "It's alive! It's alive!"

He gave it the usual uneasy glance as he pulled up his own chair. Vicki and Belinda exchanged the usual amused glance. Then Vicki settled into a chair in the corner with her needlepoint—Eric had discovered it seemed to be an unwritten rule that nannies, governesses, and *au pairs* all did needlepoint—and the music lesson began.

When Eric had made up his mind to set up as a private music tutor, he'd known that at least some of his pupils would be the same kind of over-scheduled, over-achieving, way-above-middle-class kids he had been. Kids whose parents could well afford a Juilliard graduate as a private music teacher. It would look rather odd, after all, if *none* of his pupils could afford to pay for their lessons, and he had plenty of sliding-scale and pro-bono students on his books.

When he'd made his decision to teach, he'd remembered his own experiences with private teachers—most of them had only cared about pleasing their clients, and those had been the parents, not the pupils. And his parents had only been interested in how well he performed, not whether he'd enjoyed learning.

That had been almost enough to make him abandon the idea

of teaching then and there. It had been Hosea who pointed out that it was certainly up to Eric to decide what sort of teacher he was going to be—and that if he *did* run into any parents like that in the course of his work, he'd be in the best position possible to make things better.

"*The music,*" Hosea—Eric's Bardic student and friend—had said, "*can be a great comfort, even when everything else in yore life is a mite dark.*"

That had made sense to Eric. In fact, if *he* had gotten the kind of teacher that he himself intended to be, there might not have been that incident with the Nightflyers. . . . And he just might have stuck with Juilliard the first time. But whether it was sheer luck, or whether because parents raising trophy kids went after trophy teachers, Eric had been fortunate so far. His high-end students might not see a lot of their parents. They might have schedules of activities that would drive a CEO to exhaustion. But they weren't being treated as objects—and he had it in his power to make their music lessons into times of relaxation instead of stress.

Belinda Tienhoven, for example, was studying the flute because she *liked* the flute. She was pretty good, too. He'd been better at her age—but then, he'd been practicing six hours a day. He was lucky to get a half-hour of practice out of her a day, since she was also taking soccer, ballet, riding, and French—and those were just her after-school activities.

For the first half hour of the lesson they worked on drills— fingering, breath-control—and then on a short solo piece. After that came Belinda's favorite part of the lesson: the duet. Small wonder; that was when Eric used a bit of Bardic magic to heal some of the damage that her killer schedule was doing to her. Eric had adapted a Mozart "Rondo in A" for the purpose, making sure it would be challenging but not too difficult. They alternated parts; this week Belinda had the lead.

They managed a complete play-through once without disaster, though Eric had a bit of work to keep everything on an even keel. But when he'd taken up teaching, he'd made a firm vow that if lessons weren't going to be all fun all the time—since nothing involving drill and repetition could be—they definitely weren't going to be the exercises in humiliation he remembered from his own student days. And he'd vowed that even if his pupils were so unprepared that their duet consisted of "Variations on Twinkle, Twinkle, Little Star," every lesson was going to end on a good, pleasurable note, and his pupils would finish up feeling happier and more relaxed than they'd been when they started the hour.

*Every time you use your Gift to make something better, no matter how small the change, you add Light to the World Above.* That had been Dharniel's admonition the last time he'd seen the crusty old Elven warrior. So here he was, lighting his tiny little candles in what seemed these days to be a very dark city indeed. Did it make a difference?

He had to believe it did, or what was the point?

When they brought the piece to an end, Eric was startled to hear enthusiastic clapping.

Karen Tienhoven—Belinda's mother—was standing in the doorway, still in her coat—a garment whose tailoring was so impeccable that Eric had no doubt of how expensive it was. Still, she worked hard for that money, and so did her husband.

"Wonderful!" she said, beaming, as Belinda hastily set down her flute and ran over for a hug. They looked like sisters; clear enough where Belinda got her fair coloring from. "I'm sorry to say I only heard the end of it—but you're playing *very* well, darling. I'm only here for a few minutes, I'm afraid. It's going to be another late night at work, but I thought we could have a snack together and then I could run you and Vicki up to your dance practice in the car. What do you think of that?"

Belinda squeaked, sounding like any typical eleven-year-old promised a special treat, and nodded enthusiastically. She managed to remember her manners far enough to thank Eric for her lesson, then ran off to get her dance bag. Vicki had already tactfully vanished.

Mrs. Tienhoven sighed. "Sometimes I think I'm missing her childhood, and I'm going to regret all this when she's a teenager. But this brief won't wait. And some people—naming no names of course—seem to think it's their right to pave the entire city over. But you aren't interested in a high-priced lawyer's problems, Mr. Banyon. How is Belinda doing?"

The question every teacher dreaded, Eric thought with an inward grimace. Still, even if Belinda wasn't a child prodigy, she was a good, proficient student, at or above her expected level.

"She's making real progress. And she seems to enjoy it. If you're asking me if she has the talent to be a professional musician . . ."

"Oh, good heavens, no." Karen Tienhoven waved the idea away. "It's much too soon to tell, don't you think? No . . . you see, we're planning to go away this summer. To Italy. For a month—or six weeks, if Ian and I can both get away. So if she's doing well and wants to keep on with it, I'd hate for her to stop her lessons for that long. So I wondered if you'd like to come with us? We'd pay all your expenses, of course."

Eric shook his head, smiling gently. "I really don't think I could get away for that long. But there are a lot of senior Juilliard students who are free over the summer who might be available. I know several studious young ladies who would really enjoy teaching someone like Belinda. . . . I could make some inquiries, if you'd like."

Mrs. Tienhoven thought about that for a moment—probably reflecting that, all things considered, a studious young lady might make a better traveling companion for Belinda—and Vicki—than a studly young man, like one Eric Banyon. *Danger, danger, Will Robinson!* Romantic Italy—the tutor and the *au pair* cooped up in the hotel together—

Belinda's mother smiled, and if there was a touch of gratitude in that smile for having narrowly escaped a—*situation*—well, Eric pretended not to see it.

"I'll talk to Belinda and see what she thinks. But that might be the perfect solution. Thank you, Mr. Banyon."

A few minutes later, Eric was headed cross-town, his check—in its discreet envelope—tucked into his pocket, having made a mental note to check with his former classmates to see who might be interested in an all-expense-paid trip to Italy this summer.

Assuming, of course, that Belinda was interested. She might not be. And certainly there was plenty else to do in Italy. Six weeks wouldn't make that big a difference in the playing of a child who had the normal dose of talent, as long as she kept up her practicing. And even if she didn't—well, who cared? There were plenty of other ways Belinda Tienhoven could make a living when she grew up, including following in her mother's footsteps.

Eric grinned to himself. The scene he'd just left had all the elements of his childhood but one: Belinda Tienhoven obviously wasn't a trophy, but a prize. Treasured. Loved.

The Coenties & Arundel Private Academy for Boys—known to its inmates as Cooties and Runt—was located in the East 50s. The prospectus said that it prepared its students for life. The parents of most of the students simply hoped it would prepare them for college.

Neither Eric nor Magnus had been thrilled with the idea of Magnus's enrollment there—Magnus, because he hadn't wanted to go to school at all; Eric, because he'd never had a good experience with private schools, and knew perfectly well that his younger brother hadn't either.

It was Ria who had pointed out—patiently, firmly, and, as usual, inarguably—that Magnus's academic background was spotty at best, and moreover, the false history they were constructing for him in order for Eric to gain custody of him meant that they couldn't use his real background anyway. He'd need a solid grounding at a good prep school to bring him up to speed if he wanted to get into any college at all—and according to Ria, the New York City public schools were a horror. The C&A had small classes and good security, and an excellent record of college placement for its graduates. And unlike the previous schools Magnus had attended, the security was to keep trouble *out,* not students *in.*

It was also, as Eric had quickly discovered, dauntingly expensive and impossible to get into. The first was no problem for him, and the second, as he'd discovered, was no problem for Ria. A place had been found for Magnus, who'd started at the beginning of the winter term.

Eric had fought Nightflyers, Unseleighe Sidhe, and rogue government agents long before discovering that he had a teenaged brother he needed to take responsibility for.

There were days when he thought that the Unseleighe Sidhe were less of a challenge.

Much less.

The C&A required a blazer and tie. Not only did Magnus never get tired of complaining about that, he also never exhausted the possibilities of skating near the edges of the dress code, since the C&A left the choice of tie for third- and fourth-year students—and Magnus was a third-year student—up to them.

But the major almost-fights—no actual full-scale fights; Eric had been spared that much—were always about Magnus having to go to school at all. Magnus's stated intention was to become a drummer in a rock band. Drummers in rock bands were not known for flouting their CVs. *Most of the drummers in rock bands that I've known were barely able to speak three articulate words in a row.*

Maybe it was like his theory about sopranos—in the case of sopranos, the cranial cavity was naturally empty in order to help them reach the high notes with resonance. The vibrato, much like the pea in a whistle, was the small piece of brain rattling around in the skull. In the case of rock-band drummers, the cranial cavity was naturally empty due to being so close to the amps. Any brain material left alive after the amps got done with it was compacted into the size of a thumb.

Oh that wasn't fair. There was Neil Peart and the early Phil Collins. . . .

*Then again, there's Sigu Sigu Sputnik. Wonder if Magnus has ever heard of them.*

There were times when Eric really felt his actual age. Dropping a reference to something *he* remembered as being a household word, only to have Magnus stare at him blankly, tended to invoke those times.

He reached the block of the school just as the doors opened and the students came swarming out. Some of them headed directly for the waiting vehicles—Lincoln Town Cars were the limousine of choice—others clustered on the sidewalk to talk to friends. Magnus stood at the top of the steps, looking around.

*He knows I'm here,* Eric thought with a pang of realization.

He wasn't sure how to feel about that. Magnus hadn't known he was coming today, but he obviously sensed Eric's presence on some level. Eric knew Magnus had the same Bardic Gift he did, though so far it hadn't made its presence known in any obvious way. And Magnus knew that Eric was a Bard, though they hadn't talked about it much. They were going to have to talk about it sometime, though—just as Magnus's Gift would have to be evaluated and trained.

*But not yet. And you should just be thankful that it's Bardcraft you're going to have to talk to him about, and not the birds and the bees!*

Magnus spotted him at last, and ambled over. Eric noted with faint resignation that today's tie had some sort of anime characters on it that he didn't recognize—and lit up besides, with a little flashing balloon that said "Blah blah blah." Magnus pulled it off and stuffed it in his pocket as soon as he was clear of the building.

"Checking up on me?" he asked with a cocky grin.

That, at least, was something Eric never had to do, or even think about. Magnus kept his word. He hated school, and thought it was a waste of time, but if he said he'd be there, that was where he'd be.

"Sure, I figured I'd catch you pulling a Ferris Bueller," Eric said insincerely, with the shrug that turned it into a joke. Fortunately Magnus had seen *Ferris Bueller's Day Off.* Unfortunately, it had been when the movie was on heavy rotation on one of the cable channels. Eric forbore to mention that *he* had seen it in the theatrical release. No point in hammering home the certainty in Magnus's mind that his older brother predated dirt. "I figured we could grab a taxi back Uptown, check out the homework situation, then decide what to do about dinner."

"We should go over to Ria's," Magnus said instantly. "I bet Ace would cook something. And Ria wouldn't mind. She wouldn't even be there, probably, and Ace hates wasting food."

*True on both counts,* Eric thought, as they headed away from the press of waiting cars. Ria Llewellyn was the original workaholic, spending far too many hours in her penthouse office at LlewellCo. And Ace—who had taken in Magnus when they were both runaways on the street and helped him survive, and been rescued along with him—was not only a much better cook than Eric was, she *liked* to cook. She cooked for Ria, on the rare occasions Ria was ever home to eat.

"Maybe," Eric said cautiously, as they stopped for a light.

His cellphone rang.

He pulled it out and saw that it was Ria's private office number.

"Hi," he said cheerfully.

"Try to remember you'd been having a good day up until now," Ria said, her voice at its most neutral. "Where's Magnus?"

"Right here," Eric said. "I, ah, take it you have a problem?"

"No." If she'd sounded neutral before, now Ria sounded irritated—or disgusted. Eric wasn't quite sure which. "*You* have a problem, and it's sitting here in one of my less-desirable conference rooms with its lawyer demanding the return of an object that you and I have gone to a great deal of trouble to assure them doesn't exist, if you follow me. And I think you'd better see them."

"Oh. *Oh.*" Ria was right. It *had* been a good day up until now. Because it wasn't that difficult to decode her cryptic comments.

When Magnus had surfaced last winter, Eric had promised him that, no matter what, he would never have to go back to their parents. He'd decided the easiest way to arrange that—and keep Magnus in the World Above, because it was always possible to stash him Underhill, though no one really wanted to do that, Magnus included—was to simply adopt Magnus himself. But to do that, he needed a legal claim on Magnus, and after some discussion with Ria, he'd decided the simplest thing would be to simply say that Magnus was *his* son—he was eighteen years older than his brother, after all, and it wasn't impossible that he'd fathered a child Magnus's age.

But filing the adoption papers meant surfacing as Eric Banyon, son of Michael and Fiona Banyon of Cambridge, Massachusetts.

Fortunately, Eric didn't have to worry about the government arrest warrants that had driven him and Beth Kentraine Underhill themselves all those years ago. He'd discovered that those were a dead issue in Washington, buried by a change of administration and the death of the Eighties. The statute of limitations had run out years ago, and the projects that had caused the warrants to be filed in the first place had gotten a bad rep on Capitol Hill and a lot of ridicule in the press. The fact that he looked so much younger than he ought to could be ignored most of the time, mostly chalked up to good genetics, or really good plastic surgery, and covered up by a little Bardic *glamourie* when absolutely necessary.

What Eric hadn't taken fully into account was his parents' sheer idiotic tenacity.

When he'd popped up as what he still thought of as the "real" Eric Banyon, he'd discovered that they were still looking for him—although not as hard as they were searching for their other missing child. Magnus, the trophy-child replacement for Eric. Still not of legal age, still young enough to be controlled. Or so they thought. They wanted their investment back, and they weren't going to let a little thing like Eric stop them from getting it.

And even more unfortunately, adoption proceedings were a matter of public record. They'd decided (they happened to be right, though none of the paperwork supported them) that Eric was trying to adopt his brother, not his son, and had been doing their best to block it for the last two months. Ria's lawyers had been doing a good job of keeping them away from him and Magnus so far, but unfortunately, even if he and Ria convinced everybody that Magnus wasn't their son, he'd still be Michael and Fiona's grandson, and the State of New York held that grandparents had certain rights.

Which was probably why Ria hadn't just thrown them and their lawyer out on their collective ears when the three of them had shown up at LlewellCo Tower. Eric had hoped to avoid the whole horror of a custody fight with his parents by saying Magnus was *his* son, not theirs, but it looked like he was getting one anyway.

"Hello?" Ria said into the silence.

"I'll be there as soon as I can," Eric said grimly, tucking the phone away.

Magnus regarded him quizzically. His brother was already as tall as he was, and there was some indication Magnus wasn't done growing yet. "You don't look happy."

"Mom and Dad showed up at LlewellCo with a lawyer. I need to go over there and get things straightened out."

"I'm going with you," Magnus said firmly.

Eric hesitated. He'd been going to send Magnus home.

"I have to face them sooner or later," the boy said stubbornly, though he looked just as unhappy as Eric felt. "I can do just what you told me. I'd have to do it in court—again—anyway. I did all right the first time, didn't I?"

Well, that was certainly true. Magnus had been deposed when they'd filed the original papers, and interviewed by a court-appointed psychologist as well. He'd stuck to their cover story perfectly. Of course, the parents hadn't been there at the time, but still . . .

"You did. Okay. Feel free to back out any time, though."

Magnus made a rude noise.

LlewellCo Tower occupied a prime piece of commercial real estate on Upper Sixth. When Ria Llewellyn had decided to move the main focus of LlewellCo's operations east, she'd bought a suitable building, gutted and renovated the top five floors, and reserved them entirely for LlewellCo's use, renting out the rest of the building. Every year, though, LlewellCo offices took up more space.

Eric had been here enough times to know the drill. He went directly to the security desk, showed his ID and Magnus's, and was directed to the bank of elevators that went directly to the penthouse floor.

When they opened, Ria's PA, Anita Sheldrake, was there to meet them. She was wearing a black and white hound's-tooth-check suit right out of Hedy Lamar's closet; Anita liked to project a persona straight out of vintage film noir. Anita had come from the Midwest, where she'd been in security, and those job skills transferred very well to her new profession.

"Good afternoon, Mr. Banyon, Magnus. Ms. Llewellyn asked if you would join her in her office."

Ria was on the phone when they came in, speaking rapidly in flawless Japanese. She waved them over to the bank of long leather couches that lined two corners of the room, and continued without missing a beat.

*It must be a conference call,* Eric decided after a moment, hearing her switch, first to Russian, then to French. She didn't seem to be doing a lot of listening.

A few moments more, and she hung up.

"Sorry," she said unapologetically. She pressed a button on her desk. "Derek? We're ready for you now. Sorry about the wait. Gus? Are you sure about this?"

Magnus assumed an expression of pained boredom. "My mom's name was Melissa Freewoman. Or at least, that was what she said her name was, but she was such a rampant feminist that she never would give me the name she was born with. She was an artist, a weaver. We never really settled down anywhere. I never went to school or anything. We traveled all over Europe with friends and things. I was born on a commune in Mexico—at least that's what she always told me. She never told me who my father was for most of my life. About two years ago she got sick. We came back to Canada and stayed with some friends of hers. She wouldn't see a doctor or anything but these crazy homeopathy guys and herbalists and crystal people, but when she got really sick and she got thrown into a hospice and knew she wasn't gonna make it, she finally told me my dad's name was Eric Banyon, and that I should try to find him. She said he'd told her once that he'd gone to Juilliard, so . . . I started there."

Eric assumed an identical expression. "When I was, well, about Magnus's age, after I left Juilliard, I went down to Mexico for a while, and stayed on a commune there. There was a girl there named Melissa." He shrugged. "I didn't have any idea she was pregnant when I left. When Magnus found me, I was restarting my life with my lottery winnings. If I'd known he even existed, I'd have adopted him years ago."

Ria applauded slowly. "Very good, both of you. Come on. Derek will be waiting for us."

Derek Tilford was one of LlewellCo's numerous lawyers. The year before, he had helped Kayla and Hosea cut through a lot of red tape when Eric had been lying in a spell-induced coma in a New York hospital. When Eric had needed a general counsel who wasn't fazed by the unusual, Ria had been more than happy to offer his services once more, pointing out that all her legal staff was expected to devote a certain amount of hours to "pro-bono" work, and she certainly felt that this qualified.

Eric felt that this was stretching a point, but he wasn't going to quibble with Magnus's future at stake. And as it had turned out, it was just as well he hadn't.

The four of them walked into the conference room together.

The Banyons were seated at the far end of the table, their lawyer between them. Eric had met Charles Fulton Vandewater before and hadn't liked him. He *looked* like a slick lawyer. In ten years, if Vandewater wasn't a judge, he'd probably go into politics.

Both Eric and Magnus strongly resembled Fiona Banyon; they had her coloring and her fine-boned auburn beauty. She was not ageless by any stretch of the imagination, but carefully tended to mask the footprints of age as far as possible. Michael Banyon was a dark Celt; age had given him distinguished silver wings at the temples—and deepened the lines of temper at forehead and mouth. If Fiona's rages ran cold and quiet, Michael's roaring Irish furies could rattle windows.

"That's my son," Fiona said briefly, looking at Magnus and then looking away again.

*Hi Mom, hi Dad, gee, it's good to see you again after all these years,* Eric thought, holding down his anger with an effort.

"I'm sorry," he said evenly. "Much as I hate to admit it, I am your son, but Magnus is *my* son."

"This is ridiculous," Michael Banyon said irritably. "You're not even denying his name is Magnus. That's lame, Eric, even for you."

*And here we go again,* Eric thought with weary anger. It had been over twenty years by the world's time since he'd "officially" last seen his parents—though he'd paid them a clandestine visit last year, which they didn't remember, thanks to Bardic Magic. But they were behaving as if he was still eighteen.

"Melissa named him after my great-grandfather, obviously, just as you named this supposed brother you say I have. I talked a lot about him. I *liked* my great-grandfather," Eric said, allowing his irritation to show. Great-Grandfather Magnus had died when Eric had been very young. He wondered if anything would have gone differently in his life if the old man had lived longer.

"Why don't we all sit down?" Derek said pacifically.

They sat. Eric reached out under the table to take Magnus's hand. His brother's hand was cold in his, but the boy's face was blank and hostile, giving nothing away.

"Now," Derek said, when they were all settled. "You've seen Mr. Banyon's petition to adopt his son. You're aware of the circumstances surrounding his birth. I understand your own son is missing, and has been for some time. You have our deepest condolences. But surely that has nothing to do with your grandson?"

There was a whispered consultation at the far end of the table.

Eric knew he ought to feel worse about this, but in fact the only thing he felt bad about was having to see his parents again. The way his mother had said "that's my son,"—as if she were identifying an item at the Lost and Found. Hardly the way grieving parents ought to react upon being reunited with a child who'd been missing for the last eight months!

Mr. Vandewater cleared his throat. "Mr. and Mrs. Banyon are not prepared, at this time, to accept that this is not their son Magnus. But they also wish me to inform Mr. Banyon that they intend to file a countersuit to his adoption petition to sue for custody of their, ah, 'grandson' as well."

Eric felt Magnus twitch violently, but the boy managed to stay in his seat. Fortunately, he'd been looking down, and no one could see his face.

"I see," Derek Tilford said blandly. "May we ask on what grounds?"

"The full particulars will be in the deposition, but certainly we expect the State of New York will find that Mr. Banyon cannot provide a fit home environment for a teenaged boy."

"Then there's nothing more to be said at this time," Derek said, managing to sound almost cheerful. "Good day, Mr. Vandewater, Mr. and Mrs. Banyon."

He got to his feet, escorting them out. Magnus stayed seated until the door closed behind them.

"They can't do that!" he exploded, lunging to his feet. "You told me they couldn't do that!" He spun around in place, as if he were looking for a direction to run.

"The court is going to find in our favor." No matter what he had to do to make that happen, Eric vowed silently. "You aren't going back to them. *That's* what I promised you, and *that's* what I'm going to deliver."

Magnus stared at him, wild-eyed.

"Magnus," Eric said, taking his brother by the shoulders. "If we lose the court case—which we won't—I'll send you Underhill, to friends of mine. But you aren't going back to Boston."

"They can't make me go back there," Magnus echoed, sounding desperate.

"They can't," Eric agreed. "I'm an upstanding citizen, with a trust fund, a job, and good references. I've already demonstrated that I can take care of you properly—you have your own room in a very expensive piece of New York real estate, and I've enrolled you in a good private school in which you are making good grades. I guess I could even get a desk job here if I had to, right Ria?"

"I'm sure we could find something useful for you to do," Ria said, smiling faintly. "Gus, don't worry. This is Manhattan, not some backwater holdover from the Dark Ages. Single men adopt here all the time, and our cover story of a recently dead mother and a father eager to make things right is only going to make our case stronger. If the Banyons of Boston actually go the route of petitioning to get their *grandson* turned over to them, half our work is done for us: they'll be admitting you're Eric's son, which

is the keystone of our legal position. And Eric is right. You're in
a good school, getting good grades, and on your way to college:
all of that counts with a court toward showing good intent.

"And if they keep trying to prove that you're *their* son, and
not Eric's, well . . . let's just say that the harder they try to do
that, the less they're going to look like fit guardians for anything
more evolved than a houseplant." Ria smiled one of her best
shark-smiles. "Not even a DNA test is going to prove that you
are anything except what we claim you are. I almost hope they
demand one. It should be amusing."

"You're going to do something weird, aren't you?" Magnus said
hopefully.

"If I told you, I'd have to kill you," Ria said offhandedly. "Just
believe Eric: a Bard's sworn word is gold."

Magnus wrinkled his nose in disapproval; he still wasn't entirely
comfortable at the mention of Bardcraft.

"Now why don't you go see if Anita has any pastry left over from
the afternoon meeting, while I plot secretly with Eric. I'm sure
Derek has the Vandewater party out of the building by now."

"Yeah," Magnus muttered. "Bribe the kid to get out of the way."
But he went.


"Why can't I ever get away with talking to him like that?" Eric
asked. "You herd him like a champion cowboy."

"Do you offer him doughnuts?" Ria asked whimsically, then
sobered. "The first thing they'll probably demand is a DNA test;
I wasn't joking about that. We'll need to make sure it only shows
what you want it to. There are a lot of ways you could deal with
that; I suspect the easiest would be magic—but if you find out
differently, I have a few cards up my sleeve. I've already taken
care of his birth certificate and other records, and they are gone
past all dredging up."

Eric blinked. "You made him disappear?"

"I made *a* Magnus Banyon disappear, or at least, to appear as if
he was never actually Magnus Banyon: certainly there are plenty
of eyewitnesses to the fact that there *was* a child that the Banyons
raised and called Magnus, but without those records, that child

could have come from anywhere. Adopted—purchased—kidnapped." Ria shrugged. "If anyone were to ask me, I would say he found out where he was really from, and that probably he's back with his natural parents at this very moment."

"Do you think anybody's going to believe that?" Eric asked.

"It depends on how thoroughly Derek can get your parents to unhinge in open court." Ria smiled a tight, thin smile. Eric had seen that smile before. It generally meant that there were bullets with names on them. "Oh, it isn't nice. I'm not a hypocrite, and I won't pretend that the things I have planned for them are even remotely on the straight-and-narrow. But I'd be willing to do far worse to keep Magnus out of their hands. Wouldn't you?"

"I'd rather I didn't have to," Eric said honestly. "But—I grew up with them as my parents too. Yeah. I'd do it. I'd do it twice."

He collected Magnus—who'd managed to eat most of a dozen doughnuts in the short time he'd been absent—and headed for home. Magnus seemed outwardly calm, but Eric didn't trust that. In many ways he was Eric's exact opposite—he tended to keep his feelings bottled up inside until he exploded.

Ria sent them home in one of LlewellCo's cars—by now it was getting close enough to rush hour that a cab would be hard to find. It took them the rest of the way Uptown and over to the West Side, to Guardian House.

When Eric had wandered by the old building on one of his rambles when he'd first come back to New York, he'd never realized that his nearly random choice of a place to live would have such far-reaching ramifications. He'd simply seen the "For Rent" sign in the window and gone in.

It hadn't occurred to him at the time that he was only one of a handful of people who could see it at all—and of that handful, one of a far fewer number who could make it up the front steps. For Guardian House was a place as unique as Eric himself: a building that had been home since the day it had been built—or grown as much as built, for it was as much a living thing as a work of steel and stone—late in the nineteenth century, to shelter those who gave it its name: the Guardians.

Though he'd known about them from nearly the first day he'd lived here, though his apprentice Hosea was both a Bard *and* a Guardian, Eric didn't know much more about them now than he had then. They were human Mages of great power. Their entire purpose was to guard and protect humanity from supernatural threat. When one died, another was summoned into his or her power.

But how many there were, where all of them were—beyond the four who lived in the building—where they had come from, and even the full extent of their abilities, Eric suspected that even the Guardians themselves did not know. That they worked in secret as much as possible, and in general could not offer help unless they were asked for it, was as much as Hosea had told him, though Eric knew his friend and pupil didn't mean to be secretive. It was just that there didn't seem to be much to tell, when you got right down to it. Magick was often like that.

As for the rest of the building's tenants, none of them suspected the Guardians' existence. They were simply people the House had chosen for its own reasons—writers, artists, dancers, creative people of all kinds. Kind people. Happy people, most of the time. The House, Eric had been told, needed that creativity and happiness to "live"—and certainly the city was a better place for their presence.

When he and Magnus reached the building's vintage Art Nouveau foyer, the first thing they heard was loud barking echoing off the golden marble. There didn't seem to be a dog attached to the barking, but Eric noticed the gilded cage of the very ornate—and very slow—elevator rising up from the basement. As it got closer, he heard a voice to go along with the barking.

"Come on, Molly. Come on, Molly. Come on, Molly. Sheesh, you'd think you'd never been in an elevator before."

Kayla sounded more resigned than irritated. Eric grinned to himself. From the sound of the barking, Molly wasn't the least upset, but enjoying the echo of her voice against the marble.

Kayla Smith was Elizabet Winters's protégé, currently studying computer science at Columbia. She'd been a teenaged Healer for, well, a very long time now, courtesy of a mishap with the Gates when she'd gone Underhill to improve her Healer's skills and hadn't come out where—or more precisely, *when*—she'd expected to. At least that meant she was more-or-less the age Eric "expected" her to be, from the time he'd known her Before: in fact, it had taken him quite a while to figure out that she shouldn't be. Kayla had laughed like a loon when he'd admitted his mistake.

"Elves!" she'd crowed. "They'll get you comin' an' goin', Banyon."

At least in Kayla's case, the discontinuity didn't matter that much. Her real parents had abandoned her when her Talent had begun to manifest, and there wasn't much likelihood they'd ever want her back. Elizabet hadn't minded, since she'd known where Kayla was the entire time. And Kayla didn't have that much of a paper-trail to worry about—not before Columbia, anyway.

Kayla and Molly arrived in the lobby. From the noise, Eric had expected a larger dog, but Kayla was holding the source of all that noise in her arms: a fawn and black pug. Seeing strangers, Molly stopped barking and began to wiggle enthusiastically.

"If its head pops open and a little alien comes out, I'm so outta here," Magnus muttered.

Kayla's current look, as far as Eric could tell, was a combination of *Terminator* chic and Japanese schoolgirl: short plaid skirts, Engineer boots, and the inevitable leather jacket tied around her waist. She was wearing her hair longer now, and had dyed it blonde. On *one* side. The other side was black, and she had a bright red filigree bindi stuck in the middle of her forehead. There was a matching temporary tattoo on her bicep. At least, Eric hoped it was a temp. If it was real, Ria would skin her.

"Meet Molly," Kayla said, setting the pug down and shrugging into her jacket. The little dog came bustling over to Eric and Magnus importantly, trailing a red leather leash.

"You got a dog?" Magnus said, sounding somewhere between scandalized and intrigued.

Kayla snorted. "A friend of mine, Brenda, she's gonna need a dog-sitter in a week or so and I volunteered. So I thought I'd test-drive the mutt today and see how things worked out."

"Hey, pretty cool," Magnus said. He'd knelt down in front of the dog and was scratching it gently behind the ears. The pug received his attentions with a wide grin, pink tongue lolling as it panted happily.

"Bad day?" Kayla asked. People had very few secrets from a Healer and Empath, whether they wanted to or not.

"Could have been better," Eric admitted. "Another round with Charles Fulton Vandewater, Esquire."

"Sounds like too much fun for one Bard to handle," Kayla said, her gaze intent on a point a few inches above his head. She studied his aura intently for a few seconds, her gaze unfocused. "I'd better get the mutt out for her evening walk. Then it's time to hit the books. You need anything, you give a shout. C'mon, Mol. Duty calls."

As if she'd understood—and Eric had seen far more unlikely things—Molly bounded away from Magnus and trotted after Kayla. Kayla stooped down to pick up the leash just as they reached the doors, and the two of them headed off down the street.

Magnus gazed after them for a moment, getting to his feet.

"C'mon," he said, heading for the stairs. "I'm hungry."

*After all those doughnuts?*

When Eric had first moved in to Guardian House, the one-bedroom top-floor apartment had been perfect for his needs. But acquiring a teenaged brother meant a sudden need for more space, and he didn't really want to move out of Guardian House.

Toni Hernandez—the building's superintendent—had done her best, but it hadn't been until February that she'd been able to free up a two-bedroom apartment. How she'd done it, Eric still wasn't sure; he knew it had involved bribery, persuasion, and a number of people moving within the building, but no one would give him any details. In the end, he'd only had to move across the hall.

He'd had to admit it was a relief to have his own bedroom again—Magnus had taken over the bedroom of the old apartment, filling it with the growing collection of his new possessions, including an electronic drum-kit that he practiced on for hours, and a second computer and music system, while Eric had moved out into what had been the living room. The arrangement had been less than comfortable. Eric had made sure that the magical soundproofing on the bedroom was exceptionally good, for his own sake and that of the other tenants, but it still had been difficult on both of them.

The new apartment looked pretty much like the old one: the same white marble fireplace (it didn't work, but a touch of magic could make it *seem* as if it did), same furniture: leather couch and chairs in oxblood red, same flotakis covering the parquet floors. His electronics were still in their accustomed places—a few years out of date, now, but they'd been top of the line when he bought them and he didn't see any need to upgrade just to stay with the fashion. The windows were the same size, so all he'd had to do was re-hang the curtains, buy Magnus some bedroom furniture, and they'd been good to go. He hadn't been all that sure about the William Morris chintz when Bethie had picked it out, but he'd gotten fond of it.

And the moonlilies in their blue glass vase still bloomed on the mantelpiece—elven flowers from Underhill, Kory's gift when he'd moved in; a daily touch of magic would keep them alive forever, and no matter what else was going on in his life, he, or his friends, had never forgotten to do that.

Magnus moved past him, with unerring certainty, toward the kitchen, pausing only to toss his coat and backpack onto the couch as he passed. Eric went over and tapped the computer awake. He'd been out all day, and he thought he might as well check his email first thing, then check his phone messages. A lot of his students' parents used email to keep in touch, rather than phone, and he'd hate to show up for a lesson that had been cancelled.

He scrolled down through his message queue, finding nothing urgent, and most of it spam (did anyone really believe that the diet pills and organ enlargers actually work?), until he came to one from Kory.

He opened it quickly—was everything all right at Misthold?—with Beth?—with baby Maeve?—and skimmed it quickly before sighing ruefully.

*To the Bard Eric Banyon, Laureate of Misthold, Greetings.*

Uh-oh. That was Kory in High Elven-speak. This was going to be Formal and probably involve Politics.

*The Matter of Jachiel has been put off for far too long. Your liege-lord and Prince has concluded that, while Jachiel and his Protector must and will remain so long as they claim Sanctuary, any further delay in informing his lord father of the child's whereabouts may endanger Misthold itself. Therefore, he requests and requires that you return Underhill to place that information in the hands of the Lord of Bete Noir before this mortal day is out. By my hand of write, Korendil, Magus Minor, Knight of Misthold.*

*Oh, crap.* Eric sat back. Kory was right. He'd put this off for far too long. He sighed and went into the kitchen.

Magnus was hanging over the open refrigerator, staring down into it as if it might contain something different than it had this morning. Aside from last night's Chinese take-out—which had apparently already been rejected—Eric didn't think there was much in there in the way of potential dinner.

"I, uh . . . something's come up. I'm going to have to go away this evening."

Magnus straightened up and stared at him, face blank, green eyes expressionless.

"It's Underhill business," Eric added. It was odd to feel the need to explain, odder still to realize that yes, he *did* owe Magnus an explanation if he was going to simply up and take off. "Something I should have taken care of a few months ago. I should be back by morning."

He watched Magnus think this over. He knew that Magnus believed in elves, but—as he was coming to realize more and more, Magnus didn't *like* believing in elves. Even though his closest friend—whom he might never see, or even hear from, again—was Sidhe. It didn't exactly make sense, at least to Eric.

Then again, Magnus hadn't known that Jaycie was an elf until—well, practically until just before Jaycie went Underhill again. Maybe the whole Magick thing had him spooked. After all, elves and Magick—well, that just added another layer of complication to a world that was already more complicated than Magnus liked.

"Are you going to see Jaycie while you're gone?" Magnus finally asked.

Jaycie—Jachiel ap Gabrevys—was Magnus's friend, someone he should never, by rights, have met, for the Sidhe did not allow their children into the World Above until they were much, much older than Jachiel had been when he and Magnus had run into each other. But Jaycie had been running away just as Magnus had been: from his Dark Court father and a fate he feared far more than the unknown: learning Magick. Maybe it wasn't all that surprising that they both got washed up with the other young flotsam of the streets. There weren't that many safe places to go around.

Now he and his Elven Protector had sought Sanctuary at Elfhame Misthold, and it was Eric's duty as Prince Arvin's Bard to go to Jaycie's father and explain matters—or try to.

"I don't know if I'll get to see him. I won't be at Misthold for very long. But I'll give him a message from you, if I can."

"Sure," Magnus said. "Tell him I'm still waiting for him to email me." He turned back to his contemplation of the refrigerator.

Eric stifled a sigh and went into the bedroom to change into riding leathers. Misthold had Internet access, or at least, Kory and Beth had an Internet-capable setup, but whether Jaycie would be allowed to use it was a question Eric couldn't answer. He'd never even *seen* a Sidhe child in all the time he'd spent Underhill—they were that closely kept.

And Jaycie's status was still . . . uncertain.

The son of an Unseleighe Prince, at the Bright Court of his own free will. It was an awkward political muddle. Certainly the Sidhe changed Courts—but only as adults. And children were sacrosanct. If there was any thought, any suspicion that Jaycie had been kidnapped, or was being held under duress, there would be hell to pay. Kidnapping a Sidhe child was cause for war—between Elfhame Misthold and Elfhame Bete Noir at least; between as many of the hames as each side could draw in at worst.

If it came to war.

The joker in the deck was that Jaycie had his Protector with him. Protectors were sworn to the welfare of their charges above all things. Rionne ferch Rianten would not, *could* not, let Jaycie come to harm, or remain in a place where he *could* come to harm. That was something both Courts agreed upon absolutely. So . . . so long as Rionne was with Jaycie, it shouldn't matter *where* Jaycie was, Bright Court or Dark, so long as his father *knew* where he was, and could (at least in theory) get to him, all bases should be covered.

And of course, the only person who could safely go to Elfhame Bete Noir to tell him was Elfhame Misthold's Bard. Bards were also sacrosanct, at least so long as they didn't draw a weapon. That was something else both Courts agreed upon.

When he came out, dressed head to foot in leather, the door to Magnus's room was closed. A thin line of light showed under the door, but the Bardic soundproofing kept him from hearing anything that might be going on inside. Magnus had done what Magnus always did when he was profoundly unhappy; he had retreated into his own space, possibly into his drums. Eric shook his head. And the afternoon had started out so promisingly. . . .

Lady Day was waiting for him in the parking lot. The lights of the red-and-cream touring bike flashed to life as Eric approached, and her engine began to purr—quietly, as she and Eric had had a number of talks about the stentorian engine noises that the elvensteed preferred to produce.

Sometimes Eric wondered if she got bored, sitting in the parking lot all day. He didn't get much chance to take her places these days, not even on runs around the city. Well, today would make up for a certain amount of that.

"The Everforest Node," he said, swinging a leg over her saddle. He did *not* add "as fast as lightning." Elvensteeds had a puckish sense of humor, in addition to being oddly literal-minded. Lady Day was perfectly capable of taking him at his word, or trying to. "Let's bend the speed limit, but not the speed of sound."

Magnus looked out the window and saw the flash of the elvensteed's headlight as Eric turned onto the street. He felt a pang of guilty relief. He was just as glad that this mysterious Van Helsing (Bard, yeah *Bard*) stuff had come up when it had, otherwise he and Eric would have been bouncing off of each other all night over Mommy and Daddy's latest bright idea.

Not like all of them shouldn't have seen that one coming.

Magnus shook his head. It wasn't that Eric wasn't a good guy—a great guy, really. But there were times when he seemed really naive. And what he *never* got was that Magnus wasn't a kid. He kept trying to shield him from the harsh realities of life. Magnus grinned to himself. He'd figured out all the harsh realities of life a long time ago, and they boiled down to two things. nobody loved you and nobody cared.

Except . . . he frowned. Eric loved him and Eric cared. God only knew why. He had no reason to—he'd known Magnus for less than six months. But Magnus knew in his gut, where it counted, that Eric cared about him in a way he had never been cared about in his entire life.

*Another great theory shot to hell. But it still doesn't change the fact that he treats me like I'm a ten-year-old. And I'm not.*

He supposed it was what Dr. Dunaway called "displacement"— Eric treated him like a child to make up for the fact that neither one of them had gotten much in the way of a childhood. That was what Dunaway had said, last session.

Magnus hadn't wanted to go to yet another shrink, even if it was the same one Eric was going to, but he liked Dr. Dunaway, and he had to admit that she made sense sometimes. Helped him understand Eric, anyway. She was cool with the magick stuff, too, cooler than Magnus was for sure, and Magnus couldn't for the life of him figure out where Ria had found a shrink like *that*. It wasn't as if you could put that in your yellow pages advert—*Specializing in Trauma, Stress, and Magickal Overload.*

And it looked good on the court records. After all, his supposed mom was now pushing up make-believe daisies in the Canadian wilderness, and he'd spent most of his putative life as baggage on her neo-hippie peregrinations. Anybody with that background would be badly in need of headshrinking. And Dr. Dunaway was happy to keep two sets of records—one on the real Magnus, and one on the imaginary one.

But it was still annoying to be treated like a kid.

His stomach rumbled, reminding him that it was dinnertime, and there wasn't much in the kitchen unless he wanted scrambled eggs or sandwiches. He picked up the phone and dialed a familiar number.

"Ria Llewellyn's apartment. Can I help you?" a well-known voice answered.

"Yo, Ace. How come you're picking up on the main phone?"

"Oh, the cleaning service was in today and knocked the phone in Ria's office off the desk—and after I *told* them not to go in there! Now all the lines are set to forward to the main phone, and I can't find the fool manual to reset them. I wish she'd just let me do the cleaning myself." Ace sounded irritated.

"Hey. She didn't take you in to have you slave for her," Magnus said.

"After what Ria's done for me, I'd do more than a little cleaning, you'd best believe," Ace said tartly. "But she won't let me lift a finger. She said I could do the cooking—hah! She's never home to eat what I cook. And now a perfectly good pot roast is shot to—" She stopped abruptly, as if realizing her voice was getting shriller by the moment.

It occurred to Magnus that Ace was a little more upset than an overdone pot roast would account for. She'd been living with Ria Llewellyn for long enough to know that Ria was *never* home on time.

"Hey," he said awkwardly.

"Oh, don't mind me," Ace said, sounding muffled. "I've just had . . . a bad day."

"Well, so have I," Magnus said cheerfully. "I could come over. You can tell me about yours. I'll tell you about mine. And we'll get rid of the pot roast before it can cause any more trouble. Bet you can save it, or enough of it to feed both of us."

"Well . . . sure," Ace said, sounding pleased and a little shy. "If you don't mind. I think I'm in a mood. Won't Eric object? It's a school night."

"Eric isn't here *to* object. Eric is off to go chase orcs or something," Magnus replied. "Kory sent him an email, he looked like he'd swallowed a sour pickle, and said he had to leave until morning. And anyway, we were coming over there in the first place before we got shanghaied by Bad News. We were *still* coming over when he found that email from Rivendell and said he had to split. I guess Lord Elrond can't find the ignition key for the White Ships or something."

Ace giggled. "All righty then. You come on up. And you can tell me what that email really said."

# CHAPTER 2:
## ACROSS THE BORDER

The Everforest Gate was nestled on state lands in the Ramapo Mountains, near where the Sterling Forest RenFaire was held each year. Eric wasn't absolutely sure, but he suspected that a lot of Gates were near Faires—or maybe that was the other way around. Come to think of it, a Faire made a good place to "work" if you were one of the rare sorts of elves that preferred to live in the World Above, or even to visit regularly, so maybe that was why. At any rate, this was one of the few Gates on the East Coast, aside from the Thundersmouth Gate almost a thousand miles north of here, or Fairgrove in Savannah, and though Everforest no longer had an Elfhame connected with it—if it ever had—it was a busy place, for most of the traffic going in and out of the East Coast moved through here. Technically, the Everforest Gate was part of Thundersmouth, since that was the closest Elfhame—if "close" had any meaning on the Underhill side.

Tonight, however, there might as well have been no Sidhe and no Elfhames, for all the activity in the area. It was dark and silent—to mundane and magickal senses both—as Eric turned off the main road and headed for the Gate. Just as well, really. He wasn't in the mood for any delays.

A quick twist of discontinuity, and he was through. Except for the fact that now he could *see*—for the land on the other side was lit with the eternal, unchanging, elven twilight—nothing much had changed. The area directly around a Gate tended to mirror its World Above counterpart, and so the area looked very much like the place he'd just left . . . only better.

The moment she passed through the Gate, Lady Day stopped. She shivered all over, and suddenly, in place of a motorcycle, Eric was seated in the saddle of a black mare with golden eyes. She snorted and pawed the ground, turning her head to look at him meaningfully.

"No need to nag, nag," Eric muttered. With a wave of his hand and a mental run of five notes of a John Dowland song—Magick was so easy here!—he transformed his riding leathers to the armor, silk, and velvet that Prince Arvin would expect to see him arrive in. He might not be able to *ken* a fancy outfit in the World Above, but here he wasn't dependent on someone else to change his clothing for him. There were a lot of places Underhill where the best defense was to look like exactly what you were, and a Bard had both a lot of power and a lot of protection here. Besides, it wouldn't do to show up at Prince Arvin's Court looking like he'd just come off a race track.

Lady Day whickered her approval.

The way was a familiar one, and a Bard had free passage wherever he wanted to go. Since this wasn't an emergency, Eric took the easy way out and went by the established Gates—an elvensteed didn't exactly need them to get where it wanted to go, but such a trip could be a little rough on its human passenger, no matter how much fun it might be for the 'steed.

When he arrived at the outer gates of Elfhame Misthold, he was surprised to see that Kory was one of the knights waiting for him at the gate.

Some people thought that Peter Jackson had overdone the pretty-elves business in his movies. They didn't know the half of it. Sure, elves were tall and drop-dead gorgeous—far too pretty sometimes—but they were to movie elves what racing greyhounds were to mutts. The plainest of them could beat out runway fashion models, unless they used magick to render their appearance even more exotic, in which case they looked like escapees from Cirque du Soleil. It was easy to forget they were highly efficient knights and warriors. But Korendil looked every inch the warrior in his gleaming elven armor as he stood before Misthold's golden gates.

"Eric!" he said happily, stepping forward. "Prince Arvin will be pleased that you have come so quickly."

"Well, when you asked so nicely, how could I do anything else?" Eric said, grinning as he swung down from Lady Day's back.

Kory pulled him into a hearty hug of greeting, made only slightly uncomfortable by the fact that he was wearing full plate and Eric—wasn't.

"I am glad to see you, my friend," he said quietly. "Does all go well in the World Above?"

Eric shrugged. "Well, Magnus isn't all that happy with his new school, but he isn't kicking too much. It's still winter, I hate winter, and I miss La-La Land if only for the decent weather. Toni found us a two-bedroom—I wrote you about that—so the space crunch has eased up. I wish it had a second bathroom, but you can't have everything. How's Maeve?"

"She blossoms," Kory said with quiet joy, as the two of them headed for the throne room. "You must bring Magnus to meet her."

"Maybe this summer. Unless you and Beth are planning on hitting up any of the Faires?"

"Perhaps." Kory sounded doubtful. "She grows so fast. Beth thinks it might be . . . awkward to attend the Faires, for Lady Montraille could not accompany us, and she is loathe to be parted from Maeve, even to give her into her parents' care."

Lady Montraille was Maeve's Protector, the one sworn to put Maeve's safety before everything else in both worlds. But Lady Montraille was also human, and had come Underhill centuries ago—and a human who had been Underhill long enough could never return to the World Above at all. All the years that they had spent agelessly Underhill would catch up with them in a matter of hours if they went back into Mortal Time. For now, Beth Kentraine could come and go between the Realms as she chose, but someday—very soon in elven terms—she must choose one place or the other forever. Eric knew she had already chosen Underhill . . . but Maeve was human. If Maeve chose the World Above when she was grown, would Beth regret her own choice?

"Well, we'll work something out," Eric said. "I'm just not sure Magnus is ready for the whole *Lord of the Rings* experience. He's having some trouble suspending his disbelief."

Kory regarded him quizzically. "He does not take after you, then?"

Eric shrugged. "Hard to say. Right now he's really busy not being his . . . *our* . . . parents."

They'd been walking through what looked like, to all intents and purposes, a park. Gorgeously dressed High Court elves strolled among the trees in the distance, while their lesser kindred of the Low Courts, from Low Court elves who looked more like punk versions of their High Court cousins, to every sort of Sidhe-creature ever described in myth, scampered among the low plantings or flew through the canopy on rainbow wings. As they reached a fork in the path, Lady Day flung up her head as though she'd heard someone call her name and trotted briskly away. Eric and Kory continued on the main path, and when they passed between a pair of towering oaks, they were suddenly . . . elsewhere.

If there were such a thing as Medieval Deco, Prince Arvin's throne room was a perfect example of it. The elves had no creativity—any more than the average human had innate magick—but they had an endless ability to observe and adapt human creativity, and the ability to *ken* anything they wanted and reproduce it as long as the magickal energy was there.

Misthold was one of the more "progressive" Elfhames, and Prince Arvin's throne-room bore a distinct resemblance to a cross between an old movie palace and one of those Busby Berkeley nightclubs that had probably only existed in the imagination of Hollywood. The floor was a perfect sweep of polished green Bakelite, and the walls were covered with polychrome bas-reliefs of stylized flowers and animals. A long carpet of heavy purple velvet, with a wide gold fringe, led from the doors all the way to the dais at the far end of the room. The effect was cheerful and formal (not to say a bit lurid) at the same time. Most elves were positively awash with Good Taste, but some—and Arvin was one—had never met a color they didn't like. This might have been a carryover from the old Pictish days when they still hung out regularly with humans—who also had never met a color they didn't like, preferably piled on top of every other color they liked.

Prince Arvin was seated on his throne at the far end of the throne room, with Dharniel—his war-chief, as well as Eric's teacher—standing beside him. Somewhat to Eric's surprise, so was Lady Rionne, Jachiel's Protector. Kory fell back as they passed through the doors, allowing Eric to go first.

Eric reached the foot of the dais and went down on one knee. As peculiar as it might seem in World Above terms, Arvin was his liege-lord, and he owed him the proper forms of respect in this world. Certainly Dharniel had done everything but beat that lesson into him during his training: a Bard was more than a musician and a Magus. A Bard was a diplomat and an ambassador as well. *First rule of Bardcraft: know who to kiss, what part of him or her, and when. . . .*

"Rise, Bard Eric," Arvin said. "It is good to see you again."

"It is always a pleasure to visit Elfhame Misthold," Eric said. "I am only sorry this visit is business, not pleasure."

"The matter of Elfhame Bete Noir, and the child Jachiel." Prince Arvin sighed. "You render our days . . . interesting, Eric. Still, how could we turn away any child in need, much less a child of the Sidhe? You did no less than what you must in sending him to us. But the circumstances are . . . odd." He turned to Rionne, indicating she should speak.

Rionne looked a lot different from the Rionne that Eric had first seen in the World Above. She'd shown up as this bleeding-eyed specter out of a horror movie to take apart anyone hurting a kid, if the kid had the power to call out for help magically or psychically. Not that she was any less scary now, actually. It was more a matter of if you really understood what was just beneath the surface. . . . If Kory was the archetypal Warrior of the Light, looking altogether too much like the Archangel Michael without wings for most peoples' comfort, then Rionne was his polar opposite, lacking only enormous, tattered bat-wings to stand in for a darkly handsome, utterly menacing fallen angel.

"Jachiel ap Gabrevys is a child of the Dark Court. The Prince his father is lord of Elfhame Bete Noir, and the treaties laid down between Emperor Oberon and the Empress Morrigan are clear: any may change his allegiance from Dark to Bright, or contrariwise, should he find a liege who will have him, but a child cannot choose his allegiance until he comes of age. Though Jachiel may wish to forswear the Unseleighe Court, he may not do so."

She didn't really need to state all of this, but Eric knew that this was just How Elves Did Things; they were kind of like lawyers. You had to state the obvious for the record any time you went into any undertaking. So he nodded, and kept his expression pleasantly interested.

"Yet it is also the Law that he may bide anywhere *I* choose, until the day when he is of an age to swear his fealty-oaths, and no one, neither Prince nor Emperor, nor even his own father, may constrain my choice," she added grimly. "Should Gabrevys assay to take him from my care, I should raise up my own meine to prevent it, and then there would be such a taking of heads as has not been seen in some time. It was attempted. Once."

And it was the one time the Bright and Dark Court had fought on the same side—if the song Eric had learned about the occasion was in the least correct. No, Prince Gabrevys wouldn't be crazy enough to argue with an Elven Protector who'd made up his or her mind.

"So . . . everything's fine?" he suggested hopefully.

"It is *not* 'fine,'" she corrected him firmly. "You have kin whom you cherish. If your brother vanished from your ken, would you not seek him?"

"Well, I . . . yes. Of course." Where was this going?

"Yet Prince Gabrevys does not," Rionne said, and frowned, fiercely. "I have lands of the Prince, and my steward there sends word to me. No whisper of his heir's absence has gone abroad, nor does any seek for him."

"Ah—um," Eric said, cleverly. This didn't sound right. Unless for some reason Gabrevys didn't want anyone to know that his son was gone.

Then again, if it became known *why* Jachiel fled . . . major loss of face, there.

"It is too much to expect that he doesn't know the boy is missing," Prince Arvin said. "And he may well know where he is. Therefore, I charge you, as Misthold's Bard, to ride to Elfhame Bete Noir and . . . explain matters to the Prince. Let him know that we would . . . welcome him, should he choose to visit his son and heir."

From the expression on Arvin's face, "welcome" was the last thing he wanted to do, but among the Sidhe, ties of blood trumped just about every other relationship. If Gabrevys wanted to visit his son, there was no way Arvin could deny him.

"Of course," Eric said, bowing. "I go at once."

Beth and Kory rode with him as far as the edge of the Misthold Domain. It was nice to have the company, and nicer still to see that Beth was looking settled. It was strange how, of all people, Beth had been the one to find a real home in the cloud-cuckoo-land of Underhill, while he, Eric, just couldn't find any way to be contented here.

Beth had gone back to having black hair again, which was kind of a pity, since she'd made such a good redhead. Still, it was her hair . . . and red did kind of make her look like something out of a comic book when she wore her favorite color of deep garnet.

"This is just bizarre," Beth said, when Eric had filled her in. "If Maeve was missing, you'd better believe I'd have an all-points bulletin out. And it's not like even the Unseleighe would hurt a Sidhe kid—no matter what they'd do to humans."

"But one Unseleighe Elfhame would happily hold the child of another hostage, while treating him well," Kory pointed out. "And Protectors have been slain before. Such a loss would make Prince

Gabrevys appear weak . . . and any weakness is fatal among the Dark Court. Should he have one, he dare not reveal it."

"Well, it's nice to know I'm doing him a favor," Eric said.

"Just make sure he takes it in that spirit," Beth said dangerously.

"Oh, don't worry," Eric said lightly. " 'The person of a Bard is inviolate.' "

Beth's expression turned meditative. Eric replayed his last sentence in his head and winced. Beth didn't disappoint him.

"Gosh, Eric," she said, making her eyes very wide, "And here I thought you were in green, not violet. Better get my eyes checked."

Eric groaned, and pantomimed a rim-shot—and because he could, here, he used a wisp of magic to produce the sound out of the air.

Beth bowed. "Thank you very much, ladies and gentlemen, I'll be here all week. Don't forget to tip your server. But seriously—"

"Seriously," Eric agreed. "Nobody messes with a Bard. Unless this Prince Gabrevys wants everybody from Oberon on down—and probably the Unseleighe Empress Morrigan too—coming to yell at him, I'll be just fine. Lady Day will take me over to Bete Noir, I'll perform my Official Bardic Duty, check in back here, then Gate home in time to make sure Magnus doesn't stay up all night surfing the Internet. Simple."

"I just hope it is," Beth said darkly. "I do not like Unseleighe Sidhe. I do not like them, nosiree. I do not like them in a box, I do not like them with a fox—"

"You worry too much," Eric said, leaning over to kiss her on the cheek. "And you've been reading too many children's books. Try to pick up something that doesn't have pictures for a change."

She made a face at him.

"Hurry back to us safely," Kory said.

Once Eric left the bounds of Misthold's Domain, Lady Day picked up the pace. It wasn't quite a straight shot, or an instantaneous jump between Realms—nothing Underhill was exactly straightforward—but it wasn't very long at all before Eric realized that he must be inside Prince Gabrevys's Domain.

The natural state of Underhill was Chaos—specifically, the Chaos Lands, where everything was an unformed white mist—pure, raw magick—and the unwary traveler could find his thoughts literally taking form, usually with disastrous results. The Sidhe—and everything else that lived Underhill—imposed form on that chaos, creating Domains with their own forms, rules, and physical laws. The Elfhames Eric knew of—Misthold, Sun-Descending, Never-sleeps, Thundersmouth, and Fairgrove—were all held in existence by the power of the ruling Prince and the Elven Magi that made up their Courts, and anchored to the World Above by a Node Grove as well. But he knew that there were many other ways to create and hold a Domain Underhill, and he'd never heard of an Unseleighe Node Grove.

Whatever method Gabrevys was using—and it was almost certain to be unpleasant, because that was just how the Unseleighe were—it certainly worked. The area Eric was riding through now was as extensive and—for lack of a better phrase—well-realized—as Elfhame Misthold.

But while Elfhame Misthold was all silver and gold and green—the kind of place San Franciscans thought of Northern California as being (though the weather so rarely cooperated!)—Bete Noir was the sort of place that would make a really depressed Goth feel right at home. In fact—Eric looked down to make sure, and nodded—even the grass was black. And he bet it was *always* night here, and the moon (a rather unsettling blood red one) was *always* full. A heaviness fell over his spirit, something that, had he not known from the moment it touched him that it came from outside him, would have forced him into a serious state of depression. Of course. It was much easier to impose your will on others when they were in despair. Depression sapped the will, made you too lethargic to even think of rebelling, and surroundings like this would keep you depressed, even if the spirit-killing magical aura wasn't operating.

*And probably it's always autumn, too. I know the Sidhe can't create, only copy, but you'd think they'd, I don't know . . . copy more interesting things? If this place looks this way all the time, no wonder Jachiel left. If I spent any time here at all, I'd start playing nothing but Morissey.*

As if something had heard him, the landscape abruptly changed. Suddenly Eric found himself riding through what he thought of as a "default Sidhe" landscape: rolling green hills with tall stands of trees on either side of a wide path of silver sand. Above him was the twilight sky of Underhill.

He signaled to Lady Day to stop, wondering if something was wrong. He glanced back over his shoulder. There, behind him, was the Halloween forest. The darkness stopped as if it had been cut with a knife.

It was an eerie effect.

"Some people just put up 'No Trespassing' signs," Eric muttered. "Or hang out a name-plate." He patted Lady Day on the shoulder. "Let's get this over with, girl."

Lady Day snorted and tossed her head vigorously, obviously in full agreement.

He'd thought he might have to do a bit of hunting for Prince Gabrevys's palace unless someone came to ask him his business here, since Sidhe buildings, like the Sidhe themselves, had a habit of being difficult to find when they didn't want to be. But as he rounded a curve in the road, he spotted the palace up ahead. Evidently it wanted him to find it.

It was more of a castle than a palace—make that medieval keep, heavy on the drawbridges and bronze gates. For something built by the Sidhe, it actually looked pretty normal.

Which either meant that Gabrevys didn't spend a lot of time in his Domain—or that he was a lot smarter than most of the Unseleighe that Eric had run afoul of. Subtlety really wasn't their strong point.

He thought about it for a moment. Subtlety wasn't a Seleighe strong point either, actually, especially when you considered what Beth had told him about Glitterhame Neversleeps. It was just easier to overlook when it was something you liked.

And all this philosophizing wasn't getting him any closer to going through that castle door. He was close enough now to see the guards standing on the wall, and more just inside the portcullis, ready to lower it at the first sign of trouble.

He rode Lady Day to the foot of the drawbridge, sighed, and swung down from the saddle.

"I'd better hoof it from here," he told his elvensteed. "I'll yell if I need help—but really, this should be simple. Honest."

Lady Day didn't make a sound, but he could sense her doubting disapproval.

The water in the moat was murky, but as he crossed the drawbridge, *something* broke the surface before diving deep again. Eric caught only a glimpse of a long green-gray body, like the mother and father of all eels—if an eel were as big around as a horse.

He was very glad he'd taken care to stay to the center of the drawbridge.

"Halt!" the sentry on the wall called down, when Eric had reached the middle of the drawbridge. "Who goes there?"

"Sieur Eric Banyon, Knight and Bard of Elfhame Misthold, on business from Prince Arvin to Prince Gabrevys," Eric called back.

The sentry withdrew, and Eric sensed a whispered consultation before the sentry reappeared.

"Misthold owes allegiance to the Seleighe Court. Tell us why we should not cut you down where you stand," the sentry demanded.

*Because I'm a Bard, moron.* "Does Bete Noir now offer violence to the sacrosanct person of a Bard? Is this the word of your Prince? I will go away and make a song about it," Eric said, with his best sneer.

It was no idle threat. Even in the World Above, the songs of Bards had once been feared for their power to blight or heal—and in Underhill, that power was greater still. Words had power here; words with the creative force of a human Bard behind them could melt stone at need. A song of mockery would send Gabrevys's prestige crashing down in no time.

"—Wait! I will send an escort to the gate, Misthold's Bard. You may approach."

Eric took a step forward. Just as he did, there was a violent *thwack* from below to the wooden planks on which he stood. He glanced aside, to see the eel-thing gliding by once more.

*Just like a shark, seeing if something tasty can be knocked into the water.*

If he'd been in the least tempted to forget he was in an Unseleighe Domain, that temptation had vanished. He moved forward, doing his best to get off the drawbridge gracefully before the whatever-it-was came around for another pass.

A pair of knights in black-and-silver armor met him at the gate. Their visors were down, and Eric wasn't entirely certain there *was* anyone inside the armor.

"What is your business with Prince Gabrevys?" the one on the left said.

"That is a matter for his ears alone," Eric said firmly. "Take me to him at once."

There was a pause—rather as if the two suits of armor were waiting for orders from the Mother Ship—and then they turned (silently, in perfect unison) and walked away.

Eric followed them.

He'd told Beth this would be simple. He'd almost convinced himself. But now that he was here, there was no getting around the fact that when all was said and done he was walking right into an Unseleighe stronghold with nothing but the fact that he was a Bard to protect him, and he trusted the Unseleighe Sidhe about as far as he could juggle elvensteeds. Every nerve was on alert, and he walked lightly, ready to dodge aside at the first attempt to grab him.

The interior of the keep looked nothing at all like the outside—in fact, Eric doubted it could have *fit* into the castle he'd seen, but he'd spent enough time Underhill that it didn't bother him much. The rooms he passed through (hallways, Eric had read somewhere, were a later invention, and apparently this place didn't have them) were a mix of styles and eras—none very modern, all luxurious, and all fairly close copies of things from the World Above. The effect was, oddly enough, like one of those ultra-plush Japanese hotels he'd seen in TV programs, with lots of Theme Suites. Except, of course, that the overall theme was Darkety-dark-dark, so everything was done in somber shades and there was a heavy preponderance of red and black. The few people he saw all stared at him with expressions of unblinking shock—either because he was human, or because he was from the Bright Court, or both.

At last the two faceless knights stopped before a massive set of double doors.

"Here lies the audience chamber of Prince Gabrevys ap Ganeliel of Bete Noir. Enter, Bright Court Bard, at your peril."

They turned and settled against the walls, becoming—as far as Eric could tell—suits of empty armor.

While it wasn't exactly hospitality, it wasn't—quite—open hostility. Eric stared at the closed doors for a moment. He doubted just walking forward and giving them a shove would work.

He summoned up a thread of magick and touched them gently.

The doors flung themselves away from his touch as if mortally offended, revealing a chamber beyond that was nearly as big as all the rooms he'd already passed through put together.

Here the lurid tastes of the Unseleighe were blatantly in evidence. The football-field-sized expanse of floor looked as if it had churning flames beneath it—or within it—dark-red flames that coiled and writhed like the fires of Hell, which was probably the idea Gabrevys meant to convey.

The walls were gleaming and silvery black, as if somebody had made the better sort of Gothic cathedral out of anodized aluminum. Eric kept himself from looking up with an effort; it wouldn't do to be seen gawking. It was too dark to see clearly, but he bet there was a really overdone throne somewhere at the other end of the room. He resigned himself to another long walk.

When he arrived at the far end of the chamber—as far as he could tell, he was completely alone—he wasn't disappointed. There was a huge silver throne set on a stepped dais, and the throne seemed to be made entirely of skulls. Eric wondered who Gabrevys had swiped the idea from.

The throne, unfortunately, was empty, but there was a man sitting at its foot, leaning against it.

He was dressed entirely in black velvet, holding a silver harp in his arms. His waist-length hair was the color of fresh blood—the Sidhe liked to play with their appearance—and his eyes were cat gold. He ran his fingers along the strings, and Eric sensed, as he was meant to, a faint uprush of Power.

"If you seek the Prince my master, Sieur Eric of Elfhame Misthold, he is not here. I am Jormin ap Galever, Bard to the Court of Elfhame Bete Noir. I bid you welcome in my master's name." He rose gracefully to his feet and set the harp on the arm of the skull-throne, bowing deeply to Eric.

*I don't trust him.*

Bards could sense truth, and nothing Jormin had said had been a lie, but Eric still didn't trust him. He returned the bow, anyway. No point in making an enemy. You could distrust someone, and still be polite to him. Even if his skin was crawling, and he wanted nothing more than to beat feet out of here.

"I bring a message for Prince Gabrevys from Prince Arvin of Elfhame Misthold. Can you tell me when Prince Gabrevys will return?" Eric said.

Jormin shrugged delicately. "My master has many duties to concern him. You are, naturally, welcome to wait. All the hospitality of Bete Noir shall be yours. Perhaps you will find it refreshing."

*And perhaps I'd rather jump off a cliff.* Bad enough that the place gave him the creeps, but he had the feeling that the more time he spent here, the more chances there would be for some of Gabrevys's people to mess with him. Like changing the Gates so that he returned to the World Above a hundred years from now—or in the past.

"Unfortunately, I am expected back at Misthold almost at once, and Prince Arvin will be concerned by any delay," Eric said smoothly. "I know that I can trust you to deliver my message to your Prince just as I would deliver it myself—and when next you see him."

This much was certainly true: Jormin's honor would be on the line, and Sidhe were very touchy about that. Bards were inviolate in part because you could give them a message, and they *had* to repeat it, word-for-word, inflection-for-inflection.

Jormin bowed again. "I will give my Prince your message, Bard Eric, just as you give it to me—and when next I see him."

Eric hesitated, choosing his next words with care, for if Jormin wanted to make trouble, he could easily deliver Eric's exact words—and nothing more.

"Hear then, Prince Arvin's words to Prince Gabrevys: Hail and greetings, cousin." He chose his inflection carefully too; not subservient, but absolutely, correctly polite. "Know that your son, Jachiel ap Gabrevys, resides under the watchful care of his Protector, Rionne ferch Rianten, at the Court of Elfhame Misthold until such time as it pleases her to remove him elsewhere. Should you wish to attend him in Elfhame Misthold, you may send your Bard to arrange the terms of safe passage between our Domains."

"He . . . the young Prince is at Misthold?" Jormin said slowly, sounding almost stunned.

*So they didn't know,* Eric thought with an odd satisfaction. At least Gabrevys's Bard hadn't known, and Bards generally knew practically everything about the Courts they served.

"Yes," Eric said. "I haven't seen him myself, but I've seen and spoken to the Lady Rionne." That was technically true. He hadn't *seen* Jachiel at Misthold itself, even though he'd been responsible for sending Jachiel and Rionne there.

"How came he there?" Jormin asked, sounding a great deal less haughty than he had a few moments before. "The Prince will ask me this, Bard Eric," he added, almost pleadingly.

"He was in the World Above," Eric said slowly, debating how much of Jachiel's story to tell. An Unseleighe Prince who was so terrified of magick that he ran to the World Above rather than learn it . . . he doubted that would go over too well with someone who had a throne room like this. "I cannot be sure of how he came there, but he stayed too long, and when he was found, he was—unwell. The World Above had poisoned him, and he was in immediate need of a Healer. Rionne and I found him at about the same time; the World Above had harmed her too, and she was changed and weakened thereby. He . . . did not wish to return here, and she would not compel him. I offered them the

Sanctuary of Elfhame Misthold, in Prince Arvin's name, and she and he went there together for Healing."

Jormin laughed bitterly. "Ah, Bard Eric, the Shadows will feast from your tale! You have done me a service, and now I do you one: leave this Domain as fast as you can, before the walls carry your tale to unworthy ears."

Jormin reached for his harp, and struck a few notes. Suddenly Lady Day was standing in the middle of the audience chamber, looking upset and baffled. She trotted quickly over to Eric. He could sense her tension, her eagerness to be gone.

He didn't waste time on long goodbyes, but vaulted into the saddle. Lady Day was moving before he had quite settled himself. He felt her gather herself to leap—

And then they were outside the keep, and she was running flat-out, with the penumbral edge of the Halloween Forest coming up fast—

She Gated again, and they were beyond Prince Gabrevys's Domain, but she still didn't slow down.

In fact, she didn't slow down until they were back to Misthold.


Jormin left the keep quickly, heading for the Gate that would take him back to the World Above. By now the news that the soft Bright Bard had brought might very well be making its way throughout Bete Noir—for others had spies nearly the equal of his own—and the first to bring the news to Gabrevys would be the one who was rewarded.

Would that he could have brought his master the head of the meddler who had sent the Young Prince to live among the Bright Court as well—but to interfere with a Bard would bring the wrath of the Empress down upon them all. It had been as much as he could do to remove the human Bardling from the 'hame before some of the Court fools forgot that fact in their eagerness to please their Prince.

There would be other ways for Prince Gabrevys to make his displeasure known—subtler, surer ways. And Jormin was certain his master would find them.

Meanwhile, he had his own part to play in his Prince's current affairs. . . .

When Eric reached Misthold again—finally having convinced Lady Day to proceed at something less than a headlong gallop—he found Prince Arvin out riding with a number of members of the Court. Beth and Kory were with him—no surprise there; Arvin liked Beth—but Jachiel was with him as well, riding beside Lady Rionne, and that *was* a surprise. Eric had gotten the vague impression that Sidhe kids were kept tucked off in some well-guarded pocket Domain until they reached adulthood—whatever the Sidhe considered that to be.

He looked a thousand times better than the half-dead street rat, thoroughly poisoned on Baker's chocolate and Coca-Cola, that Eric had rescued last fall. His hair was still black, but now he glowed with health. His face brightened when he saw Eric riding toward the party, and he glanced toward Arvin.

The Prince waved permission, and he spurred his elvensteed toward Lady Day. Rionne followed closely.

"Bard Eric," Jachiel said, reining in. "It is . . . good to see you return in health from Elfhame Bete Noir."

"It's good to be back," Eric said. "It was an interesting place."

Rionne made a sound that might have been a snort, and might have been a cough. "And did you find Prince Gabrevys in health?" she asked neutrally.

"Unfortunately, he wasn't home. I spoke to his Bard."

"Jormin!" Jachiel said in disgust. He hesitated, on the verge of saying something more, then changed his mind. "Magnus . . . Ace . . . are they well?" he asked eagerly instead.

"Very well," Eric said. "They miss you, of course. Magnus is living with me, and Ace is living with Ria Llewellyn—I don't think you met her."

"But I know of her," Jachiel said seriously. "She is Perenor's child, but she renounced all ties to the Dark Court—and to the Bright as well." He sounded impressed. "Some day I hope to meet her." The hero worship in his voice was plain.

*Ria has a fan in Underhill? Wait till I tell her that.* Mind, he could understand. Jachiel couldn't be entirely comfortable here in Misthold. It must be tempting for him to think that he might be able to tell both sides that they had no holds over him, and go his own way.

"And I have . . . a letter for Magnus. And one for Ace. I cannot use the Internet. The treaty will not permit it. Not yet. But Prince Arvin says I may write—if someone will take the letters," Jachiel added hopefully.

"I can take them with me," Eric said. "And Lady Day can bring back replies." He had no doubt they'd want to answer Jachiel's letters. "I'm sure we can work something out. Maybe we can use Lady Day as a courier."

"I hope so," Jachiel said. "I miss them very much."

Eric couldn't help it; though Lady Rionne tensed, he reached out and patted the boy's hand. "They miss you, too. That was the last thing Magnus said before I left, that he was waiting to hear from you, and I know Ace feels the same way. I promise, we'll work out something."

By now the rest of the party had joined them. Eric rode aside with Dharniel and Prince Arvin and made his report, repeating exactly his conversation with Prince Gabrevys's Bard.

"And so our message is delivered, and Bard Jormin undoubtedly makes all haste to his Prince's side to lay it before him," Arvin said.

Dharniel emitted a sharp bark of mirthless laughter. "Wherever he is—stirring up trouble, I have no doubt!"

"Perhaps this will distract him," Arvin said, smiling wolfishly. "Indeed, I know it would distract *me*. But that is a tale best left for the future to tell. Much as I could wish that you would stay longer, Eric, I know that you will not."

"I would if I could," Eric said. "But I'd better get back while there's a hope my apartment is still in one piece. I'll come again as soon as I can."

"A longer visit next time," Prince Arvin said firmly.

Once again, Eric collected hugs from Beth and Kory—and the letters for Ace and Magnus from Jachiel—and rode out through the gates of Elfhame Misthold.

It had been his home for longer than any other place since he'd first left Juilliard, but fond as he was of it—and the friends it sheltered—Misthold wasn't home any more. The World Above was where he belonged.

When he passed through the Everforest Gate, Eric felt the weird wrenching sensation that came with going from Underhill to the World Above, and suddenly, for the first time since he'd gone Underhill, he could tell what time it was.

*Pretty close to four in the morning. If we hurry, we can make it to the city before the commuter traffic gets really heavy.*

"Well, go on," Eric said. Lady Day snorted derisively, and a moment later Eric dropped several inches, landing with a thump on the leather saddle of his touring bike as his elvensteed became his elvenbike. He looked pretty silly sitting there in velvet and armor, he imagined, so while he was still in the ambient magickal field of the Gate, a touch of magick and a chorus of "Fine Knacks for Ladies" turned steel and velvet into the modern leather armor of a knight of the road.

Headlights flared to life, and he turned Lady Day in the direction of the main road.

When Magnus got over to Ria's apartment, he found that Ace really *was* upset. She'd overcooked the roast, and she'd already thrown out the side dishes.

But even an overcooked roast was fine with Magnus, and he said so. They shredded the beef in its own juice, then made sandwiches, and sat in Ria's enormous kitchen, while Magnus waited for Ace to tell him what was wrong.

"You'd said you'd had a bad day, too," she finally said. She hadn't eaten much, just picked at her sandwich and drunk a cup of coffee. Magnus didn't care much for coffee, but he was such a frequent visitor that the icebox was kept stocked with Cokes, which neither Ace nor Ria cared for. He rescued the other half of her sandwich and added it to his own plate. A few months on the street had given him an aversion to wasting food.

"Not one of my best," he said cheerfully, setting aside his anger in the face of her obvious distress. "The parents showed up at Ria's with their stupid lawyer and I had to see them. And then—you'll love this—when Eric told them—again—that I was *his* kid, they said, 'Fine. We'll just sue for custody of our grandson instead of our son and so there.'"

Ace stared at him, jaw dropping. "But . . . they could *do* that. And you'd still have to go back to them. Aren't you worried?"

"Not *worried*," Magnus said honestly. "Suing isn't winning. Eric and Ria are both pretty sure about that. Mad, yeah. If I had these Bard-powers that Eric talks about sometimes . . . well, I guess I wouldn't bother with lawyers. I'd just fry them."

Ace laughed. "I guess after today, I might join you. You see . . . I'm going to have to go to New Jersey."

"Where your dad is?"

Last winter, Ria had helped Ace file a Petition of Emancipated Minor Status. Ace had turned seventeen last month—her birthday was Valentine's Day—but that still meant a solid year before she could claim the privileges of adulthood that would keep her out of her exploitative televangelist father's grasp. If she could manage to get herself declared an Emancipated Minor, she wouldn't have to worry about hiding from Billy Fairchild until she turned eighteen.

She'd thought Billy was still in Tulsa, but when Ria's lawyers had gotten ready to serve the papers, she'd found to her horror that the Billy Fairchild Ministries had relocated . . . to Atlantic City, New Jersey.

"That's right," Ace said bitterly. "Daddy's bought himself a pet judge—and that means instead of the case being heard in New York, where it ought to be, I'm going to have to go down to Ocean County and appear in a courtroom, and tell some judge—who won't listen—why this upright, God-fearing, pillar of the community shouldn't get his daughter back! And *he'll* be there, sure as taxes, him and Mama and Daddy too."

"Him? Who?" Magnus asked, puzzled. She obviously wasn't talking about her father.

"Gabriel Horn," Ace said, and her face crumpled. She looked as if, given just a little push, she'd cry. And Ace never cried. "Oh, Magnus—he's about the worst man I've ever known—even including all the ones I met after I ran away! I can't let him get his hands on me again!" That was real desperation in her voice. Magnus knew it when he heard it.

"Well, he won't," Magnus said decisively. "For one thing, Billy Fairchild has a lot of money, but trust me—Ria Llewellyn and LlewellCo have more. In the first place, she likes you. In the second place, she doesn't like Billy or people like him. And Eric and Hosea and Toni and those guys talk a lot about ethics and morals and doing the right thing, but I think that all that matters to Ria is taking care of the people she cares about, and keeping them from getting hurt." Then he shrugged. "Besides, there's one place where they can't find you, and if you have to, you can go there. We both can go there." He didn't want to, but if the choice was some weird fairyland or Stalag Banyon, he'd take the weird fairyland—and he was pretty sure Ace felt the same.

Ace inspected him critically. "You're a lot like Ria, you know?"

Magnus was too smart to assume it was a compliment. "If you mean I think it's more important to protect my friends than my enemies, you're right. So when do you have to be there?"

Ace drooped. "Ten days. I got the papers today."

"Plenty of time for us to figure out how to make them really sorry they ever messed with you, then," Magnus said with malicious relish. "So . . . what's for dessert?"

# CHAPTER 3:
## DARKNESS ON THE EDGE OF TOWN

The Heavenly Grace Cathedral and Casino of Prayer was the anchor building in a twenty-five-acre business park on the outskirts of Atlantic City. So far, the rest of the park was still "under development," but it was entirely owned by Fairchild Ministries, and it was Billy's intention to make it a Christian oasis in the Godless wilderness of Sin and Vice that was Atlantic City. A television station and recording studio were under construction, and as projects were completed, Billy intended to consolidate the components of the ever-growing Fairchild Empire all in one place—as well as attract like-minded tenants.

His departure from Tulsa had not been entirely his own idea, though by now he had mostly managed to banish those painful memories from his mind and convince himself that it had been. How could his spiritual brethren have been so blind? He had been doing the Lord's work—and with Heavenly Grace gone, he'd needed to put a little pepper in his sermons to keep his market share.

"Heavenly Grace," he'd always told her, "you are the keystone of my Cathedral of the Airwaves." But she hadn't cared, the ungrateful serpent's tooth—she'd fled like the Prodigal into the fleshpots of Babylon. They'd managed to hush it up, but that hadn't done anything toward replacing her. And a man had to do something.

He'd thought he'd found the perfect solution, with Gabriel Horn's help, giving his flock a message of strength and power to bear them up in these times of conflict and uncertainty. And for a while, it had seemed to work.

Then one night he'd received an unexpected visit.

They were quiet men, men of God, men whose faces were familiar across the nation. Spiritual advisors to presidents and even kings.

They'd come to talk to him.

His wife Donna had served coffee, fluttering like a setting dove with the glory of having *them* in her house. They'd praised her and flattered her, and Billy had desperately wanted her to stay, because he knew that whatever they'd come to say, they wouldn't say it in front of her. But Donna was a good woman, with too much sense to stick around when men had come to talk man-talk. She'd gotten everyone settled and taken herself off to her part of the house.

And then they'd gotten down to business.

Oh, they'd been slick! He was outclassed, and part of him had to admire that, even while he hated them for it. They suggested it might be a good idea for him to move himself elsewhere, that he might even like to be closer to little Heavenly Grace during her schooling. They offered to buy out his holdings, find jobs for any of his people who didn't want to come with him, so that nobody would suffer by it.

And then they slipped in the steel.

*"You can understand, Brother Fairchild, that loose talk about bombing out the enemies of Christ does not go down well in Oklahoma, particularly when you're calling the FBI and the Federal Government the Enemies of Christ as well as Infidels who truly deserve to be chastised with the Lord's rod. . . ."*

Bitter memories, best forgot.

It was Gabriel Horn who showed him the honeycomb concealed within the lion's maw. It was time for him to take on a real challenge, Gabriel said. There were plenty of God-fearing Christians in Oklahoma—and plenty of blind, self-satisfied Pharisees, too. Why not take his Ministry among the pagans, the heathens, those wallowing in their sins instead? Fight the Enemies of Christ in their stronghold?

And so Billy had moved the Fairchild Ministries to New Jersey.

Of course, here his message had to be presented a little differently than it had been back home. But Billy had always been adaptable.

"First order of business . . . the casino revenues."

Gabriel Horn hated the weekly business meetings. Well, perhaps "hate" was too strong a word. They bored him desperately. But Billy thrived on them, and he wasn't ready—not yet—for an open break with his cats-paw.

"Up again this week, Reverend Fairchild. The good people just love doing the Lord's work at the tables and the slots—"

Billy nodded wisely. Gabriel Horn suppressed a sneer. It hadn't taken much effort at all to convince all of Fairchild's people that there was no sin in gambling if it was done in the name of Jesus. And the house took ten percent, and that went right back into the Ministry; truly it was blessed work! Besides, it wasn't as if the people throwing their money away were the Lord's true sheep, who deserved to be fed and guided. These were the Devil's own lambs, and deserved to be sheared. So Gabriel and Billy told them, and so they believed.

"Plus we have offering buckets scattered around the floor for praise-offerings if people feel they've been extra-lucky." Marvin Garibaldi was the casino manager, a new hire—one of the few new hires on Billy's staff who wasn't one of Gabriel's people.

"Good, good," Billy said. The various departments around the table reported in: merchandise sales were up, both in the casino and by direct mail, the publishing company would be showing a profit by the next quarter, the *Hour of Praise* had been picked up by several more stations.

"And now, I think Mr. Horn has a special treat for all of us," Billy added.

"Indeed I do," Gabriel said. He got to his feet and picked up the remote lying on the table in front of him.

There was a wide-screen plasma television built into the wall of the room behind him. The DVD was already loaded.

"Ladies and gentlemen, as you know, reaching the youth market has always been the most difficult part of our Ministry. With the launch of the Red Nails label, Fairchild Ministries is able to reach out to that market share that would otherwise not be able to receive our word, through the medium of Christian-oriented heavy-metal. The best thing about this sort of music—though I grant it may not be to the taste of everyone here—is that, properly packaged, our videos will be picked up by mainstream outlets such as MTV and VH-1, spreading our message even further. We'll be launching the label with a free concert here in just under two weeks time: Pure Blood will headline what I consider quite an impressive roster. And now, a sample."

He pressed the "play" button and sat down.

The darkness on the screen faded to reveal the leather-clad figure of Pure Blood's lead singer, Judah Galilee, standing in a field of human skulls. His waist-length hair was the lurid color of fresh blood. As he writhed and howled in torment to the opening bars of "They Killed Him," the song Gabriel intended as the hit single off their debut album, *Pure Sacrifice*, the camera pulled back to reveal a horribly tortured and very fair-skinned man hanging from a cross.

The viewers around the table gasped and recoiled.

The images on the screen dissolved and intercut with dizzying quickness: the blond muscular Jesus scourging a horde of dark, ratlike Pharisees from a shining white Temple. Jesus being tortured by those same Pharisees while a group of soft, indecisive Romans looked on. Jesus being dragged to the Cross by more dark-skinned people, while, mixed into the watching mob, other, lighter-skinned people fought helplessly to save him.

Mixed into the footage, in almost subliminal flashes, were shots of the falling World Trade Towers, burning American flags, street scenes from the Middle East. And through it all, the message of the music beat: *look what they did—look what they did—*

Gabrevys ap Ganeliel had to admit that Jormin's talents were impressive. But what Bard's weren't?

Since he'd come to the World Above to entertain himself—and Billy Fairchild could be *very* entertaining, when he didn't vex one half to madness!—Gabrevys had taken care to acquaint himself thoroughly with the petty factions of mortalkind, the better to manipulate them to his own ends. He'd discovered that there were something called Christian White Supremacists, and it had been an easy thing to nudge Billy's ministry in their direction. They had money and influence, and Billy wanted both. They wanted strife and war among the mortalkind, and so did the Unseleighe Prince calling himself Gabriel Horn.

And to recruit new young fools to their cause, these human Whites seduced their young through music, which was the easiest thing in both the worlds for one of the Unseleighe to manipulate. Jormin would craft the songs his master asked of him, and mortals would find them irresistible. Not every song would carry Gabrevys's hidden message of hatred and factionalism, but enough.

But there were markets Pure Blood couldn't touch. Most of the "Christian Rock" venue was still dominated by pretty, soft-voiced girl singers.

Like Heavenly Grace Fairchild.

Oh, she would be the perfect tool in his campaign—if she were only in his hands and under his control! Gabriel kept his face smooth with an effort. He knew precisely where she was, now—and had for several months—but he dared not attack her openly, either as Prince Gabrevys or as Gabriel Horn. She was protected from both his *personae*—by Bard Eric Banyon of Elfhame Misthold, and by Ria Llewellyn of LlewellCo.

But now . . . now the darling girl was coming home to the bosom of her family. Now he could take her, with law and cunning on his side, and no one would be able to stop him. Once he had her back in his hands—even for a few hours—there were a number of things he could do to convince her that it was in her best interests to remain with him forever.

And once he had her back, she would do just as he wanted.

She would sing the songs he wanted her to sing, and spread Billy Fairchild's new gospel far and wide.

The music video reached an end. The screen went black. There was a faintly confused silence, broken after a moment by Billy's enthusiastic clapping.

"Ain't that just the caterpillar's meow? I don't know how you do it, Gabe—that's fancier than one of those *Star Wars* movies!" Billy said happily.

"Our technicians are happy to do the Lord's work, Reverend," Gabriel said smoothly. "All Fairchild Ministries has to pay for is the computer time." Not that there'd been any computers involved, of course. No special-effects house in the World Above could duplicate what Gabriel and his minions could provide through illusion and magick. . . .

"Well, that's just great," Billy said again. He paused. "I don't suppose you could get that Judah Galilee feller to cut his hair?"

Gabriel smiled faintly. "I believe it's a part of the image. We must temper the wind to the shorn lamb, as you know."

And when the time was right, he intended to shear the Reverend Billy Fairchild. Thoroughly. Far more thoroughly than any of the suckers in the Casino.

Everything was going wonderfully well. It was clear to Billy that the Lord was smiling on the new direction his ministry was taking. He looked down at the gleaming mahogany sweep of his desk, and idly picked through the samples of new merchandise that Gabriel had left him.

New T-shirts. Not the passive victim-Jesus that Billy remembered from his childhood, the one that encouraged people to lie down and let their enemies do whatever they liked with them. This one was dynamic, a real action hero, with a scourge in one hand and a staff in the other, striking out at His enemies just as Billy exhorted his followers to strike out at theirs. And if His enemies looked an awful lot like the enemies America faced today, well, all the better. God's Ministry should move with the times. "Guts Ministry," they called it.

Bumper stickers and key chains, all with the "Red Nails" logo and the slogan "They Killed Him." Billy liked that a lot—it had a lot more punch than "He Died for You." He thought he'd work it into the next few sermons—and that would tie in to that long-hair band's CD release as well.

But good as this music thing was for the Ministry, Billy didn't intend to hitch his wagon entirely to Gabriel Horn's star. Not entirely. He'd dragged himself up from nothing—just another backwoods preacher with a bus, moving from one wide spot in the road to another, and he hadn't gotten where he was today by putting all his eggs in somebody else's basket. Gabe might have a lot of good ideas, but it was time to show him that Billy still had a few of his own.

His phone beeped gently, and Billy picked it up.

"Reverend Fairchild? Your three o'clock appointment is here."

"Thank you, Miz Granger. Send him in."

A moment later the door opened.

The man who entered wore a well-cut, well-tailored suit, but no amount of fancy sewing could disguise either the color or the fabric. It was a shade halfway between the green of a dollar bill and the lurid green of a St. Paddy's Day hat, of some dense, faintly shiny, obviously unnatural material. A pair of reflective sunglasses were hooked over a breast pocket, their lenses the same shade of green—it appeared that the man was very fond of green—and strapped to one wrist was an exceptionally large and exceptionally ugly black plastic wristwatch. It seemed oddly out of place on the man's wrist—he was the sort of man who seemed as if he would be more comfortable wearing a whisper-thin gold Rolex, such as Billy wore himself. Perhaps he wore the thing for medical reasons. Perhaps it wasn't a watch at all.

Billy got to his feet and came around the desk, holding out his hand.

"Mr. Wheatley. A pleasure to meet you."

Parker Wheatley had not been pleased to lose his comfortable and influential Washington post and see all the careful work of years destroyed overnight. However, he knew who to blame—Ria Llewellyn and Aerune mac Audelaine.

Aerune, for promising him support and then vanishing when Wheatley needed him most. Ria Llewellyn, for setting up the tissue of lies and perverted truths that gave his colleagues on the Hill no choice but to dismantle the Paranormal Defense Initiative.

Fortunately, Wheatley had been prudent. Much of the equipment Aerune had given him with which to hunt Spookies—unduplicatable by Earthly science—had been stored at a secret off-site location. He'd been able to steal it—though it wasn't really stealing, since it was rightfully his—before anyone bothered to inventory it.

But to effect his revenge against those who had destroyed his life, he needed to rebuild his power base.

With a little thought, he'd realized there was a ready market for his services. The Christian fundamentalists believed that practically *everything* was Satanic, from Buffy the Vampire Slayer to Harry Potter—and if the Spookies weren't strictly Satanic, they *were* out to enslave and destroy humanity, they didn't worship Jesus or the Judeo-Christian God, and they had pointed ears and unnatural powers. By just about any test of the fundamentalists, they qualified as demonic.

The newly christened Satanic Defense Initiative had done a booming business, if not the same sort its predecessor had. Wheatley had been in great demand as a speaker about the Satanic Infiltration of Humanity, and how the government had shut down the project to discover Satanic Agents In Our Midst due to pressure from above.

It was stomach-turning work, but Wheatley had done a number of things he didn't like in his career. Meeting with a tub-thumping—but very rich—televangelist was only the latest in a long series of such things.

"So tell me, Mr. Wheatley," Billy Fairchild said, when they were seated. "What can I do for you?"

"It's not what you can do for me," Parker Wheatley said. "It's what I can do for you."

By now, his pitch was a practiced one. He explained about the creatures that had infiltrated humanity for unknown reasons. How they were nearly undetectable—except when they struck.

"You certainly didn't call them demons when you were in

Washington, now, did you, Mr. Wheatley?" Reverend Fairchild said with a confidential smile.

Parker Wheatley allowed himself a small smile in return. The rich were rarely stupid. "You'll understand that 'demon' was not a word that would advance anybody's career in Washington, Reverend Fairchild. But I can't imagine what else they'd be, frankly. They certainly aren't human. They don't seem to come from outer space."

"And you say they're everywhere?"

"They're a lot more places than people think!" Wheatley said urgently, absolute honesty plain in his voice for a moment. "I've never captured one—not alive—but I've come close. Very close."

"But you *have* gotten your hands on a few?" Reverend Fairchild said shrewdly.

Wheatley grimaced. "Back in the early days, when we didn't really know what we were up against, we captured a few. Most of them escaped, but we managed to kill one. We tried to do an autopsy. The body just . . . dissolved. We'd had cameras running, of course. But there was something wrong with the film and the tape."

Scrubbed by high-intensity electromagnetic pulse, the technician had said. They hadn't completely understood the Spookie allergy to ferrous metal in those days, or realized that they were just as dangerous dead as alive.

"After that, we tracked them. We were able to develop a good idea of their . . . interests."

"But the government shut down your operation, Mr. Wheatley," Reverend Fairchild pointed out. "That doesn't sound as if you were doing very well."

"I can only assume they thought the PDI was becoming a little too successful," Wheatley said. "Believe me when I tell you that these creatures can look as human as you or I. And the level of influence they can exert over real human beings is literally ungodly." Wheatley lowered his voice to a confidential tone, even as he hated himself for pandering to this yahoo. "In fact, loose talk about conspiracy theories aside, I have to tell you that I think the real reason I was shut down is that They have someone—perhaps more people than just one—at the highest level under their influence. The *highest*," he repeated, nodding in the general direction of Washington. Then he allowed his voice to take on a more normal tone. "Now, I've been speaking out on the subject for a while, but to do any real good—to get my hands on some subjects for interrogation—I'll need a serious sponsor willing to put real muscle—spiritual, financial, and *political*—behind the Satanic Defense Initiative. Whoever takes that on won't have an easy time. The demons have left me alone, so I believe, because they think I'm no longer a threat. If I become one, I can't say what will happen." He blinked, and put on a brave face. "Whoever stands with me will have to have the cloak of the Lord over his shoulders."

It nearly gagged him to say that drivel. Cloak of the Lord, indeed! The cloak of the U.S. government hadn't done any good, and that was something Wheatley had possessed slightly more faith in.

"But this isn't entirely about my needs, Reverend Fairchild. I told you that when I was working for the government we'd managed to develop a sort of profile of the sort of people that attract these creatures, and believe me, sir, you fit the bill."

"Because I am a man of God, you mean?" Billy said, blinking smugly, sure of his own sanctity.

"Because you're a powerful and influential man," Wheatley said bluntly. "They're attracted to that. Sometimes they use it for their own ends, when they can, sometimes they just destroy their victims. Particularly when there are children involved."

"Children?" Billy said sharply.

Wheatley smiled to himself. He'd thought that barb would hit home. "They're attracted to children—all ages up to the late teens. We don't know why. We think it's a lot more than just that children are easier to tempt."

*As you should know, sending your buses out into the suburbs to pick up latchkey kids with promises of prizes for the older ones and candy for the little ones. And of course, how could parents object? Aren't the kids going to be safe with people of God?*

"Perhaps it's that children are easier to corrupt as well: we do know that the creatures—the *demons*—keep human slaves. A lot of the kids they target just vanish forever. Some of them show up again years later, but they're the wrong ages—years older or younger than they ought to be." Wheatley shook his head. "It's a tragedy. I've speculated that the demons are relatively few, so they're trying to build a Satanic Army out of these children, brainwashing them and turning them into recruiters for the Devil. Certainly their pawns can go where the demons can't, and that might be enough of an explanation. But your daughter's safely off in school, isn't she?"

Wheatley knew very well she wasn't. He might be a Washington outsider now, but he hadn't quite lost all of his old contacts. He knew Heavenly Grace Fairchild had run away from home several months ago. He knew she was living with Ria Llewellyn now. But if he could get Billy thinking she *might* be in the hands of the Spookies—maybe Spookies using LlewellCo as a front—

"Yes. Yes, she is," Billy said slowly. "And you think I'm at risk?"

Parker Wheatley smiled. *Gotcha, Elmer Gantry!* "I can't say for certain. Certainly you're the type of man, with the type of organization, that would attract Spookie interest—as we used to call them." He waited.

"Suppose I were interested in sponsoring your . . . Defense Initiative," Billy Fairchild said slowly. "It would have to be done tastefully, and with dignity."

"Believe me, Reverend Fairchild," Parker Wheatley said, oozing earnestness. "I'm only interested in telling people the truth, not turning the truth into a sideshow that would only discredit my—holy—mission."

"And," Billy said, a faint note of triumph in his voice, "I'd need a little something to go on with. Oh, I believe that Satan and his minions are among us, but I need some indication that these demons *are* as widespread as you claim."

Wheatley kept his face bland. Not as good as he'd hoped for, but probably as good as he was going to get. And with the Ria Llewellyn connection here through the daughter, Parker Wheatley very much wanted to forge an alliance with Fairchild Ministries, Inc.

Revenge, as the saying went, was a dish best eaten cold.

He nodded and spread his hands to indicate honest agreement. "I tell you what, Reverend Fairchild. We're both hardheaded old horse traders. You give me six months and reasonable funding. I'll start with Fairchild Ministries and work out from here, seeing what I find. We turned up a whole nest of the things in Las Vegas just before we were shut down, so who knows what we'll find in Atlantic City? If I don't find anything at the end of that time, we part ways as friends, and you'll know that everyone in your Ministry is just what they seem to be—God-fearing and *human*."

There. Plant the seed of suspicion. Make Fairchild think that he just—might—have a wolf in the fold. Make him wonder if that wasn't the reason his daughter ran away. Make him nervous and start him looking over his shoulder at shadows.

"If I *do* find something, well, you'll have nipped the canker in the bud—and between us, we may well have performed a valuable service to humanity." Wheatley smiled now, a smile of supreme self-confidence. "We'll have all the evidence that anyone could want And I don't need to tell you that good works on this scale will get you more than just a pat on the back."

*Think about the book deals and the talk shows, Reverend. Think about how much it will increase your market share if you can exhibit a real live demon in an iron cage in that fancy prayer-casino of yours.*

Billy got to his feet. "Let's shake on it, Brother Wheatley. That sounds like a fine idea. I'll have Miz Granger draw up the papers and set up a drawing account. And you can meet with Andrew about doing fifteen minutes on next week's Praise Hour, to let my congregation know that Reverend Billy isn't soft on demons any more than any other enemies of Christ. We'll go over the script together, put a little pepper in it, what do you think?"

"A fine idea, Reverend," Parker Wheatley said deliberately.

*And a better idea to get the rest of your people looking over their shoulders, too.*

Eric walked into his apartment about forty minutes before Magnus was supposed to get up to get ready for school. Fortunately today was Friday, and he didn't have any lessons to give today, so as soon as he got Magnus out the door, he intended to hit the sack for a few hours and catch up on missed sleep. It had been a long night, and he always got together with Hosea at the end of the week for a lesson in Bardcraft—not that their work together bore a lot of resemblance to the training he'd received from Master Dharniel.

But he had no complaints of Hosea's progress as a student, and he knew if Hosea had any problems with his teaching, Hosea would let him know, tactfully but firmly. The Ozark Bard wasn't the least shy of speaking his mind when he felt that the situation called for it, and he had a good sense about people—better than Eric's, Eric sometimes thought.

Eric had figured the living room would be littered with pizza boxes, or the remains of whatever kind of takeout Magnus had decided on—his brother wasn't any better about cleaning up after himself than Eric had been, well, for several years past Magnus's age—but to his surprise, the only thing in the living room that hadn't been there when he left was one very large stone gargoyle.

"Enjoy yerself on yer jaunt, did ye, laddybuck?" Greystone asked, turning his head. The gargoyle's black eyes twinkled at his own joke.

Greystone was Eric's oldest friend at Guardian House, and in a sense, Greystone *was* the House, for he and his fellow gargoyles had been—crafted?—at the same time as the House itself as a combination security system and set of guard dogs to protect both the House and its Guardian inhabitants. It had been a mixture of Greystone's curiosity about Eric that first night, and Eric's calling-on spell to find a friend, that had begun their friendship, but it had deepened all on its own. Greystone was curious about the things he could only hear from his perch atop the building—like movies and television programs—and Eric was happy to let his friend sate that curiosity with his DVD library—and even surf the Internet.

He glanced at the television. Greystone had been watching *Trigun*—one of Magnus's additions to their DVD library, and not something Eric would have bought for himself. Greystone usually preferred classic movies. But Eric supposed all popular culture was equally bizarre from a gargoyle's point of view.

He gathered his scattered thoughts and answered the gargoyle's question. "Oh, it had its moments. Sometimes I wish the Unseleighe would find a new interior decorator, though. It looked like a Gothic playpen down there, or maybe an old Frank Frazetta painting. Everything quiet here?" he asked, unzipping his jacket.

"Quieter here than where you were, I fancy." Greystone snorted. "The lad went on up to Ria's penthouse for dinner—though naturally she wasn't there for it—and got home full to the gills with bad news and roast beef. Both of which he shared with me. There's a bit of the beef left in the kitchen, and I don't doubt he'll be opening his budget of sorrow to ye by and by."

"Can I get a preview?" Eric asked, sitting down on the arm of the couch.

"Well, 'tis no secret, and he expects you and Ria between you to pull the proverbial *lapin* out of the *chapeau*, I'm warning you now. Young Heavenly Grace's father has found a judge to block the Grant of Emancipated Minor status. There's to be a hearing, and she'll have to go down in person."

Eric groaned feelingly. "That's . . . just . . . so . . . special."

"Isn't it, though?" Greystone grinned, showing a wide mouth filled with stone fangs. "You've got a bit over a week to broker a miracle, boyo."

Eric just shook his head, walking into the kitchen to brew tea. As he unzipped his jacket, the letters from Jachiel crinkled. He set them on the counter in plain sight, so he wouldn't forget to hand them over immediately.

But Greystone's news certainly hadn't been anything he wanted to hear. Of course Billy Fairchild wanted Ace's abilities back. Eric was even grudgingly willing to admit the man might be fond of his daughter, or at least as fond as anyone who considered children to be possessions could be. But her powers seemed to be the most important thing to him—from what Ace had told

them, Billy had been exploiting her Talent for years. He'd built
his ministry on them.

Like Eric, Ace had Talent. Like Eric, Ace's Talent expressed
itself through music. But while Eric, as a Bard, could cast a
variety of spells, Ace could do only one thing, though it was the
equivalent of a howitzer: when she sang, she could make people
feel whatever emotion she chose.

When she'd been younger, it had simply been the same feeling the song she was singing made *her* feel, or so she'd told
Eric, Magnus, and Ria, when she had finally been willing to talk
about her Talent. But now, she could take a song and build on
it, shape it, *twist* it. With song, Heavenly Grace Fairchild could
make people feel *anything*.

Love. Hate. Fear. Joy. Terror. Guilt. Shame. Rage. Blind panic.
Name the emotion, and Ace could conjure it.

When she'd gotten old enough to realize what she was doing,
she'd tried to stop, but her father wouldn't let her. He'd wanted
her up on the stage, leading his choir, singing his audiences into
a frenzy of adoration for him. *Lucrative* adoration.

So she'd run away.

*And now he wants her back so she can keep on doing it. Well,
who wouldn't—if they were a manipulative slimeball?*

Eric wasn't quite sure what sort of miracle was required in this
case—the real puzzle was why Ria hadn't been able to make Billy
Fairchild back off. No matter how much the Reverend Billy Fairchild
wanted his star attraction returned to center stage, he ought to
be more afraid of what Ria Llewellyn would do to him.

But obviously he wasn't.

By the time the kettle had boiled, Magnus came staggering into
the kitchen, looking like a disheveled and very grumpy leopard.
He went directly to the refrigerator, pulled it open, and chugged
half a carton of orange juice before seeming to register that his
brother was there.

"Guy can't sleep with you two making all that racket," he muttered sullenly.

*It wasn't that much noise,* Eric thought. And he and Greystone
had been careful to keep their voices low. If *Trigun* hadn't woken

Magnus, he didn't see how a little conversation could—especially through Bardcrafted sound-baffles.

But he knew from experience that Magnus wasn't a morning person. "Sorry," Eric said. "Tea?"

Magnus shuddered, grabbed a Coke out of the still-open fridge, and wandered back toward his bedroom.

When he reemerged twenty minutes later, he was dressed for school and looked more alert, and Eric was on his second cup of tea.

"So," Magnus said. "It go okay last night?"

"Pretty good," Eric said. "I saw Jaycie. He says there's a problem with the Internet connection, but he can write. I brought you a letter, and one for Ace. If you want to write back, Lady Day can deliver them, and bring his replies."

"Streetmail," Magnus muttered, as if it were the most horrible thing imaginable. "Snailmail."

Eric handed him the letter—several sheets of thick parchment, bound together with a green ribbon and sealed with a round blob of silver wax. "You might have some pity on him," he pointed out. "Part of the problem might be he doesn't know how to type, much less use a computer. Not a lot of keyboards Underhill." He tactfully forbore to mention what Jaycie had said about the treaty—no need to involve Magnus in Underhill politics any more than absolutely necessary.

Magnus gave Eric a *look,* the kind that said he wasn't sure he believed his older brother, but that if the assertion was true, he, Magnus, could not imagine a more horrifying place.

"Um . . . Ace wanted to talk to you tonight. And Hosea. If that's okay. She could get her letter then. She's got a kind of a problem," Magnus said tentatively, still holding the unopened letter.

"Greystone told me a little about it," Eric said. "He didn't think you'd mind."

Magnus shrugged, going over to the cabinet for a bowl and the cereal box. "Can't you just make this creep disappear or something?"

That was a reasonable question, from a teenager's point of view. "A . . . friend of mine always told me to keep my mind on what I actually wanted, not on what I thought I had to do to get there. What we want is to get Ace her Emancipated Minor status. Making Billy disappear might not be the best way to go about that." He countered Magnus's look of disbelief with explanation. "People like Billy don't just vanish. If he disappeared, there would be a lot of questions, and Ria would be right at the center of it because she's helping Ace. Ria's made some enemies—they'd be only to happy to 'find' evidence that Ria was involved."

Magnus didn't say anything, but he obviously didn't like the answer. Well, Eric hadn't liked it either, the first dozen times he'd heard it from Master Dharniel.

*"Life is war, young Banyon. Art is war. You would do well to remember both these things. Concentrate on the destination, not the journey. And do not allow your lust for frivolity and self-indulgence to distract you, for your enemy will use that against you. Self-indulgence is a vice no Bard—and no warrior—can afford."*

Magnus settled down at the kitchen table with his bowl of cereal to read his letter, and Eric went back out into the living room. Greystone was gone, of course—it was light enough now that his absence from the top of the building would be noticed.

Eric put away the DVD and settled down to channel-surf for a few minutes. There was nothing unusual on any of the news channels, and like every New Yorker these days, he spared a brief moment of thanksgiving for that.

After a few minutes—Eric had settled down with an old silent movie—Magnus came into the living room, ready for school.

"So," he said, sounding oddly hesitant. "Do you think that maybe you guys could come up to Ria's place tonight and kinda talk about it with us?"

*"You guys" meaning me and Hosea,* Eric translated mentally with the ease of long practice. "Sure," he said. "And hey, maybe Ria'll even be there."

"She'd better be," Magnus said darkly.

There were many things Jormin ap Galever liked about the World Above. Bringing his master bad news was not one of them.

Still it was better—oh, by far!—to be the first to bring bad news to Prince Gabrevys than to have to explain why you had not done so. Unlike some of the princes Jormin had served, Gabrevys rewarded efficiency and discretion.

Jormin was not supposed to be here now—Judah Galilee and Pure Blood were supposed to be in California, putting the finishing touches on their album and getting ready for their upcoming concert. But this news wouldn't wait. And if anyone *did* see him, it would be simple enough to explain away, after all. What could be more reasonable than that Gabriel Horn would wish to speak personally to Judah about some minor detail of the concert to come? Musicians were temperamental creatures. All mortals knew that.

But he arrived without mishap or discovery: a second *glamourie* cast over the one that gave him human seeming made him look not only more than ordinary, but encouraged all eyes to rest elsewhere. He did not even need spellcraft for the elevator, for Gabrevys had given him all their codes long ago, and he quickly ascended to the residence floor, charmed as always by the endless inventiveness of mortals.

The door he sought opened as he reached it. Jormin entered quickly, shedding both his *glamouries,* and knelt respectfully at the feet of his master.

"You would not have come yourself to bring me good news," Gabriel/Gabrevys said, after a long pause.

"I have heard better," Judah admitted, not moving. "Will you hear it, my Prince?"

"Get up. Tell me all you know. But first—who knows?"

Judah got to his feet, shaking his waist-length mane back into place. "Any who might have the wit and the spellcraft to eavesdrop on your Presence Chamber—you will know who that might be better than I. And all your court saw Misthold's mortal Bard ride into your Domain and beg audience with you. I know not what they may make of that. I saw him safe away, for your honor."

"And what purpose did Eric Banyon claim at Bete Noir?" Gabriel asked. His voice was low and even, but Judah was not fooled. His master had sounded just so when sending victims to his torturers.

When he spoke, he gave every rhythm and inflection just as he had heard them, his voice becoming an uncanny echo of Eric Banyon's. "'Hear Prince Arvin's words to Prince Gabrevys: Hail and greetings, cousin. Know that your son, Jachiel ap Gabrevys, resides under the watchful care of his Protector, Rionne ferch Rianten, at the Court of Elfhame Misthold until such time as it pleases her to remove him elsewhere. Should you wish to attend him in Elfhame Misthold, you may send your Bard to arrange the terms of safe passage between our Domains.'" He paused, then added in his own voice: "Such was the message I was given, but I questioned the Bard further, and learned more." Quickly, Judah told Gabriel everything he had learned from Misthold's mortal Bard: how Jachiel had fled to the World Above, pursued by his Protector. How he had refused to return to Bete Noir. How Eric had offered Jachiel and Rionne Sanctuary at Elfhame Misthold, in Prince Arvin's name. The longer he spoke, the more encouraged he became. The Prince was not inclined to punish his Bard this day.

"You have done well to bring me this news as swiftly as you have," Gabriel said, though to speak the words of praise nearly choked him. "Leave me now."

When Judah was gone, he got to his feet and began to pace.

His son—his only son—in the loathsome hands of the Bright Court!

But Rionne was there. His Jachiel would come to no harm with her to watch over him.

But *why* was he there? Why had he fled? Why would he not return home?

Perhaps he had discovered a plot against his life. If that were so, Gabriel would deal with it at the proper time.

And if that were so—strange as it seemed, he was safer at the Bright Court, where all eyes would be on any Unseleighe who dared to enter Seleighe lands. For now, so long as no one learned where the boy was—well, this was not all bad news. He could use his Bright Court cousins; the proper thing to do with them was to use them.

At the moment, such things did not matter. Jachiel was safe. And if he were to take his rightful place at the Unseleighe Court, Gabriel's plans must succeed here.

But to have a son held at the Bright Court, no matter the reason, was a grave insult, and one he could not afford, no matter his certainty of Jachiel's safety there. The moment it became known—and it *would* become known now that Bard Eric had come to his Court; Jormin knew that as well as Gabrevys did—his enemies would see it as a sign of weakness, and strike. But let him only bring his plans for Billy Fairchild to fruition, and he would create such a feast of blood and pain that it would be sung of all the way to the Morrigan's throne. He would be rewarded with rich gifts from her own dark hands; his power and influence would grow, and none in all of Underhill would dare raise spell or sword against him or his.

And perhaps he could discover some way to share that feast of pain in which lay his protection with the Bard—the *mortal* Bard—who had meddled so casually in things that did not concern him.

# CHAPTER 4:
## PINK CADILLAC

Around eight o'clock Friday night, a council of war gathered in Ria's Central Park South apartment. Despite his teasing that morning, Eric wasn't at all surprised to find that Ria was there: Ria was fiercely protective where Ace was concerned. He didn't say anything, but she'd never been that protective about Kayla, though the two girls were probably about equal in their ability to take care of themselves. He wondered now—did Ria subconsciously feel that Ace was the daughter she'd never had—and probably never would have? Certainly Ace looked enough like Ria to be her daughter; she was as blonde as Ria was, and few people would look past the similarity in coloring to any difference in bone structure.

Some questions were better not asked aloud.

Ace was painfully upset at the prospect of the upcoming hearing. After they'd eaten, when she couldn't put it off any longer, she spoke in jittery disjointed sentences about how much she didn't want to have to face her parents again—and it became clear to the others that while she would find seeing Billy and Donna Fairchild unpleasant, she was truly terrified at the prospect of seeing Billy's assistant, Gabriel Horn, again. And that was disturbing. What was it about Gabriel Horn that had her so spooked?

While Ria had a fairly thick dossier on Billy Fairchild and Fairchild Ministries, it didn't contain much information on Gabriel Horn.

That, to Eric, set off a faint alarm-bell. Ria's investigators were first-rate. She should have been able to name Horn's favorite toothpaste. . . .

All they knew was that he was one of Billy's personal assistants, and had joined the Ministry about a year before Ace had fled. Apparently he was very close to the elder Fairchilds, and Billy trusted him as he trusted no one else. Ace had never been able to articulate any reason for her absolute dislike-bordering-on-terror of the man. From everything Ria had been able to get out of her, he'd never behaved inappropriately toward her.

But Talents were good at reading people, even if that wasn't where the main focus of their Gift lay. All of them trusted Ace's instincts. If she said Gabriel Horn was somebody to watch out for, she was probably right.

"They may have forced a hearing, and moved the venue to New Jersey, but it doesn't change any of the facts," Ria said firmly. "There's no cause for the court to deny your petition. The Fairchilds are not fit custodial guardians—especially if Billy's denying you the right to an education and forcing you to continue to work in his 'Ministry' against your wishes. Derek has been handling your paperwork all along; I'll send him down for the hearing. He'll make mincemeat out of these twerps, trust me. And as for Horn and your parents, there's no reason you should have to be down there for longer than to make your court appearance."

"Can't you go with me?" Ace said, forlornly. Her tougher-than-nails demeanor had completely evaporated in the face of this. "I know you're really busy and all, but I just can't . . ."

"Not that busy," Ria said firmly. "If it wouldn't make things worse, I'd be right there with you. But if I went along, the press would be on me in a New York minute, and we'd have a real sideshow on our hands. That's the last thing you need right now. Once the media gets involved, this whole thing turns into a feeding frenzy that would make the last half-dozen 'trials of the century' look modest and restrained." She grimaced. "That's the problem with being visible. It's worse having been the media darling for being a corporate hero. Now they're just about ready to start looking for ways to shoot me down. And 'stealing' some yahoo preacher's baby girl would be just the ticket to make me into a monster. So far Billy hasn't played the 'trial by television' card, and I don't want to give him any ideas," Ria added broodingly.

The six of them were gathered around Ria's seldom-used dining-room table, with the summons from the Ocean County District Court on the table between them. It was odd, Eric thought, that neither of Ace's parents had sent her any kind of personal message in all this time begging her to come home. He knew Ace would have mentioned it if they had. Maybe they'd tried, and Ria had intercepted them. He certainly wouldn't put it past her.

"Eric and I can go with you," Magnus said.

"Same dirge, different key," Eric said firmly, though he hated to do it. "For one thing, if Fairchild wanted to play ugly, he could certainly ask what my relationship was to a seventeen-year-old girl—and we can't be sure he wouldn't find out I was down there with you, no matter how hard I tried to stay out of sight. For another thing, I'm pretty sure Michael and Fiona have private detectives watching both me and Magnus right now, looking for God knows what. So if I either take him out of school to go off to Atlantic City—or leave him alone to go off to Atlantic City with a teenage girl, well . . ."

"But Ah can go," Hosea said. "An Ah've got the perfect reason, too, so it doesn't matter if he knows Ah'm there."

Everybody looked at him expectantly.

"Well, go on, keep us in suspense forever," Magnus said, grinning crookedly.

"You all know Ah've been doin' a bit o' writin' here an' there these past few months," Hosea began hesitantly.

"Selling it, too," Ria said. "Don't be so modest. You're going to have to give up singing in subways soon and write a novel."

"Don't know as Ah'd be any good at yarnin'," Hosea said placidly, "but Ah do know thet if you say you're writin' an article, people'll let you go just about anywhere and ask 'em just about anything. So Ah guess Ah'll go on down to Atlantic City with Miz Ace and find me somethin' to write about there."

Ace blinked back tears of relief. "Thank you, Hosea," she said quietly.

"It's always a comfort to do a kindness for a friend," Hosea said amiably. "We've got a few days yet before you have to go. Might be Ah cain wangle me an actual writin' assignment in that time. Ah'll look around."

"I can always make a few calls, if you like," Ria said. "And all in all, I'm just as glad that Ace will be going down with the big guns in her pocket—legal and otherwise."

Hosea looked a little self-conscious. "Call it a medium-size gun an' you'd be a bit more on-target, Ah'd guess, Miz Ria. Ah'm nowheres near done learning everything Eric's got to teach me."

"Be that as it may," Ria waved his objection aside impatiently. "You may not be a fully trained Bard, but you're a full-fledged Guardian, and from all I know about them, if Ace asks you for help, you're bound to give it."

"Ayah, that's true." Hosea looked uncomfortable. "Not that Ah wouldn't help her anyway. But this Guardian business don't come to much unless there's hoodoo involved. And I don't expect any kind o' Reverend would have much truck with hoodoo."

"He used me, didn't he?" Ace said bitterly.

"Now that," Hosea said firmly, turning to Ace, "is a whole different kettle, and well you know it. That's a natural gift from God, like what Ah've got, or what Eric has, and it ain't no different than bein' able to dance or do sums in yore haid. You've seen black hoodoo, and not even the worst kind there is. You know you don't want to see it twice, and you know no right person would meddle in it."

Ace nodded, half reluctantly.

*Hmm. There's a blind spot we'll need to address some day,* Eric thought. *Some of these so-called "men of God" would use anything they could get their hands on to turn another buck, "black hoodoo" included.*

Magnus stirred rebelliously, and Eric put a hand over his,

silencing whatever his brother was about to say. Certainly neither of them had much good to think about their own parents—unfortunately, they knew them too well for that—but if Ace could manage to think well of her own parents—or at least not too badly of them—it would be for the best. Certainly Billy had wanted to use her Talent to make himself wealthy, but as Hosea had pointed out, there were far worse things in the world than a greedy fool.

Of course, greedy fools had no business raising children either. But that didn't make them Satanists.

"So Ah guess next Wednesday, you and Ah'll take a trip down to the Jersey Shore," Hosea said, satisfied. "And we'll bring you folks back some picture postcards and salt-water taffy."

Ria snorted elegantly. "I'd rather have the judge's head on a plate. But if that's settled, there's cake and ice cream in the kitchen."

"Cake!" Magnus said, as if he hadn't eaten enough to fuel a small army just a few hours before.

"I'll put on the coffee," Ace said, getting up. "You can help—" this to Magnus "—but no picking!"

When the teenagers were gone, Ria looked at Eric and Hosea, one elegant eyebrow raised.

"Gabriel Horn worries me," she said quietly.

"Ayah," Hosea sighed. "He's the frog on the birthday cake for sure."

"Claire hasn't been able to find out anything about him. Of course, he might have been using another name before he hooked up with Billy. 'Gabriel Horn'—it practically screams 'stage name,'" Ria said musingly. "And Ace has no idea why he upsets her so much. I even tried a spell of Remembering—don't give me that look, Eric, I did it with her full knowledge and consent—and there isn't even anything in her unconscious mind to go on. She was just afraid of him from the first moment she saw him. And he's *very* close to the family. Personal friend, inner circle, close advisor, you name it. And before three years ago, he didn't exist."

"Government agent?" Eric suggested. It made sense. The two sorts of organizations that dealt in cash money in large quantities were drug-rings and churches. It wouldn't be at all impossible for the former to be using the latter to launder money. Government agents gave off pretty unsettling vibes, or at least, the ones Eric had run up against did.

"I do hope so," Ria said. "Unfortunately, I had to call in a lot of markers over the Parker Wheatley thing last year; nobody in Washington would appreciate me asking any questions right now." She shrugged, irritated.

"Well, the upside is, friend of the family or not, there's no reason for him to be at the hearing," Eric said, thinking the matter over carefully. "And no reason for Ace to have to see him otherwise. Not this trip."

"Her family might expect her to visit, but there's no reason for her to oblige them while she's engaged in a lawsuit against them," Ria agreed.

"An' Ah think Ah have an idea that'll let me stick pretty close to her the whole time," Hosea said. "But Ah'll see if it works out before Ah tell you what it is."

Now Eric could put his finger on what was making him so uneasy about all this. It *looked* as if they had everything together and a good solid plan, but when he started to think about it, he realized that all they truly had was a skeleton and air. There were holes in their plan big enough to send an oil tanker through. But try as he might, he couldn't think of any solution to the problem.

"One good thing about this," Eric said, "is that nasty as this situation is, and unpleasant as it is for Ace, there's nothing the least bit supernatural about it—no ghosts, no elves, no space aliens. Just the possibility of a weird government agency."

"As if that weren't bad enough." Ria sighed. "But nothing I can't handle."

Fiona Banyon regarded the garish illuminated facade with a distaste that was nearly physical. Only a furious determination to win at all costs could have brought her to this . . . place. Of all the many things that irritated her, religious fanatics were high on her list.

"It looks like a casino." Michael's voice was absolutely neutral, betraying nothing of his feelings.

"Their offices are on one of the upper floors. They come with the highest recommendations," Fiona said tightly. Trust Michael to bring up things they couldn't do anything about after they were already committed.

Neither of them made any move to get out of the car. To do so would be the final admission that they were really here, that they were really going to do this thing.

But there was nothing else to do.

Vandewater had told them—strictly off the record, of course—that it was almost certain their petition to have their grandson Magnus's custody awarded to them would fail. He would continue to fight on their behalf—certainly he would do that—but their son Eric's case was airtight in every particular.

An attempt to have Eric declared mentally incompetent and committed to an institution on the basis of his past history, as Michael had suggested, would certainly fail. Perhaps twenty years ago that would have been possible. Now even relatives had to move mountains to prove someone was incompetent even when they actually *were*. Eric had graduated from Juilliard, he was more than gainfully employed, his circle of friends included officers of the law and the very highly successful Ria Llewellyn. No judge in *his* right mind would declare Eric incompetent.

As for their search for their missing son Magnus . . .

He was gone as if he'd never existed. Philip Dorland, the expensive and well-recommended private detective they'd hired to find him, had told them frankly that there was nothing to look for and they were wasting their money.

Fiona sneered mentally. There was no point in maintaining the legal fiction that her son was missing in the privacy of her own mind. Dorland couldn't find Magnus because Magnus was in New York, pretending to be his brother's son. She didn't know whether he and Eric had actually fooled that Llewellyn harpy, or whether she was in on their sick hoax, but Fiona Sommerville Banyon had always faced the world with clear eyes and no illusions. She knew her own children. They were weak and vicious, but they had the angels' own talent for music, and she had the drive and discipline to make up for their lack of moral fiber.

She'd failed with Eric, but she would mold Magnus into a great artist. He needed her. Magnus was too self-indulgent and blind to see it, but she was used to that.

Michael was much the same when he focused on his work. The rest of the time ... oh, he had ambition. She could never have married a man without ambition. But he lacked focus. He lacked *vision*. Without her, he would never have managed to do all that he had done with his life.

But Eric was to have been her greatest achievement: an artist that she could present to the world—famous, respected, legendary. He had failed her.

No, Fiona told herself sternly. *She* had failed. She had not understood how devious Eric could be, how weak, how selfish, how self-deluded. She should have seen the warning signs. She should have been more careful.

Magnus was her last chance.

He would not follow the path his brother had, into madness and vice.

It would have been nice if Dorland could have found a trail that connected Magnus to Eric, but unfortunately, he hadn't been able to. That left Eric a loophole that he thought he was going to squirm through, but Fiona wasn't going to let that happen. Like it or not, he was still her son. She wouldn't abandon him. Not completely. She would take Magnus back, make him see that his life must be spent in service to his great musical gifts, and perhaps ... perhaps it was not too late for Eric after all.

But her first duty was to Magnus. She was his mother, after all. And only a mother's love could give her the strength to come to this inexpressibly vulgar place in the hope that her child could be saved.

The offices of Christian Family Intervention were reassuringly bland, but it was still impossible for the Banyons to forget what they were, or escape the humiliating thought that someone might see them here—even though it was far from likely that it would be anyone either of them knew. The circles in which Michael

Banyon moved encouraged secular humanism, not religious fanaticism. Oh, there was the occasional aberration, but they were generally found in the Eastern Studies department, and tended towards gurus, not preachers. Fortunately the two of them didn't have to wait long in the reception area, but were ushered almost immediately into Director Cowan's office.

"Mr. and Mrs. Banyon. How can I help you?"

Michael was glad to see that the man behind the desk seemed to be a reasonable sort. He had the kind of distinguished professorial appearance that was insensibly soothing. In fact, it almost seemed that he wouldn't have been out of place at Harvard. In the English Department, of course.

"Our son," he began, and stopped. "Our son is a discipline problem." Yes, that covered things nicely.

Director Cowan smiled gently. "As you are no doubt already aware, discipline problems are something of a specialty of ours. What is the nature of the difficulty?"

"He's . . . well, he's run away from his school." That sounded better than saying he'd run away from home, didn't it? "And he won't go back."

"How awkward," Director Cowan said sympathetically. "Education is so very important in the young. Perhaps you could tell me a bit more about the lad."

*How odd,* Toirealach thought to himself. Unlike so many of the groundlings who came through those doors, intent on opening their budget of misery and perceived ill-usage at the hands of their children, the Banyons needed to be coaxed to speak of their son at all. From skimming the surface of their thoughts, he could tell they thought they were far too fine to come to a place such as this. He savored the rich bouquet of their tangled emotions: rage, shame, cheated fury and twisted love—a far headier brew than that usually offered up to him by his clients.

But a few spells—so subtly cast that even most Gifted wouldn't be aware of them—soon had the haughty mortalkin spilling their guts to kindly old Director Cowan, their dear friend and ally—and telling him far more than they'd intended to. . . .

But wait. Surely his master would be interested in anything involving Bard Eric of Misthold or his kin?

"A moment, please. I'd like to ask a colleague of mine to sit in on this. You'll appreciate that your circumstances—and the personalities involved—render this matter more than normally complex," Toirealach said soothingly.

"Very well," Fiona Banyon said, inclining her head graciously.

Toirealach smiled to himself. Perhaps if matters concluded to his master's satisfaction, Prince Gabrevys would give him permission to take the woman for his sport, and teach her better manners.

He stepped out of the office. It was the work of a moment to locate his master, and to let him know that the Bright Bard's parents had come to them, seeking favors.

A few moments later, Gabriel Horn entered the office.

"My colleague, Gabriel Horn," Toirealach said. "His input is valuable in our more delicate cases. Mr. Horn, the Banyons were just telling me about their son Magnus. Apparently he's left his school in Boston. The particular difficulty in the matter lies in that he's taken up with his much older brother Eric, who has been estranged from his parents for some years and is now living in New York. Eric is claiming to be Magnus's father, and is prepared to go to court to prove it—I gather there's an unfortunate history of mental instability there. Naturally the Banyons would rather settle this whole matter without unpleasantness, but this is a truly awkward situation."

"How terrible for you both," Gabriel said to the Banyons. He radiated trustworthiness and friendship; a simple enough spell, and—just as the Fairchilds before them—he soon had the Banyons under his thrall. "To lose one son—and then to face the prospect of losing another. I'm sure a day doesn't go by that you don't wish you had Eric back as well. Surely your fondest dream is that both of them will see reason and return to your guiding hand."

Both the Banyons looked faintly puzzled, as if the notion had never occurred to them before this moment. Finally, after a long, long moment, Fiona spoke.

"Why yes, Mr. Horn. Of course we'd like to have Eric back as well. But he's always been so rebellious."

"We are here to help," Gabriel said gravely. "Our mission—our *only* mission—is to reunite families. We can return *both* your sons to you as happy, helpful, supportive members of the Banyon family." He nodded at them, reinforcing his minion's spells. "There really is no reason to leave your older boy in crisis when we can save both of them so easily."

"And it can be done quietly?" Michael asked, sounding dubious. "That's important. For Magnus's sake, of course."

"We always act with the utmost discretion," Director Cowan said, taking up the thread of the conversation with practiced ease. "We feel it's important to cause minimal disruption of the family circle. For the sake of the children, of course."

*Children. Bard Eric is a man grown; more of a man than this weak limb, his father. Yet they persist in seeing him as being as much a child as the other. Blind. Willingly, willfully blind. My favorite sort of mortal . . .*

"Of course," Fiona Banyon said. "So it's settled, then? You'll get Magnus back for us? And . . . make Eric see reason?"

"Indeed we will," Director Cowan said, rising to his feet. "Now, if you'll come this way, there's the small matter of some paperwork, and then we can get started in saving *both* your children."

When the others had left the office, Gabriel Horn remained behind. He stood quietly in the center of the room, though he felt like leaping, capering, shouting for joy. Normally, by every treaty and covenant of Underhill, a Bard was utterly untouchable—but here and now, Eric Banyon's own flesh and blood had set Gabrevys and his vassals on, and that gave the prince of Elfhame Bete Noir the license to do what he would with Misthold's Bard, and still stand within the bounds of Sidhe law. Ties of blood stood above all treaty: that was the first law of the Sidhe—and had not the mortal Bard's own parents asked Gabrevys to render him a dutiful and filial child once more?

And so he would. And if, when Gabrevys and his Shadows were done with their work, Eric Banyon was of no more use to Prince Arvin of Misthold, that was no crime to be laid at Gabrevys's door, was it? He would merely have done what was asked of him by the woman who had borne the mortal Bard and the man who had sired him. No more than that. Even Oberon would have to agree, should Arvin complain.

Oh, vengeance was sweet—doubly so since he could take it within the Law!

Rubbing his hands together in satisfaction, Gabriel went to make a few preparations. There was also the matter of Heavenly Grace to consider . . .

"I can't believe you're going to interview my father," Ace said, for the seventh time since they'd left Guardian House.

"He was happy to agree," Hosea repeated once more, barely restraining a smirk.

"I just bet, once you told him you were on assignment from *Rolling Stone*," Ace said.

"It's the truth," Hosea said innocently. "Ah wouldn't lie about something like that. 'Sides, it's too easy to check."

It hadn't been all that difficult for Hosea to come up with a convincing pretext for accompanying Ace to Atlantic City after all. One of the other tenants of Guardian House was a freelance journalist, and a contributing editor to *Rolling Stone*. Dugal had read several of Hosea's other pieces and liked them, and when Hosea had asked him if he thought there might be any interest in a piece on the Reverend Billy Fairchild's "Casino of Prayer," he'd been happy to set Hosea up with the proper journalistic credentials. Of course, that wasn't a guarantee of selling the finished piece to the magazine, but it did give Hosea a good excuse for hanging around just about anywhere he wanted down in Atlantic City for as long as he needed to. He even had an interview set up with Billy for the day after Ace's hearing—and as the hearing itself was a matter of public record, there was no reason he shouldn't even attend, now, was there?

"I wish you'd let me drive," Ace said wistfully, gazing out over the vast expanse of the car's hood. "I can drive."

They were rolling down the road in a bubblegum pink 1959

Cadillac Seville Eldorado hardtop, on loan from another of Guardian House's tenants. It had white leather upholstery. There were a pair of lime green fuzzy dice hanging from the rearview mirror and a bright orange fake fur raccoon tail flying from the radio aerial. It had white sidewall tires, baby-moon hubcaps, and was about as far from inconspicuous as it was possible to get.

"A learner's permit and a history of grand theft auto ain't the same thing as bein' able to drive," Hosea said absently. "An' you know what Margot'd do iff'n Ah got a scratch on her car."

"It isn't exactly the kind of car you'd expect a writer to have. She looks so *normal*," Ace said, temporarily diverted from the reason for their road trip.

"Come to that, Ah reckon all of us look pretty normal to folks as don't know us," Hosea said reasonably. "An' Ah guess we've all got the odd kick in our gallop somewheres."

"Maybe," Ace said, unconvinced. "But most people don't paint their odd kicks Barbie-doll pink."

When they reached Atlantic City, they checked into their hotel, which was located a few blocks away from the courthouse where the hearing would be held. Driving through the downtown, they found the street names had an odd familiarity, even though this was the first visit to Atlantic City for both of them, and that puzzled both of them until Ace remembered that the streets on the Monopoly board were named after the streets of Atlantic City. The board-game street names gave everything even more of a sense of unreality than the distant glimpses of the towering, glittering casinos that lined the boardwalk did, as if she'd stepped into a cartoon.

The hotel was one of the older ones, from before the days when gambling had been legalized in Atlantic City. Ria had booked their rooms through LlewellCo, to avoid any possibility that the Fairchilds would be able to find out where Ace was staying the night before the hearing.

When Hosea went to check in, Ace stayed in the car, hunkered down low in the seat, her cap pulled down over her ears and the collar of her wool coat turned up over her neck. After a moment she reached into her purse and dug out a pair of sunglasses and put them on.

There was no reason any of Daddy's people would be looking for her here. Ria had promised her that. They'd be expecting her to come down tomorrow with Mr. Tilford, maybe, or be staying at one of those big fancy hotels on the Boardwalk.

But nothing about any of this was exactly going the way they'd expected, was it? When she'd filed those court papers, Ria had told her that she wouldn't have to go back to her parents, even though they'd have to know where she was, but she'd expected that they'd at least try to *get* her to come home. But it had been almost four months, and she hadn't heard one peep out of either of them.

She frowned. Maybe Daddy hadn't told Mama she'd turned up again, especially since she was being so undutiful? It was possible. He'd certainly do that if Gabriel Horn told him to. Daddy would do just about anything Mr. Horn said.

And maybe it was Mr. Horn who said Daddy wasn't to write her. . . .

*Soon enough you'll know,* Ace told herself grimly. *You'll see your father tomorrow. And maybe Mama too.*

Just as long as Gabriel Horn wasn't any part of it.

She shivered, and scrunched down even lower in the seat. She remembered the first time she'd ever seen him. It was a few months before she'd decided to run away. She'd been fifteen then. Not exactly naive—nobody who grew up at the center of Billy Fairchild's Chautauqua could lead a really sheltered life—but she hadn't seen a tenth of the horrors she'd see later, when she took to the road.

But nothing that would ever happen to her later—not the people who tried to hurt her, not the people who tried to take from her, not even the dark things that had chased after her, Magnus, and Jaycie—had been as terrifying as the first time she'd looked into Gabriel Horn's eyes.

Daddy had brought him home to dinner one night. That wasn't unusual; her father was always bringing home people, especially people he was thinking of taking on, and Mama took pride in her table and welcomed guests. Ben and Joshua and Andrew—all of Daddy's inside top-level folks—were there to meet him.

He'd brought Mama flowers and candy. He was dressed up fine, in an expensive suit and a shirt with French cuffs, all smiling and nice-mannered. Daddy'd been excited, Ace could tell.

"And this is my daughter, Heavenly Grace," Daddy had said, introducing her.

"Ah, the little songbird. You must be very proud of her God-given gifts, Reverend."

Gabriel Horn was a tall man, as good-looking as a movie star. He'd taken her hand and bowed slightly, almost as if he were about to kiss it. Startled, she'd looked up.

His eyes were as green as glass, and colder than ice. Something about them seemed to burn, making her feel as if she'd been stripped naked right there. She'd caught her breath in a strangled gasp. Suddenly she'd wanted to turn and run away right then, run and keep running, but nobody else had seemed to see anything wrong with the handsome dark-haired fellow, and Mama was looking at her with that firm expression that told her she'd better not forget her manners.

So she'd forced herself to smile.

"Very proud," Gabriel Horn said again, letting go of her hand. He had a deep voice, perfect for preaching, and she'd wondered for one horror-struck moment if he was one of Daddy's new deacons. If he was, she'd see him every day on stage.

And she'd known right then that she never wanted to see Gabriel Horn again.

Dinner had been horrible. Mama had flirted with Mr. Horn just as if she were a young girl again, and Daddy hadn't seemed to notice or mind. Ace had barely been able to eat a bite; at least she'd found out that Mr. Horn wasn't to be a deacon. He was going to be helping Daddy out with the business end of things. His new advisor, Daddy had said.

But that didn't mean Ace didn't see him. Mr. Horn became a frequent guest at the house—and sometimes, when he thought she wasn't looking, she'd see him watching her. Not in any sexual way—that would actually have been better. She could have understood that, though she would have hated it. But she'd had no words for the look in his eyes when he watched her.

It had been like—like the time she'd seen a blacksnake eyeing a nest of baby birds. That snake knew he was going to get those birds, and eat up every one of them. The parent-birds that were dive-bombing him and trying to drive him off knew it too. He was perfectly patient, and perfectly controlled, and perfectly avid, as if he was already feeling those babies going down his throat. The parent-birds were hysterical, knowing they couldn't stop him. It had been unspeakably horrible.

Gabriel Horn was exactly like that snake. And she was a little baby bird.

She'd known better than to try to get help from her parents. What could she say other than that she didn't like him? And she already knew that both Daddy and Mama liked Gabriel Horn just fine, and more than fine.

And Daddy wouldn't let her stop singing with the choir, and using her Gift in that bad way, and somehow she'd known, now that Gabriel Horn had come, that there would be no escape. Ever.

So she'd run. She'd thought she was free. She'd hoped she was free. But now it didn't look like she was, and if she had to see Gabriel Horn one more time, she didn't know what would happen.

Just then Hosea came back, two key-envelopes in his hand. He opened the car door—the Cadillac was like a bank vault—and got in.

"Our rooms are around the back. Ah thought we'd get settled in, an' then Ah had a mind to do a bit o' explorin', while you rested up."

But Ace had absolutely no intention of staying behind, especially when she learned what his destination was, so less than an hour later, they were on the road again, heading toward the outskirts of the city.

With only a couple of wrong turns, they reached something called the Heavenly Grace Business Park. A brightly lit archway in bright primary colors proclaimed the entrance to the Heavenly

Grace Cathedral and Casino of Prayer, but they drove past that. A few hundred yards farther down the main road there was a more conventional-looking entrance to the rest of the business park. A large sign at the entrance listed the names of various businesses located within the complex: Christian Family Intervention, Red Nails Music Publishing, Fairchild Ministries, Inc., and several others that were so utterly generic that they were completely meaningless. "Worldwide Fulfillment," for example. That could be almost anything.

"Miz Llewellyn says that the Reverend owns all this," Hosea commented noncommittally, as they drove through the secondary entrance.

Ace shifted uneasily on the wide bench seat of the Cadillac. "I never exactly knew everything that was going on," she said, her voice barely above a whisper, "but I wasn't stupid, either. There's a whole lot more money here now than there ever was in Tulsa." *Or a lot more debt.*

Neither of them voiced the obvious question: if Reverend Fairchild had suddenly become so wealthy, where had all the money come from, especially without Ace's presence to ensure the contributions of the faithful? If it had been from anything illegal, Ria would certainly have found out, and used the information to blackmail Billy into submission.

But . . . where?

They drove through the empty section of the grounds, past several obviously unoccupied buildings left over from the site's previous incarnation as a more traditional business park. Yellow sawhorses blocked the roads that led deeper into the complex, and parked in front of one of them was a car with a light-bar on the top and two uniformed security guards sitting inside.

"Touchy about their privacy, aren't they?" Hosea commented dryly.

Farther along the road that led back toward the casino, a couple of large work-trailers were parked, and it was apparent that some sort of construction project was in the early stages. Hosea slowed down to take a closer look, but a car parked next to one of the trailers—obviously another security vehicle—flashed its headlights at them in an unspoken warning to move along.

Then they reached the front of the casino.

The cathedral and casino was obviously a new building, and unlike the other buildings in the complex, which were only two or three stories high, it was a true tower: at least ten stories of gold glass and white concrete crowned the casino itself, and like casinos everywhere, the decoration of its facade would put the pipe dreams of an Oriental potentate to shame.

But not even someone familiar with the cheerful excesses of Las Vegas could be prepared for the three-story light-up cross that surmounted the entryway to the Casino of Prayer, the bright facade of lambs, lilies, scourges, crowns of thorns, fish, baskets of bread, and other, less immediately recognizable symbols, that decorated the doorway and marquee of the building. Everything that didn't flash on and off glittered with tinsel, and from within the casino—the doors were open even on this cool March day—came the sounds of familiar Gospel hymns done to an insistent disco beat, intermixed with the ringing of slot machines.

Even at this time of day, the parking lot was filled with cars. There were several tour buses parked at the edge of the parking lot, and as they watched, a shuttle pulled up to the entrance to disgorge a load of passengers before heading on its way. The Reverend was obviously not missing a trick when it came to drawing in the marks.

If this was not Hell, Hosea Songmaker reflected to himself, it was probably as close an approximation as you could achieve without actual black hoodoo. He was not completely certain, but he suspected this entire production skated pretty close to the edge of blasphemy, provided he understood the word properly. At the very least, it was a bad thing in as much as it made a mockery of God and His good things, and kept people who needed them away from them by turning them into a venal sideshow.

This was not the work of any kind of preacher that he was

familiar with. In fact, it made him begin to wonder just what kind of a preacher this Billy Fairchild was.

And it made him just as uneasy as the rest of the business park did Ace.

He wasn't quite certain why. Certainly it wasn't very tasteful, but that didn't make it either Guardian business, or something an Apprentice Bard needed to stick his nose into. And in plain fact, the better Billy Fairchild was doing for himself, the less reason he had to hang on to Ace and her Talent.

But where *was* the money for all this coming from?

Though the cathedral and casino resembled the casino hotels on the Boardwalk with its crowning tower, Hosea knew from what Miz Llewellyn had told him that there was no hotel here. The tower contained offices for the various components of the Fairchild empire, the broadcasting studio, and some private apartments for some of the senior staff. So there wasn't any hotel money, just whatever the casino brought in. There was money in gambling—Lord knew folks were both weak-willed and too hopeful, sometimes, and lost more money than they could fairly afford to. And even good God-fearing folks who would never have thought of gambling might be tempted and tried when gambling came in with the aura of false sanctity hanging about it.

But was there this much money?

Hosea's eyes narrowed as he watched the doors of the casino. This place was out in the middle of nowhere as far as the casinos went, even with the shuttles the Reverend was running. You wouldn't get any walk-in traffic from the Boardwalk casinos. And a goodly number of people would be put off by the hymns and the crosses, thinking that religion and gambling didn't mix any too well.

He reached into the back seat of the car and laid his hand on Jeanette's case.

The banjo was very old, handed down in Hosea's family for generations. It was the masterwork of a master craftsman, strung with silver. But what made it truly special was that it housed . . . a ghost. The spirit bound to it by Bardic power was a woman named Jeanette Campbell. She haunted the banjo by her own will, remaining tied to the world in order to make amends for all the wrongs she'd done when she was alive. Only Hosea could hear her and speak to her—and then, only when he was actually playing the banjo—but even dormant, Jeanette's presence lent extra power to his Bardic gifts.

He looked again at the garish facade of the cathedral and casino, trying to understand the feeling of *wrongness* that he felt so strongly, but no explanation came. Whatever the source of Billy Fairchild's newfound prosperity, it was nothing Jeanette could sense—and if it were something illegal, Miz Llewellyn would have found that out, used it against Billy in a New York minute. Hosea knew that perfectly well. Miz Llewellyn was a good woman, but she had the iron in her soul of a Good Book prophet when the need was on her. And like Jael, she used any and every weapon that came into her hand.

So the casino and cathedral, unsettling as it was, was not only mundane, but legitimate.

"Ah'm guessin' you don't want to go inside," he said to Ace, removing his hand from Jeanette's case.

Ace shuddered vehemently. "Even if I could go anywhere near the casino floor without being caught for being underage—" she said, "—no. I know it's been almost two years since any of Daddy's folks have seen me, and I look a lot different than I did then, but if any of them recognized me—if Gabriel Horn saw me . . ."

"Well, we won't let that happen," Hosea said comfortably, backing the enormous pink length of the Cadillac out of the parking place and turning in the direction of the main gate this time. "It's something to have seen the place. An' Ah'm not sure now whether Ah'm looking forward to the tour Ah'm likely to get of it myself—or not."

Earlier that same day, Billy Fairchild convened his regular Wednesday morning department meeting.

He'd learned early on—as soon as there was more to the Ministry than a broken-down bus and a box of mail-order Bibles—that while the right hand didn't always need to know what the left hand was doing, he needed to know what pockets both hands were in at all times.

Unlike the business meetings, the department meetings focused on information, not money: what was new, what was doing well, what might be introduced: new people, new faces, new ideas. They were held in a much larger conference room than the business meeting—one usually given over to "Praise Training" and "Abundance Orientation" for the new hires and junior staff. The department heads and their assistants who attended filled three big tables arranged in a horseshoe, and there was plenty of coffee and doughnuts.

Today Billy would be formally introducing Parker Wheatley to everyone. They'd be broadcasting the *Praise Hour* with his introduction tonight, and the rehearsals—without the audience present, of course—had gone very well. Wheatley was a good speaker, strong-voiced and convincing, and if he wasn't full of Gospel fire, that didn't matter too much once he got going. And if he could do what he said, and hand over a by-Jesus *demon*, then when you came down to it, Billy didn't really care if he sounded like an accountant reading a quarterly report.

But he didn't. He had a passion on him, and what was better, he had a message that would bring the Faithful bolt upright in their seats and make them pay attention, if Billy Fairchild was any judge at all of human nature. People liked signs and wonders and miracles, but even more than that, they loved horrors: they wanted to hear about the gates of Hell, the fiery pit opening wide to suck in sinners, and best of all, demons clothed in human flesh, walking among them, preying upon their innocent children. He'd learned that when he'd started running "Judgment Houses" every weekend in October up to Halloween. People'd pay good money, ten and even fifteen dollars apiece, to get scared in the name of the Lord and special effects.

And if he could do that every day of the year—

That should keep the donations rolling in.

He got to his feet and waited for the buzz of conversation to die down.

"Friends, I'd like to introduce you to the newest member of our little fellowship. This here's Mr. Parker Wheatley. He used to work in Washington D.C., until they threw him out for witnessing to the truth. Now he's come to us to get his message out, and we're glad to have him. He'll be joining me on tonight's *Praise Hour*—as some of you already know, it's going to be a very special event, and I encourage all of you who can to attend. Of course, we'll be showing it on the big screens down on the casino floor, but it's going to be something you'll want to tell the grandkiddies that you were there for in person. Stand on up, Brother Wheatley, and tell these good folks a little something about your mission."

Parker Wheatley got to his feet amid polite applause. He nodded graciously and began to speak—an expanded and slightly modified version of the speech he had given in Fairchild's office the previous week. As he spoke, the room fell utterly silent.

At the far end of one of the tables, Toirealach O'Caomhain raised his head and gazed toward his master with barely concealed horror. Several of the others along the tables were doing the same thing—all of them Prince Gabrevys's liege-folk.

If he ever discovered who among their own had betrayed them so thoroughly, Gabriel vowed silently, that one would not live either long or happily. There was no hint of magic about the green garments Wheatley wore, but there did not have to be: Gabriel recognized the work of a Master Smith.

To mortals, Danu had given three great Gifts: Healing, Bard-craft, and Smithcraft. In the days of Gabrevys's youth, those with the Gift of Smithcraft were great forgers of weapons and cunning engines, for whatever they turned their hand to, that thing they could craft with greater skill than any other mortal, but the gift of Smithcraft extended to the making of all things that could be made with hands. In ancient times, those with that Gift had spun and woven as well, both for good and ill, and their work had passed into legend as God-touched and magickal. One with that Gift could surely weave cloth so strong and fine that it would turn any spell of Seleighe or Unseleighe casting.

And someone had. Someone in the service of one of their own

had given Wheatley these weapons—or else how could Wheatley have come by his knowledge of them and their ways? And there was worse. He spoke of methods by which he could infallibly detect the presence of the Sidhe, piercing all *glamouries*, and Gabriel had no doubt that he possessed them.

Such arts have been admirable—if Wheatley were Gabriel's pawn. And even so, the Unseleighe lord had a grudging admiration for the clever trick. Only think of using a human to slay one's enemies!

But here and now, Wheatley and his deadly toys were nothing other than a terrible impediment to Gabriel's own intentions. For a moment Gabriel wondered if one of his enemies had sent Wheatley here to destroy his carefully crafted plans. If he used them—if he discovered how many of that foolish mortal Fairchild's newly hired employees were in reality the "demons" of his imaginings . . .

All would be lost.

To which Court should he look for such a subtle, elegant sabotage? The Bright Court had known for longer than the Dark how precarious Gabriel's position was; it was the Bright Court which even now held his son and heir Jachiel in its clutches; but such a feint was not Seleighe style, nor had he heard any rumors of a mortal Smith held hostage in any of the Bright Domains. And Wheatley himself might not know who had set him on.

But why concern himself with such things now? Ferret out the cause later; now was the time for direct action, before all his plans were undone!

And after his initial shock, he knew the course he must take to protect himself and his purpose.

Wheatley must die.

Proof against levin-bolts and *glamouries* his hideous garment might be, but not against a bullet. Gabriel would arrange it as soon as he could find a suitable lackey to bear the Cold Iron weapon.

And Billy Fairchild—who had brought this traitor within the gate, who had concealed his presence from Gabriel with low animal cunning—Billy had outlived his usefulness as well. He was becoming far too independent for Gabriel's tastes. Whether he had acted on his own, or had been tricked by another, he had shown himself too clearly as the liability he was to be allowed to remain alive. Gabriel was far too fond of his own life and his own power for that.

The Fairchild empire would survive. There would be, after all, a grieving widow. So much more malleable, so much more easily controlled. Gabriel was certain that not only would Donna Fairchild take strength from his presence and rise up to take over her husband's ministry, but that she would do exactly what Gabriel told her to.

Yes. Gabriel relaxed fractionally, feeling the tide of red rage receding, and even managed to smile. Tomorrow was the hearing, after which little Heavenly Grace would be coming home. A few days after that would be the concert. And then, he would have time to take care of both Wheatley and his soon-to-be-former employer thoroughly.

And permanently.

Ace had been too nervous to do anything but stay in her hotel room after they drove back from the casino and cathedral. Hosea had gone out to bring in something for dinner, and she'd dutifully given Ria a call on her cellphone to let her know that everything was all right. After that she'd tried to add a few more pages to her letter to Jaycie, but everything she'd written sounded angry and desperate. She wouldn't want to get a letter like that. Why would he?

Finally, in disgust, she turned on the television and began flipping through the channels. In an effort to lure customers away from the casinos, the hotel offered dozens of channels with crystal-clear reception; she flipped impatiently past program after program, never pausing for more than a few seconds.

Once her attention was caught by a familiar cadence. She'd stumbled across one of the religious channels, where an impassioned young man was leaning forward over the podium, making intense eye-contact with the camera.

"Jesus—" he began.

Ace quickly turned off the set.

She'd just read a book instead.

Half an hour later she was deep into Margot's new book, *Bad Companions*, reading about Prince Perigord and Azure Bowl's latest adventures as bodyguards to a temperamental princess who really, *really*, didn't want to get married. Considering that her bridegroom was a dragon, Ace could see her point. On the other hand, the princess was the sort of person that you'd want to get out of the house (or palace) just about any way you could, in Ace's estimation, so there might be some justice on both sides.

About the time she reached Chapter Three, and Princess Klepsydra was about to steal some clothes and go sneaking off in the middle of the night to get into even more trouble, Hosea came back with a couple of large bags of food.

"There's Chinese take-out for tonight," he said, as he came through the connecting door between their rooms, "and juice and muffins for the morning. And I didn't forget your coffees."

Ace took the smallest of the bags from him gratefully, and went over to set them on the dresser, out of harm's way. When she turned back, Hosea was setting out cartons of Chinese on the table beneath the window.

"Just how many people were you planning to feed?" Ace gibed. There was enough food here to feed both of them twice over, she was pretty sure, and she wasn't sure she was all that hungry.

"Well, Ah wasn't sure what you'd be in the mood for, so Ah bought a little bit o' everything," Hosea said. "There's a refrigerator in my room, so anything left over will keep."

But oddly enough, once the cartons were open, her stomach reminded her that breakfast had been a long time ago—and there hadn't been much of it, either. The food was surprisingly good, for take-out bought in a strange city where you didn't know much about the kitchen or the cook, and there wasn't much to tuck away for later when the two of them were finished.

Hosea suggested going out to a movie, but Ace shook her head, cradling her second cup of coffee beneath her chin.

"I know it's silly—I know I'm just as likely to run into *him* in New York as here—more, if he was really looking for me, but . . ."

"Well, no harm in getting your rest. We have to meet Mr. Tilford over at the courthouse tomorrow morning at nine-thirty. Then Ah'll play least in sight, just like Ah was pokin' around after a story, and you can get shut of this trouble once an' for all. And maybe there's something worth lookin' at on the television for a couple of hours."

He picked up the remote, lying on the bed where Ace had left it, and hit the "power" button.

Immediately the screen was filled with the image of a dignified man in a bright green suit. The dissociation between his face, calm and dignified, and the surreal color of his suit—like something out of a comic book—drew their fascinated attention. He was speaking with calm intensity.

"—have infiltrated our entire culture. These demons are alien in nature to everything we know and understand. There is no possibility of communicating with them on any meaningful level. Anyone who has ever attempted to do so has been horribly murdered. They have the ability not only to influence the thoughts of the weak-minded, but some people have actually become their willing slaves."

"Is this the Sci-Fi Channel?" Hosea asked doubtfully. "Ah don't recognize the movie."

"No," Ace said, sounding baffled. "This is one of the Christian channels. See that logo down in the corner?"

"Worst of all," the man in the green suit went on, "is their obsession with children. I have studied this new demonic outbreak for years, and in all cases where they show themselves, they target children. Your children are their prey, and they can lure them away from you before you have any idea that there is anything wrong. You've all seen those pathetic faces on the milk cartons, the postcards, the television shows! Where do you think they have all vanished to? I know! I *can* tell you! They have gone somewhere where neither man nor law can ever find them!"

Hosea's brows creased with puzzlement.

"But there are ways to fight these demons, these child-thieves. They can be located, they can be identified—and they can be killed. With the Reverend Fairchild's help—"

Ace gave a strangled gasp and nearly dropped her coffee. Hosea put a steadying arm around her shoulders. Both of them missed the man in the green suit's next few words, but they weren't hard to guess, from the number and address that flashed up on the screen, superimposed over the podium. Obviously this was the point in the spiel where people were encouraged to give, and give generously.

The image on the screen pulled back from the tight close-up, and now Ace and Hosea could see that the man in green was standing in front of a drawing of hideous monster with dead white skin, enormous slanted green eyes without pupils, and long pointed ears. A mane of hair as white as its skin cascaded down its back. It was naked except for a ragged loincloth, and its fingers and toes ended in long hooked talons. Its mouth was open in a snarl, exposing long curved fangs. Above it was written the words "The Enemy Among Us!"

"Tell me that ain't what I think it is," Hosea said, sounding stunned. Not half as stunned as Ace felt, though.

"Thank you, Brother Wheatley, for that inspiring message of hope." Billy Fairchild stepped up to the podium. "What's that you say, friends? 'Reverend, he's telling us demons are after our children—where's the hope in that?' My friends, my dear brothers and sisters in Jesus Christ, every day is a battle. And knowing our enemy is the first step to winning the war. It is the hidden enemies—the enemies that masquerade as friends—the enemies that we are forced to *pretend* are our friends—that do us the greatest harm—"

The camera was focused tightly on Billy Fairchild now, and Parker Wheatley had apparently left the stage. Hosea moved to change the channel, but Ace stopped him.

"No, wait," she said. "I want to hear this."

"—knowing our enemies, *fighting* our enemies, the enemies of America, whoever and whatever they are, is the first step to living a truly pure Christian life! Every time we discover a new enemy among us—a new enemy we can search out and destroy—there is new hope for our victory in this battle, new hope to create the Kingdom of God on Earth that our Lord Jesus Christ promised us would come! Did he promise it would come through peace? *No!* The Lord Jesus did not promise us peace, but a sword—and it is the sword and the gun that all good God-fearing Christians must take up now, to purge and purify God's most holy creation of the enemies of God! Only then will we be worthy! Only then will we be able to build the New Jerusalem on the sacred soil of the United States of America: God's own country!"

There was a great deal more in this vein, as Billy Fairchild whipped his congregation up into something little short of a mob. The message was clear, and not all that subtle, either: the destruction of worldly enemies brought spiritual salvation.

At last the image switched to the Salvation Choir, and Hosea hit the "mute" button. The two of them looked at each other uneasily.

"That's new, what he's saying," Ace said. She shook her head, trying to gather her thoughts. "It's . . ."

"It's the kind o' thing that can get a body into trouble—and drag a lot of other fellers down with him," Hosea said.

"And that other man," Ace said. "The one talking about—" she wrinkled her nose "—demons. The one Daddy called 'Brother Wheatley.' Wasn't that man in Washington that Ria was after named Parker Wheatley?"

"Ayah," Hosea said, sighing. "He was hunting the Good Neighbors, so Miz Llewellyn said. And if you looked at the drawing that feller on the television had, it might look a little like one o' them, if you looked at it right. If you wanted to make elves look like monsters," Hosea said, his voice a mixture of anger and disgust. The more he had time to think about it, the more likely it was that this was Wheatley—Beth had told Eric about the lurid green suits that all of Wheatley's agents had worn, suits somehow proof against all Sidhe magic.

"I thought she'd gotten rid of him," Ace said unhappily.

"Got him out of his Washington job right enough," Hosea said. "He was working with one of the Good Neighbors; well, he wasn't good at all, he's a good part of the reason why Jeanette's locked up tight in my banjo here. But Eric did for that one; put him where he can't ever hurt anyone again."

"Don't you people ever *kill* anybody?" Ace burst out. She covered her mouth with her hand. "I'm sorry, Hosea, I didn't mean that, honestly I didn't, it's just—"

"You've had a powerful fright, Ah know," Hosea said, patting her shoulder. "But Eric didn't want to kill Aerune any more than you would have if you'd been there. Ah reckon nobody with the Shine on 'em really wants to kill anything, less'n it's the only way. And Miz Llewellyn, well, Ah don't reckon she could have expected Mr. Wheatley to go off to work for your Daddy, now, could she?"

That startled a tear-filled laugh from Ace. "And now he's telling everybody that people like Jaycie are demons out to steal their children."

"Trouble is," Hosea said gravely, "there's just enough truth in it that he can make a power of trouble if he can figure out how. We'd better let Ria know, if she doesn't know already."

"You'll be delighted to know that an old friend of yours is doing well," Claire said without preamble, as she came through the door of Ria's office.

Claire MacLaren looked like a kindly old Scottish grandmother, and nothing could have been farther from the truth. She was one of the very few people in the world who had the right to walk in on Ria Llewellyn unannounced at any time, and that was rare as blue roses. She was a private investigator, one of the very best there was, and more than that, she was a friend Ria could trust absolutely to always tell her the truth. That was even rarer than blue roses; Ria was a powerful woman, even discounting her half-elven heritage, and power made people, even honest people, lie to you. Money made them search for what they thought you wanted to hear. But nothing impressed Claire MacLaren: not power, not position, and certainly not money.

Several months ago, Ria had put Claire in charge of a "watch and warn" list of people she wanted to keep track of. Some of them, Ria was nearly sure would never be seen in mortal lands again—like Robert Lintel, former CEO of Threshold. Others simply needed her watchful protection, like bookstore owner Marley Bell.

And others . . .

"Tell me," Ria said with a sigh, hitting the keyboard to save her work, and sitting back in her seat, as Claire pulled up a chair without needing an invitation. LlewellCo's business day was over, but not by more than an hour or so; a number of employees were still in the building, and Ria expected to be here for several hours yet herself. Besides, it was still the working-day on the West Coast. No point in closing up shop until the domestic operations were over. Disasters always happened five minutes before closing.

"Ye'll recall we were keeping a close eye on young Billy Sunday and his wonder show down in New Jersey," Claire said, the disapproval as strong as the Scots burr in her voice. She was good, hard-headed Scots Presbyterian; the spectacle of televangelists (which she considered to be over-prideful ignoramuses who made themselves into television stars and turned religion into a marketable commodity) grated on her nerves. "Weel, it's that hard getting someone close to him, or getting good information that isn't the open-source glad-handing and PR, but I did manage to place someone on the fringes of his merry band. It seems that bad apples flock together—to mangle a metaphor, if you'll permit. Who should show up on Mr. Fairchild's doorstep to join his crusade but our own Parker Wheatley?"

"Last seen trying to take his government spook-hunting agency private, with mixed success," Ria commented sourly. The fact that Parker Wheatley hadn't simply taken his lumps and gone into an innocuous retirement breeding fancy goldfish or collecting stamps was something of a sore point with her. The man was obsessed, a fanatic, and an ongoing thorn in her side. "I suppose it was only a matter of time before he went looking for a new source of funding, but I wouldn't have thought a respectable televangelist would touch him."

Claire tilted her head to the side. "Weel, Ria my lassie, you've got to wonder just how 'respectable' a man who got kicked off the buckle of the Bible Belt and went on to build a 'prayer casino' is. Maybe launching a crusade against the 'demons among us'—not that the silly fool Wheatley is likely to find any more of the craythurs now than he did when he was in Washington—would fit right in with everything else at Mr. Fairchild's sideshow. But I do wonder what this demon-hunting will actually involve?"

That was a good question, and where Wheatley was concerned, unlikely to have a palatable answer. Wheatley had originally been the pawn of Aerune mac Audelaine, as Ria remembered only too well, and Aerune's plan had been to start a war—not between the Bright Court and the Dark, but between humans and the Sidhe. Aerune had wanted to exterminate the mortals whom he blamed for the death of his beloved Aerete uncounted centuries before. But in forging his cat's-paw, he seemed to have imbued Parker Wheatley with a fixed conviction that the Sidhe were the implacable enemy of humanity and must be destroyed, and apparently Wheatley didn't intend to abandon his mission just because he'd lost his insider position in Washington. Obsession could be a weapon, both for the obsessed and the object of obsession. Unfortunately, Ria had not yet thought of the key to turn his obsession into *her* weapon.

"He'll want to recruit new spear-carriers," Ria said slowly, "and do as much as he can to re-create the PDI in the private sector. That will take money." *And how many of Aerune's Sidhe-hunting weapons does he have left? Any of them?* "Billy has money, maybe even enough to fund Wheatley properly, but he'll only hand over so much of it without tangible verifications. He'll want to see one of Wheatley's demons in the flesh. No one really expects you to produce an angel on demand—in fact, suggesting you could would make even the devout think about measuring you for a white coat. But say there are demons, and people will want to see something that convinces them, with or without horns."

Claire studied Ria's face, an uncompromising appraisal in her light blue eyes. "If it couldn't be done, you wouldn't be worried, Ria lass. So you think there's something out there for our Mr. Wheatley to catch—and you don't think it would be a good thing if he did."

Ria hesitated, caught unexpectedly off-guard. She hadn't expected Claire to be able to follow the argument to its logical conclusion so quickly. What should she do? If she told her that Wheatley wasn't hunting demons, but elves, the woman would think she'd gone stark staring mad.

Wouldn't she?

"I don't think it would be good for anyone at all if Mr. Wheatley caught anyone and put them in a cage on television. And as you'll remember from the Marley Bell case, Mr. Wheatley is prone to make mistakes," Ria said carefully. "And I wouldn't put it past Mr. Wheatley to manufacture whatever evidence he needed, either, at this point. He's not going to want to lose another sponsor ever again, and I think he'll come up with whatever it takes to prevent that from happening." There. That covered all bases.

"Then we'll just have to save him from himself—though saving a fool from his foolishness is a fool's errand," Claire said, giving Ria a measuring look. "Any road, he'll be appearing on tonight's *Praise Hour* to speak his piece—it shouldn't be anything too much different than the speeches he's been giving over the last few months, but I'll tape it and make a transcript for the file. You might want to watch it yourself."

"I think I will," Ria said. "Maybe you'd like to stay and watch it with me—frankly, I'm not sure I can stomach all that Hallelujah-and-send-me-your-money by myself."

Claire snorted in agreement. "And you can send out for dinner—it's nothing to be facing on an empty stomach, and that way I'll know you've had at least one decent meal today."

The two women watched the program in grim silence on the plasma-screen television that had been concealed behind the panels of an inlaid Chinese screen mounted on the far wall of Ria's office. The remains of their meals were piled up on one corner of the conference table for the cleaning service to deal with—Ria's choice would have been Japanese from Nobu, but she had deferred to Claire's taste and had sent out a messenger for the sort of thing that Claire considered a "real" dinner—in which roast beef figured prominently. Now they sat rather primly together on the leather couch facing the wall. It wasn't the first time Ria had seen Billy Fairchild's *Praise Hour*, though she'd never let Ace suspect that she watched it. Ria believed in knowing her enemy.

Claire had gotten Ria tapes of his older shows, the ones out of Tulsa, when Ace had still been leading the choir, and she'd watched them too—both for comparison, and to give herself a better idea of the range of Ace's power, since she'd never seen her young charge's Talent in action.

The difference was astounding . . . and disturbing.

Oh, the sets hadn't changed very much. The production values were a little slicker, there was the look of a bit more money, but that wasn't it.

Before, he'd been pretty much indistinguishable from the rest of his kind: love, forgiveness, hellfire, and Full Gospel. Having Ace had been what made him special enough to break out of the pack.

Now, his message had changed. Profoundly.

Oh, it was cleverly done, of course. Unless you were listening closely you wouldn't quite be able to put your finger on the difference. But now Billy was preaching hate, not love. Hate the sinner *and* the sin. Salvation through purification: purge yourself of weakness (and Billy identified tolerance with weakness), purge your country of sinners, take vengeance upon the ungodly for past wrongs. . . .

That was the heart of the problem. It wasn't enough to purge yourself of your so-called "weakness" and pack yourself full of prejudice, no, you were supposed to inflict your intolerance and prejudices on others, and institutionalize them as the law of the land.

He was calling for a crusade in the most ancient sense of the word: a real-world war against everybody who didn't share his exceptionally narrow vision of what was right.

And in the background was Parker Wheatley. Just as Claire had said he would be. And since he was right up there on the podium, leprechaun-green suit and all, it was pretty clear he was going to get his chance at the microphone before the program was over.

Right now, though, Billy was holding forth on his idea of the New Crusade. And it was ugly. This was very new, and part of the program that, had any of Billy's followers somehow missed the last several months of broadcasts, would be something of a shock to the system.

*This,* Ria thought, faintly chilled, *is very interesting. It's ratings suicide. You can't grow a market share with a message like this, not in this day and age, not for long—and whatever else Billy Fairchild is, he's a clever little demagogue who loves power and money more than he loves his version of his God. Sure, he'll pick up the hardcase audience, but at some point he'll be losing followers at the same rate that he gains them, and once he's got the fringe-fanatics, he'll plateau. Say what you like about American people, when you go to either extreme, you lose all but the lunatics.*

*So why is he doing this? Does he mean to make the Sidhe his target? Wheatley can't have convinced him of their existence this fast—and if he had, Billy would be putting out a far more focused message. Besides, he's been hatemongering ever since Ace left, from what I can tell.* Odd, that. He might have changed the message, but more than that, the intensity of the message had changed. *It's not just that he's gotten a lot more blatant about it over the last few weeks . . . he's gotten more aggressive, too.*

Parker Wheatley, as expected, said his piece. Ria nobly restrained herself from putting an expensive little antique bronze statuette through the television. But she certainly thought about all the things she would like to introduce Wheatley to, and vice versa. About the time the choir had finished singing and a message was being displayed about an upcoming free Christian music concert to be held on the casino grounds, Ria's private phone line rang.

She picked up the phone. There were only a handful of people who had that number, and she would leap out of a shower if any of them called—because none of them would call "just to chat."

It was Hosea, calling to see if Ria knew about Parker Wheatley's peculiar reappearance.

"Yes-s-s," Ria drawled. "I do have to say that I don't think green is really his color, Hosea."

She heard an appreciative chuckle from the other end of the line. "Ah'll be sure to tell Ace you said so, Miz Ria."

"Do. And tell her this certainly isn't anything for her to worry about. She just needs to concentrate on her court date tomorrow, that's all. If Wheatley wants to chase little green men that he has no chance of catching, that's his privilege. Certainly his association with Billy Fairchild isn't going to do either of them any good. I doubt that the judge is going to find the pursuit of imaginary creatures—no matter what Billy calls them—to be any sign of a stable mind."

"That's all right then," Hosea said agreeably. "We'll see you some time tomorrow."

"Don't do anything I wouldn't do," Ria said, and Hosea laughed out loud.

"Ah speckt Ah'd better mind my manners a deal better than that, ma'am," he said.

Ria acknowledged the joke with an answering laugh and hung up.

"Brave speeches to the troops?" Claire asked, with a tilt of her head towards the phone.

Ria sighed. "No sense in worrying the children. And even if Wheatley is planning to go back on the game, it will take him time to put even a small tactical force together. And unfortunately, he isn't breaking any laws that I know of by being a nutcase. Or a nuisance." *The only problem is that I can't tell from this if he's managed to find another Unseleighe patron who thinks they can play with mortal fire and not get burned. I suppose the simplest thing to do would be to ask Eric to check that out through Prince Arvin, but I hate to distract him when he's so involved with his custody case right now—and besides, I REALLY hate owing favors to elves.*

"So there's nothing to hang him on . . . until he goes out and starts kidnapping people again," Claire said grimly.

"Look on the bright side," Ria said lightly. "Maybe you'll find out he has a drug habit first. Or likes underage hookers. Or surfs kiddie-porn sites on the Internet."

"Aye," Claire said. "There's always hope. But I doubt anyone who survived in Washington as long as he did will be so cooperative."

"Oh, you never know," Ria said absently. "Sooner or later, everyone makes a mistake."

# CHAPTER 5:
## PREACHER'S DAUGHTER

At 9:30 the following morning, Ace met Derek Tilford at the red brick courthouse on Bacharach Boulevard. She'd taken a taxi there, just in case anyone might be watching—you could say a lot of things about Margot's car, but you couldn't say it was inconspicuous. Hosea said he'd be along later; even if the hearing was a closed session, a Bard had ways of being where he thought he ought to be. She hadn't been able to eat much; her stomach was too full of flutterbyes and her shoulders all in knots. Hosea had somehow managed to wolf down enough for both of them. She wondered how he could do it.

Maybe it was just that it wasn't *his* parents trying to put the shackles back on him.

Mr. Tilford was waiting for her on the steps of the courthouse. He smiled approvingly when he saw her, and escorted her inside to a conference room where they could go over last-minute details.

Her clothes had been carefully chosen for the occasion: a gray skirt, navy sweater with a white blouse, navy pumps. She looked old enough to vote. She certainly looked like someone who could be on her own and take care of herself responsibly.

She had documents showing she had a job, working in the internship program at LlewellCo, and if it wasn't quite true, the papers would certainly stand up to any legal scrutiny. Come to that, Ria probably had someone somewhere in the organization who would swear convincingly about all the work Ace had been doing as an intern. She was studying for her GED, and in a few more months she would have finished all her high school courses and gotten her diploma.

"Today's hearing should really be little more than a formality before the Court grants your petition," Mr. Tilford said. "Judge Springsteen has a great deal of experience in Family Court matters. I've looked over her record, and I haven't seen anything to worry me. The fact that you ran away from home counts against you, of course, but set against that is your parents' insistence on an inadequate level of home-schooling without proper State oversight, their failure to notify proper authorities when you disappeared, the fact that your father has insisted on your performing on stage from earliest childhood without any recompense to you, and the fact that he has forced you to continue to do so against your expressed desire to quit."

"It makes him sound like an awfully bad man," Ace said softly. Her stomach knotted again; she didn't *want* Billy to sound like he'd been abusing her! For one thing, it would make her mama very unhappy. For another, well, by Billy's lights, he hadn't been abusing her, only—

—only forcing her into a mold she didn't fit into—

—but he'd thought he was doing his best by her—

—hadn't he?

"Perhaps a bit rash," Derek Tilford suggested. "And certainly, as Ms. Llewellyn has undoubtedly informed you, you are entitled to financial recompense for your contribution to the success of Fairchild Ministries, Incorporated, over the approximately twelve-year period during which you performed as part of the, ah, Ministry."

"I don't want any of his money—I told Ria that," Ace said forcefully. "It would be like taking blood money."

"Indeed," Mr. Tilford said noncommittally. "But forgoing such a sizable and legally proper claim on the Fairchild assets, which the most conservative estimate would have to place at well over a million dollars, if not as high as five million, should present yet another inducement for the Fairchilds to withdraw any opposition they might make to your petition."

Ace blinked. She wasn't quite sure she followed what Mr. Tilford was saying, but it seemed to mean that if she promised that she didn't want to be paid for all the singing she'd done in the choir, they might be grateful enough to let her go.

One thing she was sure of: as much as Billy might say he loved her, he loved money and the limelight more.

"What if it doesn't work?" she asked.

"Then, Ms. Fairchild, we will try something else until we find something that does work. In the worst possible case, if your petition is denied and you are ordered by the Court to resume residence beneath your parents' roof, you will have at least forty-eight hours in which to comply. I have known Ria Llewellyn for many years. A great deal can happen in forty-eight hours when Ms. Llewellyn sets her mind to it."

Ace felt a sharp pang of relief. She hadn't known Ria for as long as Mr. Tilford had, but she'd certainly known her for long enough to know that he was right about that.

So even if the worst did happen, it wouldn't be *quite* the worst.

She'd still have time to escape . . . somewhere. And if that somewhere happened to be a place where Billy Fairchild couldn't get even if God Himself gave him a hand—which God Himself certainly would *not*—well, there were worse things.

Like being under Billy's thumb again. Because where Billy was, Gabriel Horn was too. And Gabriel Horn was not ever going to let her go again once he got *his* hands on her.

Maybe she'd even deliver her letter to Jaycie in person. She didn't know if she'd like living with a bunch of elves, much as she liked reading about them in books—Jaycie had hated his home so much he'd run away to New York and tried to kill himself rather than go back to his family, after all, and even if the letter he'd sent said he liked the new place he was living just fine, Ace wasn't quite convinced.

But anything—anything!—would be better than being where Gabriel Horn could get at her.

"Are you ready to go?" Mr. Tilford said.

Ace took a deep breath. "I'm ready," she said.

Walking into the courtroom was just like walking on stage had always been; a sudden sense that she was the center of attention. The feeling was just the same, even though she could count the number of people here on the fingers of both hands and have some left over. This wasn't like the courtrooms she'd seen on television. This place was old, smelled musty; the red carpet was worn thin where people did a lot of walking on it. The woodwork was dark, the walls a dingy cream.

Her father was sitting over at a table on the right, with a man she didn't recognize beside him. She looked for Mama and didn't see her, and felt a confused mixture of disappointment and relief, then let out a breath she hadn't known she'd been holding in. Gabriel Horn wasn't there.

On the right was their table. She followed Mr. Tilford up to it and sat down. It was faintly sticky, probably with layers and layers of polish that no one had bothered to remove before they added another layer.

She didn't see Hosea anywhere, but he'd warned her that she might not see him even if he was there. He'd promised her he'd come, though, and she had to believe that.

"All rise for the honorable Andrea J. Springsteen," said the bailiff.

Hosea slipped into the back of the courtroom just as everyone was rising for the entrance of the judge. Nobody noticed him, even though he was a big man and normally drew stares, one way or another, just about everywhere he went.

But one of the first bits of shine he'd ever learned—even before he'd met Eric—was the ability to make people just not pay any particular attention to him, and he'd only gotten better at it under Eric's guidance. Nobody had noticed him walk in here—even with Jeanette slung over his back—and nobody was likely to notice him sitting here in the back unless they bumped right into him.

He sat down when everyone else did, pulling the soft-sided banjo case onto his lap, and looked around. There was Ace, looking as fretful as a cat on a hotplate. And there, on the other side of the room, was her Daddy.

Only there was something not quite *right* about him.

Hosea had grown up believing in ghosts and spirits as naturally as New Yorkers believed in winning lottery numbers. In the mountains where he'd been born there were lonely places that were haunted by things that had once been human . . . and things that had never been human. People relied on modern medicine from the Flatlands when they could get it, but when they couldn't—or when it failed them—they turned easily back to the older ways of herbs and charms and spoken prayers. The loving grandparents who'd raised him had both had extensive experience of the outside world, yet neither had hesitated to turn to root-cunning and prayer to set things right. Hosea's grandfather had plowed and planted by the moon until the day he'd died, and the rocky little hill-farm in Morton's Fork had never failed to feed them.

So long before Hosea had met Eric, or Toni, Paul, José—and Jimmie, God rest her courageous soul—he'd known what magick was, and how it looked.

He was seeing magick now.

The Reverend was not a conjureman himself. Ace had talked about him maybe a little more than she'd realized, and Hosea had formed a good idea of the man. He might not be right with God according to Hosea's lights, but Hosea didn't think he was the sort to involve himself with hoodoo. Not knowingly.

But he reeked of it. He was carrying something that someone had given to him—or slipped into his pocket without his knowing it. Something that wasn't a *kindly* thing.

Hosea summoned up his mage-sight—it came a lot more easily these days—and as he did he could see a baleful red glow shining right through Billy Fairchild's jacket pocket. Worse, long tendrils, drifting as slowly as smoke, were moving inexorably toward the judge's bench.

It didn't take Bardcraft to know that if those tendrils touched the judge, she was going to see everything Billy's way.

Hosea unzipped Jeanette's carrying case and laid his hand across the silver strings of the banjo. He couldn't play it in here—not and stay unnoticed—but he needed to keep the magick in whatever fetch-bag Billy Fairchild was carrying from doing its work.

What had Eric told him once? *It's not the music, really, Hosea. The power's inside of us. The music's just the way we express it. With a little practice—well, a lot of practice—you'll be able to do what you do without the music. You can BE the music."*

He guessed he was going to have to skip the practice and get straight to being the music. Right now.

He pressed his fingers hard against the strings, feeling the silver press into his calluses. There was a faint silvery shiver from the banjo, as if Jeanette were trying to waken into life. He let his mind fill with the music he knew so well: "Callie's Reel," and "Sally Goodin," and the far-too-appropriate "Devil Went Down to Georgia": rollicking tunes, filled with life and power and force. And with them he called up a mighty wind, a wind that existed only in the same place that the red tendrils existed, blowing them back toward Billy Fairchild, away from Judge Springsteen.

With his mage-sight, he saw the ghost-tendrils bending backward, like the streamers of smoke they so resembled, blow away and dissolve. But as soon as he stopped willing the power, they reformed, stronger than before, and he had to begin again. Only now it was a little harder to think of the tunes, to hold them in his mind, and a little harder to call up that ghostly wind. The baleful power wasn't weaker, though. If anything, it was pushing harder, as if his opposition had made it stronger.

Hosea felt a twinge of alarm.

If Eric were here, he could have destroyed the fetch-bag, or put a shield around the judge that the smoke-things couldn't get through, or done a dozen other things, but Eric had years of training. All Hosea could do was keep sweeping the baleful power back, knowing that his ability to do even that was growing steadily weaker.

The hearing went on for a very long time. She'd thought it would be quick, with the judge just looking at her papers and making up her mind, and that only the lawyers would have to talk. But she read everything over carefully, listened to both the lawyers say why her petition should—and shouldn't—be granted, and then she wanted to ask Ace and her father both a lot of questions.

They both had to come up in front of the judge by them-selves, and it took all Ace's will to walk those few short steps to stand beside her father. Daddy was just as mad at her as she'd ever seen him. He didn't like that she'd cut her hair, he didn't like that she was wearing makeup—although she'd had to wear makeup for the broadcasts, he and Mama had never let her wear any out on the street—he didn't like her clothes. The clothes Mama had bought for her had always been lacy and frilly—"real pretty dresses," Mama had always said, to make her look like Daddy's little angel. She'd never worn a pair of jeans in her life until she'd run away. Now she looked—well, she looked like a girl fixing to be a professional woman, an independent woman, a girl who wasn't reckoning herself to be a girl anymore. Daddy didn't like that, not one bit. He wanted her to still be "Little Grace" who always did what she was told and never questioned anything.

But he was smart enough not to go on at her with the judge watching. All he said was, "Your mama misses you, Heavenly Grace," in that sorrowful way of his, when they were both stand-ing before the judge.

Ace knew better than to answer back. She clamped her mouth shut—hard—on all the things she longed to say. *Misses me so much she never wrote me, or called me—and neither did you. I wonder why that was?* She looked up at the judge, trying to make her face say nothing at all.

"Reverend Fairchild, I've heard what your lawyer has to say, and I've heard what your daughter's lawyer has to say. Now I'd like to hear what you have to say."

"I'm a man of God, your Honor," Billy said solemnly. "I have nothing to hide."

Judge Springsteen raised an eyebrow. "Let's start with the claim that your daughter was forced to participate in your . . . evangelical activities against her inclinations. What do you have to say to that?"

Billy's face was a study in honest amazement, and Ace gritted her teeth. "Your Honor, my daughter always loved to sing! Her voice was a gift from the Lord Jesus! Ever since she could walk, she'd climb up on stage and sing right along with the choir. I never thought for a single minute . . . but if she don't want to do that any more, I won't ask her to. Just so she comes home where she belongs."

"And the matter of her schooling?" the judge asked, shuffling through the papers.

"Honey, you know your mama and I just want what's best for you," Billy said, speaking directly to Ace now. "You come home and we'll talk about it. If you're really set on going away somewhere to college, I guess we've raised you so you can tell right from wrong."

The judge turned her attention to Ace. "You've heard what Mr. Fairchild has had to say. Are you willing to withdraw your petition, Ms. Fairchild?"

He sounded so reasonable—so reasonable—and how could the judge know that the second he got her back in his hands he'd go back on every promise he made, every pledge, that even if the judge made him swear on a mountain of Bibles he'd hold that no promise made to the "ungodly" was anything but a pledge made to be broken?

"I'm sorry," Ace said, looking down and shaking her head. "I can't do that."

"Now you listen to me, Heavenly Grace—" Billy began, the heat coming into his voice, and that hard tone she remembered only too well.

"Please remember where you are, Mr. Fairchild," Judge Springsteen said, rapping her gavel once. After a moment, she continued. "Emancipated minor status is a major step, not to be undertaken lightly. Your parents would like to try again to become a family with you. I can appoint a social worker to make regular visitations to your home to make sure your legal rights are respected. I can also order the three of you to attend family counseling sessions with a counselor of my choice in order to ease the transition, if you agree to return home."

*Yes, and how long before the counselor is bought off with Daddy's money or Daddy's charm? How long before the social worker gets tired of making visits?* Ace knew, from the talk she heard over at Guardian House, just how strapped all the Social Services were for money to pay for personnel. Seemed like the politicians in charge liked the way that people like Daddy handled their family affairs, and aimed to see there weren't many resources to interfere with suchlike. The judge could order all she liked, but Ace wasn't being beaten—not physically, anyway—nor sexually abused, and she'd be pretty low on any social worker's already too-crowded checklist. Ace could imagine all too well what would happen. Two, three weeks at the most, and the visits would become phone calls, and quick ones at that, and the counselor would write *The End* to the counseling sessions in order to tend to somebody who had a habit of whipping his kids with an electric cord.

"Well, now, Heavenly Grace, that sounds like the best—" Billy began.

"No." Her voice was barely a whisper. "*No,*" she said again, more loudly. "I don't want to go back. I don't want to live with them. They won't change, because they don't see any reason to change, no matter what. They think they know best, and that won't change either. You don't know him, Judge Springsteen. I do. I know what he'll do. *No.*"

But there wasn't any anger in her words, only a kind of mournfulness. She hadn't thought saying that would make her feel so sad. It wasn't as if she thought she could go back and live like a family, even if Gabriel Horn weren't there to turn her life into a nightmare. There was no way Judge Springsteen or anyone else could remake Billy Fairchild's character; make him anything other than the charming, selfish, manipulative, *driven* man Ace had grown up with. Oh, he was all fine words and promises now, but if she could go back, if she did go back, Ace knew just what would happen. The judge could appoint as many social workers as she liked, order as much counseling as she liked, and Daddy would find some way to sweet-talk his way around all of it, just the way he'd always sweet-talked his way around anything that didn't suit him. Or, now he had money, *real* money, change-the-world money, he'd buy his way out of what he didn't want to do.

The judge looked disappointed. "You may return to your seats," she said.

Hosea could hear the words being spoken in the courtroom, but they came to him only faintly and almost without meaning. Sweat ran down his brow with the effort he was making; his shirt was soaked with it.

If he failed, Ace would lose her case. Each time Hosea had swept the red tendrils back, a little more understanding of their purpose had seeped into him. The charm Billy Fairchild carried was meant to bend the judge's will to his, and Billy wanted his daughter back beneath his roof.

If Ace was told to go back to her parents, she'd run away again, and one of the few places left for her to run was Underhill. No one wanted that.

And then Billy and Ace got up from their seats and stepped toward the bench. Hosea saw the red tendrils rise up—almost triumphantly—and reach toward Judge Springsteen. Now they didn't have as far to go to get to her.

He could not let them touch her.

He gathered up the last of his strength, and knew it would not be enough.

He thought about all that Paul and the others had told him about the Guardian's gifts—little enough, save that it was unlike the power of a Bard in every way. Not something you were born with and practiced at—something you were lent by a greater Power; a gift that worked through you for reasons of its own. Something that came and went at its own will; called into the world by need, and vanishing as soon as the need had gone.

There was need. And Ace had asked for his help.

Hosea swept his hand across the banjo's strings, making them ring softly.

*If yore going to come, come now.*

The judge stared at them all for a long moment before she finally spoke.

"I'm not going to rule on this today," she finally said. "There are a number of points that complicate this petition, including the fact that the petitioner is only eleven months away from her majority. It's possible that there's a third solution that would best serve the interests of both parties. I'd very much like to see either the petition or the opposition to it withdrawn. You can expect my final ruling on this case a week from today."

She raised her gavel to bring it down, and then her gaze lengthened, focusing on something behind the litigants.

"Young man," she said sharply. "What are you doing in my courtroom?"

She'd seen him. His charm to stay invisible had broke wide open, and she'd seen him. "Ah'm sorry, ma'am," Hosea Songmaker said meekly, getting to his feet. "Ah 'spekt Ah got lost."

Before she could question him further—or order her bailiffs to throw him out—he ducked out the doors at the back of the courtroom. As the doors closed behind him, he heard the rap of her gavel.

He'd barely managed to keep the hoodoo away from the judge—and he wasn't quite sure he'd managed it completely, or whether the Guardian gifts *had* come, there at the end, because she hadn't ruled one way or t'other, now, had she? Maybe it had only been his Bard's shine, because he'd brought in real music, instead of just the music in his head. At the end, he'd had to risk playing a few notes on Jeanette, and that was why she'd seen him.

But if Ace hadn't gotten the ruling she'd wanted, then neither had Billy Fairchild. And a lot could happen in a week.

He stood on the court steps, breathing deeply. The cold air felt good in his lungs—the calendar said it was spring, or close enough, but March in the Mid Atlantic States was nothing like the March weather where he'd grown up, and Hosea missed the mountains. Still, just now, he could do with the chill; he was sweating like he'd chopped a whole month's worth of firewood, and he was just about that tired, too. He shrugged the strap of the banjo case higher onto his shoulder. He wanted to have a good long chat with Jeanette as soon as possible, and get her thoughts on what had happened in that courtroom today.

He hadn't recognized the style of magick that had been on the Reverend, and that troubled him. In his time with the Guardians, he'd thought he'd seen just about every kind of magick there was to see—black, white, and plaid. He knew he'd recognize the kind he'd seen today again if he saw it—all forms of magick had a distinct signature—but as it was, he knew he couldn't even describe it well enough for Paul to begin to make an educated guess as to who—or what—might have whipped up the original charm. He hadn't seen the thing itself, after all: only its effects.

And that wasn't even the most urgent question that needed answering. The important question—and one somebody had better get an answer to right away—was who close to the Reverend Billy Fairchild had the power and the skill to make something like that, and what else were they doing?

Was it a Guardian problem or a Bard problem? This was the dilemma that Hosea always faced at times like these. He'd managed to knock the hoodoo back on its heels with his Bardcraft, but if the Reverend's fetch-bag had been created by a black magician, he was pretty sure that made this a Guardian problem.

He sighed. Best to take himself out of sight now. Since he was one hundred percent sure he'd be calling on Reverend Fairchild later, he decided he didn't want to be caught loitering here.

Just in case that influence charm wasn't the only charm in the Reverend's pocket.

Ace glanced back just in time to see Hosea leave the courtroom. Billy didn't care; all *his* attention was elsewhere, and he was too full of anger to pay any attention to something as trivial as who'd snuck into the courtroom. The judge's gavel came down, and then the bailiff was commanding them to "all rise" again. They stood while the judge left the courtroom.

She kept her eyes straight ahead, but at the edge of her vision she could see Daddy arguing with his lawyer in furious whispers.

Before he could come over to their table, Mr. Tilford was on his feet and had the two of them out and into the corridor. He walked quickly, so that Ace had to hurry to keep up, and within minutes they were seated in his car in the parking lot across the street.

"You did very well in there today. Now we have a week to encourage your parents to withdraw their opposition to your petition," Mr. Tilford said, starting the car. "I'm afraid you'll have to return for the final ruling, though. Fortunately, the judge didn't make any restrictions regarding your place of residence in the interim. I can give you a ride back to the city now, if you'd like."

It was tempting—she felt safe in New York, even if that safety was an illusion. Hosea could bring back her things.

But then she realized that she didn't want to leave just yet. She wanted to talk to Hosea.

She had a suspicion—something not even really strong enough to call a hunch—that something that had been supposed to happen in that courtroom today hadn't happened.

Something bad.

Gabriel was in Toirealach's office when Billy found him. He'd been making last minute arrangements to welcome the Bard and his young brother—everyone was so distracted by their preparations for Friday's concert and the expected crowds that they would hardly notice any of the small plans that Gabriel footed on his own, and Christian Family Intervention operated almost as an independent fief beneath the larger umbrella of the Fairchild Ministries anyway.

Many months ago, Gabriel had taken a minor department of Billy's organization—mostly concerned with publishing dreary pamphlets on the Christian Family and funneling money into suitable outreach programs—and remade it in his own chosen image, filling it with a hand-picked staff. Some of them were human—for those cases where all that was needed was a kidnapping and a good scare, followed by a little talk, to make the children of his clients see reason. But the rebellious children of the sort of folk who would come to a place like Christian Family Intervention were generally not so amenable to simple manipulation—nor was Gabriel inclined to waste such tender, tasty morsels. So the larger part of the staff was not recruited from the ranks of humans. Most of them were Sidhe—simple spells could do what all the rehabilitation programs in the mortal world could not.

And a great many of the children who were brought into CFI were sent to the grey room to meet the Soul-eaters, and none of their parents had ever complained afterward about the spineless puppets they'd gotten back. Well, most of those parents wanted spineless puppets, if it came down to that. So long as the child could parrot whatever his parents said, stayed close to home, and never, ever spoke a rebellious word again, they were happy. And if the bright, gifted creature that they *had* once called "son" or "daughter" was replaced by something that would probably grow up to an adulthood that featured being fitted with a paper hat, a uniform in primary colors, and a nametag and a preoccupation with French fries, well—too bad.

Gabriel was certain Michael and Fiona Banyon would not complain either. Or at least, not immediately. And his revenge upon the Bright Bard who had stolen his Jachiel from him would be complete, for when Bard Eric left the Chamber of Silences, his Gift would be gone, along with his will.

"We have the name and location of the boy Magnus's school," Toirealach said. "We'll take him there, and use him for a dagger at the Bard's throat. The mortal Bard will not know who has him until the silver fetters are on his wrists—and then it will be far too late."

"Very good," Gabriel purred gloatingly. "And then—"

The doorknob rattled. The door was locked, of course. A furious pounding immediately followed.

"Gabriel!" Billy Fairchild could thunder like a righteous summons to God's judgment onstage, but just now, there was a whining undertone to his bellowing that set Gabriel's teeth on edge. "Open this door! Open this door right now! How dare you lock any door against me!"

*I will not have to listen to that much longer,* he promised himself. He swept his mortal *glamourie* back around himself—noting as he did that Toirealach O'Caomhain had done the same—and went to open the door.

Billy was standing on the threshold, his face scarlet with anger. What immediately drew Gabriel's attention, however, was the state of the talisman he had slipped into Billy's pocket before he'd sent him off to the courthouse this morning.

The Sidhe could create enchanted objects—a cloak, a cup, a sword, boots filled with magic—that would render their wearer invisible, nourish (or poison) him in ways mortal food could not, slay a dozen enemies at a blow (and cause wounds that would not heal), allow their wearer to run faster than the fastest horse. But it had been centuries since such things had been done as a matter of course. Such toys were only of use to mortals, after all—the Sidhe could do all these things and more by drawing directly upon the power that infused the very air of Underhill, and was available, albeit in a weaker form, here in the World Above. Since the Great Withdrawal, most of the Sidhe had been far less inclined to put objects of magickal power into the hands of mortals, lest they find them turned against their own kind.

But what Gabriel had slipped into Billy's pocket was not something as simple and straightforward as an enchanted object. What he had given him was no less than Magic Itself.

The Sidhe cast spells as naturally as they breathed, but few of them could have done what Gabriel had, for the art was nearly lost. Take a spell, give its components solid form, turn it into an amulet or a talisman that anyone, mortal or Sidhe, might carry and wield.

Of course, such devices lacked the power of a spell freshly cast, one with the caster's own will directly behind it. And that had been just as well in the case of the Talisman of Compulsion Gabriel had given Billy Fairchild, for had the empty-headed fool been exposed to one-tenth of Gabriel's natural power, he would have been burned to ash.

But the talisman should have ensured Billy's victory in the courtroom today, and Gabriel could see from Billy's thoughts that it had not. Worse, its power had been thoroughly drained, and Billy himself reeked of Bardic magic.

"Is something wrong?" Gabriel asked, as if he didn't already know. "The hearing—"

"Come on up to my office," Billy said, glancing meaningfully at Toirealach.

Once the door to Billy's private office had closed behind them, Billy went over to the liquor cabinet and poured himself a stiff drink. His hands still shook with barely suppressed anger.

"That heathen bitch said she couldn't make up her mind!" he snarled, gulping down the whiskey as if it were ice water. "She looked right at my little Heavenly Grace—oh, Gabriel, it would have broken your heart; she stood right there dressed like a man-woman and painted up like a harlot—and said she couldn't make up her mind it was God's will that a daughter belonged with her parents!"

"But she hasn't ruled against you?" Gabriel asked, wanting to make sure the matter was clear, at least in Billy's mind.

"Said she'd give her answer in a week." Billy slammed his empty glass down on the top of the credenza. "Said she'd like it best if one of us gave in before then—what good's that fancy lawyer I hired if he can't win a simple case like this?"

"You haven't lost yet," Gabriel said soothingly. "I suppose the judge wanted to avoid too much adverse publicity."

"*Publicity?*" Billy yelped. "There wasn't anybody in that court-room but me and her and that high-toned New York lawyer bought and paid for by that Ria Llewellyn that's trying to steal my child!"

So whatever Bard had spoiled his plans—and Gabriel was fairly sure it wasn't Eric Banyon; he knew where Bard Banyon was—Billy hadn't seen them. Which meant the Bard must be a powerful Bard indeed, to conceal him or herself and still cast the spells that had foiled Gabriel's.

After all the work he'd gone to—putting pressure on judges, distracting and misleading Ria Llewellyn, expending all his most subtle *glamouries* to get the case heard in New Jersey instead of New York—that there should *still* be a Bard arriving to foil his plans at the final hour nearly maddened Gabriel.

And even if he *personally* cast a *glamourie* on the judge, making sure she would rule the way he chose next week, there was no guarantee that the Bard would not be there again, and break it.

No. The judge must rule the way Gabriel wished of her own free will. And that meant something important must change in Heavenly Grace's family in the next seven days.

But first, he had to soothe this fool. Otherwise Billy would rampage around like a maddened bull, wrecking everything in his path. There were too many important things going on this week, too many delicate situations Billy's rantings could overturn. So much as it made Gabriel's back teeth ache with clenching, Billy would have to be appeased and patted. "I wouldn't worry about it too much, Billy. I'm sure she's taking her time simply because she knows you're such an important man. Unfortunately, Ria Llewellyn is also an important woman. Before the judge rules in your favor, she needs to give every indication of fairness and impartiality." With the words, Gabriel put forth the force of his will, to smooth the ruffled feathers and ease the anger.

As usual, Billy answered to the pull on the reins as he'd been conditioned. The anger oozed out of him.

"So you think next week my little angel will come home?" Billy asked hopefully.

"I am confident that next week the judge will find a compelling reason to deny Heavenly Grace's petition," Gabriel said smoothly. "If she hasn't already withdrawn it herself."

Derek Tilford brought Ace back to the hotel, and parked in front of the entrance.

"Are you quite sure you'll be all right here?" he asked.

"I'll be fine," she said, though she wasn't really convinced of it at all and was trying hard not to panic. She looked around the parking lot, and didn't see the pink Cadillac anywhere.

Maybe Hosea was taking the long way back. As soon as she got inside, she'd call his cellphone and find out where he was. Then she'd call Ria.

"You're sure?" Mr. Tilford said again. He sounded doubtful.

"Right as rain," Ace said, summoning up her sunniest smile.

She popped out of the Mercedes before Mr. Tilford could think of a good reason to keep her, and hurried off across the parking lot toward her room.

Neither she nor Derek Tilford noticed the nondescript man in the nondescript car that had followed them from the courthouse and waited until the Mercedes left before driving away.

Hosea drove only a few blocks—enough to take him well away from both the hotel and the courthouse—before parking again, sliding over to the passenger side of the front seat, and taking Jeanette from the case and slipping a set of silver picks over his fingers. He had questions that wouldn't wait, and right now, there was only one person who might be able to give him some answers. Thank Heaven the Caddy's heater was efficient; there was nothing worse than a cold banjo for being out-of-tune.

"Hello, Sweetheart," he said softly, as he began to play.

He felt Jeanette's flash of annoyance—she hated pet names nearly as much as he liked to tease her—but she quickly grew serious.

:You stink of Sidhe magick,: Jeanette's ghost said succinctly. : Unseleighe magick. What the hell have you been up to, Hosea? If you get us both killed, I'll—I'll find some way to haunt you personally, I swear it—:

"Killed" in Jeanette's case was a relative term, but if the banjo that she haunted were destroyed, she'd have no chance to finish her redemption and pass on. She'd simply cease to exist with grim finality.

But all that was far from Hosea's mind at the moment. Not when she had just given him the key to what was puzzling him, and it was a key he had in no way anticipated.

"Unseleighe magick?" Hosea said, so startled he stopped playing.

That made no sense. He'd faced Aerune mac Audelaine in battle. He should recognize an Unseleighe spell.

And more to the point, what was Parker Wheatley doing launching his crusade from Billy Fairchild's pulpit, if Billy had an Unseleighe Magus casting spells for him—or on him?

With an effort, he resumed playing—a version of "Danny

Deever" he'd written himself. Nearly all of Kipling's poetry did well set to music. "*'What are the bugles blowin' for?' said Files-on-Parade...*"

"Jeanette, are you sure?"

*:Oh, no, I'm just talking to amuse myself,:* the ghost snapped irritably.

Hosea grinned, despite his worry. Jeanette hadn't been much of a "people person" in life, and death and an afterlife hadn't done a lot to sweeten her temper. But irritable or not, she was a good friend and ally when it counted, and had proved herself again and again.

"How much of what went on in the courtroom did you see?" Hosea asked.

He felt rather than heard her wordless snarl of exasperation. *:WHAT courtroom, you gormless farmboy? I see what you see, I hear what you hear—when you're playing this damned yammer-stick. The last thing I saw was your hotel room last night. Did we win, by the way?:*

"Yes and no." As the bright rills of music ebbed and flowed through the car, Hosea filled Jeanette in on what had happened at the hearing, seen and unseen.

*:You're in trouble,:* she said succinctly, when he'd finished. *:If you want my guess, this Sidhe you're hunting isn't working with Billy. He's working with Wheatley. Wheatley and Aerune had a partnership. Aerune's gone. So Wheatley needs another partner; working with an Unseleighe Sidhe worked once, so Wheatley's gone back to the same well.:*

"And Billy's fetch-bag?" Hosea asked.

*:Wheatley needs Billy's organization since he doesn't have government funding any more. What better way to ensure it than to be able to do Billy-boy a few favors? If I were him, and I wanted to persuade him I'd helped him out, I'd say I'd blackmailed the judge, though, not that I'd slipped him a magick spell,:* Jeanette said judiciously.

All that made perfect sense; all the dominos were lining up. "Ayah. That's be the way to play it, I reckon." Hosea chewed on his lower lip for a moment, thinking on it.

Just then his cellphone rang. He set the banjo aside and rummaged in the pocket of his jacket until he pulled it out.

"Hosea Songmaker."

"Hosea, where are you?" Ace's voice was skittery with worry, just on the right side of panic. He felt guilt; she was the one who'd been up there in the cross hairs, and she had to have felt it, felt like she was all alone. She'd had to stand by the side of Billy Fairchild and stick up for herself, and then get told she was going to have to wait to hear what was going to happen. And here he was, gallivanting around, without telling her.

"Just sittin' on a side-street, havin' a little chat with Jeanette," Hosea said. "Didn't mean to worry you none."

He heard Ace let out a long breath. "Are you coming back soon?" she asked plaintively. "I want to talk to you."

"Ah guess Ah'm about done here," he said. "Ah'll be along."

He picked up the banjo again just long enough to tell Jeanette he was going back to the hotel, then put the instrument back in its case. He checked his watch. He'd have just about enough time to shower and change and make a phone call or two before driving out to keep his appointment with the Reverend Billy Fairchild.

And any members of the Unseleighe Court he might have watching over him.

Magnus squirmed in his seat, while trying not to catch the teacher's eye. It was hard to keep his mind on his schoolwork today—or even to look like he was. Not that History was his favorite subject. Who cared about the Treaty of Ghent? He bet whatever country it had been signed in wasn't even there anymore anyway.

History was the last class of the morning; Magnus made a desperate effort to keep from yawning, his mind wandering, as Mr. Goulburn continued to lecture. If The Ghoul wasn't the most boring speaker in the entire history of the universe, he was definitely in the top ten.

Magnus knew he ought to pay more attention to the lectures, but deep in his heart he knew he really only had to show up in class, do the reading, and somehow manage to pass the tests, and he didn't need the lectures for that. His math and science grades were high enough to pull his average up to respectable levels—his English grades were fair—but he truly hated history.

Today more than usual.

The tasteful, expensive, and oh-so-classic dark wooden student-desk (dark wood didn't show ink) felt like a set of Colonial stocks.

Eric had promised he'd call the moment he heard anything about how Ace's hearing had gone. The school insisted that students turn their cellphones off during class hours—and confiscated any that weren't—but his multifunction watch was set on "stun," and even his techno-Luddite brother Eric could handle text messaging. He'd get the news as soon as there was any.

Magnus wished he'd gone to the hearing. It wasn't like the world was going to come to an end if he missed a day or two of school. And it couldn't really make *that* much of a difference to whether the State of New York decided to roll over and play nice, he told himself. Sooner or later Eric was going to be declared his legal guardian . . . and if he wasn't, well, now that Magnus had gotten a taste of freedom, he bet that within six months he could have his parents *begging* Eric to take him off their hands.

Just then there was the faint hiss that indicated the classroom intercom had come on. It was funny: there were cellphones and computers everywhere, and practically every student at least had a pager, but the Administration still relied on the hot new technology of half a century ago when it wanted to tell them something. Goulburn broke off in the middle of a description of the Battle of New Orleans—which was actually starting to get Magnus's attention—and waited to see what would happen.

"Magnus Banyon, please report to the principal's office at once. That is all."

Magnus sat bolt upright as every eye in the class was riveted on him. What the hell?

He knew he wasn't being called out of class because he'd done something violating the many rules in the Cooties & Runt Code of Conduct. Other than his neckties—and the rules only specified that the students must wear ties, not what kind of ties—his conscience was entirely clear. If there was one thing Magnus knew well, it was how to skate close to the edge of a set of rules without falling off. Magnus looked down at his wrist, but there were no messages there. He glanced at the time. Eleven-thirty; Ace would probably be out of court by now, but she might not have had time to call yet. But maybe Eric was here to take him out of school for something else.

He got to his feet amid restless stirrings and stifled snickers from his classmates. Goulburn cleared his throat sharply for attention, and the noise subsided.

Magnus stuffed his history books back into his backpack and slung it over his shoulder, then walked out the door.

Even in the hallowed halls of the Coenties & Arundel Private Academy for Boys, discipline reigned supreme. The paneled oak halls were silent. The stained glass windows glowed serenely. The scent of lemon-wax permeated the atmosphere. Only the faintest hum of higher learning emanated from the classrooms Magnus passed on his way to the staircase.

*Jerks,* he thought succinctly.

He'd been here long enough to know what most of his classmates intended to do with their lives, and there wasn't an ounce of fun in any of it. Even though they were all within a few years of his age, they already had their futures all planned out: law, medicine, politics . . . a few wild and crazy souls were going to become architects or bankers. The right Ivy League university, the right contacts, making the right friends, and then a serene slide into the Old Family Firm or something like it. One or two were going to teach—at the university level, of course. Nothing so plebian as public high-school or elementary-school teaching for them.

The thought of having his life planned out that far in advance—and such a *boring* life, too!—made Magnus's blood run cold. Was there such a thing as a Stepford Teenager? If they wanted a life without challenges, without surprises, without *fun*—why not just buy a pine box now and lie down in it? Because Life was supposed to be unexpected.

He walked sedately down two flights of stairs—the wide oak banisters were made for sliding, and the stairs just begged to be taken three at a time, but both actions earned major demerits, and there were always hall proctors around even when you couldn't see them—to the first floor, and turned down the hall that led to the principal's office.

And slowed.

And stopped.

Because it had suddenly occurred to him that there was something very, very wrong with the scenario he was walking into.

The principal wasn't calling him to the office for some disciplinary action. That meant someone had shown up asking for him. He'd immediately assumed it was Eric, but he'd just realized that was impossible. Or pretty unlikely at the very least.

Eric wasn't the brightest crayon in the box by any means, much as Magnus loved his brother, but even he should have thought to message ahead to tell Magnus he was here.

So whoever had called Magnus down to the principal's office wasn't Eric.

There was a really short list of people who weren't Eric that Magnus was willing to go anywhere with. Ria. Hosea. One or two of Eric's other friends from Guardian House. And every single one of them would have messaged ahead.

It would be just like his parents to try something at his school.

He stepped quietly out of the middle of the hall and moved slowly along it. The principal's office was around the corner, but the door into the outer office had a glass pane in the top half, and directly at the end of this hallway was a marble-topped table with an antique gilt-framed mirror hung over it. The mirror was large, and heavy, and angled slightly out from the wall. If you stood in just the right place, you could see the office door reflected in it.

He didn't like what he saw.

There were two men in black suits standing at Ms. Castillo's desk. They were as tall and as wide as professional wrestlers, and as alike as two clones. Ms. Castillo was sitting at her desk, but she was doing absolutely nothing, simply staring straight ahead, eyes wide open, as if she were asleep sitting up.

He couldn't exactly see Principal Kinross, but he could see part of a grey business suit standing at the edge of Castillo's desk. It wasn't moving either.

Weirdness. Very bad weirdness. And actually, Magnus didn't care for weirdness even when it was good. He backed away quickly the way he'd come, and when he could no longer see the doorway in the mirror, he turned and ran.

He didn't really have a plan—all he intended to do was run until he'd opened up enough distance to feel safe enough to stop and call Eric—but he didn't get that chance.

By the time he reached the street he knew his grace period had run out—they were after him now in earnest, and he knew that whoever they were, he had no intention of letting them catch him. He felt it in his gut, in the back of his neck; he didn't have to look back. There was a Presence back there, and he fled from it like a homeboy from a SWAT team.

Midday, midweek, midtown; the sidewalks were crowded with pedestrians. Magnus shoved through them recklessly, hoping they'd slow down his pursuers as much as they slowed him. He felt his backpack fall and didn't stop to retrieve it.

He got to the corner and plunged into the street, crossing with the light but running dangerously close to the edge of the moving cars, where the human traffic was thinnest. He gained the sidewalk again, and as he did, he heard screaming behind him, mixed with the screech of brakes and the blare of horns.

That *was* enough to make him look back; there were few things that could make a New Yorker stop and take notice.

Two black wolves the size of ponies were loping along the sidewalk on the other side of the intersection. People were running out into traffic to get away from them.

His nerves screaming with atavistic fear, Magnus turned and ran again. At least the fear was giving him an energy and a speed and strength he hadn't known was in him.

Now he wasn't being even marginally polite about the people he shoved out of his way: when you had monsters chasing you, all the rules changed. He scrabbled in his pocket for his cellphone, not taking his eyes from the sidewalk ahead of him; both Eric and Ria were on his speed-dial, and right now, he didn't care which number he hit.

Just as his fingers closed over it, another giant wolf bounded out in front of him. He didn't see where it had come from—it was just *there*.

It jumped at him. The people around him shouted and ran. Magnus hit the sidewalk with bruising force, staring up into the impossible red eyes of the wolf, and felt as if his heart was going to explode with terror.

The red eyes seemed to grow larger. . . .

The sun shone into Eric's bedroom, illuminating the desk in the corner. Music paper was spread out across it, several bars of an unfinished composition jotted down with a music pen.

Although a Bard improvised music as easily as he breathed, and improvisation had always come easily to Eric, at Juilliard he'd also learned the more rigorous discipline of traditional classical composition. There was a certain appeal to writing down a piece of music that would be played the same way—more or less—every time, a piece of music that could be handed on to someone else, and even though it was no longer something he was required to do, Eric liked to keep those skills in practice. Besides, there were very few things he could give his Sidhe friends as presents, but a piece of original music was something a wealthy, nigh-immortal elf couldn't make—or buy—for himself.

He set his pen down for a moment and glanced at the clock. Still too early for any news.

Maybe this weekend they'd all do something—Eric grinned at the unfamiliar concept—*fun*. Maybe they could go down to Six Flags, or something. Magnus would pretend to hate it, but Eric bet he'd jump at the chance to stuff himself with junk food and ride things guaranteed to subject the human body to more G-force than the average astronaut. And Ace could use a major chance to blow off steam—that kid was wrapped way too tight. Maybe he could even talk Ria into coming along. Provided he could come up with a suitable form of bribery. Although it might take blackmail to get Ria onto the Nitro Mega Coaster. . . .

Just as he was about to pick up his pen again, a sense of unfolding disaster struck him with the force of a physical blow.

Everything had been fine a moment before, but suddenly the room seemed dark and cold, even though nothing had changed. He felt as if a shadow had come into the room and whispered horrors in his ear, and he didn't know what, or why.

All he knew was that there was some warning of danger that had slipped through the wards of Guardian House as if they weren't even there.

"Greystone?" he said aloud. "I got a red alert! What's happening?"

*Nothing,* the gargoyle's mental voice answered promptly within his mind. *If it's a warning, it's one that only you can hear. Be careful, laddybuck.*

Fear was a powerful motivator. Five minutes ago, Eric wouldn't have thought he had the energy to run down the stairs rather than wait for the elevator.

If he was the only one who could hear the warning, if it was something that could pass through the formidable shields that protected Guardian House from harm, then the warning had to be about someone closely connected to him.

And that was a short list, Eric decided, as he ran toward the parking lot to pick up Lady Day.

Greystone had already alerted Toni Hernandez, and there were few things a Guardian couldn't take in stride. Eric didn't know where Kayla was right now—he was pretty sure Columbia was on break—but Toni would track her down and check in with her, just to make sure she was all right. Since Kayla had moved into Guardian House, she'd become something of an unofficial mascot to the Guardians, and they'd keep her from coming to harm.

Ria . . . well, he pitied the trouble that tried to take Ria on, actually.

That left Magnus. Magnus, who was no kind of Mage, and all alone, at school.

Vulnerable.

He flung his leg over Lady Day's saddle. She'd caught his emotional turmoil from several flights away; almost before he'd settled his weight in the bike's saddle, the elvensteed had backed out of her parking spot and was flying down the street toward Magnus's school.

His stomach was a cold knot of dread, as he bent his head against the wind of Lady Day's passing. He'd been worrying about Magnus from the moment he'd known there was a reason to worry. Magnus was a good kid—no, a *great* kid—but his stubborn insistence on shutting out the uncanny aspects of the world (hard to do, living in Guardian House with a talking gargoyle for a friend, but Magnus managed) was going to get him into trouble some day. Maybe today was the day.

Eric turned Lady Day onto Broadway—it was fastest, even at this time of day—and the elvensteed settled down to making serious time, dodging taxis and pedestrians and ignoring any traffic laws that didn't happen to suit her, such as the speed limit.

They'd only gotten as far as Columbus Circle when suddenly half-a-dozen enormous black shapes came lunging out from among the other cars toward them. After a moment's stunned incredulity, Eric realized what he was seeing.

Wolves.

Wolves—but worse. They were to normal wolves what a birthday candle was to a forest fire—they were all the primeval terrors of night and the ancient forest given fur and fangs and flesh. And what made them so horribly wrong was that they were *here,* on a New York City street on a raw March day. Their pupilless eyes glowed Unseleighe red, and they seemed to know what he was thinking—and be laughing at him. Fire and ice crawled through his veins as he made eye-contact with them.

He didn't dare start a full-blown duel in the middle of Broadway. And worse, Eric didn't know if they had anything to do with the warning he'd felt, or were just an awful coincidence. Elves didn't *do* New York. But then, elves didn't attack Bards, either.

He threw a shield around himself and Lady Day just as one of the beasts dodged in, snapping at his foot. Lady Day swerved and tried to evade them, but they herded her—slamming against Eric's magickal shield and dashing in front of the elvensteed—toward Central Park. They couldn't touch him—but they could overset Lady Day by allowing her to hit one of them, and send her and Eric under the wheels of a truck or car.

All around them, brakes screeched and horns blared. Another urban legend in the making? Maybe. Eric didn't have the leisure to think about it.

Lady Day put on a burst of speed, dodging through the oncoming traffic, slamming up over the sidewalk, and bouncing bone-jarringly up over the low wall surrounding the park. The Unseleighe dire-wolves fell back, but only a few paces, letting her run, and as soon as she was headed deep into the park, they closed up again.

There were people in the park, but not as many as there were on Broadway. Now he could fight.

Or better yet—run. He could be in Misthold before they had a chance to—

But suddenly he heard a jangle of disharmonic harpsong, and his shield was ripped away.

Before he could react, he felt powerful jaws clamp down on his ankle, yanking him from Lady Day's saddle and hurling him to the ground. One of the dire-wolves landed on top of him—it weighed more than Eric did—knocking the breath from him, and beneath it all, the harp played on, like Stravinsky on crack, making it hard to think. He thrashed under the wolf's weight, but it wasn't moving, and every time he tried to take a breath, the wolf got heavier—

He could hear Lady Day fighting, hear the yelps and stifled yips of the other dire-wolves, and beneath those sounds, the sound of a powerful automobile engine approaching.

The dire-wolf sitting on his chest backed off.

Eric rolled to his knees, gasping for breath. He felt strangely weak, and cold all over.

Lady Day—in horse form now—stood like a stag at bay, surrounded by a panting half-circle of dire-wolves. Just beyond her a black limousine stood parked. Eric readied his spells.

The back door of the limousine swung open.

Jormin ap Galever sat in the back. He was holding Magnus against his chest, with a silver knife to Magnus's throat. Magnus's head lolled limply; he was unconscious, but Eric could see from the rise and fall of his chest that he was still alive.

"Will you join us, Bard?" Jormin called cheerily.

Eric gritted his teeth and got to his feet. He kept his expression as stony as he could, even though his heart felt as if it had stopped, and his thoughts were running in panicked circles like frightened mice. The unspoken message was clear: resist in any way, and Jormin would kill Magnus. And no elven treaties protected Magnus.

"Fine." He turned to Lady Day. "Go home. I'll tell you what to do later." *This is not the time to argue about this, girl. . . .*

Through the link they shared he felt her reluctant obedience, and felt a pang of relief. He didn't trust Jormin to let her go once Eric's back was turned, and captured elvensteeds were great prizes for the Dark Court. . . .

Lady Day sprang backward, out of the circle of dire-wolves, and galloped away. In seconds the sound of hoof-beats was replaced with the mournful howl of a high-powered motorcycle engine receding in the distance.

Someone yanked his hands behind him. Automatically he started to struggle, but Jormin pressed the knife closer to Magnus's throat, and he stopped.

He felt the touch of something cold and heavy on his wrists. Bracelets?

Cold . . . the cold seemed to seep into his blood, flowing through his veins with every beat of his heart, until it was a struggle to breathe. He felt his knees grow weak, and the day darkened around him.

And then he knew nothing more.

# CHAPTER 6:
## SELL IT AND THEY WILL COME

"I'm always happy to get out God's message any way I can, Mr. Songmaker," Billy Fairchild said, smiling as he welcomed Hosea into his private office, "but I've got to say, I'm a mite puzzled. Isn't *Rolling Stone* one o' them rock and roll magazines?"

Billy Fairchild didn't look like a man who'd suffered a crushing setback in his personal life only a few hours before, nor like a man who was grieving over the absence of a beloved daughter. For that matter, he didn't look like a crazy religious maniac. He had the practiced charm of a good politician, a way of making whoever he was talking to at the moment feel that they were the most important person in the world. Hosea had seen con-games tried on by experts, but there was a *genuineness* to Billy that made him almost doubt himself. There was only one explanation for that particular conundrum. Whatever Billy Fairchild happened to be saying at any particular moment, he had the knack of really believing it himself.

Which made him doubly dangerous; a pathological liar of the worst kind. You couldn't tell if he was telling the truth by any signal that he would give you; he'd be able to pass a lie detector test with flying colors. And even Bardic truth-sense was likely to fail in the face of such utter conviction.

And the fetch-bag—Unseleighe magick, he now knew, with Jeanette's help—was gone. His mage-sight detected no sign of it.

"Shore is," Hosea said easily in answer, sitting down in the offered seat beside Billy's polished mahogany desk. "But it also does a lot of stuff it thinks people that listen to rock'n'roll might be interested in—like a preacher that runs a casino. Ah can't say they'll print what I write, y'know, that's the risk a freelancer takes, but they said they were interested. An' heck, if *Rolling Stone* don't take it, somebody else might. I jest like to try the big dogs first."

"Can't ask for fairer than that," Billy said. "And—well, say, I just got a notion, maybe you can stay a few days—I can get you a free ticket to the concert we've got coming up. If a music magazine is interested in a casino, they ought to be twice as interested in a rock band."

Fairchild made it sound like he'd "just" had that idea, but this time Hosea was able to tell he was being played, that Billy Fairchild had planned this from the time he agreed to the interview. This was a "bait-and-switch" tactic. He was probably planning that *Rolling Stone* would prefer to cover something about what Hosea assumed was another "Christian Rock" band, and hoped to get the article refocused. Hosea responded as Billy would want, looking surprised and interested. "Cain't say as a preacher bringin' up a rock band seems any more likely than a preacher runnin' a casino."

Billy laughed, deprecatingly. "I don't much care for that kind of music myself, but the Lord Jesus didn't preach to the people in fancy high-toned talk they couldn't understand, you know. He used the words they knew. So if I want to get the Lord's message out to the young, I have to use their music to do it, and that's why I've started Red Nails Music. But Gabriel can tell you more about that—that's his bailiwick. I just pick good people and let them run—at heart I'm just a backwoods country preacher doing what I can. But I expect you know that. From the sound of you, you aren't too long out of the hills your own self."

"Ayah," Hosea agreed shamelessly, taking his microcassette recorder out of his shoulder bag and setting it down on the desk. "Why don't you start with a little of yore early days, an then maybe tell me about how you came to build this place?"

The one thing a certain kind of person was most willing to talk about was themselves, Hosea had found, and Billy was certainly that kind of person. He heard plenty about Billy's humble beginnings as a traveling revivalist preacher, and nothing much about his daughter—except that "the whole family pitched in, of course, to spread God's Word."

"Is yore daughter planning to follow in your footsteps?" Hosea asked, making the question seem as idle as he could possibly manage.

"Of course she is!" Billy said fervently. "My little angel wouldn't have it any other way. Why, she's been a part of my Ministry ever since she could walk! She wouldn't leave me now."

The sad thing was, Hosea reflected, that there was probably a part of Billy that actually believed that was the truth. The trouble was, there was another part of Billy that was determined to make sure that "truth" was what came to pass—regardless of anything Heavenly Grace wanted.

But Billy was going right on, oozing sincerity. "I'd sure like for you to meet her, but she isn't here right now. She should be home soon, though, and maybe if your article isn't done, you can come back and visit with her then."

"I'd like that," Hosea said. As far as he could sense the truth in Billy's words, nothing Billy had said was an outright lie. It was true that Ace wasn't here . . . and for some reason, Billy Fairchild had a strong belief that not only would she be coming back soon, but she'd be happy to talk to reporters.

That was worrying. And Hosea couldn't tell if the belief was because Billy had convinced himself that it would be so—or because Billy other reasons besides that.

Billy, however, was sailing on to other subjects. "But deeds speak louder than words, and I expect you'd be glad of a chance to stretch your legs. Why don't we take a turn around the casino floor, and then I'll bring you back upstairs and introduce you around a bit? I'd love to jaw all day, but Miz Granger, she's got a notion that work ought to get done around here, dear lady, and I suppose I can't blame her," Billy said, grinning conspiratorially. "You put in that article of yours that I'd be lost without her, mind. Been with me twenty year."

"Ah surely will," Hosea said.

The two men got to their feet and headed toward the elevators. On the way they passed Mrs. Granger's desk. She glared fiercely at Hosea as he passed, daring him to even think anything uncomplimentary about her boss. Billy's private secretary was a type Hosea was familiar with—the backbone of every church, big and small—determined, efficient, and formidably loyal to her office master. Billy Fairchild could be sacrificing black cats by the dark of the moon and it wouldn't change Mrs. Granger's opinion of him, which had been set in stone long ago.

They took the elevator down to the lobby of the office building—that entrance was on the opposite side of the building from the casino—and then Billy walked over to a door in the wall marked "Employees Only" and pressed a quick series of numbers into a keypad lock before opening the door. He opened the door and ushered Hosea through into the sensory overload of the Heavenly Grace Cathedral and Casino of Prayer.

Billy's enthusiasm ought to have been infectious. He happily explained to Hosea how he'd taken a personal hand in every aspect of the Casino of Prayer's construction, from the design of the slot machines, to the games offered, to the decoration. The idea to make the House's percentage ten percent—"a real Biblical tithe"—had been his, as had been the free-will love offering boxes scattered freely about the casino. All the gaming tokens used in the machines had Biblical verses stamped on them—that had been Billy's idea, too—so that people could be constantly uplifted and refreshed in spirit while they gambled. Even the decks of cards used at the blackjack and poker tables were specially printed, with the Twelve Apostles replacing the face cards, the Dove of the Holy Spirit replacing the aces, Jesus instead of the Joker, and the Fairchild Ministry logo on the back.

They were for sale in the gift shop, of course.

There were other things to do in the casino besides gamble, of course. You could listen to live gospel or "spirit" music—none of the bands from Billy's new label, he said regretfully, not yet—watch highlights from Billy's previous *Praise Hours* on a thirty-foot screen, dine in four different restaurants (one of which offered "Authentic Food of the Bible Lands!") and Hosea saw a sign for an evening show promising a Genuine Simulated Reenactment of the Miracles of Moses Before Pharaoh! Whatever that show might be, its contents probably didn't bear thinking about too closely . . . though surely it took the place of the usual Vegas-style magic act.

Everyone recognized Billy, of course, and wanted to talk to him. People clustered around him as he glad-handed and greeted them, giving a good imitation of a campaigning politician. It effectively discouraged any interview-type questions from Hosea, but he got an earful just the same.

"Reverend, I saw your show last night. Is it really true what that Mr. Wheatley said about the demons?" An elderly woman in bright pink stretch pants and a Casino of Prayer logo sweatshirt put a hand on Billy's arm as he passed her seat at the slot machines and regarded him anxiously.

"Sweet thing, there's not one thing said on my program that isn't the gospel truth," Billy said firmly. "But we're gonna root those ol' demons out no matter where they're hiding and send them all back to Hell, don't you worry. We've got big things planned—and you can be a part of the Liberation Army. Just keep watching my program and praising Jesus, and you'll see what you need to be doing."

Most of the questions had to do with Wheatley's startling revelation, naturally, and from Billy's answers, Hosea got the impression that in a few weeks the advice from the pulpit on what to do about the "demons" was going to become a good deal more prescriptive. But a number of the people who stopped Billy on their tour simply wanted autographs, or to have their picture taken with him, or to tell him what a difference he'd made in their lives. Some of them asked about Heavenly Grace, and to them, Billy gave the same answer he'd given Hosea—that she was away right now, but that she'd be back soon.

There was no doubt in Hosea's mind that Billy was the sort to thrive on the attention, never turning anyone away—and why not? He was obviously a natural showman.

It saddened Hosea; here was a man who had been given so many good gifts—health, energy, intelligence, good looks, the ability to understand people . . . he could have done truly good things with them. He could be showing people how to make the most of their own lives—he could be using the money brought in to feed the hungry and tend the sick, instead of building mockeries like this so-called Casino Cathedral.

In fact, by his own words, and from what Ace had said, he had not been a very bad man until Gabriel Horn had arrived on the scene. Or at least, he had not been doing near the harm he was now. And between the hate and fear he was preaching, and the way he was preying on peoples' weaknesses here in this casino, he was doing a lot of harm.

On the whole, Hosea thought it would be very interesting to meet Gabriel Horn.

Hosea glanced around the casino, and wondered if the Reverend Billy Fairchild was familiar with the Bible verse about the children crying out for bread and being given stones.

At last they ducked out through the side-door again. Hosea had gotten so used to the din in the casino that the silence on the other side of the door was nearly deafening.

"Any time I need a little pick-me-up I just go down and walk around out there for a while," Billy said, grinning. "Sets me right up. You can just feel the love rising up out of all those good Christian souls."

Hosea smiled, but his heart wasn't in it. All he could think of was that love didn't have a great deal to do with what Billy had been preaching last night.

And that Billy was probably a great deal more "set up" by all the money being sucked out of all those good Christian pockets.

"*There* you are, Reverend! When Mrs. Granger said you'd gone down to the casino, I was afraid we wouldn't see you for the rest of the day," a new voice said.

Hosea turned and regarded the speaker. The man was as tall as he was—and there weren't many who were. While Billy wore an expensive handmade suit in a way that managed to make it look "just folks," there was no mistaking the stranger's suit for anything but custom couture tailoring.

"Well, just the man I was going to be looking for next!" Billy said sunnily. "Hosea, this is Gabriel Horn. I couldn't run this place without him. Gabe, this is Hosea Songmaker—he's come down here to do a little article on us."

"A reporter?" Gabriel Horn said, his voice dark with suspicion.

"More like a freelancer journalist, even if that's a kinda fancy word. *Rolling Stone* sent me down," Hosea said, carefully putting on a respectful and opaque mask, "and if they like what Ah write, well, might be they'll print it."

He really did wish there was enough time to take care of Billy Fairchild properly and with thorough care, Gabriel thought wistfully. From what black cauldron of fool's inspiration and raven-kissed luck had he drawn the notion to summon a Bright Bard to his side and give him a tour of the inner workings of the Ministry?

Of course, it was unlikely in the extreme that Billy knew that this so-called journalist was, in fact, a Bard, obvious as the fact was to Gabriel. And it might almost have been seen as a stroke of good fortune—if Gabriel had been in a better humor—for surely this was the busy meddler who had seen to it that Gabriel's own spells had gone awry this morning. Was there any chance whatsoever that there were two Bright Bards sniffing around Billy Fairchild at this moment? Improbable, to say the least.

"I am delighted to meet you, Hosea Songmaker," he said, holding out his hand.

Yes—he knew it when their palms clasped—the flavor of the magic was the same as that which had wrapped and drained his talisman. This, then, was little Heavenly Grace's champion.

Swiftly, he considered how the interloper might best be served.

A quick and merry death? Gabriel dismissed the possibility with regret. At the moment what he could do was very limited. It had taken every ounce of his power to send his Hunt into New York City in broad day to take the Bright Bard Eric and the boy his brother and bring them away safe again, and undoubtedly Jormin would be complaining about it for the next hundred years. The mortals' blighted iron city was no place for the Sidhe—only Aerune the Mad, who had owed allegiance to no Court, and who had dared Oberon to bring him to heel, had made it his own—that place that mortals had once called cursed because *he* dwelled there, and in a strange retribution, had made it into a place where no Sidhe dared linger.

So for now Gabriel's powers were spent . . . and more mundane "accidents" took time and care to arrange, and were better left for the hours of darkness.

So this Bard's death would have to wait. But at least he now knew the face of his enemy, and with care, he'd be able to take the measure of the mortal as well.

"Maybe you could show Hosea around the place a little—the behind the scenes stuff," Billy said, foolish and open and gormless, with no more notion that he was giving succor to the very person that had thwarted his will than a suckling babe. "Tell him all about the concert this weekend, and see if we can't persuade him to stay and give it a listen. I figure that's just the thing his magazine would like to hear about."

Suddenly, Gabriel felt much more cheerful. Out of the mouths of babes— *Oh, yes.* If the Bard stayed for Jormin's concert, that would give Gabriel plenty of time to recover. He already knew where Heavenly Grace was staying. No doubt the Bard laired there too. He could take the Bard at his leisure and feed him to his Soul-eaters; not a light feeding, but a heavy one. Not even his bones would remain. And then there would be nothing standing between him and acquiring the maiden.

Nothing.

"I'd be delighted to," Gabriel said warmly. "I hope you'll be able to stay for the concert. It's going to be an amazing event. Come this way—I'll take you up to the Red Nails office."

" . . . I think we've signed the finest in Christian heavy metal today: Pure Blood, Holy Sacrament, Lost Angels, Revelations . . . they'll all be at the concert on Friday."

The offices of Red Nails Music occupied most of a floor of the Fairchild Tower, and bore a superficial resemblance to any other creative workplace: messy desks, harried employees, walls covered with posters and every flat surface heaped with promotional items. In fact, there really wasn't much difference between this office and the offices of *Rolling Stone*.

Gabriel talked as he took Hosea on a quick tour, and there were some profound differences between Gabriel's style and Billy's. Hosea noted that while Gabriel's staff was happy to see him, and didn't hesitate to approach him for help, there was a certain *formality* in the exchanges that hadn't been present between Billy Fairchild and the people he met. Gabriel Horn wasn't the type to let people forget, even for a minute, who was the boss. Billy preferred his underlings to act—at least while Hosea had been there—as if he was as much friend as employer.

"The concert is free—we're holding it to launch Pure Blood's debut album—and we're expecting several thousand people to show up," Gabriel was explaining. "We didn't want too big of a crowd, you understand—one of the reasons we're holding it on a weekday and only doing minimal advertising. Too many people could pose a crowd-control issue. But it should be enough to get the word out—and there's still plenty of room here in the business park; we shouldn't have all of the subsidiaries of the Ministry moved in and the rest of the space rented out to compatible corporations until late next year."

"Does that include moving in Parker Wheatley's demon hunters?" Hosea asked. He did want to know if everybody at Fairchild Ministries was as pleased with Wheatley as Billy was, and besides, an interviewer ought to ask an awkward question or two.

While Gabriel Horn made him uneasy—though he didn't have quite the same effect on Hosea as he'd had on Ace—Bardic powers or not, he couldn't say what bothered him about the man any more than she'd been able to. It was a great pity he hadn't been able to bring Jeanette along with him to the interview, because without her, his ability to see what lay beneath the surface of things was limited. His mage-sight would show him magick and things unseen—if he could find an undistracted moment to use it. And if it didn't happen to come up against a power greater than his.

Now there was a comforting thought.

He could also tell, usually, when someone was telling the truth. But Gabriel Horn very carefully had not said anything that was not purely factual. At least, not until this moment.

Gabriel Horn hadn't liked his question about Wheatley at all, though he did his best not to show it.

"Mr. Songmaker, one of the reasons Billy and I get along so well is because I let him deal with the matters he considers important and he extends me the same courtesy. I'm sure that if he wants Mr. Wheatley to have resources, he'll give them to him."

*That's true. And he knows it.*

But what Gabriel Horn wasn't saying was how he *felt* about that. No, he was going to skim right past that little roadblock. "If you'd like, when we're finished here, I can turn you over to Andrew Wyath—he produces the *Praise Hour*, and he's been working closely with Mr. Wheatley—and you can see if you can get a few minutes of his time."

"Oh," Hosea said dismissively, glancing over Gabriel's shoulder at an enormous poster of Judah Galilee, wearing leather pants, clutching a blood-red guitar that matched his hair, and looking as if he were undergoing electroshock therapy, "that's all very well, and Ah do thank you for the thought, Mr. Horn, but . . . Ah think mah readers might be more interested in music than demons."

Gabriel smiled, obviously recovering his good mood with a bit of an effort. "Then by all means, let us give the people what they want. I can give you a press-kit and some CDs—Lost Angels is a popular local band, and Revelations had some success in the Detroit market before they signed with us, put out a couple of CDs on an indie label, but I think we can take both of them to the top. As for Pure Blood, well, once you've seen and heard

Judah Galilee, I think you'll have to agree that he's going to cross over. The boy is absolutely brilliant, and very appealing."

"These people don't just walk up and knock on your door," Hosea said, making it a half question.

"You'd be surprised," Gabriel said with a faint smile. "But in the case of Pure Blood—"

One of the office staff approached Gabriel hesitantly. "Excuse me, sir, but Judah Galilee is waiting for you in your office."

"Well, this should be interesting," Gabriel said. "Come along, young Songmaker. This is your chance to meet a modern-day Bard."

Gabriel's offices were at the end of a long corridor that wouldn't have been out of place at LlewellCo—expensive wooden paneling, the real thing and not veneer, and thick carpets that had never come out of an industrial-supply warehouse. Hosea had to hurry to keep up with Gabriel, and even so he kept falling a few steps behind. That, he suspected, was another bit of power-play, designed to put him in his place. Gabriel had all the moves, all right.

There was something just the slightest bit off about all of Gabriel's reactions, but Hosea couldn't quite put his finger on it. It was as if Gabriel was playing a part, somehow, playing it well, but playing it for Hosea's benefit, and try as he might, Hosea could not imagine why that should be.

Hosea was looking for an Unseleighe Magus, probably one working with Parker Wheatley, who had had Unseleighe allies before. Someone who had given Billy a charm that would win his court case for him. And so far, he hadn't seen any sign of one.

While Gabriel Horn was the original bad hat, Hosea was prepared to guarantee Gabriel wasn't working with Wheatley. There was only one thing he was prepared to feel sure of about Gabriel Horn, and that was that the man resented Wheatley at the least, probably disliked him, and certainly was not at all happy about Billy Fairchild's involvement with him.

They reached the door, and Gabriel opened it.

His office had a breathtaking view, though mostly of empty office buildings and half-finished landscaping at the moment, and mercifully it was one of the few places in the complex from which it was not possible to see the facade of the Casino and Cathedral of Prayer. There was a long sleek black leather couch under the window, with a long sleek musician dressed mostly in black leather lounging on it.

Judah Galilee looked as if he were barely out of his teens. His eyes were a startling shade of gold—and not from contact lenses, either, Hosea decided, looking closely. His hair, which was definitely enhanced, was bright crimson and waist length. He looked up when Hosea and Gabriel entered, but not as if he intended to move at any time in the near future.

"Hosea is a member of the press, Judah; you may speak freely in front of him," Gabriel said.

And that was a flat untruth, the first Gabriel had uttered in his presence. Of course, it might simply be a *joke. . . .*

"I just wanted to talk about the supplies for our trailer for the concert. We don't want any red M and Ms in the candy. Red M and Ms are Satanic," Judah said, a faint whine in his voice.

"'No Satanic Candy,'" Gabriel recited, as if making a note. "Judah, are you *quite* through jerking my chain?"

"Actually, I've got a really long list of stuff," the singer replied with an impish grin, sitting up and swinging his long legs off the couch. "And then there's what Abidan wants, and what Coz wants, and what Jakan wants—" He turned to Hosea, getting to his feet. "But it can wait. Gabriel says you're a reporter. Are you here to cover the concert?"

"Among other things," Hosea said.

But he had clamped his mask of slight deference and interest down hard over his features. Gabriel had called Judah Galilee a bard a few minutes ago, and at the time Hosea had thought he was making another of his oddly skewed jokes. But now that he saw Judah in the flesh, he knew Gabriel had been telling the simple truth.

Judah *was* a bard. No, a Bard. A Bard as Eric was, as Hosea was learning to be. No wonder Gabriel was so sure that Pure Blood was going to be a success, if Judah was its lead singer.

For Hosea could feel Judah's Gift as clearly as he could sense

Eric's, and it took all his will and training not to let that knowledge show on his face.

Hosea knew—Eric had made sure he knew—that just as a Bard's Gift could be used to heal, it could also be used to destroy, but healing, *creating*, was the wellspring and foundation of Bardcraft. Not so for Judah Galilee. He possessed all the power of a Bard, but somehow Hosea knew that if Judah ever created anything, he did so only to destroy it. It was as if everything sane in the world had been turned to madness: if there were such things as demons walking the world in human flesh, Hosea thought in that moment he might be looking at one.

And he knew with a sinking feeling that if he'd recognized Judah as a Bard, then Judah had recognized him as well.

Did Gabriel know what Judah was? Hosea suspected he might.

And that meant he was in a lot more trouble than he had time to think about right now.

It was an enormous effort to make conversation, to ask the sort of questions a person in his position ought to ask, to pretend he'd sensed nothing simply because he didn't know how much either of them knew, and to let them know that he'd sensed anything at all might trigger the worst sort of disaster. His hotel room key was in his wallet—he'd thought nothing of it at the time, but if something happened to him here, that key would lead whoever took him down right back to Ace . . . and Jeanette.

And that would be the worst kind of disaster.

Half an hour later he was out of there, feeling as if he'd escaped the lion's den only because the lion hadn't happened to be particularly hungry that day. It was nearly six o'clock. He was carrying a press-kit for the upcoming concert—actually a large shopping-bag full of tapes, CDs, and other promotional items—a press pass that would get him through the gate and backstage on Friday, and half a dozen tickets to give to his friends. Gabriel had even promised to help him get a chance to talk to Parker Wheatley sometime before the concert, and Hosea had thanked him politely, even though he didn't really expect to keep that appointment.

He suspected that Gabriel knew that as well.

It was already dark when he walked out of the building. When he'd walked in that afternoon, he'd never expected to be so purely grateful to leave. He threw the bag onto the passenger seat of the pink Cadillac and drove quickly away from the building, unable to repress a shudder of relief as he did so.

"So that is Sieur Eric of Misthold's apprentice?" Jormin ap Galever said, after Hosea had left. "Unimpressive. Yet odd." He shrugged elegantly, dismissing the anomalies he had sensed in Hosea's magick. The mortal was hardly beginning his training; as a Bard, he was inconsequential. He probably could not work magic without actually playing or singing, and that, for a Bard, marked him as the merest tyro. Insignificant. "A pity for him that he has not chosen to make his manners to Prince Arvin and accept the protection of Elfhame Misthold—or is it that Bard Eric did not think to extend such protection?"

"It will not matter soon," Prince Gabrevys said, dismissively. "I *will* be rid of him, of course; he stands between me and my rightful prey, Fairchild's Fair Child. He thwarted me once; he shall not do so again. His death will not be laid to my door—indeed, it cannot be, at least, not by the Bright Court; they have no agents that are practiced enough to trace back my movements here in the World Above. Nor indeed by any other of the Sidhe, not even the High King himself. There will be a terrible accident here on Friday, one that will claim the lives of a number of people. I'm afraid Sieur Eric's inconvenient apprentice will be just another tragic casualty. Pity, that."

"Not that Sieur Eric will either know or care," Jormin gloated, still delighted with his own cleverness. Though the boy Magnus had somehow sensed the presence of the Hunt and run, he hadn't gotten far, and had been easily taken by Abidan, Coz, and Jakan. And the fury, fear, and despair on the Bard's face when he had seen Jormin's hostage had been wine of a heady vintage indeed. "By the time I take the stage, he and his brother will be well on the road back to Boston. His parents will be lucky if they don't drool on themselves. As for this Hosea Songmaker, I can play him in circles for as long as I please. He'll be no trouble to you, my Prince."

"I will hold you to that, Jormin," Gabrevys said softly. "He may be untutored, but he surely will have recognized you for a Bard, if not as Unseleighe. I wish him to stay here and keep Heavenly Grace at his side until she hears word of her father's tragic death. She will have to return to her mother's house, then, to comfort her in her bereavement. Once there, I can move the Apprentice into position to eliminate him, and once the Apprentice Bard is gone, I may move to take the maiden at my leisure."

Jormin cocked his head to the side, his hair falling over his shoulder like a spill of blood. "So you mean to move at last! To be the butt of mortal's japes suited you ill, my Prince. This is happy news. I shall ready my most subtle enchantments . . . against two Gifted mortals, you will have a day, perhaps two, before they become suspicious at their own delay—after that, I can still hold them as long as pleases you, but they will begin to wonder at their own behavior, and perhaps might suspect and ready their own crude magic to counter me."

"It will not be so long as that, my Bard," Gabrevys told him, dark pleasure in his voice. "Only keep them here until the day of the concert. After that, it will be too late. Now here is where you must go. . . ."

Once Hosea left for the business park, Ace checked her watch and phoned Magnus. Although it was lunchtime by now, his phone returned an "Out of Service" message.

She made a face. She knew he wouldn't have forgotten to turn it on—it was more likely he'd been caught trying to use it between classes and gotten it confiscated again.

She tried Eric next, but she got the same message from his cell, and nobody picked up at the apartment. She sighed in annoyance. He was probably off giving a music lesson and had his phone turned off, and she had no idea when he'd be back to pick up his messages at the apartment.

She called Ria next to give her the bad news, not that Ria didn't already have most of it, courtesy of Mr. Tilford.

"So when are you coming back to New York?" Ria said. "I can't say this thrills me—especially the part about your father having an Unseleighe Magus somewhere on the payroll, whether he knows it or not—but having Parker Wheatley launching a demon-hunting crusade under the aegis of Fairchild Ministries does give us a bit more ammunition to pry you loose. As soon as Derek gets back, I'm going to have him put together a short précis of Mr. Wheatley's recent career—kidnapping, torture, subversion—to present to Judge Springsteen. An environment containing a man like that is no place for an impressionable young girl like you. Not to mention what kind of unpleasant experiences he might expose you to, nor the kinds of unwanted attention he'd bring in the way of people who might be looking for revenge. He hurt a great many people, and no few of them hold grudges." She paused a moment, and Ace could practically hear her thinking. "I might be able to shade enough of what I've got to make it look as if he has mob connections—and you know, the three places that deal in a lot of untraceable cash are organized crime, legalized gambling, and churches. A church is a logical place to use to launder money—make that a church running a casino . . . I think I can throw out enough red herrings to make the judge start feeling a bit alarmed. I'd like you back here, though."

Despite herself, Ace managed a smile. "Well, it's a little too far to walk. I thought I'd wait until Hosea got back from his interview, and see what he's found out."

"Call me then," Ria said. "And be careful."

"I will," Ace promised.

After that there was nothing to do but watch television, pace, and wait for Hosea to return from interviewing Billy. She used up all the coffee in both the in-room coffeemakers—hers and Hosea's—and began to think about going out to get coffee and maybe something more appetizing than the leftover Chinese food in the refrigerator, but no matter how much she tried to convince herself it was perfectly safe, she couldn't quite bring herself to do it. She called Eric's apartment several more times, but nobody ever picked up the phone, and by the time she made the last call, it was well after the time Magnus should have been home, even if Eric wasn't.

Something was wrong.

She started to worry in earnest.

Magnus knew her hearing was today. He was mad to find out how it had come out. Even if Coenties & Arundel had taken his phone, he would have called her from another one as soon as he could.

Unless something had happened to him.

She knew their parents were fighting Eric over custody . . . had something happened? Were they tied up in court somewhere? Or stuck in a lawyer's office? Had the parents somehow managed to get them arrested?

She thought hard, gnawing at her lip. There had to be somebody she could ask. Not Ria. For one thing, she didn't want to wind Ria up about Magnus and Eric's parents any more than she already was, and for another, she hated to keep going to Ria with every little thing, and she'd already promised to call her as soon as Hosea got back. And there might be a perfectly reasonable explanation for what was going on that she just couldn't think of right now.

Kayla. Kayla lived in the same building. She and Eric had been friends for years, and Ace suspected that Magnus kind of liked Kayla too. Besides, Kayla knew things about people. If there was something funny going on, Kayla would know. And if there wasn't, she'd tell Ace to stop being a jerk and then Ace could go take a cold shower or something.

She dug around in her bag for Kayla's number. Her phone was a new one, and she hadn't gotten around to completely programming it yet.

The phone rang, and there was a connection. For a moment Ace heard nothing but wild barking, then: "Molly—Molly—Molly, I don't know who it is, but trust me, they ain't callin' for you!"

"Kayla?" Ace said doubtfully. The barking subsided—or rather, became stifled, as if its source had been wrapped in something.

"Yeah. Ace? Are you okay?" Kayla said. "Good girl!" This last did not seem to be directed to Ace.

"Why shouldn't I be okay?" Ace demanded suspiciously.

"Well, this morning Eric took off like the proverbial bat, and Greystone told Toni he'd gotten some kind of vague mumbo-jumbo warning, like only Bards get—and I guess Too-Tall didn't get one, or you would have called earlier and you wouldn't be nearly this calm now—so when I got back from walking Molly, everybody jumped on me just in case I'd got kidnapped by space aliens, which I hadn't, thank you very much. Drop that, Molly! Sheesh! If this is what having kids is like, I'm becoming a monk."

"I haven't been able to get through to Magnus on his cellphone all day," Ace said flatly. "And Eric isn't answering the phone in the apartment."

Kayla let out a long breath. "Actually, we were all sort of hoping you wouldn't notice that."

"*What happened?*" All the apprehension that Ace had felt all day spiraled up into a sudden flash of terror, and suddenly her hands were shaking so hard she could barely hold onto the phone. Something *was* wrong, something horrible had happened to Eric, Magnus, or both!

"Breathe," Kayla told her firmly. "There's nothing you and Too-Tall can do from down there. The big guns are on it and we didn't want you worryin' about somethin' you couldn't fix. All I know is what Toni told me that Greystone told her. He didn't sense anything directly, either. Whatever it was came straight through to Eric, and all *he* got was a warning of trouble. He took off on his bike for Gussie's school, and about half an hour later, the bike was back. Empty. When it showed up, Toni called Ria, and Ria called the school. They checked, but Magnus wasn't there—his history teacher said he'd been called down to the office. That was about the same time somebody turned a pack of wolves loose in Midtown, according to the news reports."

"Wolves?" Ace said faintly.

"Or something that looked like wolves to most of the people that saw them," Kayla said grimly. "Odds are they weren't. Paul's trying to get a line on what they were and where they came from right now, and Ria's looking for Eric and Gus."

Wolves in Manhattan—that had to be magic. Lady Day coming

back alone. Eric and Magnus missing—Ace felt paralyzed and helpless—she didn't know anything about this magic stuff, only what she'd seen since she met Eric, and that was hardly anything—

"Look, I know it sounds stupid, but—try not to worry. Eric's survived a lot of weird stuff. Hell, he's even been *dead,* and it didn't slow him down much. Wherever he and Gus are, he'll make sure they both get back safe. Right now, you've just got to make sure that the two of you stay safe too. It's only been a couple of hours."

"Yeah," Ace said faintly. She could feel tears building in the back of her throat, and gulped them down. She wasn't going to cry in front of Kayla. Kayla was counting on her to keep herself under control. If she lost it, she'd just be a liability, not a help. She took a deep breath. "Okay. Call me if you hear anything, okay?"

"Sure," Kayla said. "I just wish I didn't have to give you more bad news on a day like this."

"Oh, you know how it is," Ace said, trying to feign cheer, "bad things happen in threes."

Once she'd disconnected, she wondered why she'd said it. So far today, only two awful things had happened.

Hosea arrived very soon after that, and though she managed to keep her vow not to burst into tears, the sight of his face nearly made her break it.

He looked frightened.

She'd never seen Hosea afraid—not even when he'd been facing down Jaycie's Protector with nothing more than a banjo and the wild guess that he'd solved the riddle of her true identity rightly. If he'd been wrong then, Rionne would have torn him to pieces, but he hadn't looked the least bit scared.

"You don't look like you've had a better day than Ah've had," Hosea said, with the ghost of a ragged smile.

"Eric and Magnus are missing," Ace said, struggling to keep her voice even. "And from what Kayla says, it wasn't natural."

Hosea sighed deeply, and bowed his head. "That might not be the best news Ah've ever gotten," he said. "Ah did want to ask Eric about a few things." He shook his head. "Cain't be helped, though. What exactly did Kayla say?"

Frowning in concentration, Ace recited back everything she could remember from her conversation with Kayla. The more she said, the less good it sounded.

Hosea ran a hand through his pale blond hair, making himself look a bit like a scarecrow in a cornfield. "Well, Paul's the best at sorting things like this out, and there isn't much that gets past him. Something that went right for Eric and Magnus, though, Ah'm bound to say, odds are it's the Good Neighbors, and vexin' as it is, even something like this, it could be their way o' askin' for help—or givin' help—or payin' a social call as much as bein' unmannerly. Cain't be sure until we can ask Eric. Last time one o' the Good Neighbors set out to do him a kindness, they kidnapped him out of a hospital and bespelled the whole place to think he'd never been there in the first place, which gave the rest of us quite a turn until he showed up again," Hosea added with a crooked smile.

*Oh yes, mortal fools, set your fears to slumbering,* Jormin thought to himself. His fingers moved over the strings of his harp, weaving a subtle spell of Misdirection. His shields were strong; they would neither see nor sense him, and the spell was the sort that even the most canny Magus Major would have difficulty detecting, for it was not something imposed from without. No, the beauty of this spell was that the chains of its binding were forged within the hearts of its victims.

Jormin's silent music plucked up every strand of their own desire to stay here and investigate further, every desire to believe that all was well with their friends, and strengthened them, while suppressing those urges that would lead them to seek outside help, or leave.

In the end, they would be sure they had made up their own minds.

Freely.

"So he could be all right? Both of them could?" Ace asked hopefully.

"And probably are," Hosea said reassuringly. "And as soon as

they get things sorted out Underhill—which is where they probably are right now—they'll be back. Count on it."

Ace took a deep breath, willing herself to be calm. Hosea was
right. She was sure he was. He had to be.

"So . . . what happened to you today?" Ace asked. "How did
the interview go?"

"Well, that prayer casino is a pretty piece of work," Hosea said
thoughtfully. "And that's one slick operation. Ah expect it could
give LlewellCo a run for its money, in its own way."

Briefly, he described what he'd seen of the casino, and his
interview with Billy Fairchild.

"He seems pretty convinced you're comin' back—o' course, that
could just be moonshine for a dumb reporter," Hosea said. "Ah
met Gabriel Horn, too. Nasty piece o' work, but Ah jest cain't
put my finger on what bothers me there. Doesn't quite seem to
fit in with the rest of the folks. And surely isn't fond of Parker
Wheatley, either, though there could be a lot of reasons for that.
He was happy to tell me all about his new record label, and the
free concert they've got comin' up on Friday. Gave me a whole
batch of free samples, too. Pity this place don't run to a VCR,
or we could look at some o' them tonight."

"I'm not sure I want to," Ace said, and Hosea shrugged in
agreement. He sighed, and Ace got the sense he'd saved the worst
news for last.

"His star turn is a band called Pure Blood, and while I was
there, their lead singer, a feller called Judah Galilee, dropped in.
And I guess I know why Mr. Horn is so sure that Pure Blood is
going to be a success, because Galilee is a Bard."

It took a moment for the words to sink in.

"A Bard?" Ace said. "A magic Bard? Like you and Eric?"

"That's the trouble," Hosea said, looking even more weary than
he had when he'd come in. "Not like me and Eric. This Judah
Galilee is all meanness and twisted up inside. Ah don't know
what his music's like, but it's sure to hurt people. What Ah do
think Ah know is that Mr. Horn knows exactly what he's got by
the tail."

Ace took a deep shaky breath. "What are we going to do?"

Hosea grimaced. "Ah'd been going to ask Eric that, until you told me he'd upped an' vanished. Now . . ." There was a long pause. "Ah'm not sure Ah want to bother the folks in New York with our problems down here until they've found Eric. Or he's turned up by himself."

Ace nodded. That made sense. Magnus might be in trouble, and right now, they weren't. "But you told Ria you'd call. She'll worry if you don't."

"Well, Ah 'spect Ah can tell Miz Ria about my day without tellin' her *too* many stretchers. And maybe Eric and Magnus are already back, and we're frettin' for nothing."

But when Hosea made his call to Ria, and gave her a very carefully worded account of the day's events—yes, he'd seen Billy Fairchild and Gabriel Horn; yes, he'd gotten a tour of the casino; no, he hadn't seen any Unseleighe, nor did he have any better idea of who it was who'd crafted the charm that Billy had carried into court—the two of them found that Eric and Magnus were still missing. Nothing that Ria or the three Guardians had been able to do had enabled them to trace their whereabouts.

Ace had to admire Hosea's performance. Absolutely nothing he said was a lie—in fact, everything he said was absolutely true. But the impression he managed to give with all that truth-telling was 180 degrees from the actual truth of the situation, and he left out the Black Bard entirely. He created an impression that the two of them were quite secure where they were, and that they could get far more done if they stayed put and out of the way of the search for Eric and Magnus.

"Actually, Ah'd like to poke around for another day. Ah've got an interview with Parker Wheatley set up for tomorrow, and maybe Ah can find out a little more about this demon-busting crusade o' his. And Ah guess Miss Ace is just as safe here as anywhere, don't you think?" Hosea said into the phone.

"She's agreed—and she'll skin me alive if anything happens to you," he added unnecessarily, as he folded up the phone.

Ace didn't say she could take care of herself. If there was one lesson she'd learned far too well in her seventeen years of life, it was that there were a lot of things out there that were bigger and stronger than she was, and some things that were smarter. She could use all the help she could get.

"Are you really going to go back and talk to Parker Wheatley?" she asked.

"Ah'd rather not," Hosea said surprisingly. "Ah'd rather not ever go near that place again. But let's see what Jeanette has to say."

Hosea went off to his room and brought back the banjo case, sitting down on a chair. Ace settled down on the bed to listen. She loved Hosea's playing, no matter what the circumstances were, and maybe listening to him would help her to think of something.

From his vantage point outside, Jormin felt the unfamiliar magic he'd sensed before, much stronger now. What was it? As a half-trained mortal Bard, Hosea Songmaker's power was no match for his own, he knew, and though the Sidhe were as susceptible as any to Heavenly Grace's Talent, she had not yet come into the fullness of her strength—and, he knew from his Master, she did not wish to use her Gift.

He hesitated, wondering if he should alert Prince Gabrevys, but whatever the apprentice Bard was doing, it did not seem to pose any threat to him.

At last the web of his spell was set tight, past any undoing. It would follow them wherever they went, feeding on their hopes and fears, keeping them from either leaving the immediate area or seeking outside aid.

Oh, he would have to return in a few hours of the World's time to reinforce it again and make sure it was running as it should, but for now, his work here was done. . . .

:Well?: Jeanette demanded instantly.

Hosea told her the most important things first—Eric and Magnus were missing, and that there was a Black Bard fronting one of Gabriel Horn's bands. He went on to tell her all he'd told Ace, trying to bring his sense of *wrongness* into focus.

But it was still as if he couldn't think clearly—or couldn't think of the right questions to ask.

"Ah didn't find that Unseleighe magician you told me to look for, sweetheart, but Ah didn't get a chance to meet everybody in Billy's organization. And after today, Ah'm not all that sure Ah want to go back. Galilee knows me for what Ah am, you cain take that to church."

Jeanette made a rude noise, for once not even bothering to object to the hated endearment. :*Oh, you think you didn't see any Unseleighe, farmboy? I'd bet you dollars to doughnuts—assuming I had any dollars, or any use for doughnuts—that your Judah Galilee is an elf-boy. And I'd double that bet and say Gabriel Horn is holding his leash, which means you've got another one, because Sidhe don't truckle to mere mortals.*:

"Elves?" Hosea said, feeling utterly stunned. How had he missed that? "Both of them?"

:*Did you look?*: Jeanette demanded. :*REALLY look? Or were you just too distracted for some odd reason to ever use your mage-sight on either of them?*:

Hosea thought back. There'd never been a really good time to take a close look at Gabriel Horn, and he'd known Judah Galilee would know what he was doing, so he hadn't tried using the Sight on him. But maybe he should have been a little more aggressive about trying.

Maybe he should have been a lot more aggressive.

:*The timing works,*: Jeanette went on. :*Billy's a ratbag, but his snake-oil show apparently didn't really start to go to capital-H Hell in a handbasket until Brother Gabriel showed up. And in a very short time it's bigger and sleazier than ever before, with a big influx of money from a source nobody can quite put their finger on, even your money-laundering girlfriend Ria with her pocketful of lawyers. Want to bet Gabriel's the funding source? I bet he's got big nasty plans for Fairchild Ministries. And if you're still thinking that Eric's disappearance is a coincidence, I've got to say, you're even dumber than you look.*:

"What would the Sidhe want with a televangelist?" Hosea asked blankly.

:*The Unseleighe like to break things,*: Jeanette answered bleakly. :*And Fairchild Ministries would make a nice big hammer.*:

Ace could see Hosea's lips moving, and knew he was talking to Jeanette, but she couldn't hear him over the sound of the music. From the expression on his face, though, Jeanette was giving him quite an earful, and nothing that he liked. At last he set aside the banjo, and sighed.

"Jeanette has a theory," he said.

The more Hosea talked, the more it all made a kind of awful sense: how everything had gotten particularly bad at home just after Gabriel Horn had shown up, how Daddy would never even think of hearing a word against him—and Billy Fairchild was a man who hated competition as much as he'd loved his own way.

"But . . . Bards are human, aren't they?" she asked, confused.

"Some are," Hosea agreed. "But just like Healin', it's a Talent that shows up extra-strong in particular elves, too. Eric said the Elven Bards are the most powerful magicians the Sidhe have, the ones who make the Gates, and anchor the Nexus-points to the Node-groves to anchor an Elfhame to the World Above."

"Sounds like physics, not magic," Ace said dubiously.

Hosea smiled faintly. "Paul says that they're pretty much the same thing when you take them far enough. Ah wouldn't know. What Ah do know is we've got us a fine mess here—and all our big guns are on a huntin' expedition somewheres else."

"But maybe we don't need them," Ace said slowly, thinking it out. "You said that Gabriel Horn doesn't like Parker Wheatley. And Ria said he started out hunting elves, and whatever he's calling them now, it looks like he's still doing it. If I can get to him, and tell him that Gabriel Horn and Judah Galilee are 'demons,' he'll use his bag of tricks on them—if just to prove me wrong. But I won't be." *I hope.*

"Besides," she continued, "I bet Mr. Wheatley doesn't like Gabriel Horn any better than Mr. Horn likes him. I bet he knows good and well that Mr. Horn doesn't want him around. And I bet he's thinking he'd like Mr. Horn out of the way, and maybe take over in his place. If he can do something to get rid of Mr. Horn, you know he will!"

"And what if Jeanette was right about the other thing, too, and Wheatley's working for another Unseleighe?" Hosea said.

"I don't get the feeling any of those guys like each other very much," Ace said, remembering what Ria had told her. "And Mr. Wheatley's just showed up. Maybe Gabriel Horn doesn't like him because he thinks he's poaching on his territory. Maybe Mr. Horn doesn't know about the other Unseleighe, if there is one."

But Hosea was frowning at her. "It's too dangerous," Hosea said.

"No it isn't," Ace said, excited now. "I can just sneak in to the building, get into Mrs. Granger's files, and find out everything I need to about Mr. Wheatley, including where his office is and his home address. Hosea, if anybody sees me, it's probably going to be somebody I've known all my life and grew up with, and from what you've said, Daddy's told everybody I'm away at Bible College somewhere, so why shouldn't I come back for a visit?" She took a deep breath. "And if I get into *real* trouble, I can sing my way out. You know I can. If we can start Mr. Wheatley and Mr. Horn fighting with each other, that would be good, wouldn't it? And if we could get our hands on some of those "demon hunting" weapons that Mr. Wheatley has, that would be better."

The more Hosea considered the matter, the more he thought she was right—not because he wanted to go back to that unhappy place, but because he couldn't leave something that dangerous alone.

Judah Galilee and his band would be playing before an audience of several hundred people—at the very least—Friday at noon, and Hosea hated to think of what the Black Bard might do with the energy he could raise off such a crowd.

He wasn't sure that either Judah or Gabriel were Sidhe—Jeanette was only guessing, after all—but if they could get Parker Wheatley to turn his elf-hunting obsession on Fairchild Ministries, it should convince Billy Fairchild to get rid of one of the two. Either he would convince Billy Fairchild that Gabriel was a demon, which would rid them of Gabriel Horn, or he would so outrage Billy that Fairchild would throw Wheatley out on his ear. And that was the worst that would come out of it.

And at best, it might solve a large number of their problems. Horn and Wheatley might actually lock horns and destroy each other, and it might happen in a public enough forum to bring down Fairchild Ministries as well.

"All right," he said reluctantly. "But we'll wait until we're sure everybody's out of the offices for the night. And you be as quick as you can."

"I will," Ace said soberly.

They'd gotten the call that afternoon. Fortunately, Michael didn't have classes that day, and they'd been able to fly down immediately.

Fiona was both pleased and a little irritated that the call had come so soon. She couldn't precisely decide where the source of her irritation lay; perhaps this seemed too easy? In her experience, nothing worth having was obtained easily, and if bringing Magnus and Eric to heel could be done so quickly, then the implication was that it was something that she and Michael could have accomplished themselves.

They would see.

Once more—for the last time, she told herself—they drove to the offices of Christian Family Intervention. When they got there, the girl had already left for the day, but Director Cowan was waiting for them in the reception area.

"Mr. and Mrs. Banyon. Do come in. It's wonderful to see you again, and on such a happy occasion for us all. I'm sure you remember Mr. Horn?"

"Yes, of course," Michael Banyon said, holding out his hand.

Gabriel smiled as he took Michael's hand, regarding the Banyons with deep satisfaction. The woman fairly seethed with haughty impatience, as if she wished nothing more than to snatch her plaguish brats from his hands and flee. But he had no desire to return her children to her just yet. No, in a few hours he would go and explain to the Bard what a treat lay in store for him, and then give him a few more hours to savor the anticipation of it. The feeding pen was quite secure, as were his bindings. There would be no escape for him, only horror. In the morning, well before the concert started, he would send the Bard and his brother off to their new life. Meanwhile, he would have the parents as further hostages, should the necessity arise.

"I'm sure you're both anxious to see your sons. Believe me, nothing gives us greater joy than the opportunity to reunite a family." He smiled again, broadly, at Fiona's reaction.

"Sons?" she asked sharply. "I thought—"

"Ah, I know you had not anticipated recovering your eldest, Eric, yet we have managed to convince him how misguided he has been," Gabriel interrupted, unctuously. "They're both here in the building right now, and looking forward to their reunion with their parents. Truly, the Prodigal Son returns to the arms of his family. We're just taking care of a few last-minute details, our legal staff is making sure that all of the legal mess poor Eric instigated is cleared up so that you won't be bothered with any of it anymore. Just getting all of the niggling details tidied away, then you can see them. It won't be long. Why don't you have a seat while you're waiting?"

Looking skeptical, Michael seated himself on the couch that Gabriel indicated, and, reluctantly, Fiona followed his lead. As they settled themselves, the prepared spell was triggered. Their faces went slack, their eyes closed, their bodies settled limply against each other.

"Good," Gabriel said with satisfaction. "You do excellent work, Toirealach."

Toirealach O'Caomhain bowed to his liege-lord. It was a fine thing, to have competent underlings. That was one mistake that altogether too many Unseleighe didn't understand. One needed to keep an iron fist yes, but in a velvet glove. If your underlings could not be sure of reward, they would not serve you without overmuch supervision. "They will slumber here until they are waked, and they will have no sense that time has passed. A bit of meddling with their memories will convince them that they came on the morrow instead of today, and all will be well."

"Then there is nothing more for you to do than hold yourself ready for the pleasures of the coming day," Gabriel said.

Toirealach rubbed his hands together. "Ah, what a grand feast you spread before us, my Prince! Blood and pain, and the deaths of children! Truly, you are the greatest of the Dark Court!"

*Not yet, perhaps,* Gabriel thought. *But I will be.*

# CHAPTER 7:
## MY FATHER'S HOUSE

Ace had left Hosea parked on the road outside and walked in, because Margot's pink showboat was just too darned noticeable. Fortunately the casino was doing a booming business even at this hour, and that had covered her approach.

Getting into the building wasn't a problem. It might be Atlantic City instead of Tulsa, but Daddy hadn't changed the locks. He still used numerical key-pad locks, and the access codes were various Bible verses. The one for the elevator was still John 4:13—the elevator was locked down for the night, but she typed in "5646413," and the elevator began to move. It played Muzak versions of praise-songs softly through its speakers. She shuddered at the banality of it.

She reached the top floor—of course Daddy's offices would be in the penthouse. The doors didn't open, and she punched in "628848," her mind automatically supplying the citation: Matthew 4:8. *Again the devil taketh him up into an exceeding high mountain, and sheweth him all the kingdoms of the world, and the glory of them.*

The doors opened. She stepped out into the corridor, listening hard, but everything was quiet.

She'd never been here before, but the place had a creepy similarity to her father's offices in Tulsa—not that it looked like them, because it didn't—rather, it looked like what he'd *wanted* them to be like. As if this place were the realization of a dream. It was easy to know where to go, and where everything ought to be—this was just the old Fairchild Ministry World Headquarters, redone and enlarged, but designed by the same mind just the same. She wondered what those men who'd suggested he leave Tulsa—Ria had told her about that—would think if they could see where he was now.

If they were smart, they'd be wondering where the money had come from.

At the end of the hall was a set of big mahogany double doors touched with gold leaf. The doors were closed now, but during the day, they'd be open, she knew. There'd be a big outer office and reception area, with Mrs. Granger's desk in the middle of it in front of another set of big mahogany doors, and behind those would be Daddy's private office and personal study, the one that would be in all the publicity photos.

She hurried up to the doors and punched in the keycode, automatically reciting the Bible verse in her head. The light on the lock went from red to green, and Ace eased the door open.

It was darker in here than it was out in the hall, and she risked using the little LED flashlight she and Hosea had picked up on the way over here. It put out a lot of light for its size, but the beam was really small, and probably wouldn't be seen from outside so long as she didn't shine it at the windows.

The room looked very much as she'd expected it to—larger and grander than the one in Tulsa, of course. There was a big oil painting of Daddy on the wall, and the same large glass cases holding some of the trophies and awards he'd gotten over the years. There were large silver bowls of fresh flowers on the side tables, though. That was new.

Ace shuddered again. The place reminded her of a high-class mortuary.

If this was a dream in realization, it was one that had died and been mummified.

She moved quickly over to Mrs. Granger's desk. There was nothing on it; as always, everything was locked away for the night, including her Rolodex. The desk was locked, of course, but for as long as Ace had known her, Mrs. Granger had kept the desk key under her blotter, and Ace found it easily.

She held it in her hand, hesitating. Mrs. Granger had been with them ever since Ace had been a little girl. She'd been one of the first people Daddy'd hired. She'd baby-sat Ace when Mama'd gone to the beauty parlor, and helped Mama pick out Ace's dresses when the money started to come in. Breaking into Mrs. Granger's desk seemed almost more wicked than breaking into the building.

*I have to do it. I won't mess anything up, I promise.* She took a deep breath and put the key into the lock.

She found the Rolodex quickly, but to her dismay, the card for Parker Wheatley only showed a Maryland address. He couldn't still be living there, could he? There was no office listed, or internal phone number, but he had to have an office in the building if Daddy was having him launch the crusade she'd seen on television. She kept looking.

The card for Gabriel Horn gave his home address as this building. Ace frowned. Was that possible? It gave his office, too: she memorized that as a place to stay away from.

She quickly checked through the file folders in the desk. Nothing useful.

Her neck ached with tension as she considered her options. This should have been easy; it wasn't. All right, then, it just wasn't going to be *as* easy as she'd thought it should be. That didn't mean it was going to be hard.

Ace eyed the doors behind the desk nervously, working up her courage. *I have to go in there.* Daddy would want Mr. Wheatley where he could keep an eye on him. The Ministry ran on paperwork; she knew that much. If Mrs. Granger didn't have the file, it had to be in there.

She knew it was perfectly safe. It had to be, at this hour. Everything was dark in there. Daddy would be at home, wherever that was now. She could find out where Mr. Wheatley's office was, get what she needed, and leave.

She quickly put everything in Mrs. Granger's desk back the way she'd found it, tucked the key back under the blotter again, and headed for Billy Fairchild's office.

He'd actually been thinking of getting an apartment at the Tower lately—not that Donna wasn't still an everlasting helpmeet and joy, praise the Lord, but with Heavenly Grace still gone—and thankfully he'd taken Gabriel's advice not to burden Donna with all of this nonsense about the girl living right there in New York City and refusing to come home—Donna seemed just a bit peaked these days. With as much as he had to do at the Ministry, he didn't want to tax her with its problems when she was feeling so poorly. Not everyone had his natural vitality, Lord knew. It wasn't fair to ask it of her. Maybe putting in an apartment just off his office wouldn't be a bad idea. On late nights like this, Donna wouldn't sit up, worrying about him until he came home. He could just call her and let her know he was going to stay overnight, and she could just relax, and have a night on her own. Maybe watch one of those old romantic movies she doted on so much. And when Heavenly Grace came home again, they could have a Girls' Night again, pop popcorn and watch the old Shirley Temple movies she used to love.

At least with all this new business—the Crusade, the upcoming concert, he was spending less time than ever at home, so that was a blessing. He'd had a late meeting with some of the commissioners about some casino business, and some last-minute details about the concert. Hand-holding, really, and nothing Billy hadn't been doing one way or another since he'd cut his wisdom teeth. It had all gone without a hitch. Now he was headed back to the Cathedral and Casino of Prayer to see Gabriel. Gabe had said he had a few more last-minute ideas about the concert himself, and Billy had to admit that Gabriel's ideas were usually good ones. Just about as good as his, in fact.

He met Gabriel in the elevator, and they rode up to Billy's office together.

She'd just started to search Daddy's desk—it was going to take longer; he wasn't nearly as organized as Mrs. Granger—when

Ace saw light flare under the door and heard voices in the outer room.

*Someone was here.*

And she was trapped.

Billy opened the door of his office and flicked on the lights.

"—went real easy. All they want to know is that they aren't gonna have another Woodstock or Altamont on their hands. Well, I told them that this is good Christian music we're going to be playing, and besides, we'll be hiring plenty of professional security to handle the crowds, none of these Hell's Angels or anything like that. Showed 'em the contracts we already have with the firm that handles the casino business, and told 'em we were gonna bring on more people just for this concert."

Billy sat down behind his desk, his hands stroking the smooth grain of the polished wood as if it were a beloved pet.

Gabriel smiled. "Of course. That was very wise of you. Now, on the whole, I thought we ought to go one step better for the concert venue itself. I've brought in a special private security team. They're professionals, experienced with crowds and concerts. There won't be any unexpected trouble. Of course, that's what I wanted to talk to you about."

He went to the sideboard and poured them both drinks. He passed one to Billy and sat down in the chair across from the desk. The office was a complex interweaving of spells, his own *glamouries* and those of the other Sidhe who had infiltrated Billy's organization over the last few years; everywhere his eye rested, he noted the subtle nets of persuasions and compulsions that he had woven around Billy Fairchild. There was a certain danger in this, of course. Another Sidhe would sense it at once. Fortunately, after Friday, there would be nothing to sense. . . .

Time to bring up the next step in the plan. "As you know, publicity thrives on controversy. And your . . . bold . . . stance has gathered its share of protest."

"Let the heathen rage," Billy said, sipping his drink and grinning with foolish triumph. "I'm not the man to back down from a little controversy."

"Precisely," Gabriel said approvingly. "In fact, the more they object, the more it proves that you're right to take the position you have, both on America's enemies, and in the way you promote the Gospel. And so, I think the faithful deserve to see a palpable demonstration of the rightness of your cause. A passion play, as it were. And as we both know, a passion play requires a sacrifice, or at least the appearance that one might be forthcoming, in order to have any impact."

Fairchild wasn't entirely stupid. "Go on," Billy said, leaning forward intently.

Gabriel waved his hand in the air. "You know that you receive hundreds of threats every week. And so far, thanks to our own care and foresight, nothing has ever come of any of them. What if—during the concert, when the media is here, not to mention our own camera crews—there were a bombing attempt on the Casino and Cathedral of Heavenly Grace? The main stage is going to be set up right outside. If a bomb were to go off there, the carnage would be incredible."

"But it won't go off," Billy said cautiously.

"Oh, of course not," Gabriel said soothingly. "We can arrange for the bomb to be so badly constructed that there's no possibility of its actually exploding. We might time the discovery of it near the end of the concert, so it doesn't disrupt things too much. But its presence will underscore a higher truth: that your Ministry is surrounded by those who wish to destroy it. That there is a Great Evil willing to kill perfectly innocent victims in order to get at you. In fact, seen that way, a bomb isn't really a hoax: it's just a tangible symbol of a greater truth."

Billy sat back in his chair. "'A greater truth,'" Billy said admiringly. "I *like* that! Gabe, you've got a good head on your shoulders. Now, I don't want to know anything more about this. I've got to be able to act natural when the time comes, you see."

*And to convince yourself that you knew nothing about it, you pompous canting fool—!*

"Don't worry," Gabriel said. "I'll take care of everything."

Crouched behind the half-open door to Billy's private study, Ace heard every word. Her blood turned to ice in her veins, and she felt the hair on the back of her arms lifting in horror.

She could easily believe that Gabriel Horn would do something so awful, but what she couldn't believe was that her father was going along with it.

It was true that he'd said a lot of things in the past that weren't quite true, but that was worlds away from something like this. Setting up a bomb scare was not only cruel and self-serving, it was far from harmless. From everything she'd heard, there were going to be at least a couple of thousand people out there Friday morning listening to this Judah Galilee, and when the discovery of the bomb was announced, they weren't all going to relax. They were all going to riot. People would be hurt, trampled, even killed. And that wouldn't be the end of it, either. People would start pointing fingers, looking for someone who could have planted a bomb, making accusations, maybe even taking the law into their own hands when they thought they'd found the perpetrator. And all the time the people responsible for it would be watching and saying it was out of their hands....

Billy Fairchild had always been greedy and selfish, and Lord knew he wasn't any kind of a good Christian, but three years ago, if someone had suggested doing something like this, he would have said no. He'd known better then. He wouldn't have set up innocent people to get hurt so that he could look like a martyr.

He sure wouldn't have sat there and gloated about it, and said he didn't want to know any more details so he could act innocent!

Tears gathered in her eyes, and she fought to remain silent. Gabriel Horn was the Devil Incarnate, she was sure of that now. She and Hosea had to get rid of him—send him back Underhill, if Jeanette was right about him.

And they had to stop the concert, or the bomb scare, or both.

Finally Daddy and Mr. Horn got up and left, but for a long time she couldn't bring herself to move, though Billy's office was dark and silent once more. She knew Hosea would be worrying about her, and at last the fear that he would try to come into the building after her gave her the will to get to her feet.

This time she found what she was looking for immediately: Parker Wheatley's employment application, and a bunch of pamphlets and clippings about something called the "Satanic Defense Initiative." The address on the application was the Maryland address from Mrs. Granger's Rolodex, but there was a note on a Post-It, scrawled in Billy's handwriting, with a local hotel address. He was probably living in a hotel until he could find an apartment.

She copied the address on a piece of paper and stuffed it into her jeans. Riffling through the file further—the pages were in no particular order—she found the memo from Ben about the offices he'd assigned Mr. Wheatley to. So now she knew where to find him in the building—and any Sidhe-hunting tricks he might have, too.

It was time to go. Definitely. She had the feeling she was already pressing her luck.

She was pretty sure that Daddy had left the building, but now that she'd seen Gabriel Horn again, and knew that he lived in the building, she was afraid to take the elevator, for fear she might see him.

Fortunately she doubted he'd be on the stairs. She couldn't for one minute imagine him doing anything that would raise a sweat.

The fire door with the glowing green exit sign over it opened noiselessly, and she closed the door behind her slowly and with painstaking care. The stairs were in stark contrast to the offices; bare concrete walls, rough concrete stairs, industrial metal railings. Any sound made in here would be amplified. She moved carefully, trying to keep her steps from echoing, glad she'd worn her sneakers. Fifteen flights, and then she'd be down on the ground floor and out of here. She'd get back to Hosea, they could leave, they'd call Ria and tell her everything, she'd stop Gabriel Horn from setting the bomb, they could go to Parker Wheatley tomorrow and tell him whatever they liked. . . .

And she'd be on her way back to New York. She never thought she would ever have thought of New York City as being "safe," but it was a sure sight safer than this place.

Voices in the hall beyond the stair-landing caught her attention when she'd only gone a few flights. She flattened herself against the wall beside the door, heart hammering.

"—and now, my child, let us go and visit a Bard. Yes, a true Bard. His name is Eric Banyon, and in a few hours we are going to destroy him, but it is only proper that we give him time to relish his fate first."

She recognized Gabriel's voice and risked a glance through the window set into the metal fire-door. Gabriel Horn was walking down the hall, along with someone she didn't know. His back was to her. She watched as he opened a door and stepped through it.

Eric? Eric was here? She stepped back and pressed herself against the wall again, breathing deeply.

This was worse than bad. Kayla had said he and Magnus had been kidnapped. Hosea thought they might have just gone Underhill, but he was wrong. They were here. And if they were in Gabriel Horn's hands, they were in the worst of trouble.

She pulled out her phone and dialed Hosea's cellphone.

She thought it connected, but she wasn't sure, and she didn't hear anything but static. After a moment, she closed the phone in frustration.

*Think, stupid!*

She couldn't go back inside and use any of the phones in one of the offices. The switchboard was shut down for the night, and if she tried to get a line out, it would light up on the Security desk. Whoever was down there on duty would know that somebody was where they weren't supposed to be, and come looking. Even if she did take the risk, Hosea couldn't get in without the elevator codes.

And what was she going to do alone? Hit Horn with her shoe? She'd told Hosea she could sing her way out, but that had been when she'd only thought she was going to run into ordinary people. Not Gabriel Horn. This wasn't a television show; she wasn't Buffy, to run in there and rescue them before the commercial break. She didn't even have a brick she could use as a weapon.

She hated the thought of leaving Eric here, but from what she'd overheard, Gabriel Horn wasn't going to do anything to him yet. No, if this was a television show, she had to be smart. She needed to be Lassie, not Buffy.

*Run and get help, girl!*

That was the smart thing to do. Run and get help. She could get Hosea—they'd come back in.

She ran down the stairs. Now that she knew where Gabriel was, she wasn't as worried about being heard, though she still struggled to compromise between speed and silence. She couldn't afford to be stopped now.

She was gasping and breathless when she reached the bottom of the stairs, and had to force herself to stop and look before she opened the door to the lobby.

Empty. With a shaky breath of relief, she eased open the door and stepped through it.

She'd just reached for the keypad to the outer door to unlock it when a heavy hand came down on her shoulder.

She let out a faint gasp, too shocked to scream.

"Why, it's little Heavenly Grace, isn't it?" an unfamiliar voice said. "Yes, I'm sure it is. What an unexpected pleasure. For me, of course—not you."

Sleep was one of the many baffling and entertaining things that mortals did, and Jormin had returned to the hotel at a time when he thought his master's two prizes would probably be engaged in that peculiar activity to set his spells deeper in their minds. Mortals could be induced to forget much while they slept, even Gifted mortals, and in their vulnerability, he might have the chance to unriddle the mystery of the strangeness in the apprentice Bard's magick.

But when he'd arrived, they were not there.

It did not worry him. They would not have run far, and with his magick upon them, they were easy to follow. It was a merry jest indeed to discover that they had fled directly to his master's feet.

He saw the apprentice Bard stopped upon the edge of the road in his Cold Iron chariot, and gave him a wide berth; he was not the greater prize, in any event. He followed the girl to the tower, and what he saw in her mind as she emerged made him decide, regretfully, that the little vixen must not be left to run free any longer. The matter must be set before his Prince at once.

Ace spun around. The man she was staring at was elusively familiar, and at last she recognized him. Judah Galilee. Hosea's Black Bard. As if he had stepped right out of one of those posters Hosea had brought back with him.

"Oh, *do* try to fight," he said cordially, smiling a cold smile. "Try your arts on me, worldling, and I vow by the Morrigan, I'll turn your bones to water, and believe me, I shall deeply enjoy every moment as much as you will regret it."

"Oh, please," Ace said hopelessly, pleadingly. "Just let me go. I can't hurt you. I just want—"

His smile widened, and grew even colder. "Now, pretty child, we both know I cannot, for this night you have seen and heard that which it were far better you had not. You're clever enough to know that—but not clever enough to come willingly, I do vow. So struggle, do, and despair. I shall enjoy that. I shall enjoy that a very great deal."

Judah looked like a rock star—from his long hair and flashy jewelry to his head-to-foot black leather—but he talked like something out of Masterpiece Theater. Like Jaycie had talked, at the very end, when he'd stopped pretending to be human.

Jeanette had been right. He was Unseleighe. There was nothing else that he could be. And the Unseleighe knew no mercy.

Something deeper than fear made her duck under his arm and bolt for the stairs. She knew even as she did that it wouldn't do her any good.

But she tried. She had to.

Eric struggled slowly toward consciousness. For a very long time all he had was the sense that he *ought* to be conscious, and a nagging sense of despair and wrongness. Nothing more. As if—when he *did* finally awaken, it would be to great sorrow.

But for now, all he could do was drift, barely aware. As if his very *self* had been stolen away.

At last, as if he were remembering the punch-line to an old joke, he realized why he should be awake. It all came back to him with a jolt, and all at once.

He was Eric Banyon, Bard of Elfhame Misthold. He'd received a warning. He'd been going to rescue his brother Magnus—but he'd been too late.

They were prisoners.

Of the Unseleighe.

As he strained toward consciousness, he heard someone calling his name.

"Eric. *Eric.*"

Magnus didn't know if his brother heard him, but he had to keep trying. He had no intention of giving up. They were going to get out of here, and then somebody was going to hurt. A lot. He didn't know who, yet, but he bet that Eric would be able to tell him.

He'd awakened a while ago—he thought it was about an hour now—so abruptly that at first he'd been completely disoriented. It had taken him a few seconds to focus on where he was; to realize that whole thing about history class and the giant wolves hadn't been a bad dream, likely as that was, but reality. More of that magic stuff, only at this point even he was able to figure out that trying to deny that magic existed was only going to make things worse. No, he'd just better suck it in and deal with it.

He remembered nothing between the time the wolf had jumped out of the alleyway and knocked him down, and here.

He'd woken up tied to a metal chair. His ankles were tied to the legs of the chair with some kind of soft white rope, and his hands were tied behind the back. He had a pretty good idea of what his bonds must look like, because Eric was right there, in another chair set at right angles to his, just a few feet away, and they were probably tied up the same way.

Kinky.

This stuff was lots more fun when you saw it in the movies, when you were sure nobody was really getting hurt and besides, the good guys were going to get out okay.

The one good thing about this was that it was nothing to do with the 'rents. They'd send lawyers. They'd send cops. They wouldn't send giant wolves. Definitely.

And they wouldn't bother to kidnap Eric too. Why should they? He was about a thousand years old, and there was no way they could make him do anything. No, whoever it was that had decided to grab both of them had some other ideas in mind.

He looked around the room. Grey. Hard to tell what size, when everything—walls, floor, ceiling—was the same color, and looked sort of like it was coated in Teflon. Magnus shuddered. He wished he hadn't thought of that. Ace was always telling him how easy Teflon was to clean, because everything washed right off it. He didn't like what that made him think of.

He couldn't see a door, but there had to be one.

The room was dimly lit, but he couldn't see a light source, either, or where the light was coming from. If Eric and the other chair hadn't been there, it would have been easy to get dizzy in the dimness, but they gave him something to focus on.

He strained at his bonds, but they held fast. Besides the ropes, Eric's hands were shackled. The restraints were big, heavy things, like something out of an old pirate movie, and they looked like silver, not iron.

More kink.

When Magnus shook his own wrists he didn't feel a similar weight. He guessed the shackles must have something to do with magick.

He'd tried to wake Eric then, but Eric was out cold. He didn't look very good either—not bleeding or anything, but just not good. The way his head lolled was wrong, and he wasn't sleeping, he was stone cold out, and in a bad way. Magnus bet that if he could see clearly, Eric would be really pale.

Like a drug overdose. Like the way Jaycie had looked there,

towards the end, when he was mostly unconscious from all that cola and chocolate.

For a brief moment, Magnus tried to convince himself that this was an ordinary kidnapping, that they'd both been drugged, that whoever had drugged them had just given Eric too much. But he couldn't manage it. Even if an armful of tranqs would work on an Ascended Jedi Master, or whatever the hell Eric thought he was, there were still those wolves. And those weird guys in Mrs. Castillo's office. And the kinky silver handcuffs

And the fact that he was pretty sure the chairs were silver, too.

Who the hell would make a whole *chair* out of silver?

They were in real trouble. It was magick everywhere, and magick was the one thing he *didn't* know how to MacGyver himself out of.

He wondered if getting those cuffs off Eric would help. Maybe if he could get his chair over to Eric's, he could do something about them.

But when he tried to rock the chair, it didn't move at all. Like it was welded to the floor.

Magnus took a deep breath, forcing himself not to panic. He'd been in trouble before. He was still here. They'd get out of this. And then someone would be in deep, serious trouble.

"Eric?" he called. "Eric? Hey, *stupid*, wake up! Eric, wake up!"

"—up. Eric, wake up."

Eric forced his eyes open with a shudder and a gasp.

Grey. Everything was grey.

"Are you all right?" His voice was a croak. But it was Magnus's voice that had awakened him, so Magnus was still alive, and, presumably, still with throat uncut. So they were that much ahead of the game.

"Better than you are."

For all Magnus's bravado, Eric could hear the undercurrent of fear in his brother's voice.

He tried a little bravado of his own. "No . . . I'm good."

But he wasn't. He was awake, and that was a definite improvement, but his wrists . . . burned. He tried to summon up his magick, but every time he tried, it wouldn't come clear in his mind. Something was stopping it.

"Eric? We're going to get out of here, aren't we?" Magnus demanded.

"One way or another," Eric said firmly. He wasn't going to lie to Magnus, but there was no reason not to share what hope he had. "Greystone knows there's a problem. If we've both gone missing, he'll call in the cavalry." Ria. Toni and the other Guardians.

"You can't get us out of here, can you? Because of those things on your wrists?" Magnus said flatly.

"That's probably the reason," Eric said, doing his best to sound calm. "I think it's some kind of Binding Spell. I can probably overload it, given enough time. Meanwhile, tell me what you know."

Magnus's tale was quickly told, and Eric shared what he knew about his own capture as well, but it made no sense to him. For Prince Gabrevys to attack a Bard of the Bright Court would not just mean war between Elfhame Bete Noir and Elfhame Misthold—it would mean swift punishment from Oberon himself.

And if Eric was Gabrevys's target, why involve Magnus at all? There'd certainly been ways to capture Eric without involving his brother. And if Gabrevys meant to kill Eric, it would have made more sense simply to not let him wake up at all . . . because once he was awake, he had the potential, at least, to cause trouble. There was some piece of this that was missing, but the sense of it, even the shape of it, eluded him.

Missing pieces—better tell Magnus everything he knew. Shielding him wouldn't help, and might hurt. "Look, Magnus. There's something you don't know about all this," Eric said.

Magnus snorted eloquently.

"The Sidhe Lord who's got his hands on us . . . he's Jaycie's father. And I'm pretty sure he blames me for the fact that Jaycie's at Misthold."

There was a long silence.

"So he's just like Mom," Magnus said at last, bitterness in his voice. "Jaycie's happy now, and he'd rather be dead than go home, but this guy doesn't care."

"If he shows up here *don't* tell him that," Eric begged. "In fact, don't say anything to him if you can manage it. And don't believe anything he says—no matter how much you want to. Remember that the Dark Sidhe lie as easily as breathing. Easier. They love deception. They live on lies. They'll do and say whatever they can to cause the most pain; it's like a drug to them." He wracked his brain, trying to think of every possible thing he could warn his brother about while there was still time.

"Jaycie used to cry at night—and scream," Magnus said grimly. "When he was asleep."

*Elves don't sleep,* Eric thought, but then remembered that when Magnus had known him, Jaycie had been lost in Dreaming most of the time.

"If you see—" Eric began, but just then there was the sound of a door opening.

There was the sound of two sets of footsteps behind them, faintly muffled as if they moved over a rubbery surface.

They walked around and into Eric's field of vision: a tall man in a dark suit, accompanied by a dark-haired boy about Magnus's age. The boy had a pleasant, open expression, but there was something terribly wrong with him.

Hosea had always said that people with the Gift seemed to be more vividly *there* than people without it. At its simplest, Talent was human creativity, and everyone had it to some degree. What Eric was seeing now was something he had not thought could exist: a human with no spark of that most essential element of humanity, and it was painful to see.

The tall man smiled. "This is Devon Mesier. Say hello, Devon."

"Hello," Devon said pleasantly. He seemed completely uninterested in the fact that there were two people tied to chairs in front of him. It seemed to have no impact at all on him.

As for his escort, well, Eric might not know who he was, but he certainly knew what he was. The man tilted his head to the side. "What, Sieur Eric? No pleas for mercy for your brother? No haughty reminders of your inviolate status as a Bard of Misthold? Would that you had showed as much wisdom when you stole my son from me!"

*Oh shit.* Though the man before him remained cloaked in human seeming, Eric knew who he was now. And the excrement had definitely hit the rotating blades.

"I did not steal him," Eric answered evenly. "I offered Sanctuary to Prince Jachiel and his Protector, Prince Gabrevys, as you well know. He fled your Domain and would not return, and his Protector will not force him. Go and ask him yourself. Prince Arvin has offered you safe-passage."

Gabrevys smiled hollowly. "Oh, I shall . . . when I bring to Prince Arvin the tragic news of what has befallen you. Then shall the Law be *my* shield, for do I not act at the behest of blood? I shall not harm one hair of your head, nor spill one drop of your blood, nor do one thing that I have not been commanded to by the woman who bore you and the man who sired you. Aye, Bard Eric—if you can act within the Law, so can I!" Gabrevys threw back his head and roared with laughter.

Eric stared at him, stunned. His parents? His *parents* had made a pact with Prince Gabrevys? They couldn't have had any idea of what they were doing.

But that didn't matter, he realized with a sinking heart. It didn't matter what Gabrevys had done to trick them into it. They were his parents. By the Law of the Sidhe, Gabrevys's actions would be legal. He was following the request of Eric's own parents, the only way he could work against a Bard and get away with it.

"Let Magnus go," Eric said, desperately, now.

Gabrevys cocked his head. "Not so haughty now, eh, Bard Eric? And how shall I do that, when the bargain was for both of you? Return to me both my sons, the woman said. Make them my dutiful loving children once again, she begged. And so I shall. Come the dawn, you both shall be as young Devon here—obedient and compliant to her every whim. Alas, those gifts and talents she prizes in you will be gone, ravished away by my Soul-eaters, but she asked only for your obedience, my word upon that. No longer will you meddle in the affairs of your betters—nor will you remember them, or care."

Oh, this was bad. He might not be able to cast a spell, but Eric still knew truth when he heard it. Prince Gabrevys was telling the truth.

"Think carefully before you do this," Eric said. He forced himself to speak calmly. "You'll be acting within the Law, it's true. But you'll make a lot of enemies. And not all of them are bound by Sidhe law." Ria Llewellyn, just for starters, who'd never met a law she couldn't turn into a pretzel when it suited her. Beth. The Guardians? Possibly. Beth and Kory had allies that they could call on, too.

"Ah, do you pin your hopes on your foolish apprentice? Alas for you, that he will be dead by tomorrow's sunset," Gabrevys purred.

Just then Eric heard the sound of the door opening again. Gabrevys looked up and past him. Eric would have been willing to swear that for one moment the Unseleighe Lord looked utterly startled.

"Your reasons?" he snapped.

"She spied upon you, my Prince," another voice said. "Such a thing cannot be allowed. I have not harmed her." Since the door was directly behind Eric, he couldn't see the speaker, but Magnus could, and his face went absolutely white.

Whatever, whoever was behind him, it couldn't be good.

No, he knew from Gabrevys's smile that it wasn't good at all.

"Dear child, is it not entertaining that after so long attempting to avoid my company, you should come and seek me out?" Gabrevys said, his voice velvet over steel.

"I wasn't looking for you, Gabriel Horn," Ace snapped. "If you were drowning, I'd pour water on you. *Ow!*"

Eric abruptly felt as if someone had hit him in the stomach, and not just because Ace had suddenly been added to the hostage list. Prince Gabrevys was Gabriel Horn?

Everything suddenly made more—and less—sense.

Why Ace had been afraid of him without knowing why. Where Billy's sudden inexplicable wealth had come from. The bizarre dark turn his ministry had taken. The weird twists and turns in Ace's court case.

But why would an Unseleighe Prince be spending so much time on someone like Billy Fairchild? That had started long before Jaycie had run away.

A second Unseleighe—also wearing human *glamourie*—stepped into Eric's line of vision, dragging a wildly struggling, but now grimly silent Ace with him.

"You leave her alone!" Magnus shouted, thrashing wildly in his chair. "You sick piece of shit—you think Jaycie isn't going to find out about this? Kiss your kid goodbye, Darth Vader."

Eric winced.

"Magnus!" Ace gasped.

"My son is my concern," Prince Gabrevys said, all trace of humor gone from his face. "He will see reason, once the inconvenience that the two of you represent is removed." If not for the terms of his pact, Eric would have feared for his brother's life, but Gabrevys would honor his oath to the letter. They were safe—for now.

But Ace wasn't.

"And what is it that you think you heard, my bold and pretty child?" Gabrevys said, moving forward to where Jormin stood with Ace. She'd stopped struggling now, but her body was tense with hopeless defiance.

Gabrevys cocked his head as if listening, and Eric knew he was reading Ace's thoughts. He'd asked her what she'd overheard, and of course she couldn't help thinking of it now.

Gabrevys smiled, and ruffled Ace's hair, his good humor restored.

"You're thinking of the false bomb meant to be discovered in the late afternoon of tomorrow's concert, and how sad it is that your father has been so corrupted that he will permit such a thing. But allow me to ease your mind. There won't be a false bomb at all. It will be real."

Eric kept his mouth shut, because otherwise it would have dropped open. Bomb? Was there any end to the twists this thing was taking?

"I dislike Parker Wheatley a great deal, you know," Gabrevys continued in conversational tones, "And Billy Fairchild has grown quite inconvenient. It occurred to me that an elegant solution to so many of my trifling difficulties would be reached should both of them die in a very large explosion. I believe I shall frame Wheatley for the deed—the man is obviously unstable—and implicate your leaders in attempting to shut down Fairchild Ministries. The explosion will kill most of the attendees at the Pure Blood concert as well, generating what I believe is called 'a new rock legend,' and best of all, my people will be there to film it all, and carry away the tale, as will assorted members of the rock press—at least those who survive. Many of them will not. As will also be the case with your young disciple, Bard Eric; I'm very much afraid if by luck he will survive the explosion, he will tragically perish soon after, one way or another."

Eric felt his mind reeling. How had all this managed to happen without anyone noticing?

"Then Fairchild Ministries will be mine to do with as I will. It is such a lovely tool with which to sow hate and dissension among the mortals. Why, the footage of the bombing alone should provide a lovely feast of agony for my liegemen every time it is shown—all those dead and maimed children! And not at a distance, either. Close. In detail. Every nuance caught on film. The pleading of the dying, the screams of the injured. What an exquisite thought."

He reached out to cup Ace's chin in his hand, and stared deep into her eyes for a moment. She made faint mewling sounds of distress, but was unable to look away.

At last he released her, sighing in disappointment.

"I had, of course, hoped that the tragic death of your father would cause you to abandon your bid for freedom and return to your mother's side to comfort her," he said. "But now I see that even if I removed all memory of this evening from your mind and sent you on your way, you would be of little use to me. You have grown far too rebellious to make an appropriate pawn. No, I am afraid you must wait here with the others, meet with my—allies—and give them what they most desire so that they may give me what I require. In the morning, you may give your father a few brief hours of happiness before sharing his fate." If a smile could drop the temperature of a room, his plunged it to freezing. "What a tragedy! Billy Fairchild, newly reunited with his daughter, only to have the two of them perish at the hands of the ungodly!"

"Don't do this," Eric begged. "Prince Gabrevys—"

"Try my patience, Bard Eric, and I can kill her now," Prince Gabrevys snapped. "Her body will be found in the rubble either way. Or perhaps you would prefer I gave her to Jormin for a night's sport? Would you like that, my pretty one?"

"My master is kind," Jormin said softly.

"Choose, Sieur Eric—" Gabrevys began, then paused, his eyes full of unholy shadows. "No. I shall let the boy choose."

He turned those eyes towards Eric's brother. "Come now, young Magnus. Your brother has doomed you to terror and agony and to spend the rest of your life as a creature barely half alive. Shall the girl share your fate? Or shall I give her to Jormin?"

"She'd rather stay here," Magnus said, his voice filled with hate. "And so would I."

Gabrevys shrugged, as if it didn't matter in the least to him. "Very well. Jormin, tie her up."

Jormin flung Ace away from him, sending her sprawling, but before she hit the floor, ropes like those that bound Eric and Magnus appeared around her wrists and ankles, binding her ankles together and tying her hands behind her back. She hit the floor hard.

Gabrevys chuckled appreciatively, then crooked his finger in his minion's direction. "Come, Jormin. We will find you other entertainment. Come, Devon." The two Sidhe and Gabrevys's human victim walked from the room as if the other three had ceased to exist.

"I'll kill him," Magnus growled, an undercurrent of frenzied hysteria in his voice. "I'll rip out his heart with my teeth and *feed* it to him—!"

Eric concentrated on Ace. There was nothing he could do

to get through to Magnus right now; in fact he wasn't really sure that Magnus would hear him if he spoke. He'd never seen Magnus so angry—he was completely consumed with rage, and the closest Eric had ever seen to someone who was in classic berserker-mode.

Too bad there was no useful way to employ that much anger.

Ace had rolled to her side and gotten to her knees. Her face was white with shock, and her eyes brimmed with tears, but Eric was glad to see that she seemed to be holding on to her control, if only barely.

"Where are we?" he asked her, perhaps more harshly than he had intended, but he was afraid if he sounded soothing, she'd lose it.

She made a faint sound of surprise. "Welcome to the Heavenly Grace Cathedral and Casino of Prayer in Atlantic City, New Jersey," she said. Her voice wavered, and she took a deep breath. "Magnus, *shut up*," she added in exasperation.

There was a sudden silence.

"What's going to happen to us?" Ace asked, looking straight at him. "You know, don't you?"

"At dawn—unless I can get these cuffs off and get us out of here—something called Soul-eaters are going to come in here and turn the three of us into zombies like that boy Devon," Eric said flatly. At this point, there didn't seem to be a lot of point in prettying things up.

"Courtesy of Mom and Dad," Magnus added, still sounding furious. "Who expect to get back a pair of musical prodigies, but are going to get a couple of 7-11 clerks instead."

"Apparently they eat Talent," Eric explained reluctantly. "*All* Talent. Creativity, imagination, will. Spirit. Real emotion. Anything that makes life worth the living."

He tried again to summon a spell—any spell. Nothing. But was it his imagination, or were the cuffs on his wrists not quite as cold as they had been?

"It won't work," Ace said desperately. "Hosea's waiting for me to come back. They think they're facing down a Bard, but he's a Guardian, too. And Ria knows there's something wrong down here—if I go missing, this is the first place she'll look."

"Yeah, that big explosion tomorrow'll probably clue her in," Magnus said sullenly.

Ace shot him a burning look. "Why don't I just see if I can get you untied? We've got a good few hours until dawn."

Struggling awkwardly, she began working her way around to the back of Magnus's chair.

One piece of business done, another yet to do. Sending Devon to his rest—the boy's parents had been so happy to get him such a respectable position as an intern at Fairchild Ministries, and Gabriel found his presence eternally amusing—and releasing Jormin to his pleasures—any untidiness could be concealed in the aftermath of the concert disaster, after all—he went to keep an appointment he had made several days before.

His destination was a tavern in the poorer part of town. Such places never changed—from a turf-covered hut at the village's edge with a hole in the roof to let the smoke out, to a rough wooden building at the edge of the high road with the drinks served across a bar made up of kegs and planks, they were all the same: places for mortals to seek out oblivion and trouble.

The mortal was waiting for him in a booth in the back. Gabriel sat down opposite him.

"I was afraid you weren't coming," he said anxiously.

"I had a little trouble getting away without anyone seeing me, LeRoy," Gabriel said. "You know how important it is that nobody see us together."

"Because *They're* always watching," LeRoy LaPonte said.

Gabriel had first become aware of LeRoy LaPonte a few months before, while looking through Billy's fanmail. To say that he read it would be entirely incorrect: he sifted through the letters as a mortal might sift through the grains of sand at a beach, looking for something that might catch his attention.

LeRoy's letter had. Painfully misspelled, nearly incoherent, it had rambled on about the New World Order and how Billy was surrounded by enemies who would try to stop him.

The letter had made no sense. But it had been filled with power and passion.

Gabriel had written back. He had shared his growing fears that nameless forces close to Reverend Fairchild were perverting his holy mission and causing him to waver in his commitment to purity. He had told LeRoy about the concert—having learned long since that LeRoy was a great fan of such music—and encouraged him to attend.

He had always intended that LeRoy should make a disturbance at the concert—it would be good publicity—but when his plans had changed, he had decided that LeRoy should make an even larger disturbance. . . .

"That's right," Gabriel said. He extended his *glamour* around LeRoy: no matter what he said now, LeRoy would believe it absolutely. But it was hardly necessary. "I have hard news for you. But I know you're strong, and I know you can take it like a real man."

LeRoy nodded solemnly.

"Reverend Fairchild has fallen to the Dark Forces. He's decided to sell out the music. At the concert tomorrow he's going to announce that he's shutting down Pure Blood and the other bands and is renouncing his Purity Crusade. The New World Order has gotten to him, LeRoy. You have to stop him. You're our only hope. You know what you have to do, don't you?"

"I have to stop him," LeRoy said. "I am the Sword of the Lord, His Avenging Angel of Light."

Not for the first time, Gabriel wondered what went on in mortals' minds. LeRoy's thoughts were so tangled and fragmented that they were nearly impossible to read.

"That's right," he said solemnly. "You are the Lord's Avenging Angel of Light, and Light shall be your weapon. The only way to save Judah Galilee and all the others is to blow up Billy Fairchild's false cathedral at the very moment he's trying to stop the music. Then he'll see he was wrong."

"Nobody will get hurt, will they?" LeRoy asked anxiously.

Gabriel stifled a sigh. Why did they always ask that? Mortals were as bloodthirsty as a pack of rabbits.

"No, LeRoy," he said. "Nobody will get hurt. An Avenging Angel wouldn't hurt anyone with innocence and repentance in their hearts, after all, would he?"

"No," said LeRoy, brightening. "I guess I wouldn't. But . . . the concert's tomorrow, and all, and I—"

"I have all the tools that you need to carry out your holy mission," Gabriel said smoothly. "I will show you what you need to do, and where to place it."

And when he was done, LeRoy LaPonte would not remember Gabriel's part in this at all. When he was caught and confessed—for Gabriel certainly meant for him to survive—the evidence that would also be found would link him with another Fairchild Ministries insider.

And then the fun would begin. . . .


Hosea was long past having second thoughts. He was well onto tenth thoughts by this time. And all of them were the same. This was a bad idea.

He'd been trying to talk himself out of the notion ever since Ace had gotten out of the car and started walking up the road. The trouble was, Hosea didn't have a better idea. She'd been right all the way down the line: she had the best chance of committing what was, when all was said and done, this burglary, and getting away with it safely. She knew how her dad thought; she probably knew not only how to get into any place he owned, but how it was likely to be laid out. And most anyone she met *would* think she was just back from whatever school Billy claimed she'd gone to.

But the longer she was gone, the more he remembered that the best chance wasn't a dead solid certainty.

Finally he *knew*, with a sinking sense of disaster, that she'd been gone far too long. Something bad had happened. He took a chance and moved the car into the business park.

Like its brethren along the Boardwalk, the Casino of Prayer was a 24/7 operation, and even at this hour, there were plenty of cars parked right outside. He was unsurprised to see how many of them were clear examples of people who were suckers for a fast talking salesman, and with more money than taste—and not very much money, when it came right down to it. The pink Cadillac fit right in, sad to say. If anything, it seemed tame.

There were other distractions as well. Horn's concert was tomorrow, and kids were already coming in to wait for it, settling in with blankets and sleeping bags and chairs around the main stage. Security wasn't even trying to keep them out, nor paying any particular attention to them, even though Hosea saw bottles being passed around and caught the sweet scent of pot. At least that meant Security wasn't paying any particular attention to Hosea, either. He parked in front of the casino without incident. Multicolored neon from the building's facade slid over the car's paint-job, turning it orange, purple, lurid magenta. . . .

He thought about going inside. It would be easy enough to say he'd just come back looking for a little background color for his story if anyone happened to recognize him from earlier in the day.

But wherever Ace was, she wasn't wandering around the casino floor. And from what she'd told him, he wasn't sure it would be all that easy to get into the office tower. Not without a touch of shine, anyway.

Just then his cellphone rang.

He whipped it out, but there was no one on the other end, only static, and the signal wasn't even strong enough for it to show a number.

He regarded the tower grimly. Only one person was likely to be phoning him at this hour of night—one person who couldn't get through, anyway. And Ace wouldn't be phoning from inside the building unless she was in a power of trouble indeed.

He got out of the car, and slung Jeanette over his shoulder. As an afterthought, he dug through the bag in the back seat that Gabriel Horn had given him and pulled out the laminated "All Access" pass on its scarlet lanyard and looped it around his neck.

It took him a while to make his way past the stage and through the small crowd, but, as he'd hoped, the pass gave him the perfect disguise. Though every instinct screamed at him to run, he moved at a purposeful walk, and if he didn't quite blend in to the crowd, at least he looked as if he belonged.

He was within sight of the doors to the tower lobby when he saw Ace come dashing toward them. But just as she reached them, Judah Galilee appeared behind her.

Hosea stood very still. One moment the lobby had been empty—he would have been ready to swear to that. The next moment Judah had been there. He watched from several yards away as Judah dragged Ace back toward one of the elevators.

*Lord Jesus, protect that child,* Hosea thought simply. He'd follow as quickly as he could, but he did not think his power was any match for Judah's, and he dared not risk being caught himself.

*The Good Lord helps those who help themselves,* Hosea thought, heading for the doors once he was sure the lobby was empty.

It did not occur to him to wonder why he did not stop to call Ria Llewellyn.

The outer doors were locked, but that was not enough to stop even an apprentice Bard. Mage-sight told him which buttons to press on the keypad, and in what order. The lock light went from red to green, and he was in.

He considered the elevator, and hesitated. It was too easy to get trapped in an elevator. From the direction he'd seen Ace come, she'd taken the stairs coming down, so that was the way he'd go up.

There was another lock there. It hadn't been used as recently, so the traces were harder to read. Hosea settled for just asking it to open. It took a little more work, but he managed it.

At each door on the way up he stopped, testing it, but Ace hadn't passed through any of them, and there was no one on any of the floors that he passed. From his tour, he remembered Billy saying that the whole building wasn't occupied yet. He and Gabriel Horn had offices on the penthouse floor. The record company's offices were on the floor below. The broadcasting studios and the Ministry offices occupied the three floors directly above the casino, and Billy's extensive publishing and mail-order empire occupied the three floors above that. But the only thing between floors six and fourteen was something called Christian Family Intervention on the tenth floor, as far as Hosea knew.

Of course, that might just mean that the other seven floors were occupied with offices and conference rooms.

Or there might be something on ten that needed a *lot* of elbow room. . . .

When he got to the fire door on ten, he took a good close look at it, and read emotional traces all over it, traces he recognized. Ace hadn't opened it, but she'd stopped here, and seen something that had frightened her badly.

Had she seen Judah? Had she been running from him, and been brought back here? Hosea simply didn't have enough information to be sure. What he *did* know was that he was only a few minutes behind Judah, and he'd do well to hurry.

For the first time, he felt a stab of regret that he'd never accepted the sword that Toni Hernandez had done her best to urge upon him ever since he'd become a Guardian. A sword—not an enchanted banjo—so she said, was the proper sort of weapon for a Guardian to carry into battle. And right now Hosea had to admit that it might be a little more practical if he had to face down Judah Galilee and whoever he had with him.

But when all was said and done, a sword just wasn't his style. And he was as much a Bard as a Guardian. The music magic had been his long before Jimmie Youngblood had bequeathed him her legacy. Whoever, whatever it was that was in charge of Guardians was just going to have to adapt to Hosea's style and choice of weapons.

It would have to be enough.

He eased open the door into the hallway and stepped out.

Without the distractions of earlier in the day, the crowd of other people getting in the way, he could sense the strange wrongness in the air that told him Judah and Gabriel were probably somewhere near. It still didn't "read" to his perceptions as Unseleighe magick—it felt, for example, nothing like what he'd experienced when they'd fought Aerune—so either Aerune hadn't been a typical Unseleighe, or these two weren't, or they were doing something to conceal their magickal signature.

To search the whole floor would take more time than he suspected he had, but Jeannette could search it faster than he could. He needed to get somewhere out of sight to call up her help—you could say a lot of things for Bardic magick, but it wasn't generally a quiet thing.

He glanced up and down the corridor using his mage-sight. Some of the doors glowed a dark baleful red, as if they'd been heated red-hot. Some were only faintly red. Some had no scarlet glow at all. Hosea picked one of those and told it to unlock itself—and just in time, too, for he'd barely eased the door most of the way shut when he heard footsteps in the hall.

He shut the door and dropped to the floor. They'd see a door that was open even a crack, but there was space beneath the doors. From his unorthodox vantage point, Hosea watched three pairs of feet walk by—a pair of gleaming black loafers, a pair of more ordinary lace-up shoes—and Judah Galilee's distinctive silver-heeled boots.

They passed out of sight and stopped. A few moments later Hosea heard the elevator rumble to a halt on the floor and stop, and the sound of footsteps entering it. The elevator went away. All was silence again.

None of the three had said anything, and that was frustrating, but only in bad novels did the villains stand around discussing their plans among themselves just so the hero could be enlightened. The villains already knew what their plans were—why should they bother to tell them to each other?

He'd just have to find out, which meant finding Ace first.

And pray he wasn't searching for her body.

He came out into the corridor again, and headed for the door that glowed most deeply scarlet—the offices of Christian Family Intervention. No surprises there, but a lot of worry; it was supposed to be a family counseling organization specializing in troubled teens. If this was the heart of the Unseleighe infestation . . .

The doors on this level didn't have keypad locks, but they were locked just the same. He looked at the knob and whistled a few bars of a melody. There was a distinct click, and Hosea turned the handle.

The outer office was an ordinary receptionist's office. In the glow from the hallway, he could see that it did not have an outside window, so he risked turning on the lights. He searched it quickly, just in case, but there was no one here. The door to the office beyond was locked as well—the sign on the door said "Director Cowan"—but Hosea opened it easily.

Here, too, there were no windows—but they would have spoiled the whole English Headmaster look that someone had been striving for, rather as if C. S. Lewis had shopped at Wal-Mart.

And there were people here.

Hosea checked, but they were no threat. A man and a woman, sitting on a leather couch that was against the far wall of the office. They were slumped against each other, eyes closed, deep in spell-bound Sleep.

He could try to wake them later. Right now finding Ace was more important, and there was another door to try. He stopped long enough to take Jeanette from her case and sling her strap around his neck. The way the door looked to his mage-sight, he would need all the help he could muster against what might lie beyond it.

Disturbingly, this door was not locked. One hand firmly wrapped around the neck of the banjo, he eased the door open. . . .

It always seemed simple in the movies—but in the movies, the ropes didn't slither under your hands like live things, doing their level best to re-tie themselves as fast as you tried to untie them. And she was working by touch, with her own hands tied behind her back. It really didn't help that Magnus was growling—there really wasn't any other word for it—and kept forgetting to keep his wrists together to give her as much slack as he could.

At least neither of them could see that she was crying.

No matter what had happened in her life before this, she had never actually felt as if there was no hope. There had always been hope; hope that Daddy would see reason, that Gabriel Horn would go away, that she could run away from home, that she and Jaycie and Magnus could manage to keep body and soul together, that one day they would have a real place to stay—

There had always been a hope.

There wasn't. Not anymore. She knew that; knew it blood and bone deep, with a despair that had no bottom. They weren't going to get out of here. They were going to end up like that dark-haired boy that Gabriel Horn'd had with him, the one that Eric had said had gotten all the Talent sucked out of him. But it would hardly matter, because then he was going to kill her, and her Daddy, and hundreds of other innocent people. And then he was going to go home to her Mama, and smile, and smile, and smile. . . .

Ace choked back a sob. She almost had one of the knots undone, but just as she pulled it free, she felt the rope pulling back the other way, trying to pull itself back into the knot again.

She looked up at the sound of the door opening.

"Hosea!" she gasped, in an urgent whisper. "Oh, quick—*what time is it?*"

It wasn't the oddest question he'd been asked by someone he was rescuing, but people the Guardians rescued tended to want to know things like the year, the country, and—on one memorable occasion—what planet they were on when help finally arrived. Hosea glanced at his watch. "A little after four."

Ace gave a choked laugh of relief that sounded just on the edge of hysteria; she looked as if she might burst into tears at any moment. "I *told* you he'd rescue us," she said to no one in particular.

"Sunrise is around seven," Eric said urgently, looking up at Hosea, and straining at his bonds. "We've *got* to be out of here before then."

"Happy to oblige," Hosea replied. He slung Jeanette over his back and pulled out his Leatherman multi-tool.

He'd expected to have to cut through the ropes, but they simply shriveled away at the touch of the iron blade. More of that Unseleighe muck, he reckoned. What he'd do if they ever managed to make themselves immune to iron and steel, he didn't know. Ace and Magnus stood up and hugged each other hard, as he knelt down and got to work on Eric's bindings.

"We have to get out of here 'cause there's a bomb," Ace said quickly, over Magnus's shoulder. "Gabriel Horn is setting a bomb to blow up tomorrow at the concert and kill everybody."

"Well, that does sound like his style," Hosea said mildly, getting to his feet after freeing Eric's ankles. Somehow, after all this, he wasn't too terribly surprised. "No wonder he was so anxious for me to have a front-row seat." He walked around to the back of the chair and regarded the silver cuffs. "Ah don't suppose you cain sing your way out of these?"

"Sorry," Eric said, looking hangdog, as if he somehow blamed himself for not being able to get out of trouble this time. "It's some kind of binding spell."

"Let's let Jeanette an' me give it a try then. Ah cain try cutting through the metal as a last resort." He smiled a lopsided smile. "Things hereabouts don't seem to like Cold Iron much, now, do they? We'll haveta see jest how they like a little Bard-shine."

He swung the banjo around in front and took a moment to tighten the strings. He supposed if he'd known he was going to become a Bard who needed to summon up the music magic at a moment's notice, he'd have picked a less temperamental instrument to carry around, like a guitar or a fiddle. But the banjo had been in his family for a very long time, and he trusted it, and besides—he had the feeling that there had always been a certain amount of shine in it, even before Jeanette had made it her home.

He struck a few experimental notes, then broke into a rendition of "Billy in the Low Land," a fiddler's reel that he'd always liked, and had adapted for the banjo. If you were looking to set something free, this was the tune to do it by.

It was a bright bouncy tune—the banjo wasn't a mournful instrument—and as the music spilled over his fingers, Hosea concentrated on the silver shackles.

Most magick glowed. This, embodied in the silver cuffs, ate light instead. He'd hoped he'd sense a locking mechanism, however artfully concealed, but there was nothing. However much it looked like a length of chain and two wide bracelets to his open eyes, to his magickal senses, it was just one seamless block of stubborn, swallowing Eric's hands up to the wrist, and sucking his magic out of him.

But Hosea was stubborn, too.

The reel came around to the repeat, and he picked up the pace. If there was nothing to open, maybe he could change the shape, or the substance, or turn them back into what they'd been before they were shackles. Anything to get them off Eric's wrists. *You get off'n there, you!* he thought at them. *You don't rightly belong here, and you oughtta git back to where you come from, right quick!*

He'd just about made up his mind that he was going to have to saw through them when there was a faint, ear-splitting wail; Ace and Magnus winced and covered their ears, and the cuffs turned themselves inside out and vanished.

Eric gave a faint startled yelp and leaned forward, rubbing his wrists.

"Thanks," he said, getting shakily to his feet. "Now, let's get out of here."

"There's a couple of people outside we're going to have to bring along," Hosea said. "All wrapped up in magick, just the other side of that door."

"It's locked," Magnus announced.

While Hosea had been working on Eric's cuffs, Ace and Magnus had gone over to the door. There was no handle on this side, only a dark door-shaped line in the wall.

"If they could open it, so can I," Eric said. Now that the Binding Spell had been lifted, he was himself again, as if a missing puzzle piece had been dropped into place. It had been—horrible. He never, ever wanted to find himself in that position again. If he ever saw someone coming at him with silver handcuffs like that—

Well, that wasn't important right now. What was important was that he get the kids away. The kids and Hosea, to keep them safe. Ria would kill him if anything happened to Ace. Scratch that, she'd kill him, then resurrect him so she could kill him all over again.

They'd get out of here, he'd send the other three back to New York—and then he'd figure out some way to stop that bomb from going off.

He summoned up his Flute of Air and played a few experimental notes, then a stronger skirl.

The door swept inward, spilling the strong light of the room
beyond into the grey room. He'd never been so glad to see ordinary
light before. It was like god-rays coming through black clouds.

The four of them stepped through the door in single file, Eric
coming last, holding himself back by sheer force of will from
rushing the open door.

"I am *so* glad to get out of there," Ace said fervently, turning
to face him.

But Eric had stopped, staring at his parents, sitting side-by-side,
unmoving, on the sofa.

"What are *they* doing here?" Magnus demanded, his face cloud-
ing. He started forward, but Hosea put a hand on his shoulder.

"Ah'd reckon they're here to pick the two of you up come the
morning," he said, reasoning it out. "And Gabriel wanted them
here early, just in case."

"Leave 'em," Magnus said flatly. "They came here on their own;
we've got no responsibility to them."

"We can't do that," Eric said, immediately, feeling a sick anger
even as he said it. He wanted to agree with Magnus—but he
couldn't. Like it or not—he couldn't. Even if they had forfeited
any right to his concern as a son, he still had a responsibility
towards them as a Bard.

"Don't tell me you *care* what happens to them!" Magnus burst
out. He sounded as if he were trying to keep from crying—or
screaming. "You ran out on them the first second you could and
never looked back. And don't *you* say anything," he added, turning
on Ace. "It's not like you're trying to do anything but get away
from *your* parents!"

Ace turned red with anger, and slapped him. Hard.

"Stop it," Eric said. He didn't raise his voice, but it cut right
through the emotional storm about to break, and shattered it,
leaving absolute silence behind. "No arguments. I'm not leaving
anybody where Gabrevys can get his hands on them. And you
owe Ace an apology, Magnus. If you can't figure out why on your
own, maybe you'd better ask her politely to tell you."

He didn't look back to see what Magnus did; there wasn't time. He concentrated on the spell surrounding his parents. No way they were going to be able to drag them out, asleep as they were. They'd have to get out under their own power.

It was a Sleep spell, but not a simple one. Gabrevys was a Magus Major, and had had centuries to perfect his magick. Gabrevys might be able to break the spell with a touch, but Eric had to unravel it carefully, lest he cause further damage.

And they had to hurry.

He studied it for what seemed like an agonizingly long time, still in that complete silence that had fallen over all of them at his rebuke.

At last he summoned up his flute and began to play. Mozart. He'd always liked Mozart. Not as mathematical as Bach, but somehow more suitable on this particular occasion. There was spontaneous life in Mozart, and joy. They needed joy, here.

The spell appeared to his magickal sight as a darkly glowing cocoon of thread. Each strand must be teased loose and dissolved, and in the right order, too. Otherwise—

Well, he didn't know for certain what would happen, but he suspected it would somehow wrap more tightly around its victims, perhaps sending them into a sleep from which there would be no awakening.

At last the spell broke free—and as it did, Eric felt a flare of warning. There had been something incorporated into the spell that he hadn't expected—a kind of alarm.

Wherever Gabrevys was, he knew the spell had been broken, and he'd be coming back to find out why.

They didn't have much time.

"We've got to get out of here—*now*," Eric said.

Michael and Fiona opened their eyes, looking around in confusion.

"Eric—Magnus," Fiona Banyon said, getting to her feet. "Are you . . . are you ready to go home now?" She looked around the room, obviously searching for someone she didn't see. "Where are—"

"You have to come with us now," Eric said carefully. "Gabriel

Horn lied to you, and so did the people who were working for him. You're in danger here."

His father gave a sniff of contempt. His mother frowned. "Eric, what are you talking about? Are you out of your mind?"

"No, no more than usual; he's the same old Eric," Michael Banyon said with a wry smile. "Fairy tales, or hallucinations; delusions of persecution. Well, Fi, at least we have Magnus. Come along, Magnus." He held out his hand peremptorily.

Magnus exploded. "*Fuck you!*" he shouted. "You think I'm going anywhere with you! After what you tried to do to me! You've spent all your lives trying to turn me into an obedient little puppet, and when nothing else worked, you hired a couple of thugs to do it for you. I wouldn't turn a dog over to you! Well I've got a surprise for you!—the thugs you hired didn't happen to be human. It would have worked great, only that precious musical talent that's the only thing you care about would have been gone for good."

"For God's sake, Magnus," Michael said in exasperation. "Don't you start too—I've heard more than enough fairy tales from your brother—"

"Where's Mr. Horn? Where's Director Cowan? What have you done with them?" Fiona demanded, interrupting him.

"They aren't here. They left hours ago, after they . . . drugged you," Eric said, hoping that if he sounded rational, they might actually pause long enough to listen to him, at least a little.

"Come on, Fiona. We'd better go get help," Michael said suddenly. He put a hand on her arm, drawing her toward the door.

*Oh hell. That'll bring Gabrevys right down on us—*

Eric summoned up his Flute of Air. His parents didn't recognize the truth when they heard it—small wonder—and there was no time to convince them. He'd just put a come-along spell on them . . .

Hosea put a hand on his arm.

"No," the Ozark Bard said quietly. "Iff'n you use magick to force them to do what you want—even for the best o' reasons—how are you better'n Gabriel an' his lot?"

Fiona exchanged a look with Michael, and the two of them

edged towards the door, keeping a watch on Eric as if they expected him to suddenly leap on them.

"But—" Eric protested—

Then he let out his breath in a painful sigh, letting the flute dissolve.

He couldn't. No matter if they did bring Gabrevys down on them. Hosea was right. To take away another person's free choice by magick was wrong. And they didn't have time for anything else.

Fiona and Michael reached the door, snatched it open, and bolted out, slamming it behind them.

"You warned them," Hosea said. "You've done your part."

"Not that it will do any good," Eric said grimly. "Let's get out of here. And hope we're lucky enough to get out of here before the hunt shows up."

Hosea nodded; Magnus just snarled. Ace didn't say anything, but her face was white again. They ran out into the outer office, and then into the hallway. No point in trying to be quiet or subtle now—their only hope lay in getting out of the building before Gabrevys found them, or all four of them would probably end up back in that grey room.

He didn't see his parents anywhere.

He was definitely going to write to the Better Business Bureau about these people, Michael thought angrily, if not bring them up on civil and criminal charges both. He was positive that they'd both been drugged—his watch said it was nearly five A.M., and the last thing he recalled was that it had been midafternoon.

And as for the grateful, compliant offspring that Director Cowan had promised, Eric was the same irrational, delusional, defiant boy Michael remembered, and Magnus had grown much, much worse. Dangerously violent, in fact. No wonder Fiona had been terrified.

To make matters worse, they seemed to be trapped on the tenth floor. All the elevators were locked down for the night. They searched the entire floor, trying doors, finding nothing and no one, while Michael kept his ears open for sounds of Eric and his band of hippies. The look on Magnus's face had made him both angry and alarmed.

The door to Christian Family Intervention was still open, however, and the others seemed to have gone. Michael quickly urged Fiona inside and closed the door behind him. It shut with a comforting click.

The phone on the secretary's desk was shut off, which was infuriating, and so was the one in Director Cowan's office.

"I suppose you expect to simply wait here until he shows up in the morning?" Fiona demanded icily.

"All of this was your idea," Michael reminded her. Belatedly now, he checked his cellphone, but he hadn't charged it in a couple of days, and as he feared, it was dead.

"And I suppose *you* didn't want your son back?" she snapped. She strode over to the door at the far end of the office. "Come on, Michael—show some initiative for once. All of these offices probably interconnect. Maybe someone's left another cellphone in a desk." She flung open the door and ushered him in ahead of her.

The door closed behind them.

As their eyes adjusted to the dimness, they could see that whatever this was, it was no office. The room was empty except for two silvery chairs.

"Well that was another brilliant notion of yours," Michael said. He turned around to leave.

There was no handle on the door.

# CHAPTER 8:
## EVERYBODY'S LOOKING
## FOR SOMEBODY

Gabrevys entered Toirealach's empty office. The reek of his destroyed spell still filled the air, and it took no Art to know that his prey had escaped. That was unfortunate, and for more reasons than just the obvious. Once summoned, the Soul-eaters must be fed, or else they quickly grew uncontrollable, even for a Magus Major. Apprehension pricked him, but he dismissed it. There was no reason for apprehension at this juncture. It would be a simple enough matter to find them food from among the feckless mortals gathering for the concert if the Bard and his brother could not be recaptured by the time the *peu de porte* automatically opened a few hours hence, but. . . .

Perhaps it would be best to be prepared.

With a thought, he summoned Jormin, and as he waited, he approached the door that led to the feeding pen and laid his hand against it lightly.

He raised his eyebrows in faint astonishment. The feeding pen was not empty. And now he knew where the two that had been left in the outer office had gone.

Perhaps he had underestimated the temper of Sieur Eric's

character. Rather than taking his parents with him, the Bard had left them in the feeding pen, as a sacrifice in his place.

An elegant solution, one worthy of an Unseleighe Prince. Once the Soul-eaters had fed upon them, they would never again be able to make such a covenant with any of the Sidhe as Gabrevys had used against Misthold's Bard on this occasion. Perhaps the Bard was sending another message as well—that just as he would not again be bound by ties of blood, so Gabrevys must look for his own ties of blood to be used against him?

He had not looked for such subtlety from a human. Perhaps apprehension *was* in order.

He turned slightly, as his underling's presence impinged on his consciousness.

"My lord?" Jormin entered and, quickly sensing his master's mood, knelt and bowed his head.

Gabrevys looked down on him, broodingly. "Sieur Eric and his followers have escaped. Find them and return them here by dawn. Take with you as many of the folk as can be spared from our work here. See to it that the Bard and his cohorts warn no one of what is to come."

"I hear and obey," Jormin said, bowing even lower for just a moment, before springing to his feet and running from the room, as if he was running for his very life. Which was just as well, because, in fact, he was.

With Hosea and Eric covering the rear, and Ace in the lead, the four escapees burst out into the lobby, and with shaking hands, Ace punched the lock-code into the door. They ran out into the night, not caring this time if they were noticed.

But there was more to worry about than the night-shift rent-a-cops. The parking lot was filled with people—

For a moment Eric was stunned at the crowd gathered here in the middle of the night, but then the hasty explanation back in the Grey Room dropped into place:

*Free concert.* Hundreds of—if not precisely innocent, then certainly uninvolved spectators—were assembling in a potential combat zone. Oh, now wasn't that just what they needed. . . .

People would be arriving hours ahead of time to make sure they got good places.

This was not the time to stand out as running out of a building in a panic.

*Right. Now's the time for my favorite "pay no attention to the man behind the curtain" number.*

With a few bars of "Mr. Cellophane" from *Chicago* running through his head as the key and foundation (damned useful, that song), Eric quickly cast a spell over the four of them so that they could pass through—or around—the crowd unseen.

But while it would work on the humans gathered here, it wouldn't fool the Sidhe chasing them. Not for one second. The Sidhe *invented* that "Don't see me" spell, and they knew every counter for it.

And he knew pursuit was right behind them. Gabrevys wouldn't just give up and go home because Eric and Magnus had escaped. If he could get the four of them back before dawn—and back into that room—he'd still have won whatever game he thought he was playing. And without them free to tell what they knew, he'd still be able to carry out the rest of his plans—at least he'd think so.

Eric still wasn't entirely certain what else was supposed to have happened in that room. Except that Gabrevys had seemed awfully certain when he'd left them all there that Ace, Eric, and Magnus would be happy little puppets by dawn. Too bad he must have read the Evil Overlord Checklist; he hadn't stood there and gloated nearly long enough, so Eric was not at all clear on the details. The only thing that he was clear on was that by not only consenting, but *asking* Gabrevys and his minions to snatch the two of them and turn them into good, obedient, mindless drones, the elder Banyons had completely nullified any protections that Eric's status as a Bard gave him.

*Thanks so much, Mom and Dad.*

So maybe Gabrevys really would win, if he could get them back in there.

*So we just have to make certain that doesn't happen.*

They reached the car.

"Whoa—nice wheels," Magnus said shakily, as Hosea unlocked the doors.

"Solid Detroit iron, which is more to the point just now," Hosea said grimly as they all piled in—he and Eric in the front, Magnus and Ace in the back seat. "Might spike their spells a touch." He backed out carefully; the last thing they needed right now was to run over someone. Ace already had her phone out.

"It's dead," she said in frustration.

"Try mine," Hosea said, handing it over.

But by the time Hosea had reached the road, they'd discovered that none of their cellphones worked. Possibly the Grey Room's spells had drained them   technology and magick were an uneasy combination at the best of times.

"Crap," Eric said flatly.

"We'll call Miz Ria from a payphone—" Hosea began, but Ace cut him off.

"Her phones screen out everything that comes from a payphone and sends them to an answering machine. She doesn't check it herself; her secretary does, and that won't be until *she* comes in at eight!" Ace wailed.

Magnus shook his head. "I don't remember anybody's number," he confessed uneasily. "I just put 'em in the SIM so I won't have to."

"We've got to tell somebody about the bomb!" Ace cried, tossing her phone to the floor in frustration. "You saw all those people back there—and more coming. They're gonna be killed!"

"Do we?" Eric said in a strained voice. "Who do we tell—and what do we tell them?"

They'd gotten out of the business park now, and all of them breathed a little easier, although it didn't mean they were safe, yet, by any means. Eric was turned sideways in his seat, looking back out the car's rear window, but saw no sign of pursuit yet.

Of course, their enemy wouldn't necessarily be so lawabiding as to be using headlights. . . .

"We tell the police," Ace said, looking quite beside herself. "I was right there when Mr. Horn and Daddy planned it all out, and you better believe the police take things like that seriously these days."

"And then Gabriel told you that it wasn't going to be a fake, like he told your father, but a real bomb—when he had you tied up in a back room of Christian Family Intervention waiting to get your brains sucked out by creatures from Underhill," Eric finished for her. "And even if you don't tell them that part—and I think you're smart enough to leave that out—they'd want to know how you came to overhear the first conversation. And even if you had a good answer for *that*, you're in the middle of suing Billy Fairchild. It doesn't make you a very credible witness."

"So make it an anonymous tip!" Magnus said belligerently. "They'd *have* to check that out."

"And he'd use magick on any police that showed up," Ace admitted bitterly, after a long pause. "And make them believe anything he wanted them to believe. It wouldn't work, would it?"

Eric nodded.

"Ah 'speckt not," Hosea said regretfully, keeping his eyes fixed on the road ahead. "Then, what *do* we do, Eric?"

Fortunately, he had an answer for that.

"Ria," Eric said. "We find something that isn't a payphone, and call her on it. Or better yet—call her service and talk to the live person, who *will* put us through." Fortunately, that was one number he *did* remember; unlike Magnus, he hadn't lived most of his life with cellphones available. Ria certainly screened her calls—but the service knew him, and he had the right code-phrase that would tell them to put him through. The advantages of having a live person on the other end of the line could be enormous. "Ria will believe us, and she'll be able to make the right people believe *her*. We just have to get to a phone to call her." *One that works. One we can defend for long enough to tell her enough of the details.*

"There's a phone back at the hotel . . ." Hosea began doubtfully.

"First place they'll look," Magnus said instantly. "Hey, can't this thing go any faster?"

"It better," Eric said. "I don't think we can take Gabrevys and his Bard both if it comes to a fight. So we've got to stay out of their reach, and warn Ria—and both those things are about equally important."

"Seems to me this'd be a good time to whistle up Lady Day and go see Ria in person," Hosea said, after a moment's thought. He was making random turns, heading south and west, back toward the city proper.

"No," Eric said. "They attacked me while I was riding her before. They might be able to track her."

"So we're stuck!" Ace asked.

"I think if we—*Hosea, where are you going?*" Eric demanded suddenly.

"Ah . . . Ah don't rightly know," the Ozark bard said, sounding shaken. He applied the brakes and the Cadillac bucked to a sudden halt in the middle of the deserted road.

"Back to the hotel," Ace said, answering Eric's question. "But we shouldn't go back to the hotel . . . should we?"

No. And right now, Eric didn't have time to get to the bottom of the question of why Hosea was going there.

"Let me drive," Eric said. He got out of the car, and Hosea slid over on the wide bench seat without comment.

Driving the pink Cadillac was like navigating a tugboat, especially since most of Eric's recent driving experience had been not only with elvensteeds, but motorcycle-shaped elvensteeds at that. But he got it in gear and took off again.

"We need to get out of the area," Eric said, gathering his thoughts. "They'll expect us to head north, back to our home base, so I'm going south. The Parkway's full of rest stops. The first phone we find, we'll call Ria. Hell, if her phones screen out pay-phones, I'll just *buy* a damned pay-as-you-go cell and call her from that!" *And I'll find out what's wrong with you,* he added silently to his Apprentice.

But if the Cadillac handled like a barge, it accelerated like *The Millennium Falcon,* and by the time they found the on-ramp for the Garden State Parkway South and reached the speed-lane, it was cruising along at a smooth eighty-five. A little Bardic *glamour* would ensure that they weren't stopped by any troopers, and as for other drivers, at this hour on a Friday morning, south of Atlantic City, the Parkway was just about empty.

For the first time since he'd awakened in the Grey Room earlier that night, Eric began to feel hopeful. There was no chance Big Pink was bespelled—not with all the Cold Iron in her—and it was just possible they'd either managed to outrun their pursuers, or misled them. . . .

"There's some guys behind us," Magnus reported in idle tones. "Looks like bikes. Good time for a run." There was a pause, then he spoke again, sounding worried, "They're coming up awfully fast."

"Eric—" Ace said, alarm in her voice.

Suddenly there was an ear-splitting wail, and every pane of glass in the Cadillac shattered.

Eric flung up an arm to protect his eyes as the wind whipped pebbles of safety glass and shards of mirror around him. Suddenly he was driving blind, with the eighty-five-mile-per wind whipping into his face. But he didn't dare slow down.

Adrenaline thrummed through his veins, as Ace shrieked behind him. He summoned his armor and slammed the visor down—it wasn't as much protection as a motorcycle helmet, but it would have to do.

Eric pushed the pedal all the way to the floor. Automatically he glanced down, but the face of the speedometer was a spiderweb of cracks. They had to be doing over a hundred, though.

Not good enough.

There was a *thump* on the roof, and a groaning, tearing sound as *something* began to pull at the roof of the car. There were long, curved black talons hooked around the edge of what had once been the windshield, and Eric thought he'd really rather not see what they were attached to.

Behind him, Magnus was invoking the "F" word at a machine-gun rate and at the top of his lungs.

Now Eric could hear the sound of hoofbeats, even over the sound of the howling engine and the wind.

"Get down!" Eric shouted to the others.

Hosea reached for the wheel, steadying it and freeing Eric's hands. That trick would only work for a few seconds, but a few seconds would have to be enough.

He turned in his seat—the angle was awkward—summoned the *1812 Overture,* and blasted the roof with all his might.

It was already weakened. Now it blew free, and took with it whatever had been tearing at it. Eric heard a shriek as their arcane passenger was dislodged, and then more shrieks as the mass of Cold Iron tumbled into the middle of the riders following them.

He turned back and grabbed the wheel from Hosea, yanking the now-convertible back into the middle lane, and jamming the accelerator all the way down again.

"I thought they couldn't touch iron!" Magnus yelled from the back seat. He'd climbed out of the footwell and was looking over the back deck again.

"Some of them can," Eric shouted back. "If they aren't Sidhe." And Gabrevys had apparently come to the World Above prepared for every eventuality.

With three bars from the first thing he could think of, which happened, ironically enough, to be "Ein feste Burg ist unser Gott," *(thank you, Martin Luther!)* he flung a shield over the top of the car. It made a poor windshield—it was like looking through a thin bubble of water—but it cut the icy blast of wind and it was better than nothing.

And it would protect them from a levin-bolt, if the riders started firing at them.

There wasn't a lot he could do while he was driving, and while he was willing to risk changing drivers at a hundred miles an hour if he had to, he wasn't sure what Hosea would do once he was behind the wheel. Maybe turn right back the way Gabrevys wanted them to. Maybe stop. Either would be bad.

Hosea had slung Jeanette's strap over his shoulder, and was getting ready to play, but looked uncertain, as if he couldn't think of anything appropriate.

*Remind me that I have to increase your repertoire, Apprentice.*

"They're coming back," Ace announced. "What can we do?"

"Your power will work on them as well as on humans," Eric said. "If you can think of some way to make them decide to go away, now would be a good time to try it."

Ace gave a strangled hiccup. More than anyone Eric had ever known, Ace hated and feared her Gift.

"Here they come," Magnus said grimly.

The thunder of hoofbeats got louder. Even though they seemed to be riding horses—or nearly—the riders were overtaking them easily. The rearview mirror was gone, of course, but when Eric risked a glance over his shoulder he could see them clearly: black-armored riders, still nearly a dozen.

He was just glad there was no one else on the road now.

"'Fighting for Strangers,'" Ace said. "*Quick!*"

She took a deep breath and sang as the banjo sparkled into life. Not the usual sort of thing that Hosea played; this was a grim tune, full of hollow melancholy.

"'*What makes you go abroad—fighting for strangers—when you could be safe at home—free from all dangers—*'"

Hosea's strong baritone joined in on the counterpoint—if there was a folk song that Hosea didn't know, Eric had yet to discover it. Ace's pure soprano soared above his voice and the banjo both, carrying its message: *give up, go home, you'll only get badly hurt if you fight. . . .*

Eric felt the power of Ace's Gift wash over him, raising the hackles on the back of his neck. It took all his determination and will not to stop the car right there and get out. Ace reached out and put a hand on his shoulder, and the desperate desire to surrender eased slightly.

Magnus began to drum on the back of the seat with his hands in time to the song.

"'*You haven't an arm and you haven't a leg—The enemy nearly slew you—You'll have to go out on the streets to beg—Oh poor Johnny what have they done to you?*'"

There was a wildness and a sorrow in Ace's singing that made Eric want to lay his head down and cry, right there. It was not about this fight, right here: it was about every fight, every battle, since the beginning of Time—every time someone had left their home, for good cause or bad, and come back maimed, changed . . . or dead.

No reason for it. No good reason. Ever.

Fewer riders now.

"'What makes you go abroad—fighting for strangers—when you could be safe at home—free from all dangers—'"

No wonder Billy had wanted to keep her—no wonder Gabrevys had wanted to take her. No wonder Ace feared her own Talent so much. It was the ultimate seduction, the ultimate compulsion . . .

Much more of this and he was going to drive off the road. He had to stop. But not on the Parkway, and not at a rest stop. Now that he'd seen what Ace could do, Eric thought they had a chance against the rest of them, but he didn't want to involve any innocent bystanders.

There was an exit coming up. He took it at speed.

The other three never faltered until the jouncing became too great to ignore. Eric didn't think they'd noticed until then, lost in that place where good musicians go. He pumped the brakes, disastrously reminded when it was far too late to change his mind just how much heavier a good old fashioned piece of Detroit iron was than a modern piece of road-plastic.

*Go-fast doesn't help much if you don't have slow-fast too.*

Maybe their pursuers would overshoot. But it wouldn't matter. The nightmares they were riding were a lot more nimble than Big Pink. And if he put her in a ditch, it would take serious magick to get her out again. And they didn't have time for that.

But he reached the bottom of the ramp without incident. The exit put them on a two-lane country road with nothing on either side but fields and trees, and here, as opposed to the Parkway, the road was foggy. He'd stop right here, except for the fact that in his experience, there was always a lone traveler coming down these back roads doing eighty at just the wrong moment. He glanced back over his shoulder.

Through the spell-shield, he could see that the remaining riders—only four now—were gathered at the top of the ramp. Their eyes, and their mounts', glowed red.

Eric gunned the engine.

Two miles down the road he found what he was looking for. In season, it was probably a roadside cider stand. Right now it was nothing more than a wide spot in the road. He yanked Big Pink off the road so violently that the car spun completely around and ended up pointing back the way it had come.

But it was off the road.

He got out of the car, drawing his sword. On the other side, Hosea got out too, his hand pressed against the banjo's strings.

"Five-fifteen," Hosea said, glancing down. "Sunrise is 5:51. Don't know what dawn would be."

It was already a little less dark, but not dawn by any stretch of the imagination, and cold as only a March morning in New Jersey could be.

And Eric could hear hoofbeats in the distance. Coming slowly— why should they hurry? They knew precisely where Eric and the others were.

Eric looked around. They couldn't run. And fighting was starting to seem more and more like a losing proposition.

"Come on—quickly!" he said. "I have an idea."


Judah, Abidan, Coz, and Jakan—who in another time and another place answered to four quite different names—rode slowly down the road. They were the strongest of Gabrevys's Court—strong enough to resist the siren enchantment of the girl's Gift, when the others had turned and fled, sobbing like children.

Of course, having the chunk of Deathmetal dropped in their midst had hardly improved things. It had killed two of the mounts outright, and taken some of the fun out of the chase. If the four of them had not taken care to ride well back, they might have met the same inglorious fate—only think of the ignominy of being taken from a Hunt in full career by fleeing prey!—but Jormin had been more wary than that. He had met Bard Eric before. The mortal boy was clever, and the Deathmetal chariot was a weapon to be reckoned with.

And now at last the mortal Bard had chosen to fight, not flee. That might be entertaining in its own way. It was true that now he knew that he could not be harmed in body, nor could his brother, but the two hostages to fortune he rode with possessed no such sureties. What price would Bard Eric place on their safety?

The four reached the place where the Deathmetal vehicle was, and stopped.

It was empty.

Jormin rode forward, suspicious of a trap. His mount shied in the presence of so much iron, and he rowelled its sides ruthlessly.

He rode all the way around the vehicle. Nothing. No tracks leading away from it, no scent of them in the trees beyond. Only the reek of iron befouling his magick.

He swung down from his saddle and stepped forward, glancing up at the sky. Far less than an hour till the *peu de porte* opened, and the Soul-eaters came from their feeding pens in Bete Noir to feast. If Bard Eric and his brother were not there then to receive their attentions, Jormin was not certain they would still be lawful prey. What he *did* know was that the Soul-eaters could not be summoned again until another feeding pen was constructed, for this one would be gone in the spectacular display that Prince Gabrevys had promised them all.

He heard breathing.

It was coming from the back of the Deathmetal machine.

*They were hiding within!*

He clawed at it until the leather of his gauntlets smoked, and the pain of his burns made him hiss with rage, but he could not pry the closed compartment open. With a scream of fury, he brought both fists down on the metal, leaving a deep dent in it, then sprang back in dismay. If he crushed the compartment in which they had secreted themselves, he might kill the mortal Bard and his brother—and the punishment that would come to him for that made him shudder.

He backed away from the chariot, growling in anger. No spells he could summon would transport the entire object back to his master, and he could not open it. He could destroy it here, but to kill Sieur Eric and the boy Magnus outright would be a far more terrible failure than to simply fail to bring them back. Escaped prey could be captured later—but not all of Jormin's arts could re-animate the dead.

But if this *vehicle* would not yield to him, at least it would not serve its cowardly masters any longer. He lashed out at it with a levin-bolt. The iron made the magick ricochet spectacularly about the clearing—causing the other three to swear and dodge, and all four mounts to buck and shy—but the levin-bolt had its desired effect. For a moment the entire iron car was outlined in an eerie violet halation as the paint boiled up on the vehicle's surface, and all four tires melted.

There! The iron dragon would carry them no further at least.

Jormin did not like to confess failure. But at least he could wrap the tale in some success. He had marooned the worldlings here in the middle of nowhere. It would take them hours to reach civilization, and longer still to convince anyone that their tale held truth. And before they could manage that, the Prince could send mortals to retrieve them.

"Come, friends, let us away," he told the others. "The hour grows late—and we have sweet music to make!"

*Okay, so maybe hiding in the trunk hadn't been such a good idea,* Eric thought to himself. But it was still better than a full-on magickal brawl with four of the Unseleighe Court, especially when Hosea and Ace could be killed at will and Magnus—as far as Eric knew—didn't have any way of fighting back.

Of course, one good titanium crow-bar and their goose would have been cooked, but when he'd seen that Gabrevys hadn't been with their nightmare-riding pursuers—and remembered how *feudal* Elfhame Bete Noir had seemed—he'd played a hunch that these weren't exactly cutting-edge forward-thinking Unseleighe. That, powerful as they were, they were *old*—which meant just a bit set in their ways. Elves weren't big on creativity in the first place. Gabrevys might be able to come up with the idea of a Sidhe rock band of evil—he'd probably gotten the idea from a book—but unless he was on Fairgrove's restricted e-mail list, he wouldn't be current with the latest in nonferrous technology adaptations.

Still. Four people crammed into a car trunk. . . .

Of course, once they'd locked themselves into the trunk, the problem remained of getting *out*. . . .

"I can't breathe," Magnus complained in an undertone.

"If you can talk, you can breathe," Ace whispered back. But she sounded a little breathless herself.

It *was* stuffy in here—stuffy, hot, and very, very cramped, even though the Coupe de Ville had a trunk about the size of some of the smaller New York City apartments that Eric had seen. The dent in the trunk hadn't helped matters any; it was pressing hard against Eric's left shoulder, and he was pretty sure it was going to leave a bruise.

"Are they gone, do you think?" Hosea asked—with remarkable calm given the circumstances. Eric didn't know what all Jormin had done besides bang on the trunk: he did know that the car had rocked violently a couple of times and then settled sharply lower in a way that didn't bode well for the tires. "Ah cain see light around the edges of the trunk," Hosea added.

"I think so," Eric said. "I'm pretty sure I heard them ride off. We can't stay in here forever, anyway."

"*You* might be able to," Hosea said ruefully. "It's a bit of a tight fit for me."

"You had to bring the damned banjo," Magnus groaned.

"Hey—watch it!" Ace said. She sounded indignant rather than scared. Which was an improvement.

"Okay, everybody, hold still," Eric said. "I'm going to try to get the trunk open."

Eric was pretty sure he knew how sardines felt by the time he was done getting into position, and he didn't dare try a really high-powered spell, like the one he'd used to blow the roof off earlier. There was too much chance he'd just cook the lot of them.

He felt around for the lock mechanism, and piece by piece, humming "Step By Step" under his breath, he made it trickle away, until there was nothing there but a hole in the trunk. Now he could see out, and—fortunately—a lot more fresh air could get in.

Hosea was right. It was dawn.

And shouldn't the trunk have sprung open?

Eric pushed at it as best he could from his cramped position. It was almost impossible to get leverage, or, for that matter, move at all, with the four of them in here—it was just a good thing he'd changed back from armor to street clothes before they'd all piled in, or they'd never have managed it.

But the trunk lid wasn't moving. Jormin's blow must have jammed it shut.

"Stuck, is it?" Hosea said quietly.

"Yeah," Eric said with a sigh. There was no point in concealing the obvious.

"Anythin' you cain do?"

"One thing." One spell he knew—one of the handiest—was to make an inanimate object "remember" its original condition. Kory used it, back in their digs in San Francisco, to help restore the old townhouse to its former Victorian glory. It could be used to make old things new—for a time, anyway, at least when he did it, since it seemed to work better for elves than it ever did for him. And like most spells, it had its converse—though, oddly enough, the effects of this one didn't wear off. He could hurry an object's natural aging span, making it break down and decay—or *rust*—in a matter of minutes. If he did that here, the car should corrode to the point that they could get out of the trunk.

Of course, Margot would skin them all for destroying her ride. But that would be later.

He really hated to destroy such a beautiful machine. For a moment he hesitated, hoping there was another way. But there wasn't—nothing safe enough to use at such close quarters for all of them.

He'd better try it. Because just because Jormin and his pals had ridden off just now didn't mean they'd given up.

Eric placed a hand against the inside lid of the trunk, letting his mind fill with music.

Rust spread from his palm as if it were frost, and soon the air was filled with choking metallic dust—a side effect he hadn't anticipated. Eric closed his eyes tightly and held his breath, concentrating on the spell. His fingers sank into the suddenly rust-greasy metal, and he could feel Hosea adding his power and effort to the spell.

There was a shuddering groan as the Cadillac sank further to the ground with a squeal of protest as something within the frame gave way, and at last the trunk lid flew up in a cloud of rust and decaying carpet. Coughing and choking, the four refugees clambered out.

"Jesus," Magnus said comprehensively, staring at the car.

The tires—which appeared to have previously melted to puddles—had decayed to dust, and the wheel-rims were bent and rusting. The car rested on what was left of its door-panels on the gravel, as the jolt that had freed them from the trunk had been the last of the suspension giving way.

Both side-mirrors had fallen off. Every exposed bit of chrome that remained was pitted with green and brown corrosion. The roof, of course, had been torn off earlier that morning, and the twisted shears of tortured metal stood up like the stubs of decayed teeth. The headlights and tail-lights were shattered, as was every piece of glass and Bakelite in the cockpit. The (formerly) white leather seats were split and tattered, and had turned an ugly greenish-grey with age and mold. The stuffing and the springs were foaming out through the split and flaking leather like strange growths.

But it was the car's metallic pink paint-job that had undergone the most bizarre transformation, and one that owed little to Eric's spell. Most of it was gone entirely, the bare metal beneath red with rust where it had not flaked away entirely. But where the paint still remained, it was a sort of soup-green, and had bubbled up as if it were diseased. It was almost as if someone had turned the *idea* of the other color inside-out.

"Margot's going to kill you, Hosea," Ace said when she finally stopped coughing.

"Ayah," Hosea agreed glumly.

"Can you, like, fix it?" Magnus asked doubtfully. "We can't exactly walk out of here."

Eric shook his head. "Not fast enough." *Not at all. I don't think even Monster Garage could do anything with this car now.* He concentrated for a moment. "But Lady Day's on her way. I think it's safe now. When she gets here, I can talk her into turning into something to get the four of us to a phone—or back to New York. And there's something else I need to do while we're waiting."

For the first time since they'd opened the door out of the Grey Room Eric wasn't either running or fighting for his life. He dropped into mage-sight and took a look—a really *good* look—at the other three.

Magnus looked perfectly normal—no sign of any lingering spells around him at all. Eric breathed a sigh of relief.

But Ace and Hosea . . .

Both of them *shimmered,* ever-so-faintly, with spellwork.

Compared to these, the ones cast on his parents had been coarse and clumsy things. No wonder even Hosea hadn't noticed them. Eric stared at them intently: he needed to know what they were before he destroyed them, lest he do more damage.

"What is it?" Hosea asked, seeing the intensity of his stare.

"You've been bespelled," Eric said absently, most of his attention still on the spell. "You and Ace both. It looks like Jormin's work—" There! He had it now—a compulsion, very subtle, to keep them both in the immediate area where it had been set. They'd do anything they thought they had to in order to fulfill it; in fact, if Eric weren't here to stop them, they'd probably start heading back to Atlantic City soon—coming up with some reason why that was a good idea and managing to forget all the reasons it wasn't. No wonder Ria wasn't already down here, guns blazing. They'd probably kept everything they'd known or suspected about Gabriel Horn to themselves, without knowing why they'd done it.

Ace stared at him for a moment, then suddenly burst into tears. Hosea put a comforting arm around her.

"You could of been a mite more tactful about that, Eric," the Ozark Bard said mildly.

"I can fix it," Eric said quickly. "Not fix it, but . . . Don't worry. I can make it unravel."

He filled his hands with the Flute of Air, and suddenly the misty clearing was filled with the pure spiraling mathematics of a Bach prelude. The notes seemed to coil round and round, describing golden spirals in the air, each one alone and only, making shining helixes in the air. They rose up like motes of light to his inner sight, and then began to settle slowly over Ace and Hosea.

And everywhere they touched, a strand of the Unseleighe magick melted away.

At last it was gone. Whatever spells had bound them against their will and knowledge bound them no longer.

"What did it do?" Hosea asked, when Eric had stopped playing.

"I think—I'm pretty sure—Jormin placed a *geas* on both of you to keep you from leaving the immediate area." Eric sent the Flute of Air back to where it came from. "It was good. Really good. You'd have to have a lot more experience in magick than you do to have known it was there, or that he was putting it on you. You didn't know about it, but unconsciously you'd do whatever you had to in order to stay there."

"Includin' not callin' for help—when that would o' been the smartest thing to do," Hosea said in disgust.

"Hey, if you'd been smart, bro and I would be zombies by now," Magnus said. "So it ended up being a good thing," He leaned back against the fender of the rusted Caddy. It promptly tore loose and dumped him onto the ground.

"Serves you right," Ace said promptly. But she reached down and gave him her hand.

"Hey," Kayla said from the side of the road. "Oh, shit—is that Margot's *car*?"

*Get a dog and you'll never need an alarm clock again.* Kayla reminded herself that it could have been worse.

Brenda could have asked her to baby-sit a real kid for a weekend.

*Why couldn't Molly have been a cat?* She'd had a vague idea that her Spring Break would be a time when she would actually get a chance to *catch up on her sleep.* What Brenda hadn't mentioned was that Molly would see no reason to change her morning schedule just because Kayla had the rare chance to sleep in. Molly was up bright and early—*very* early—to take care of a dog's morning needs (which meant that Kayla was up and dressed, since she couldn't very well hand Molly her leash and send her out by herself), after which Molly wanted breakfast, after which Molly wanted (you guessed it) another outing.

After that, of course, the pug was perfectly happy to curl up again and snuggle and even go back to sleep for several hours, but by that time, like it or not, Kayla was wide awake. She'd never had that ability to just doze off whenever she felt like it.

Still, it wasn't Molly's fault that Brenda was a (shudder) Morning Person. And Molly was so charming and full of fun that it was impossible to be mad at her, even when you were being awakened at oh-dark-thirty by a sloppy face full of wet pug kisses. How could you be angry with anything that could maintain that level of enthusiasm from the time she woke up to the time she went to sleep?

But if she ever got a dog of her own, Kayla was going to make sure that the mutt understood that morning started at a reasonable hour—eight-thirty, say. Or maybe noon.

On this particular morning, though, Molly hadn't had to wake her up. Kayla hadn't gotten much sleep, and she was pretty certain she wasn't the only one in the building suffering from the insomnia.

Eric was still missing, and so was Magnus. And Lady Day was here, fretting, but unable to tell them why, and it was too much like the last time that had happened for Kayla's peace of mind. Ria had already checked all the hospitals, and Toni and Paul had checked out the "giant wolf" sightings near Gussie's school, but—frustratingly!—Toni had said the Guardians couldn't do anything more. Or at least, not as Guardians, and what they could do as Eric's friends was minimal.

"It doesn't seem to be Guardian business, Kayla. I'm sorry," was all Toni could say, shrugging helplessly.

At least the last phone call Ria'd had from Hosea, last night around seven, sounded as if there wasn't too much in the way of trouble going on down there—if Kayla knew Too Tall at all, he'd be back today to help look for Eric. Maybe he was already on the way back.

Maybe he was already here, and looking.

Not that there was any place to look for Eric.

Which left Kayla to pace, and worry, spend a mostly sleepless night worrying about things she couldn't do anything about, and take Molly for an extra-long post-breakfast walk to relieve her nerves. Not for the first time, she wished her particular Talent was for something besides Healing. Finding, for instance. That would be pretty useful right now.

She was just heading back toward the apartment along the street that bordered the small parking area behind Guardian House when she saw a sudden flare of headlights in the lot.

That caught her attention; she made it her business to notice anything out of the ordinary in and around Guardian House. It was a little early for anyone to be leaving for work, and almost everyone took the bus or the subway anyway, since parking in New York was a nightmare. Maybe someone was taking an early weekend?

No.

There was only one bright-red motorcycle in the lot, and it was the one doing the moving. And there wasn't anyone on it.

It was Lady Day. The elvensteed was going somewhere. Alone.

*Not a bloody chance.*

Without thinking twice, Kayla scooped Molly up under one arm and ran toward the bike. Lady Day was just starting to back out of her parking slot as Kayla vaulted into the saddle, holding the enthusiastically wriggling pug tightly against her chest. She didn't really want to bring Molly along on this adventure—excellent or otherwise—but she had no choice: she knew Lady Day wouldn't wait for her to put Molly back in the apartment. Lady Day *might* not want to let her come along—but Kayla wasn't going to take no for an answer.

"Wherever you're going, girl, I'm going with you," Kayla said firmly. "If Eric needs you, he probably needs some rein-forcements."

Like she'd be much in the way of reinforcements. . . .

At least Lady Day didn't try to buck her off. Well, the elvensteed had let Kayla ride her before. And if she was going where Eric was, odds were he'd need a Healer, like the last time he'd gone missing. She'd be of that much use, anyway.

The bike turned onto the street and sped up, heading in the direction of the George Washington Bridge. *Okay, I don't need to steer, so*—Holding on to to Molly in case the idiot dog got the idea to try to jump off, and wishing she had a third hand, Kayla unstrapped Eric's spare helmet from the back of the bike and shoved it onto her head. Good thing the chin-strap had a Velcro fastener in addition to the buckle, because you couldn't buckle anything with just one hand. Fortunately she was already dressed for the weather—which meant gloves and boots and her leather jacket. She held on tightly to the handlebars with one hand and Molly with the other; the pug barked enthusiastically, obviously enjoying the ride.

"I just hope we get there fast—and there's no tolls," Kayla said. She had her purse with her, slung crosswise over her shoulder, SOP in New York to deter purse-snatchers, but she wasn't sure how the toll-booth attendants would react to her furry passenger.

She needn't have worried. There were toll-booths, but Lady Day didn't stop for them. Lady Day didn't stop for anything: traffic lights, yield signs, oncoming traffic. Kayla had no idea how fast they were going, but none of the other drivers seemed to notice them—a good thing, too, as she didn't think even all of Eric's elf-*kenned* gold could pay for the speeding tickets they should have gotten . . . not to mention driving through the toll-booths. But the alarms on the booths didn't even go off. It was as if they were ghosts.

They crossed the bridge and headed into New Jersey. Kayla muttered a despairing curse when she realized that wherever Eric was, it was probably a lot farther away than Hoboken. Lady Day went faster.

Then something really, really odd happened. The world itself stopped obeying the laws of physics as Kayla understood them. By the time they reached the Garden State Parkway, the outside world had become nothing more than a bright blur, whipping by literally too fast to be seen, like something out of an old science-fiction movie. There was a faint high humming in the air that seemed to waver up and down a note or two, monotonously, but other than that, an eerie silence.

And instead of the blast of wind that she expected—that ought to be there, if she was riding on a motorcycle traveling as fast as this one had to be traveling—there was nothing more than a faint breeze.

Magick. Eric had told her that the elvensteeds had some way of traveling fast and invisibly in the World Above. She'd believed him, but hadn't really thought about the mechanics of such a thing. It wasn't lightspeed, of course, but it sure seemed as if Einstein would have taken one look at what was happening and gone off to shoot himself.

She didn't want to try stepping off to test how far the magick ran, though.

And even Molly was quiet. Finally.

After a few minutes of that—just as Kayla was starting to get used to traveling on Twilight Zone Motorways—the elvensteed began to slow. The world outside took on form. Nothing but trees—for an instant Kayla wondered if they'd gone Underhill, but the road was still here, so she guessed they hadn't. Lower New Jersey, then; outside of the industrial wasteland where the state was still rural and (so she'd heard) really pretty.

Slower still, maybe in the lower three digits now. Green road signs flashed by, much too fast to make out. The center line was still one continuous blur. Instinctively she gripped the handlebar and tucked her head down behind the windscreen.

The high humming began to be replaced with the roar of the wind, and the faint breeze became stronger by the moment.

Slower still—ninety? a hundred? A sign for someplace called "Cape May" flashed by. Now the wind was a real wind, pulling at her jacket and whistling over the helmet. She tucked Molly's head tightly against her chest, wishing that somebody made pug-sized biker-goggles. Or at least, that she'd thought to stick Molly inside her jacket while they were still traveling their own private wormhole.

There was a flash of pink at the side of the road. It whipped past almost before she'd registered it.

*Oh, god. Is that—?*

It had *looked* like part of Big Pink, Margot's car.

Had there been an accident?

*Oh, no, please.*

Kayla flinched inwardly, bracing herself for what she might encounter with a sense of pure nausea. Sure, she could *heal* damage, but what people tended to forget was that before she could fix injuries, she had to feel them, most of the time. There was no way you could call that fun by any stretch of the imagination. And there was always the problem that if someone was hurt bad enough, she could get sucked into their pain and need and they'd both die. . . .

Lady Day slowed still further, and Kayla saw a sign: MYERS CORNERS EXIT: 1 MI.

They took the ramp. Someone had laid serious rubber all the way down recently, she noted. Her tension eased a little. Maybe not an accident.

Lady Day coasted down the side road in an eerie silence, and it took Kayla a moment to realize that she wasn't hearing engine noises from the elvenbike. Well, they were pretty much optional.

And up ahead . . .

There were four people standing in a little knot at the side of the road. From their body language, things were uncomfortable, but not critical. And nobody was hurt.

Eric. Magnus. Ace. Hosea. Alive and well.

And . . . Margot's car?

No. . . .

"What are you doing here?" Eric demanded, as Kayla swung off the elvenbike and walked toward them. For some reason, she had Molly-the-Pug with her, and the little dog danced around in circles at the end of her leash, barking joyfully.

Well, at least someone was happy. Poor little flea-bait probably hadn't seen real countryside in her entire life.

"I was out walking the furkid when your ride lit up," Kayla said, shrugging. "I figured she was going wherever you were, and

I didn't want to miss the fun. An' it wasn't like your bike was going to wait for me to park the dog with Toni or anything. So what the hell's going on? The Unseleighe Court set up shop in Jersey?"

She'd meant that as a joke. Unfortunately, of course, she could probably tell by his face that it wasn't. And he had decided it was time to break chapter one of the Book of Bad News to her.

"Actually . . . yeah," Eric said. "And we need to get to a phone pronto."

"Well," Kayla said, dropping the leash—Molly immediately ran to Ace and began making shameless overtures—and digging in her backpack, "how about if a phone comes to you?"

She retrieved the phone and held it out, still not quite able to take her eyes off the wreck of the car behind the four of them. "Fully charged. I checked this morning before I went out."

It was six-twenty in the morning, but Ria Llewellyn had already been at her desk for over an hour. A multinational holding company didn't sleep, and if there was one thing the Threshold disaster had taught her, it was that the price of "clean hands" at the corporate level was eternal vigilance over the doings of one's underlings.

Fortunately, eternal vigilance was a little easier on someone who was half elven. Elves didn't sleep as such, and half elves, while they did need to recharge, didn't need a *lot* of sleep; two hours, maybe three. Which was proving to be a good thing.

Especially these days, when the world seemed to be taking the fight against terrorism as a blank check to impose measures large and small that had nothing to do with anti-terrorism, and everything to do with the convenience of government and big business. What was it Jefferson had said about a government big enough to supply everything you needed was big enough to take away everything as well? Ria had no objection to making money herself—money could buy so many pleasant things—but there were sane and reasonable limits, which one had to fight tooth and nail to maintain, it seemed. . . .

The Arabs had a saying too; if you let the camel's nose into the tent, pretty soon you had the whole camel in there.

But LlewellCo wasn't the only thing occupying her at the moment. Would that it were. The charter for the Ria Llewellyn Foundation was an ongoing series of minor annoyances, as was the purchase of a suitable large and isolated parcel of land on the East Coast to build what Eric insisted on calling "Hogwarts West" upon. There was deciding how best to settle the matter of Michael and Fiona Banyon once and for all. Reviewing Derek's latest memorandum to Judge Springsteen on Billy Fairchild's unsuitability to retain custody of his daughter.

But positively the most urgent and desperately annoying problem was that of Eric and Magnus's kidnapping.

The list of Unseleighe with the power to operate effectively in Manhattan was short—if you defined "effective" not just as the ability to walk around and sight-see—Kory could do that, and he was only a Magus Minor—but to shape-shift, spell-cast, and muster up enough power to take out a fully trained Bard. A few days ago she would have said such a list was nonexistent. Obviously it was not.

There was the possibility that whoever this was had found allies that had no trouble with Cold Iron. It wasn't unheard of, but the Unseleighe were not noted for their cooperative spirits.

And why would the Seleighe take him without telling her? Especially after that last time—she'd made her feelings perfectly clear. The chill in her message to Prince Arvin probably kept his drinks cold for a month.

The first thing she'd done after they'd learned that Eric and Magnus had been taken was to write down as much as she knew and courier it up to Inigo Moonlight in Carbonek. The elven "Confidential Inquiry Agent and Researcher of the Arcane" had far more Underhill contacts than Ria did: if Eric were Underhill—in either Court—Mr. Moonlight would be able to locate him, and, just as important, tell Ria *why* he and Magnus had been taken.

Doing that bought her time to think sensibly and carefully. If the kidnapping was a side effect of some annoying Sidhe vendetta, and had nothing to do with Eric personally, the very last thing she wanted to do was tell Elfhame Misthold about it. She'd spent the first few decades of her life listening to her Unseleighe father plot long elaborate schemes and vengeances against a constantly expanding enemies list, and knew exactly how long Sidhe memories could be—and how their quarrels could escalate. Eric had been caught up in one once. Never again. Telling Arvin would only bring Misthold in on the quarrel and make things worse for decades to come.

She'd also used her own spellcraft to try to locate Eric. Ria was a sorceress: neither an Elven Magus nor a mortal magician, her unique abilities were a peculiar blend of both sides of her mixed-blood heritage. And she'd come up with precisely nothing. Not scrying, not psychometry, not pyromancy—no form of divination or clairvoyance that she tried had revealed either Eric or Magnus's location. True, she wasn't primarily a scryer nor a far-seer; she hadn't the practice in it that specialists did. Nevertheless, the fact that she was drawing a blank bothered her profoundly.

All that left was a waiting game, and she didn't like it. Maybe Hosea would have better luck than she'd had—he was Eric's apprentice, after all. Maybe there was a link there that he could follow. She'd wait till a slightly more civilized hour and call him. Whether he'd found any traces of the Dark Court beyond the spell he'd detected at Ace's hearing or not, she still wanted the two of them back here where she could keep a closer eye on them. And come to that, something about everything going on down in Atlantic City just didn't add up. . . .

The phone rang. She glanced down. Her private line, and Kayla's number. She grabbed for it.

"Ria."

"Hi, Ria. Don't worry, we're all right."

She closed her eyes in relief. Dear gods, those were the words she wanted to hear more than any others right now. . . .

"Eric!"

"But that's just about all the good news," Eric went on. "First things first: there's a free concert today at the Heavenly Grace Cathedral and Casino of Prayer. Gabriel Horn has set a bomb to go off during the concert. I'm pretty sure it's somewhere in the casino—it's being closed down during the concert—but I'm not sure."

Trust Eric to show up out of nowhere and present her with a full-blown disaster as casually as other men would offer her a bouquet of flowers.

*Yes, but that means he knows deep down where it counts that you can handle disasters, and you can probably do something about them.* There had been men in her life who had taken one look at her and assumed she had gotten where she was by accident.

"What do you need me to do?" Ria asked simply.

She heard Eric laugh a little raggedly.

"None of us here would make the most credible witness—Ace overheard Horn telling Billy about it while she was burgling his office, but Horn told Billy the bomb would be a dud, to whip up support for Billy's White Power Crusade. Horn told us he intends it to be the real thing—but that was while he was holding Ace, Magnus, and me prisoner. That's because Gabriel Horn is Prince Gabrevys ap Ganeliel—Jachiel's father—and he blames me for the fact that his son is at Misthold. Among other things, he wants revenge. Lots of it, probably involving pain, dismemberment, and emotional suffering beforehand."

*Elven vendetta,* Ria thought aggrievedly. *I knew it. I swear, you'd think that with their long lives they'd have figured out something better to do with their time.*

"But he can't just take out a Bard," she said aloud. Not because she believed it, but because she wanted to figure out *how* the little bastard had created bonsai out of the treaties and laws that governed Underhill to allow him to take out a Bard.

By the sound of Eric's long-suffering sigh, she wasn't the first person to have said that to him lately.

"He can if the Bard's parents set the Bard up by accident," Eric said. "Long story. I'll tell you later. Anyway, nobody's going to believe any of us if we report the bomb, and if the authorities try to check out the warning with Horn or any of his people—and I think he's got a lot of his own people into the Ministry by now—he'll just englamour them and make them go away thinking everything's all right."

"So you thought of me," Ria said dryly, thinking hard. Surely, with all of this so-called "War on Terror" nonsense, she could find someone, somewhere whose paranoia she could use as a crowbar to lever this mess open, or a hammer to beat it into submission. "When is this bomb supposed to go off?"

"I think he'll want to go for the biggest mess he can make," Eric said. "The concert's supposed to start at noon, but there were people already there the middle of last night. Oh, and Kayla's here, if you're looking for her I summoned Lady Day and she, uh, sort of hitched a ride. But that's a good thing, it turns out, because none of our cellphones are working for some reason, and hers is."

*It lacked only that, it really did,* Ria thought. She also thought about ordering him to send Kayla right back on Lady Day, reckoned the odds of that actually happening, took a deep breath, and banished the problem of Kayla from her thoughts before she spoke.

"I'll do everything I can," Ria said. "I wish I could promise, but the two of them—Horn and Fairchild—seem to have their hooks into things pretty deeply down there—and now we know why." Something else occurred to her, as she allowed her head to shift into the twisty paths that the Unseleighe—and, come to think of it, government officials—usually took. "And Eric . . . you *do* realize that Horn might have known that Ace was listening to the original conversation all along and just *lied* to Billy, knowing that Ace would overhear it?"

There was a stunned silence from the other end of the line. No, obviously Eric hadn't considered anything like that. But Eric hadn't grown up as a pawn of Perenor's plots and counterplots.

"But he told us the same thing when we were his prisoners," Eric said blankly. "It has to be true. And no matter what . . . we can't just ignore it."

*No, we can't. No sane person could. But the Sidhe, especially the Unseleighe Court, aren't sane by any definition of the World Above. Certainly Gabrevys would lie to someone he was preparing to kill. Certainly he'd want to put Ace in the position of having to go to the police with the story that her father was involved in a plot to blow up his own casino. And certainly he'd like to take me out of the game now by making me cry "wolf" in this spectacularly public fashion about something that turns out not to be true. . . . And certainly he is capable of thinking of a hundred plots and counterplots on the spur of the moment. Nothing is too tangled a web for him to weave.*

*But we don't dare take the chance he's bluffing. . . .*

"I'll do as much as I can do from here," Ria said. "But this time, Eric . . . I can't make any guarantees." She thought for a moment. "Where are you? Do you want me to send a car for you?"

She could almost feel him grin, ruefully.

"Actually, I'm not sure where we are—but I *am* sure it wouldn't be a good idea for us to stay here long enough for your car to get here. We managed to out-think the Unseleighe so far, but I'm sure Gabrevys has plenty of plain old mortals on his payroll, too. His guys went away when they couldn't get past the Cold Iron box we were hiding in, but they know where they left us. We need to haul ass away from here before they decide to wake up a mortal or three and send them with shotguns. Lady Day can get us back to the Garden State Parkway, and we'll do our best to get back to Atlantic City from there. Maybe there's some place around here we can rent a car."

"Or steal one." Ria laughed. "Good luck in convincing your elvensteed to become a charabanc. And . . . be careful."

"I'm always careful," Eric said virtuously.

# CHAPTER 9:
## COUNTIN' ON A MIRACLE

"The first thing we have to do is get out of here," Eric said, handing the phone back to Kayla. "What I told Ria was right; it'll take time for Gabrevys's flunkies to get back, roust out mortal thugs, and send them here, but they do know where they left us, and as far as they know, we've got no way to leave in a hurry."

"We could always walk," Kayla said, regarding Lady Day cynically as she stuffed the phone back into her backpack. "I don't see her turning into a stretch-cycle. And even if she could, we'd kind of attract attention."

"Can't that thing, um, turn into other things?" Magnus said, surprising Eric. "Besides a bike, I mean." He hadn't thought that Magnus had been paying that much attention to the Otherworldly aspects of Eric's life—willingly or otherwise.

"Within limits," Eric agreed. "She did a car once, but it was a pretty small car. I'm not really sure she can turn into something big enough to hold five of us."

"And a dog," Kayla added.

Molly trotted back over to Lady Day to sniff at her front tire in a speculative fashion. Lady Day responded with a loud engine howl, and flashed her lights menacingly. The pug—not particularly daunted—scuttled backward, barking cheerfully.

"Whatever she's going to do, could she do it soon?" Ace begged. "Because I don't know how far we are from Atlantic City, but I'm sure you're right. Mr. Horn already knows he's got to send somebody else after us, and they're probably already on their way."

"C'mon, sweetie," Eric said to the elvensteed. "The five of us really need to get out of here, and you're our only way. Gabrevys isn't going to be happy that we got away from his knights. I need you to turn into something that will carry all of us."

The moment the words were out of his mouth, he *knew* he should have been more specific. Lady Day shivered all over, there was a kind of blurring around her, and suddenly, in place of the cream-and-red touring bike, there was . . .

"What's that?" Magnus asked after a long moment. "It looks like a Volkswagen. But . . . not. Um. A whole lot of not. Is there room in it for an engine?"

"Real impressive, Banyon," Kayla drawled.

"It's a Citroen," Eric said, inspecting the folding windows. "Just be glad she didn't pick a Reliant Robin." The goggle-eyed red-and-cream car—almost small enough to have fit into the Cadillac's trunk—*did* vaguely resemble a mutant Volkswagen. Fortunately Lady Day only *looked* like a Citroen; they wouldn't have to deal with the little French car's notoriously underpowered two-cylinder engine. Since she was still herself, there didn't have to be room for an engine. And with the rag-top down, they could all fit inside. Barely.

"Pleased with yourself, aren't you?" Eric said to the elvensteed. This was probably her revenge for his telling her to leave him and Magnus with the Unseleighe. But—yes, it could have been worse. She could easily have picked a Reliant Robin.

Lady Day flashed her headlights in her equivalent of uproarious laughter. Eric sighed inwardly. His fault for not being more specific, but on the other hand, she really couldn't turn into something much larger than this, so there was no point in wishing for something like, say, a Jeep Cherokee. There was a kind of mass limit, apparently—though one or two of the Sun-Descending and Fairgrove Sidhe had elvensteeds that could, and did, reliably replicate real sports cars.

Maybe it was an available power thing. Maybe it had something to do with seniority. Or rank. Or the fact that he wasn't Sidhe.

"Pile in, folks," Eric said with a sigh.

"Shotgun," Kayla said instantly.

They backtracked to the Garden State Parkway South entrance, and headed along it, looking for the nearest exit that would lead them to the northbound Parkway.

It wasn't the most comfortable ride Eric had ever gotten from his elvensteed. Even though there was no engine in the engine-compartment so he actually had somewhere to put his legs (and so did Kayla) it was still like being crammed into Big Pink's trunk. With the driver's seat pushed all the way forward to give the three jammed into the Citroen's miniscule back seat as much room as possible—and one of them was Hosea, who was *not* a small man—he felt as if the steering wheel was going to wear a groove in his hips, just to begin with. Plus, there was the fact that he was freezing: Lady Day's version of the Citroen's heating system was, Eric suspected, far better than the real thing, but even though it was turned up full-blast, it couldn't quite compensate for the fact that March was not convertible weather here on the Jersey Shore.

If Kayla weren't a touch-Empath, it would have made more sense for her to have been in the back seat with Ace and Magnus, but as wound up as the two of them were, Eric was sure it was pushing the limits of her shields just to be this close to them. Sitting in their laps would have been intolerable. And unfortunately, she wasn't wearing anything that would actually insulate her from them. He vowed to get her a set of silk long johns as soon as possible.

While neither Ace nor Hosea were complaining, Magnus was more than making up for their silence. And, sad as it was, the wind of their travel was not drowning him out, not completely. According to Magnus, the trunk of the Cadillac had been roomier.

At least, sandwiched between Hosea and Ace, he didn't have

to worry about freezing, though of the five of them, he was the only one not dressed for the weather. Eric had been kidnapped from the back of his bike; Kayla had been out walking Molly when she'd jumped into Lady Day's saddle; and both Ace and Hosea had been wearing winter coats when they'd had to make a run for it, but Magnus had been kidnapped out of his classroom at Coenties and Arundel, and all he was wearing was his school blazer (the tie had gotten lost somewhere along the way).

However, when Magnus was complaining about things, Eric had long since learned, he wasn't either particularly hurt or particularly upset, and Eric let his brother's griping go pretty much in one ear and out the other while he worried about more immediate—and more urgent—problems. It was probably Magnus's way of coping with things. Ace wasn't telling him to shut up, so she must have gotten used to it.

Besides the discomfort of all of the passengers, he could feel Lady Day's uneasiness as well. The strain of carrying five passengers (and a dog, Eric footnoted mentally) was telling on her. Elvensteeds were enormously strong, and had incredible stamina, but they had peculiar limitations as well. Maybe it did have something to do with the fact that he wasn't Sidhe. She could run as a bike from here to the coast and back, but stretching into this form was draining her. No matter how much he wanted to get back to Atlantic City quickly—and no matter how convenient it would be for all of them (if cramped) if they could simply *drive* there in Eric's elvensteed, he had to let Lady Day revert to her elvenbike form as soon as possible. And evidently, in this shape, she couldn't ramp up to the warp-speed that would get them there in minutes.

He found an exit and took it, anxious for her, anxious to get back to the Ministry, anxious—hell, beginning a quiet panic—about what they'd find when they got there. Fortunately, the on-ramp for the northbound GSP was clearly marked, and almost as soon as they got on, he saw a sign for a rest stop a couple of miles ahead. *Food Gas*, it said. Presumably the former wouldn't give you the latter.

*That's it. We'll have to find another way from here.*

They pulled into the rest stop. Fortunately, at this hour of the morning—not even seven yet, and on a Friday—the place was fairly deserted. Eric was relieved to see that it was a "full service" stop with the usual road food places: a Nathan's, a TCBY/Dunkin' Donuts, and a McDonald's, in addition to the gas-station mini-mart. The world might be coming to an end, but he really couldn't remember the last time he'd eaten anything, and his stomach was assuring him it was more than time to fuel up. And if he felt that way, the teenagers—and certainly Hosea, who ate more than anyone he'd ever seen before—must be feeling as if their stomachs were in too-close proximity to their backbones.

"Everybody out," he said. He pulled out his wallet and handed Magnus several twenties as soon as his brother had squirmed free of the back seat. "Go get some breakfast."

Magnus didn't have to be told twice. He took the cash and headed for the Mickey D's. The others followed. Come rain, come shine, come the end of the world, a teenager was going to want fries and a coke.

Kayla stayed behind, proving that her teenage years were behind her—somewhat. "What about you, Bard-boy?"

"Gonna see a man about a bike," Eric said.

Lady Day was perfectly capable of driving on her own, but just because the rest stop was mostly deserted didn't mean it was completely deserted, and he didn't really want an audience for what was about to happen. Eric drove around the back of the buildings, looking for more privacy.

He got out of the Citroen, and almost before he could close the tiny clown-car door, Lady Day shuddered and resumed her preferred form. Eric would have been willing to swear that the elvensteed gave an audible sigh of relief at the transformation. He patted her gas-tank sympathetically. "I'm sorry, girl," he said apologetically. "We'll find another ride. I won't put you through any more of that."

But now what? They were stuck in a rest stop a long way from Atlantic City without any practical way of getting back there quickly. Certainly Eric could call Ria from here and see if she could get a car to them, but the same things that had kept him from asking her to do that back where they'd been stranded still held. Getting a car to them would probably take hours, and Eric suspected they didn't have hours—either to stay ahead of Gabrevys's hunters, or to do what they could to make sure that what he planned didn't happen. If there was no other way, he'd ferry the others up the Parkway one by one, but he'd really prefer to find another solution. Running Lady Day at warp would probably leave a magical signature, and besides, that would be splitting the party. If there was one thing that bad horror movies and the occasional RPG had taught him—not to mention practical experience—it was this: never, ever, under any circumstances, split up the party. Do that, and the bad guys always got you.

Maybe something would come to him.

He left Lady Day parked behind the building and walked back to the McDonald's. When he got there, to his surprise, Kayla was standing out front, Molly cradled in her arms. At his puzzled look, she shrugged.

"Dogs. Restaurants. Not a good mix. We're not in France, you know, Banyon. Too-Tall said he'd bring us out something, an' there's tables over there. We'll manage."

"Hey, it's way too cold to eat outside, and I bet Molly's a lot cleaner than half the patrons. I bet if you bring her inside nobody'll notice her." And a touch of Bardic Magick would make certain of it. He winked at her, and raised his eyebrows significantly. "They'll probably look right past her."

*Cellophane, Mister Cellophane, should'a been my name . . .*

Kayla grinned, and Molly panted. "Guess we're in France after all, hotshot."

Eric held the door for her, and she followed him in. Whoever would have thought that a musical about gangsters would come in so handy?

Ace was holding down a table while the other two were at the counter ordering for all of them. Eric and Kayla sat down, with Kayla holding Molly on her lap. Just as he'd promised, nobody gave Molly a second glance. In fact, as the song promised, they looked right through her.

"Is your bike okay?" Ace asked. She must have picked up on his anxiety. Then again, she was a lot more sensitive to body language than the average teenager. Say, Magnus.

"She's fine," Eric said, and shrugged. "Unfortunately, she can't take the five of us any farther than this. It's just too hard on her."

When the others arrived at the table with breakfast, they convened an impromptu council of war. First casting a spell, this time using the "Uncle Ernie" song from the Who's musical *Tommy* to make certain they couldn't be overheard—though any strangers overhearing their conversation would probably think they were a bunch of gamers—Eric told the others everything he'd learned from Ria.

"—so while she'll do what she can, she can't be sure that Horn won't be two jumps ahead of her all the way. Or that the whole thing isn't some sort of long, complicated Unseleighe trap to rope Ace in," Eric finished. He shook his head. "That's the trouble with dealing with the Unseleighe. Everything is complicated with them, and they've had centuries to learn how to make really tortuous plans."

"So it might just all be up to us, is what you're saying," Kayla said, looking both discouraged and stubborn at the same time.

"Could be," Eric answered reluctantly. He hated the fact that this was the only answer he had to give, but it was. Sitting here, in this utterly *normal* place, he had absolutely no idea how he and Hosea could possibly find Prince Gabrevys's bomb and neutralize it, let alone solve all the other problems that an Unseleighe Prince who'd become the best buddy of a power-mad televangelist cozying up to a bunch of White Supremacists represented. *If this was a TV show, Ria and her private army would be showing up about now. Instead we've got two teenagers, a couple of musicians and an Empathic Healer. And not one of us is a MacGyver.*

He supposed they'd have to wing it. As usual. He was getting awfully tired of the universe throwing its problems at him and expecting him to solve them.

"So all we have to do is actually get back there," Hosea said. "And right smartly at that, since the concert's going to start around noon, from what Mr. Horn told me. Pity it's a mite too far to walk in the time we have." His brows furrowed as he spoke; he wasn't being ironic. Eric had the feeling that he was perfectly prepared to try to hoof it back.

"An' too bad we've all got such high moral principles we can't just steal a car—not that there's all that many of them around here to boost just now," Kayla added. "Of course, the fact that none of us know how to hotwire anything that isn't fifteen years old probably doesn't help." She raised an eyebrow at Eric. "Unless that Bardic magic can disable a car alarm and get it moving without a key?"

"Not without knowing a lot more about cars than I do," he admitted. "The magic can only do what I tell it to, and I have to know what I'm doing first."

"So how *are* we going to get there now that your ride's punked out on us?" Magnus asked.

There was an awkward silence. The best answer Eric had been able to come up with so far was riding to the nearest town and renting a car—only he didn't know where the nearest town with a rental place was, or how long it would take. "Rent something?" He had a vague recollection of a rental company that came to pick you up . . . if only he could remember which one it was. And if there was one close enough.

"Well," Ace said, "can't we just hitchhike back?"

The others stared at her in surprise.

"Five of us?" Kayla asked doubtfully.

*And a dog,* Eric thought. *Don't forget the dog.*

"That's got to be one of your dumber ideas," Magnus finally said. Ace's face hardened, but her expression was the kind that a tough little girl took on when she'd been hurt. Eric tried to kick him under the table, but he couldn't reach him.

"We can ask," Ace said stubbornly, her chin set. "We can do that." She got to her feet and walked out. "How's it hurt?"

"Time to drain the dog," Kayla said instantly, and followed, Molly in her arms. Considering that Molly'd made a second breakfast off most of an Egg McMuffin plus a whole hash brown patty, Eric thought walking the dog might be a really, *really* good idea. Not to mention that it would be a good idea for someone to go with Ace.

Hosea gave Eric one of those meaningful-yet-inscrutable looks the Ozark Bard was so very good at and said he'd see if Ace needed any help.

That left Eric alone with Magnus. And from Magnus's sullen expression, he was pretty sure Magnus thought he was in for a lecture on manners.

Only Eric had gotten every lecture in the mythical book on manners himself—from his parents. And if he'd gotten them, Magnus had certainly gotten them. Probably twice over, since the 'rents had figured they hadn't filled Eric's ears nearly enough.

So he wasn't going to do that.

"If you don't like her any more, you don't have to see her again once we get back to New York," he said instead, pretending that he thought Magnus's rudeness was due entirely to dislike rather than teenage-male stupidity. *Oh yeah. I remember being that stupid.* "Just try to hold it together until then—I mean, assuming we all live that long—because she's had it pretty rough lately. She could stand a lot of kindness about now, or I think she might crack up on us." *And if she goes to pieces, I'm not actually sure I can put her back together. And for that matter, if she goes to pieces in a Talented kind of way, she could take the rest of us with her without much problem, from what I've seen so far.* "I know things have been rough on you, too, but—well," he shrugged. "You're a guy. You're tough."

That actually got Magnus's attention. "Don't *like* her?" he said, surprised, then demanded. "Why wouldn't I like her?"

"I don't know," Eric said carefully—Magnus's emotions ran close to the surface at the best of times, and they'd been rubbed especially raw by the news that his parents had hired Unseleighe Mages—knowingly or not—to turn him into a mindless vegetable. "But it's possible that she might have just gotten the idea that you don't like her. I've done a lot more dating than you have—" Kathi, and Traci, and Donna, and just before he got mixed up with Kory, there'd been the spectacular melt-down with Maureen "—and the one thing I know for sure about ladies of any age is that they kind of hate being called 'stupid.'"

Magnus thought that over for a while, while he finished the

extra-large chocolate shake he'd ordered to go with breakfast. "I didn't call Ace 'stupid,'" he finally said. "I said her *idea* was stupid."

Eric winced mentally. "Well," he said mildly, "she really might not like that much either right now. And the way she's feeling, well, if you say things like that, she's gonna be oversensitive, and she'll take it to mean you're talking about her."

"It *is* a stupid idea," Magnus said stubbornly. "Nobody's going to give a ride to five whackos and a dog."

"Maybe not," Eric agreed, trying to resist the urge to slug his brother. "I admit it doesn't sound very likely. But Lady Day can't carry the five of us at once, I'm not sure how fast Ria could get a car here—or I could get a car—and I really can't think of anything better right off hand than asking around to see if someone will give us a ride. What's it going to hurt? If that doesn't work, we'll try something else."

Magnus stared down at the table and began to tear a napkin into tiny strips. Eric had a good idea that Ace's idea of hitching wasn't really the issue here. And in a moment, Magnus confirmed that.

"They hired those guys," he said quietly. "To suck out our brains and turn us into robot-kid-zombies."

That was what was really bothering his brother. Eric understood, and sympathized. He himself had had almost two decades to come to terms with how their parents had treated him, so this was only another drop in the bucket. For Magnus, it was different—and much more immediate, in a way.

"They didn't know what they were doing," Eric said quickly, hoping, in a way, to soften the blow.

"No, Eric," Magnus said, gazing up at him with those disconcerting green eyes. He sounded chillingly adult, as if it were he, not Eric, who was the many-years-elder. "That's the whole point. They knew exactly *what* they were doing. What they didn't know was *how*. They didn't know it was going to involve woo-woo magic and alien brain-eating monsters, sure. I betcha they didn't think too hard about what was going to go on, but if you put a gun to either of their heads and they *had* to take a wild-ass guess, they'd say, hey, maybe drugs, maybe some new and exciting form of lobotomy-lite. And yeah, kidnapping. We can't forget that. That was in the plan from the start and they knew exactly what they were doing when they signed on for that. But they would have said it was all worth it because it was all going to be so *convenient* once all the messy stuff was over with. 'Just don't bother me with the inconvenient details that I'll have to work hard to forget later.'"

The depth of bitterness in Magnus's voice was something Eric had no words for. Had he ever felt such bitterness, such—not even hate, but despair? He didn't think so—no, it seemed to him that he'd been thinking about other things entirely. Fear of the Night-flyers, and fear for his own sanity had trumped everything else. He'd been thinking more about running away—and just plain not thinking—than thinking about his parents. Then he'd been thinking about keeping food in his belly, and then—quite quickly, actually, once he'd discovered the Rennies and the busking in L.A., he'd been mostly thinking about playing music and having sex and getting high, and not necessarily in that order. But Magnus didn't have those things to worry about, and except for that short stint on the streets, never had. He'd been able to concentrate on his relationship with his parents to the exclusion of all else.

And Eric couldn't say Magnus had drawn the wrong conclusions, either. Their parents *had* hired Christian Family Intervention to get Magnus back—and not just to get him back, but to return him to them docile and obedient. To return *both* Magnus and Eric in that condition, in fact. They hadn't asked how CFI was going to accomplish this. They hadn't asked any of the questions that people who cared about anything but their own way would ask.

And at last, Eric felt—cold. And angry. And for one moment he wanted—

But no. The anger of a Bard could kill. No matter what they deserved, it wouldn't be his hands that dealt the cards. Karma could come back to bite their asses on its own. The best revenge he could get would be the one he was taking now; to remove himself and Magnus from their control forever, and let them stew in their own juices.

"Yeah," Eric said softly, "you're right. And that sucks. And the only good thing about any of this is that the fact that they kidnapped you is going to be great for our custody case if we can figure out how to use it. Just . . . don't beat Ace up over it, okay? Watch who's in your backlash. Save it for the people who deserve it. Think how they're gonna look when you tell the judge all about this."

"Yeah, okay," Magnus muttered, tearing the napkin into further tiny strips. By now he had what looked like an enormous mound of confetti in front of him. "I guess I'll go tell her she isn't stupid, okay?"

*I hope she takes that in the spirit that it's intended.* "Yeah," Eric said. "That would be a good start."

When they got outside, Eric walked around a bit, looking for the others. He finally located Ace over by the gas pumps, talking to a man standing in the back door of a Winnebago that was pulled up to the pumps.

He ambled over in that direction. As he got closer, he could see that the 'bago had been custom-painted on the side, with the legend "Wild Bill's Geese." But instead of the wildlife picture Eric expected to go along with something like that, there was a design of a gold laurel crown surrounding a sable oval on which was placed a gold spearhead, point up.

Now, Eric was familiar with both SCAdians and Rennies, and this didn't look like anything that either of those groups would have painted on the side of an RV. And while there were a fair number of SCAdians who were getting long in the tooth these days, he didn't think too many of them were collecting Social Security.

Besides, there were none of the other medievaloid trappings that the SCAdians tended to bedeck their vehicles with. No "I Stop For Dragons" bumper stickers, no rack of rattan weapons tied to the back, or pavilion lashed down to the top. In fact, the bit of art had a sort of military precision about it, as if it was some sort of insignia.

*Okay. That's a little freaky,* Eric thought. *Those geese must be really fighting back.*

The man was quite old—Eric judged him to be well over eighty—and his skin was dappled with the spots of age. He held himself erect with the aid of an aluminum cane. What little hair he had left was snow white. But for all the fragility of age, there was a vitality and good humor about him that made Eric smile in spite of his current problems. And he was treating Ace with gentlemanly courtesy that was, at the same time, not at all condescending.

"Eric!" Ace called, waving at him. "This is Mr Jedburgh. He and his son are going up to Atlantic City to see a show, and he says he'd be more than happy to give all of us a ride."

Eric approached, trying to get more of a feel for the man, and getting nothing but good vibrations. "Not a problem, sonny," Jedburgh said. "I had more than one set of wheels, ah, give out on me in my time. Always at the worst possible moment, too. There are five of you, the young lady said?"

"And a dog," Eric said.

"Always liked dogs. Adam Jedburgh, at your service, as the young lady told you," he added, holding out his hand.

"Eric Banyon. This is my—" Whoops! He caught himself just in time, and finished smoothly " son, Magnus." It wouldn't do to blow his cover story now. They had to live with it all the time, not just in the courtroom.

Eric shook the proffered hand. For all the man's age, his grip was dry and firm.

"You look a little young to have a son that age," Adam Jedburgh said shrewdly. "I'd have taken you for brothers."

"I'm a youthful indiscretion," Magnus said promptly.

"Very youthful, and very indiscreet," Eric said, with a grin. "Thank you very much, Mr. Jedburgh. We really appreciate this. Ace, Magnus, you stay here, and I'll go round up Hosea and Kayla. I'll be back in a minute." And that would give him a little time out of sight to toss a bit of *glamourie* over himself so he looked a bit closer to the age he ought to be by the World's Time.

"Don't dawdle. Slot machines wait for no man," Adam Jedburgh called cheerfully after him.

Eric found Kayla and Hosea over in the designated dog-walking area. Hosea had Jeanette slung over his back in her soft carry-case, and Kayla had the end of Molly's red-leather leash looped over her wrist as the pug wandered aimlessly about. She glanced up as Eric approached, her gaze turning expectant as she saw his expression.

"Believe it or not, Ace found us a ride," Eric said. "Not just that, but a comfortable and friendly ride."

Hosea grinned. "She said she'd do better at it without me around to scare people off, and Ah guess she was right after all."

Kayla grinned. "Girl power!"

Eric shrugged. "Something like that, I guess."

"Let's go, then," Kayla said. "Come on, Molly. Manners."

When they got back, the Winnebago had pulled up past the pumps and was waiting among the parked eighteen-wheelers. Another man—a younger version of Adam—climbed down from the driver's side door and walked back toward them.

"I'm Douglas Jedburgh, Adam's son. Is this the rest of you?" He looked friendly, but cautious. Eric didn't blame him. He was taking a risk, no matter what his father had promised. Five strangers, three of them young men—could be trouble.

Then again—five strangers and a pug? Not the kind of combination you expected to be pulling carjackings. . . .

Molly barked cheerfully and he reached down to ruffle her ears.

"This is all of us," Eric agreed. "I'm Eric, this is Kayla and Hosea. You've already met my son"—he'd nearly tripped himself up again, and once again, caught himself at the last moment—"Magnus, and Ace. We're really grateful for the ride."

"Well, we were going that way anyway. Dad said I should get out of the house and stop moping just because Mary wasn't there, and he wanted to see the fleshpots—we're from Minnesota, you see," he added, as if that explained everything. "Normally I wouldn't pick up hitchhikers, but Dad's a good judge of character. He's had to be."

Eric glanced sideways at Kayla. She looked perfectly serene. Whatever had motivated Douglas and his father to take off for the wicked city, it wasn't Douglas's grieving widowhood, though that would be a reasonable guess for a man his age. So the wife probably wasn't "the late."

"So where *is* your wife?" Eric asked. "If I'm not being too nosy."

"Well, I did lay myself open to the question. Climb on in and we'll get moving. Dad'll be happy to answer it in great detail."

As they walked up to the RV, Eric saw Hosea blink in startlement at the design on the side, but the big man climbed in without comment, and Eric and Kayla followed, climbing in through the middle door.

A lot of the more well-off Rennies Eric had known had possessed RVs. Some of them had gutted the insides and completely redone them. Some of them had left them pretty much the way they were. They'd run the gamut from shabby-but-serviceable to works of art, like Suleika the dancer's vintage Airstream trailer.

This one had a military neatness to it. While obviously several years old, well-used and well-loved, everything was well-cared-for and in its place. The cabinets were secured with widgets to keep the doors from flying open accidentally when the RV was moving, and seatbelts—bolted to the frame of the vehicle—had been added to the couches in case of extra passengers.

"Belt up and we'll get rolling. It's going to take us at least ninety minutes to get to Atlantic City," Douglas Jedburgh said. When he'd heard the clicking of seatbelts, he shifted into gear, and pulled out onto the access road leading to the Parkway.

*Follow us and don't be seen*, Eric told Lady Day silently, and felt the elvensteed's equally silent assent.

Driving an RV was like driving a small house, and it accelerated about as well. But by the same token, it was pretty hard to miss, so they weren't really in any danger of being hit, and fairly soon they'd reached cruising speed.

"He was asking where Mary was," Douglas said to his father companionably.

"You were complaining again," Adam Jedburgh corrected him good-naturedly. He turned his seat—the passenger seat in the Winnebago could turn to face the back—and grinned cheerfully at Eric. "This young feller was going to sit around the house and mope for six weeks just because Mary was off helping Kimberly bring my great-grandbaby into the world and making sure Kimmie had a little help around the place. Oh, it's not that Mason's a bad boy, you understand, for a grandson-in-law, but he's on the road six days out of seven, and Kimmie's at home, and with the new baby, what girl—even a great big grown-up girl that we're all supposed to call 'women' these days from the time they can walk—wouldn't want her mother there to help out and tell her that new babies don't break? So Mary went, and I didn't see any reason for Dougie to sit around the house waiting for her to get back like a retriever pining for duck season when he could be indulging me instead of driving his neighbors crazy. The way he carries on, you'd think Mary'd gone to Heaven instead of Amarillo."

Douglas Jedburgh grinned, but said nothing to contradict his father.

"Boy or girl?" Hosea asked with interest.

"Doctors say she's going to have a boy," Adam said promptly. "We'll know for sure in a week or so. In my day, you had to wait until the baby was born and take what you got."

"Ah guess that's still the way, when you come right down to it," Hosea said. "Ah don't think we've been rightly introduced, sir. Ah'm Hosea Songmaker, and Ah couldn't help but notice what you have painted on the side of your RV. Ah guess you were in the OSS in the war?"

Adam looked surprised, then pleased. "Well, Mr. Songmaker, that's a pretty good guess. Not too many people remember the OSS anymore."

"Didn't have to guess," Hosea said modestly. "Mah grandaddy served with them. Name of Jeb Songmaker."

"Jeb Songmaker!" Adam did a double-take, and a grin spread across his face until it nearly met at the back of his head. "Dougie, this is Jeberechiah Songmaker's grandson! You remember I told you about him!" Adam said excitedly. "Good Lord, Jeb's grandson! Talk about a small world—I never would have thought it!"

"Oh, wow, this is just . . . weird," Kayla said in an undertone.

"The OSS wasn't that large an organization," Eric said. "Not like the CIA is today. It isn't all that unlikely that two agents would know each other." At Magnus's blank look, he explained further. "The OSS was the first American intelligence agency, formed by William Donovan during World War II. At the end of the war, it was replaced by the Central Intelligence Agency."

He was trying to be unobtrusive, but he could have been shouting his explanations for all the attention that Adam was paying to them. No, it was Hosea that had all of his attention. Hardly surprising. Meeting Hosea must make Adam feel as if he was somehow catching up to an old comrade.

"So what happened to Jeb?" Adam asked eagerly. "We lost track of each other—"

"He got through the war right enough," Hosea said, with a nod. "Went on home to his farm—he must of talked about his parcel o' land—and married my gran'ma Dora. My gran'parents had the raisin' of me, but Gran'pa Jeb never did talk much about what he did during the War, leastways not to me."

"I'm glad he got back," Adam Jedburgh said simply. "A lot of good men didn't. I met Jeb during training in England—a long skinny drink of water with a hill-country accent you could cut with a knife. Me, I was there for the same reason a lot of other guys were: German had been the first language in my house growing up, and I spoke it like Uncle Adolf's brother."

"Dad—" Douglas Jedburgh said warningly.

"Dougie, I'm too old to change my spots. Oh, I know, I know: we won the war and they're all our friends now, and every one of them is a Good German. But they weren't then. Or do you think I'm boring our guests?"

"Please," Eric said quickly. "Nobody's bored. And we'd all like to hear about this." It *was* fascinating—how often did you get a chance to listen to living history? Especially living *secret* history; a lot of what the OSS did was still under lock and key. Besides, this had to be good for Adam Jedburgh, to find out what had happened to an old friend. And if Adam Jedburgh was talking, neither he nor his son would be asking awkward questions about Eric and his friends—questions they might not be able to answer.

He'd already come close to slipping up twice over Magnus, and none of them had known they'd need a cover story.

"There. You see? *As* I was saying, there was Jeberechiah, looking like he'd never had shoes on before in his life—no offense, Hosea, but back in '41, a lot of kids joined up who'd never been off the farm and still had straw in their hair, and your granddaddy looked like a prime example—with his old violin and an ugly yellow dog that none of us knew how he'd managed to smuggle onto the troopship, let alone get it onto the base, but there it was, and an accent that just about ensured he'd be shot the moment he set foot anywhere in Europe—and as far as any of us knew, he didn't speak a word of anything but English, and that not very well, and I could not imagine how he had managed to talk his way into Wild Bill's command. I remember one time . . ."

For the next several miles Adam Jedburgh had them all laughing helplessly with anecdotes of clever—and highly trained—young men on the loose in wartime England. Eric wasn't sure how much of these stories to believe, but apparently Jeb Songmaker had been the ringleader in a series of practical jokes that would have put the pranks of any collection of modern college students to shame.

There was the still-fondly-remembered incident of the local farmer's prize cow smuggled into the colonel's office.

The exceptionally-well-concealed (and exceptionally productive) still.

The exploding mashed potatoes.

The night maneuvers that had left the "enemy" searching for them all night in a freezing downpour while Jeb's team had spent the night sleeping warmly in a barn ten miles outside the combat area—and sitting down to a good country breakfast cooked by the farmer's wife in the morning.

But one thing puzzled Adam Jedburgh greatly, and he returned to it once more.

"Thing was, if Jeb Songmaker was with us in England, he had to be heading for somewhere in the European Theater. And he had to have already gotten through our training course back home. Well, I worried about how he was going to manage. There was no way he was going to sound like anything but a GI Joe—heck—begging your pardon, girls—the local folks could barely understand a word he said, he came from that far back in the hills—and that wasn't going to do him any good east of Calais. I tried to teach him enough German to get by, but it was hopeless. So one night when we were down at the local pub, I asked him what he was going to do if he had to talk to anybody over there. And he said, in that country twang of his, 'I'll get by.' "

The old man shook his head, obviously still unable to believe it even after all these years. "And I guess he did, because he always came back, no matter where they sent him."

"But Ah guess you lost touch with him?" Hosea asked.

"Oh," Adam said off-handedly, "I went over to France to help out the Resistance, and I decided to stay for a while. We had to do a little improvising when our supplies ran out, but our biggest hole-card against Johnny Boche was always laughter. The one thing fascists of all stripes hate most is being ridiculed, and we found out that we could do as much damage if we could make people laugh at them as by blowing something up. I owe that lesson to your grandfather, Hosea, and I'm happy to be able to pay it back, even in this little way."

They'd been seeing signs for Atlantic City for the last several miles, but now they were starting to get close.

"Well," Adam said, after clearing his throat and glancing at an exit sign, "looks like we're about to drink that parting glass, so to speak."

"We're staying at the Trump Taj Mahal—Dad says if you're going to go to the devil, you might as well do it up brown," Douglas Jedburgh said with a small smile. "We could take you there—or is there some other place we could drop you?"

Eric had been thinking about how to answer that one for almost an hour. "You can just drop us at any parking lot along the way that's convenient, thanks. We can call a cab from there." That much was perfectly true—they *did* intend to call a cab—and a touch of Bardic Magick encouraged their Good Samaritans not to ask any of the obvious questions, like where their hotel was, and why they shouldn't just drop them there.

Going back to Ace and Hosea's hotel room would have been logical and easy—but it was also fairly likely that it was staked out by goons either mortal or Unseleighe.

"You're sure you'll be okay?" Douglas Jedburgh asked.

"They're sure, Dougie," Adam told his son firmly. "Probably can't wait to get away from all your chatter," he added, winking at them. "But if you need anything else, you come around to the Taj Mahal and ask for Adam Jedburgh. Dougie and I will be there for a week, seeing the sights before we head on down to Texas. Figure we'll give Mary and Kimmie a little surprise and I'll get an early look at my great-grand-baby."

"We'll do that, sir," Hosea said. "Iff'n there's need. That's a promise. An' here—" He paused to fish in his pocket, and came up with one of the business cards Eric had insisted he have printed up. *Because you never know when you'll need one.* It looked good to have them when you were busking, and better still to have them in case someone actually might offer you a gig. They were simple enough, just his name, a phone number and address, and *Musician: blue-grass, country, and folk.* "You cain always get ahold of me here."

Eric sighed with relief. This was even better. Hosea had just proved that they had permanent addresses. Adam would be a lot less curious now.

"Well, good," Adam said firmly. "Wild Bill's Geese stick together, and that goes for their families as well."

A few minutes later, Douglas Jedburgh found a place to stop, and expertly maneuvered the Winnebago into a strip-mall parking lot. He stopped the RV, and the five of them got out.

As he drove away, Kayla turned to Hosea. "You know the weirdest people," she said, setting Molly down.

"Ah wasn't the one who knew him, but mah gran'pappy. Ah guess it was in the family, though," Hosea said reasonably. "Ah sort of suspected things might fall out that way when Ah saw what was painted on the side of the RV. Gran'pa didn't talk about the war all so very much, but he did have his unit patch, an' it looked just like that. They weren't authorized, and they were all supposed to be destroyed, but Ah guess one or two of them got away."

"He was there to help us when we needed help," Ace said, as if she were pronouncing a sort of judgment.

Magnus sighed. "It wasn't a dumb idea, okay. But it *was* kind of a long shot."

Ace smiled at him. Apparently he was forgiven. "Sometimes you just have to take a chance."

Just then there was a faint flurry in the air. Suddenly a cream-and-red touring bike of no exact make sat parked in an empty parking slot a few feet away.

"Took you long enough to get here," Eric said to the elven-steed.

"Now what?" Kayla asked.

"We call that cab," Eric said. "And we head back out to the cathedral and casino. If we can't do anything else to stop what's happening there today, we can at least make sure that Gabriel's bomb doesn't go off."

*I hope.*

"At least we can make sure we get everybody cleared out before it does," Ace said, with the same finality. "Somehow."

The taxi arrived promptly—the first thing that had gone completely right in quite a while—and the driver had no objection to taking Molly as a passenger. The four (five) of them rode in the taxi while Eric followed on Lady Day.

By the time they reached the road that led toward the Heavenly Grace Business Park, it was a little after eleven o'clock. Traffic was heavy—all apparently on its way to the concert—and a lot of the cars had bumper stickers like "Keep America Pure" and "White is Right" on them, and symbols that were almost—but not quite, of course—Nazi flags.

They were still at least five miles from the gates, but traffic had already slowed to a crawl. Eric stood up in his seat and looked ahead—he could already see people just giving up and starting to pull off on the verge and park. Soon traffic wouldn't just be slow, it would be stopped entirely.

No matter what Magnus thought, Eric wasn't quite old enough to have been at Woodstock I, but nobody of any age could have missed the endless retrospectives of the event, so Eric was perfectly aware of how snarled the traffic around a big outdoor concert—especially one that really *was* free—could get. Very soon now the cars weren't going to pull off to the side of the road to park. Their drivers were just going to abandon them in the middle of the road and start walking in to the concert, and then the fun would *really* begin.

He flagged the taxi down and pointed for the driver to pull off. Fortunately there was a cross-street ahead; he saw Kayla speak to the driver, who turned into it—a better idea than Eric's—and stopped.

Eric pulled up beside the driver's side window.

"I had no idea the traffic was so heavy," he said, digging into his jeans for his wallet. "You'd better turn back. We'll walk from here."

The others, taking their cue from him, began piling out. Eric added a generous tip to the amount on the meter. It wasn't going to be easy getting out of here.

The driver must have agreed, for instead of turning around, he simply drove off down the road in the direction he was headed.

"And once more I say, 'now what?'" Kayla said, when they were all standing on the side of the road.

"We walk in. I'm sure it won't be the first time you snuck into a rock-concert," Eric said.

"Yeah, Bard-boy, but it's definitely going to be the first time I snuck into a Neo-Nazi rock concert. Did you see some of those bumper stickers?" Kayla answered.

Eric simply shuddered. New York might be the most cosmopolitan city on Earth, but there were a few things its inhabitants were insulated from. And now it finally started to feel real. He found himself clenching and unclenching his fists, and he was getting the beginning of the cold he always got in his belly at the start of a fight.

A fight. And he was taking Ace and Magnus, both utterly unacquainted with fighting, into the middle of it. And Kayla, utterly unsuited.

But if he stopped to ask himself what he thought he was doing—he would stop. And so would they.

And people would die.

"Are you going to be okay if we go in there?" Eric asked.

Kayla shrugged. "Unless I run into one of your heavy hitters, I'm going to be more than fine. That's the really sick thing, Eric. All those people out there right now? They're really happy. They think they're good people surrounded by other good people and having a great time. They just think some other people—blacks or Jews or gays or Muslims or pick your label—have to be killed, or put in camps, or gotten rid of some other way. But most of them don't even hate those people. Not usually. They just think it's their duty, and it's right, and it's sad but it's something that has to be done. And the people that make me want to scream are the ones that convinced them that this is the truth."

"I guess you're going to have to scream later," Eric said. "We'd better start walking. But the minute we get this bomb thing dealt with, I'm going Underhill and coming back with either a good strong leash for Prince Gabrevys or a really good reason why I can't have one."

*As soon as we get this bomb thing dealt with. As if I had any ideas how.*

"Hmph," Hosea grunted. "Ah'm thinkin' if you cain't put a leash on him, Ah'm gonna. An' about now, Ah'm thinkin' it oughtta be made outta Cold Iron."

Eric nodded; he hoped he'd be able to get help from Misthold in dealing with Prince Gabrevys, but he was already considering the possibility that he couldn't. He wasn't sure what he was going to do in that case—the last thing he wanted to do was start a war Underhill, but the next to last thing he wanted was to have to watch his back every moment for the rest of his life just because an Unseleighe Prince had decided to start a vendetta.

"Count me out," Kayla said, shaking her head. "I've had enough of Elf Hill for a lifetime."

*Maybe, Punkette—but Elf Hill has a habit of not letting go.*

They headed back up the road toward the gate, cutting through the traffic as soon as there was a gap. As far as any observers could see, Eric was wheeling his motorcycle along beside them, but in fact, Lady Day was doing all the work, and he was just resting a hand on one of her handlebars.

The closer they got, the colder he became. Because ideas still weren't coming to him.

*Wish we'd been able to ask old Adam for some advice.* Someone from the OSS now—there was someone who would have had some creative notions for this situation.

As they got closer, they started to hear music in the distance—not live, Eric thought; probably something canned being run through the amps on whatever stage was set up.

They were walking right back into the dragon's lair—which was an insult to the few dragons Eric had ever met, none of whom could ever have come up with something this vile—and Eric still didn't have any clear idea of what he was going to do about the problem when he got there. Worst of all, the people he was bringing with him were by no stretch of the imagination a crack commando team.

Kayla was an Empath and Healer. Great after the battle was over, but not a lot of use in a fight. In fact, the fight itself would probably lay her out cold.

Magnus didn't, as far as Eric knew, have any expressed magick at all. He'd been lucky enough to escape with his life once, and now Eric was dragging him right back into danger. The trouble was, there were no safe places—even if Magnus agreed to stay somewhere out of harm's way, it was just as likely that Gabrevys would find him wherever he was and use him as a weapon against Eric and the others. And stashing him somewhere would be splitting the party again. Nope. It was ab-so-lutely guaranteed that if the party got split up, both parts would end up in trouble.

Ace was a powerful Talent, it was true. The only trouble was, her power worked just as irresistibly on her own side as on the other side, and once she'd created an emotion in people, she couldn't direct how they responded to it. In a controlled environment like Billy Fairchild's Praise Hour, that didn't matter. In the chaotic venue of a rock concert, it could matter quite a bit.

Hosea was Eric's apprentice, and a Guardian. Both of those

things counted for a lot, but Eric had no illusions: the magickal muscle they were facing could eat the two of them for breakfast and not even get indigestion. A trained, Unseleighe Master Bard, an Unseleighe Magus Major, and who knew what sorts of allies. Some of which he already knew were resistant to Cold Iron.

*Why are we doing this?* he asked himself. But he knew the answer.

*Because we're the good guys, and we have to try.*

Around them, more and more people were starting to walk in. The line of cars heading toward the gate had slowed to a crawl, moving at barely two miles an hour now. The people on foot were easily outpacing those still in their vehicles.

Kayla picked up Molly and cradled her in her arms. The little pug was gallant and willing, but there was no way she could walk all the way to the casino and cathedral, and she'd only slow them down if they kept to her pace anyway.

"Your purse is ringing," Magnus said to Kayla.

Kayla passed Molly to Ace and dug in her backpack. The ringing sound got louder. She flipped open the phone, and after listening a moment, she passed it to Eric.

"It's for you," she said with a smirk.

"Um . . . hello?" Eric said.

"Where are you?" Ria asked.

*Oh, please tell me you have a crack SWAT army ready to storm this place.*

"A couple of miles up the road from the concert site," Eric said. "The place is jammed. We're walking in."

*Please tell me you want us to turn around and leave.*

"That's the best news I've had all morning," Ria said. "I hope you can do something when you get there."

*You hope we can do something. That is not what I wanted to hear.*

"That doesn't sound good," Eric said. "I don't mean to sound cranky, but weren't you supposed to be calling the cavalry?"

"Put it this way. I've got some good news and some bad news. The good news is that there were a few favors left for me to pull in, and I used them. The bomb squad is all set to go in and take the casino apart."

A familiar sound overhead caught Eric's attention, and he looked up. There were three helicopters in the sky over the casino. Two of them were obviously press. The third one looked a lot more businesslike. Ria's? Or Horn's?

Or someone else's? There was always Wheatley to think about.

"And the bad news?" he asked.

"They can't get in. I don't know what it looks like from where you are, but there are almost five thousand people packed in at the site down there, and Pure Blood, the other bands, and the local bikers and skinheads have got the crowd so worked up about 'Federal persecution,' Waco, and Ruby Ridge, that the sight of anything that even looks like an agent of the government is going to start a full-scale riot. Bottom line: they aren't sure about the bomb, and they *are* sure about the riot. They're talking with someone in the organization about arranging to get a team inside quietly, but that's going to take time."

"And time is what we probably don't have," Eric said grimly. "But they're set to go in?"

"The moment it's clear," Ria said.

"I guess what we have to do is clear it," Eric said. "Thanks, Ria."

"Thank me after they find the bomb," Ria said. "If there is one."

He handed the phone back to Kayla, and summarized Ria's conversation for the others.

"Mr. Horn said he'd hired security, too," Ace said miserably. "*Special* security."

"I guess the Feds aren't going to get in there one minute before he wants them to," Kayla said.

"But we need to get in there now," Hosea said. He dug around in his pocket and produced a brightly colored plastic rectangle on a lanyard; the press-pass Gabriel Horn had given him two days before. He hung it around his neck. "Ah guess if we run into any of that 'special security' of Mr. Horn's, Ah'll tell them Ah'm with the band."

Magnus gave a cynical snort.

Up ahead they could see people climbing over the low wall that separated the business park from the road. It wasn't very high—less than five feet—and more a matter of decoration than security.

"I think that's our cue," Eric said, nodding toward the others.

Hosea boosted the others over the wall—Kayla and Ace first, then Molly, then Magnus and Eric. Then he handed Jeanette over the wall to Eric, then heaved himself over, swinging himself across the top of the wall like an Olympic gymnast working out on the vaulting horse. He dropped lightly to the grass on the other side.

"Hey, what about your bike?" Magnus said.

"She's coming," Eric said. "Look."

For a moment, it seemed a black mare hung poised in the air over the wall, legs outstretched in a leap. Then she landed, neat-footed, and there was only the touring bike again, looking as pleased with itself as a machine could look.

"What if somebody saw that?" Magnus said, sounding scandalized.

"Think they'd believe it?" Kayla asked. "Everybody knows motorcycles don't turn into horses and leap stone walls. And I don't care if these are supposed to be Christian bands, I'll lay you good money more than half this crowd is stoned on something already. Trust me, I'm a Healer, I can tell these things. C'mon, Gus, let's get going."

Eric put a hand on Lady Day's handlebars again. It might make sense for them to split up—it would certainly be faster, and he could take one passenger with him on Lady Day—but now more than ever Eric knew they should stay together. Apart they were too vulnerable. All of them.

*Don't split the party.*

They began to walk as quickly as they could toward the concert venue. The music got louder; an insistent primal beat.

They were moving through crowds of other people, all heading in the same direction. Apparently the cars were being diverted down to the far entrance, because the road that led right past the casino held nothing but pedestrians, and looking back, Eric could see that the casino entrance was blocked with bright yellow sawhorses and cars, and several men wearing black security uniforms were standing around beside the cars. They were letting pedestrians in, but no vehicles. Despite the fact that the road was empty and available, the pedestrians were walking across the lawns and the landscaped areas toward the music. Eric wondered if Billy Fairchild'd had any idea of what he'd been letting himself in for when he'd agreed to host a free concert here. Tomorrow this place was going to look as if it had hosted a tractor-pull, not a concert.

*It's going to look a lot worse than that if you can't pull a rabbit out of your hat, Banyon,* he told himself grimly. By now the ice had taken over his gut and was edging up his spine. Strangely it was not fear. Maybe he'd been in too many fights already for that.

Maybe it was just hubris.

Ria had said that this was a flashpoint crowd on the edge of riot, but Eric neither saw nor sensed any sign of that here on the fringes. The thing it reminded him of most strongly was the Eloi moving toward the Morlock's call: docile, eager, and oblivious.

At least the lack of cars made their progress faster now. They soon drew even with the Casino and Cathedral of Prayer.

To Eric's mage-sight, the building shimmered with darkly scarlet wards so dense and many-layered that the building itself was nearly invisible. From that he could assume that there was, in fact, a bomb inside, but he couldn't sense it. He doubted he could even walk through the door.

He blinked, banishing his Othersight. What he could see with his regular vision didn't look any better. Standing in front of the side door of the building were about a dozen of those skinhead bikers Ria had mentioned, looking armed for bear. Even if they could take the muscle out, they couldn't get into the building—he doubted anyone with the least scrap of Talent could.

He heard Kayla take a sharp breath.

"Oh, god," Ace said in a choked voice, looking up and pointing.

The others looked where she indicated.

There were people, crowds of people, clearly visible at the office windows of the upper stories of the casino and cathedral looking out over the crowd: the casino itself might be closed, but either the rest of Billy Fairchild's empire was open for business, or he'd offered it up as a coign of vantage for those interested in seeing the concert but not mingling with the groundlings.

Eric felt a pang of something too deep for horror. *How many people does Gabrevys need to kill to do whatever it is he's trying to do?* he thought with frustrated indignation. That Gabrevys should try to destroy him and Magnus was almost reasonable in comparison—that was revenge, and revenge was understandable.

But this . . . ? This huge amassing of unnecessary deaths, just because you could—that was pure Unseleighe evil.

Having reached the building, they'd reached the edge of the concert crowd as well. The audience filled the entire space between the clear-space at the foot of the stage—kept clear by more of the biker-Security—and the empty building at the other side of the parking lot. It was one of the original buildings that had been here when Billy had bought the place; a long low building only two stories tall, and just far enough away that none of the audience had yet been tempted to climb up on its roof to get a better view of the bands.

Eric suspected that Ria's estimation of the number of attendees had been conservative. There were a lot more than five thousand people here. Either Billy had underestimated the draw of the bands on the bill when he'd talked to Hosea, or Gabriel Horn had been lying. There might be as many as ten thousand people here already.

The entire parking lot had been cleared of cars. The stage had been set up directly in front of the casino and cathedral—which meant that the giant light-up three-story cross was directly behind it. At the moment the stage was empty, but two giant video screens flanked it, playing music videos.

The stage itself was draped in red, white, and black—instead of blue—and some of the audience were carrying home-made banners and placards. Some of them bore crosses.

Some of them didn't.

"Welcome to Nuremburg," Kayla said to Eric. Her voice was a little slurred; she sounded slightly drunk on the intense emotions of the crowd. "I hope you've got a plan?"

He did. Seeing the crowd, the stage, one had come to him.

"Some people are getting up onto the stage," Hosea reported. "Warm-up band, Ah guess."

"Perfect," Eric said. "Now here's what we do . . ."

# CHAPTER 10:
## WHERE THE BANDS ARE

A band called Lost Angels was deafening the audience—and the five of them—with its second number by the time they had everything they needed.

Eric was counting on the fact that they still had a little time. There would be at least one whole set by the warm-up band, and a couple of songs by the main attraction before the place went up. Jormin was the lead singer of Pure Blood, and no Bard could resist the chance to perform for this large an audience. Eric had to have at least until Pure Blood took the stage and did a couple of numbers.

But he intended to deny Jormin his audience. Long before then, he and his friends would Bard-Out the people assembled here. They'd undo the frenzy that Gabrevys and his minions had whipped them into, calm them, and convince them to simply *leave*. The combination of his and Hosea's Bardcraft and Ace's Talent should be able to accomplish that.

But all those people wouldn't be able to hear them over the amps down there, even with magick to help. So they needed to improvise. . . .

They were able to move around fairly easily behind the stage.

Nobody was back there; the road crew was standing out in front with Security, watching the show. Until the time came to change the set for the next act, there wouldn't be anything to do.

Eric cast a *glamourie* over them that didn't exactly change their appearance, but did make them seem to belong there. They didn't have to worry about running into Jormin—he was playing his part of Being a Rock Star, and would be waiting in one of the two trailers that served as green rooms until it was time for Pure Blood to take the stage.

As for Billy Fairchild and any speeches he might be going to make, Eric suspected they'd be timed for just before Pure Blood's appearance as well. He'd want his audience all worked up and ready for him, just as if this were one of his Praise Hours. Besides, Pure Blood was *his* trophy band; he would want to introduce them.

As big and as ugly as this whole thing was, it still had more than a little in common with all the RenFaires Eric had worked through the years. The stage crew had their mind on the performers, and anybody who looked as if they belonged where they were and were doing what they were supposed to be doing would pretty much be ignored.

For that matter, the number of trained and reliable roadies around was finite. These guys probably didn't care who or what they worked for, as long as they got their paychecks. This year, it was Christian metal; next year, it could be a thrash-rock group, a bunch of Goths, a boy-band or a punk revival. Whoever had a bankroll and a payroll.

The five of them loaded several flatbed carts with what they needed. There wasn't anything big enough to shift the drum-kit and the keyboard, but Lady Day obliged them there, transforming herself into a very shiny four-wheeled "motorized" cart.

"Hey. Wha'chew doin'?" one of the road crew said, wandering over. He was wearing a "Red Nails: Leap of Faith" T-shirt and had to shout to be heard over the band, even back here behind the amplifiers.

"We've got to move this stuff out of the way to make a clear path to the stage," Eric said, extending a thread of Bardic Magick toward the man to make what was actually a pretty lame excuse become completely believable. "They told us to take it over by the trailers."

"Well, hell, we'll just have to move it back over here again when Pure Blood comes on, but if that's what they said, go ahead. Wouldn't want the sky-pilots to trip over somebody's ax. Need any help?"

"No, we've got it. Thanks."

"Look out for souvenir hunters. Judah's been having trouble hanging on to his panties. The ladies think he's really hot." The roadie ended with a snort that said, wordlessly, *and so does he.*

Eric just grinned and waved, keeping up his impersonation of someone who was with the tour. Lady Day started rolling, and he did his best to give the impression he was controlling a heavy load.

It seemed as if it took forever before they were safely buried in the middle of the crowd—safe, because the people surrounding them would do a lot to mask them from magickal detection, assuming Gabrevys's people were looking for them here. The spells Eric and Hosea cast kept them from being trampled: the people might not quite register that they were there, but they moved out of the way anyway.

Once they'd worked their way around to the front of the stage, the music was even louder than before. Eric hadn't thought it was possible. He'd never been a real fan of this stuff: his own tastes had always run to classical and traditional music.

Even Magnus and Kayla, who *did* like what Eric privately referred to as "that head-banging noise" (Kayla liked techno-House; Magnus was a fan of Black Metal) didn't seem to care for the current offering. Well, they could probably make out the lyrics. . . .

Ace and Hosea simply looked grim. And Molly, who was riding atop one of the carts, had flattened down as far as she could, her ears pressed close to the sides of her bowling-ball-shaped head. If the music was stunningly loud to human hearing, Eric could barely imagine how it must sound to a dog.

The crowd began to thin as they neared the other building. Everybody wanted to be close to the music.

*Right. Bottom of the ninth and bases loaded. You've been here before.* Nevertheless, his stomach was knotting up. He felt a terrible need to hurry, although they were moving as fast as they could, and if they flat-out ran, they might attract the attention of any of the things around here that could see through Bardic *glamouries*. There was a lot they were counting on to make this work: most of all, that Prince Gabrevys shared the fatal obliviousness of all the Unseleighe Sidhe, and would simply never imagine (not that any of the Sidhe were any good at imagining, and as far as Eric knew, Gabrevys had no human advisors) that an enemy he'd last seen running for his life, an enemy that Gabrevys *knew* he was more powerful than, would simply turn around and sneak right back into his mortal stronghold.

And beyond that, they were counting on the fact that Gabrevys ap Ganeliel was a feudal prince who took his ruling style from the *real* Middle Ages—which meant that the way he wanted to do something was the way it was going to be done, period. And *that* meant that even if any of his underlings happened to have any initiative, they certainly wouldn't use it. If Gabrevys had a bunch of people looking for the five of them in South Jersey and said that was where they were, *nobody* would be looking for them here if they knew what was good for them.

Meanwhile, just as Eric had said to Magnus what seemed like a thousand years ago, repeating what his own mentor had told him: *"Life is war, young Banyon. Art is war. You would do well to remember both these things. Concentrate on the destination, not the journey. And do not allow your lust for frivolity and self-indulgence to distract you, for your enemy will use that against you. Self-indulgence is a vice no Bard—and no warrior—can afford."*

They weren't here to take out Gabrevys or his Bard—or even Parker Wheatley and his new "Demonic" crusade today. All they wanted to do was shut down this crowd so that Ria's specialists could come in and find the bomb. *They* wouldn't have any trouble getting into the building—provided they didn't have Talent, anyway.

Hosea tapped Eric on the shoulder and pointed. Between the music and the roaring of the crowd, talking was impossible. He could have cast a bubble of silence around them to shut out the noise, but he really didn't want to use any more magick than he had to. Enough magick of the wrong sort would probably attract Gabrevys's attention.

He looked where Hosea indicated.

There were two guards in casino security uniforms standing in front of the main entrance to the building they wanted to enter, obviously to keep spectators from getting in. Getting around them wouldn't be a problem—a quick look with his mage-sight told Eric they were ordinary mortals, and so the *glamourie* he had cast to conceal the five of them would hold, and they could probably just walk right past them—but if there were guards here, there'd be more around the side, where the service door was, and those would take more dealing with.

He was right. As they angled around the side, he saw two more of the uniformed guards. But he was not at all prepared for what happened next.

He was ready to put them both to sleep, but he needed to catch their attention in order to do it. But the moment their attention was on them, he didn't get the reaction—irritation, anger, even fear—that he expected. Instead they looked resigned and faintly amused.

"Is this the rest of the stuff for the guys upstairs?" one of the men asked. He had to cup his hands over his mouth and shout to be heard.

"Uh . . . yeah," Eric said. *Guys? Upstairs? This does not sound good.*

But they could deal with them when they got there—they'd have to—and right now he was going to take the guards' mistake as a gift from whatever gods protected improvising musicians. He simply waited as one of the guards opened the unlocked door for them and held it to let them move their equipment through, cracking some joke that Eric and the others couldn't hear.

At least once the door was shut, the music was damped to a dull roar. They moved away from the entrance, down the dark hall, lest the Security people should think twice about letting them in. Next thing they had to do was find the stairs—and then find out whose little helpers those guys had mistaken them for.

But was something else weird going on.

This building should have had all the charm of a wet sock, even in the middle of March: stuffy, airless, and damp with the fact that it had been uninhabited and without power for who knew how long. But although it was obviously untenanted, there was air circulating here.

"Power's on," Magnus said, coming to a stop. He flipped a wall switch. The overhead lights came on. "Yup."

"Elevators," Kayla said, turning back. With elevators they wouldn't have to drag this stuff up quite so many stairs, and from the second story, they could find the roof access.

"Why?" Hosea asked simply.

"Somebody else in this building needs power for something," Eric said. "Electrical power, not the other kind. And they must be running enough equipment off it that the guys at the door figured we were with them, bringing in more."

Kayla found the button and pushed it. The rumble of the elevator indicated that all the building's systems were, indeed, live. It descended to ground level and the doors opened.

Kayla started to wheel her cart into it, but Eric stopped her.

"If there are freaky people upstairs, Hosea and I had better deal with them first," he said.

"Here, Little Bit," Hosea said, slipping his banjo off his shoulder and handing it to Kayla. "You hang on to Jeanette for me until I get back."

"Aw, geez," Kayla muttered, taking the instrument gingerly by the neck. "First dogs, now haunted refugees from the Grand Ol' Opry. Hurry back, you guys."

Her tone was light, but her pupils were dilated. Eric just nodded at her.

The elevator doors opened, and Hosea and Eric walked in.

Eric took a deep breath, doing his best to *feel* as far away as he could, trying to sense danger ahead—or possibly behind. He wasn't sure whether to feel pleased or irritated that he didn't sense anything at all.

The elevator stopped.

The lights were on here on the second floor, at least in the back half of the building, but like the old joke said, nobody seemed to be home.

Neither Eric nor Hosea were inclined to raise their voices though—or even, really, to talk. Both of them could feel that there was something *wrong* here, as wrong as if all the closed doors they passed in the hallway concealed stacks of murdered bodies. They just weren't sure, either of them, what it was.

And for some reason, they could hear the concert better here than they had downstairs.

Could the bomb be here, instead of over in the cathedral and casino? Eric paused to consider that. It was so . . . unlikely . . . that he simply didn't think that Gabrevys would have thought of it, and he couldn't imagine that the Unseleighe Prince would have warded that building and not this one if the bomb were here.

But because the stakes were so *very* high, Eric took the time to look, using his mage-sight to look not only through the building, but *through* the building, as if it weren't there, searching for anything that thought of itself as a bomb. Nothing on this floor, or the floor below, and the building was built on a slab besides—buildings near the coast didn't tend to run to basements—so there wasn't a basement to worry about.

Nothing.

Whatever was the cause of their uneasiness, it was something else.

When they found the fire stairs at the end of the hallway— fortunately the building wasn't very large, not in comparison with the Cathedral and Casino of Prayer—they also found a nest of extension cords running from various outlets and rushing up the steps like a Medusa's hair. The door itself was propped open—the music was *very* loud now—and ice-cold outdoor air came blowing down the short flight of stairs that led to the roof. The air brought with it a rank *organic* scent—maybe somebody had been dumping garbage up here?

"Somebody shore needs a lot of power for his radio," Hosea said. Eric couldn't hear him now, but he could read his lips.

Eric nodded. "Let's go see," he mouthed back.

They moved cautiously up the stairs, Eric in the lead. The door at the top hadn't just been propped open, it had been ripped off its hinges. Well, that pretty much explained why the music was so loud.

Ripped off the hinges . . .

*This is not good.*

Cautiously, Eric looked around the edge of the doorway.

The power cables snaked out to the center of the roof to three state-of-the-art video cameras on tripods and their peripherals, all trained on the stage across the way. The set-up wouldn't be visible from the ground—well, *they* hadn't seen it, after all.

And baby-sitting the equipment were three werewolves.

They weren't "real" werewolves—as much as the term had any meaning. They were seven-foot-tall fur-covered tailless bipeds with wolfish heads, hands with long talons, and doglike haunches: horror-movie werewolves. They weren't anything Eric had a name for, but Gabrevys had already proved he had allies from something other than the Celtic-based Unseleighe Realms.

*Must be Low Court, or something like it, or they would have spotted us on our way here,* Eric thought automatically. Low Court Seleighe Sidhe couldn't survive away from their Node Grove; in fact, none of the Low Court creatures on the Light Side of the Force that he had ever run across could get far from their anchoring point in the World Above. He didn't want to think about what their Unseleighe counterparts did to manage.

Or had done for them.

If they were Unseleighe, he *could* try playing the Bard Card: of course, if they weren't Sidhe after all—and they might not be; there were some very weird things Underhill—it wouldn't matter at all to them whether he was a Bard or not. Only the Celtic-inspired creatures had any respect for Bards, or fear of them.

Hosea came up behind him and peered out over his shoulder. The big man saw what Eric had seen and jerked back with a sound like a stifled and indignant cough of laughter.

Eric could only share his feelings. There was something weirdly silly—and horrible at the same time—about watching a bunch of shaggy nightmares peering through lenses, adjusting recording equipment, and generally acting like techie-geeks, while knowing they must be here so that Gabrevys would have a nice detailed wide-angle souvenir of the explosion and its aftermath. And knowing, too, that the moment they saw the two humans, they'd come for them and rip them to bits. And probably eat them.

He didn't want to fight. He'd been in one full-scale elven battle—the one Perenor had so kindly arranged back in Southern California—and he still had nightmares about that.

Maybe he could just get them all to go to sleep . . .

"Nice puppies," Eric muttered under his breath, conjuring up his Flute of Air.

The notes he blew weren't precisely music: they were music and more—color and light and scent; the idea of rest, comfort, deep, dreamless *sleep*. They spread out from the shimmering body of the flute in a sparkling swirling fan and arced over the werewolves as if Eric had cast a net.

The spell had no effect.

Except one.

All three of them pricked up their ears as if somebody had just rung the dinner bell.

As one, they swiveled their long heads and stared.

And with a flash of fangs, all three of them came loping across the roof toward the doorway. The wolf-legs on the almost-human torso gave them an odd tippy-toe gait that looked uncomfortable, like sprinters in high heels.

Except they were coming really fast. And it didn't look as if they were eager to shake hands. Rip the hands off, yes; shake them, no.

Ice and fire mixed ran through his veins, and everything went into Matrix-style bullet-time.

Run? No real place to go. If he and Hosea ran, they'd only lead the werewolves back to the others—who were even less prepared to defend themselves than Eric and Hosea were—and when push came to shove, they *needed* this rooftop as a staging ground for their spell.

No matter who was on it now.

They had to fight. And as little as Eric liked the idea, they had to kill, because he didn't think there was any way short of that to stop these creatures without magick.

Eric stepped out onto the roof. He summoned up his armor—of all the spells he had at his command, this was one of the easiest—and drew his sword. *So much for Bardic inviolability; even if they are Sidhe I've just forfeited my rights to that by drawing first. . . .*

Just for good measure he summoned up a levin-bolt (major chord; crash of violins) and with everything he had in him, he threw it at the nearest one, full-strength.

A levin-bolt was pure raw magick, as lethal as lightning: Sidhe, mortal, or King Kong, a levin-bolt would destroy them all.

But he wasn't particularly surprised—just a little disappointed—to see the blast of energy slide sideways in every direction at once—at least that was what it looked like—without any effect.

Not Sidhe, then. He'd been pretty sure when he'd seen how they'd reacted to his first spell, but now he was *really* sure. Some of the creatures that lived Underhill, oddly enough, all things considered, were utterly magick-null. Magick simply didn't affect them.

They made great shock troops.

Now his senses all began to speed up, until they caught up with real-time.

Right about the moment that the werewolves closed on them.

The lead werewolf clawed at him, growling, and Eric ran sideways along the roof, opening up room to move. The other two followed; he could see the three of them barking—or whatever they did—but he couldn't hear a thing over the music. He danced out of the way, muscles reacting before his brain finished going *Oh shit!* He jabbed at the monster with his sword, making it keep its distance. One good swipe from those talons and his head would come right off.

He ducked under a clumsy swipe and slashed at the arm, and was relieved to see that the blade bit deep into the shaggy flesh, and that it seemed to hurt—at least enough to make the monster backpedal a bit. Dharniel had been insistent that he learn more about swordplay than Terenil had had the time to teach him, saying a Bard must be a master of all the arts. While Eric would never be the equal of someone who'd had centuries to spend practicing with a blade, he wasn't exactly incompetent. And his body was trained now, the way a gymnast's body was trained. He didn't have to think anymore to fight; just react.

The other two stayed behind the leader, trying to decide what to do. In a moment they'd spread out and try to surround him, and then things would get—Eric grimaced at himself, but was unable to resist the pun—hairy. Behind them, he saw Hosea running toward the camera equipment. They hadn't noticed that Eric had brought a friend yet.

Dharniel had always told him that the outcome of a fight was decided in the first moments of engagement. He didn't have time right now to wonder if that was true, and in fact he'd never really figured out what the Elven War-Chief meant by it.

What he *did* know was that suddenly for just a moment he had an opening, and a werewolf right in front of him that he'd made just too mad with his constant sword-pricks to realize that running straight into a sword probably wasn't a good idea.

It was a perfect stop-thrust, even though his sword wasn't really designed for fencing moves, and he'd had to bring it up two-handed. Nausea rose up in his throat as the length of elven blade slid through hair and skin and *meat,* but it did what it was designed to do. It killed. The werewolf made an odd gargling sound, and dropped, sliding off his blade even as Eric withdrew it.

That left two.

Eric danced back, moving automatically, trying not to think too hard about what he'd just done. It wasn't the first time he'd been responsible for things and people dying, sure, but it was the first time he'd done it so up close and hands on. And this was not the time to have a melt-down over it. He might have killed one, but there were two left.

And whichever one he went for, the other one would go for *him.*

"Hey-yah—doggie!"

Hosea's words echoed loud in the few seconds of silence between the end of the music across the way and the start of the crowd's cheering. He came running across the roof, one of the tripod legs from one of the cameras in his hand. As a makeshift spear, it was probably as good as they were going to be able to come up with on short notice.

One of the two monsters turned its attention to Hosea. Eric shifted his attention to the other one. The music started again.

*How many numbers is this? Are they near the end of their set? Is Pure Blood the next band to go on, or do they have another warm-up band? Dammit, we've got to finish this!*

Either the new werewolf was smarter than the one Eric had just killed, or it had learned from the leader's fatal mistake. It circled around, forcing him to keep turning to face it, growling meaningfully deep in its throat—Eric couldn't hear it, but it *looked* as if it were growling—and slashing at him with those long-taloned hands.

And he kept slashing back. But he inflicted only superficial cuts; not enough to disable, not enough to kill. Perhaps not even enough for it to feel.

It was waiting for him to get tired, he realized. Or careless. If it could get inside his defense, it could tear him to pieces. And he was distracted, wanting to know what was happening with Hosea and knowing he didn't dare look.

He'd wounded it a dozen times—small cuts on its forearms—but they weren't even slowing it down. And he *was* getting tired. He was going to have to think of something new. And fast.

He dropped his sword, turned, and ran.

He'd had his back to the camera equipment when he'd done it, and the sheer apparent stupidity of the maneuver got him a good five-second lead. He reached the cameras first and turned.

The werewolf was in midair, springing for the kill, fangs bared, talons spread.

Eric called his sword.

It snapped into his palm with a stinging impact. He barely had time to bring the point up before the monster landed on it.

And him.

*Ah CRAP!*

All the breath was driven out of him, as the mass of fetid fur threw him to the surface of the roof.

His armor saved him from broken bones, but there was no way that having a couple of hundred pounds of werewolf land on you from six feet up could be called fun by any stretch of the imagination. He did his best to roll with the impact, but it still knocked the air out of him completely, and it was several seconds before he could shove the smelly mass off him and get to his feet.

*Star Wars* had always been his favorite movie. He'd driven Dharniel crazy practicing moves from the dueling sequences. Now he was glad that —

*Hosea!*

He looked wildly around.

Hosea was standing over the last of the werewolves. Its throat gaped open as if it had been sliced. The improvised spear stuck up out of its abdomen at an angle as well, but that obviously hadn't been enough to kill it.

Hosea saw him and smiled, but not happily. He held out his gloved hands, and now Eric could see that there was a thin red cord looped between them.

"Banjo string," Hosea explained. "Ah keep extras in mah pockets 'cause they do break at the darndest times, an', well, Ah figured that a lot of uncanny things don't like silver much."

*And, silver or not, a metal banjo string makes a pretty good garrote,* Eric thought.

"Come on," Eric said wearily. "I don't think we have much time."

Dead, the creatures were vulnerable to magick. Eric used a spell to burn the bodies to ash. He really didn't think the others needed to come up here and see a roof full of dead werewolves.

Getting the equipment upstairs took two trips, and when they were done, Eric locked both elevators open and took a moment to summon a spell to lock all the downstairs doors: the doors to the outside as well as the doors to the fire stairs. It wouldn't stop anybody who was really determined to get in for very long, but it would buy them time.

Without Lady Day, getting the drumset up the last half-flight of stairs would have been a major undertaking, but the elvensteed simply rolled up the stairs as if she were one of the Mars Rovers. Molly followed her, scampering around the roof, and sniffing curiously at the scorch-marks that were all that remained of the werewolves.

"Um . . . trouble?" Kayla asked, watching the pug.

"Some," Eric admitted. Not that Kayla couldn't take a pretty good guess. He knew those things had needed to die, and had probably deserved to die besides, but he wasn't sure how he felt about being the one to kill two of them, and he didn't really have time to sort out his feelings right now.

Eric had played with Beth's band, Spiral Dance, enough times to know how to set up a band's equipment, and he knew Kayla had some experience herself. They got to work, clearing the space they'd need.

"These amps aren't going to be anything like big enough," Magnus said, as he uncovered the drum-kit and began setting it out. As soon as he removed the last piece of equipment from Lady Day, the elvensteed shuddered and resumed her "natural" form—looking rather relieved to do so, Eric thought. "They'll never hear us."

Magnus pulled out a set of sticks and twirled them experimentally, frowning.

"Magick will take care of that," Eric said, setting up the keyboard. The gods bless Dharniel and Juilliard for their mutual agreement that a Bard should be a master of many instruments. The keyboard certainly wasn't his favorite instrument, and he wasn't wild about the elven harp either, but he could play both of them. He started transferring the power cables from the recording devices to their equipment.

Kayla had already slung a metallic-purple Stratocaster over her shoulder and was fingering it experimentally, her face neutral.

Eric kept his mouth buttoned—but he hadn't known until this moment she could play guitar. Maybe it was something she'd learned while Underhill—just as Dharniel had insisted that he learn swordcraft, the Healers had seen to it that Kayla learn to play and sing. It would make sense. The elves had a notion that a person should be well-rounded that dated back to the training of a medieval knight.

Ace picked up a microphone and was checking it. "Just like old times," she said. She flipped switches on its accompanying amp and nodded.

Hosea would be playing Jeanette, of course. He'd set up a microphone close to her soundbox, and another one on a stand so he could sing and play at the same time.

Eric found the microphone that belonged in the stand attached to the keyboard and clipped it into place.

No time. No rehearsal. And the stakes just about as high as they could be.

And Magnus the key to all of it, because a band without a drummer wasn't a band.

He looked at Magnus. Magnus raised his sticks in salute and smiled ferally.

"Okay," Kayla said. "Let's rock the house. With what?"

"Doesn't matter," Ace said absently. Her eyes were far away. "The music's just a vessel. I'll make it do what you want."

"Something as different from *that* as possible," Eric said firmly, indicating the band on the stage across the way. He brought his hands down on the keys with a theatrical crash.

He was alone for the first few bars until Magnus realized what he was playing. His brother shot him a look of agonized disbelief, then laid down the rhythm, clear and strong.

Kayla and Hosea came in right on cue, and then Ace.

"*'I thought love was only true in fairy tales—'*"

A silly trippy hippity-hoppy song, first made a hit by the Monkees when Eric had been younger than Magnus was now, and recently covered by Smashbox in a movie about a big green guy who marries a princess and lives happily ever after.

A happy song. A hopeful song. A song about finding out things weren't so bad after all. About *believing*.

Ace poured everything she had into the song. Eric could feel exactly what she was doing: everyone who heard her—and thanks to Bardic Magick, that was everyone here—felt happiness. Felt *love*. Felt a desire to be kind, and most of all, to *help*.

It was the best thing she could have done. If she'd focused on making them all want to *leave,* she would have triggered the same kind of riots they'd come here to avoid. But calm happy helpful people would cooperate with the Bomb Squad, and would certainly leave in an orderly fashion if they were told to.

He concentrated everything he had on feeding her *more* power, and he knew Hosea was doing the same.

And out of nowhere, he felt that power *increase,* as if somehow, the whole was more—far more—than the sum of two Bards and two Talents.

No.

*Three* Talents.

*Magnus?*

Eric glanced over at his brother. To all appearances, Magnus was lost in a world of his own, his hands blurring over the drums as he laid down a complex underpinning for the song. His head was down, his hair plastered to his forehead with sweat. He'd even taken off his blazer.

And he—*glowed*—with power. Eric could see its threads, reaching out to all of them.

*No Gift of his own that anyone can see—but the power to make the Gifts of others stronger . . .*

"I'm A Believer" came to an end. Without a pause, Eric called for "Istanbul" by They Might Be Giants.

Judah Galilee paced back and forth in his dressing room irritably. His master had truly not been pleased when he had been forced to return empty-handed this dawn, and only the fact that his presence was vital at this entertainment—and for others of his master's plans in the days to come—had kept him and his men from going to feed the Shadows. But it had been made clear to him that he stood in disgrace: the hunt for Misthold's mortal Bard—and the rewards for its successful conclusion—were to be given to others. Mere underlings! Worse. *Mortals.* Weak, mayfly mortals!

*Oh, let the Prince attempt to build his Domain upon the prowess of mortals!* Judah thought rebelliously. *Others have gone that*

*road, and the Chaos Lands have taken them! He will see in the
end that only his own blood may be trusted.*

Judah smiled. But Prince Gabrevys's own blood *couldn't* be
trusted, could it? His own blood had betrayed him, fled to the
Bright Court, hiding there behind the skirts of the spineless milk-
toothed Seleighe. Oh, the song he could make of that would cast
his master down so low that not even the Morrigan herself—should
she wish it—could raise him up again.

Perhaps . . . just perhaps . . . it was time to remind Prince
Gabrevys of that fact, and seek a greater share in his master's
power.

Or seek another Court.

But not just yet. Not until he was sure there was no greater
prize to be won here.

Suddenly Judah felt a ripple of magic spread over the lovely,
murky, anguished currents of the Festival. A small thing at first,
but it grew, spreading like oil on a turbulent sea, leaching away
the anger, the power, that he and the others had so carefully
nurtured here.

He flung open the door of his dressing room and rushed
outside.

The others were standing in the hallway. They'd felt it too.
They weren't Bards, of course—he wasn't foolish enough to keep
such competition close, but even minstrels, Court singers and
entertainers with minor magicks, were neither blind nor deaf to
magick.

He thrust open the door to the outside and glared around
wildly.

There!

Atop the building across the way. Judah's lips pulled back in
a feral snarl. His master's quarry and all his friends, here in the
heart of Prince Gabrevys's power, working such magick as was
an affront to his master and all his careful plans. Already the
audience was turning away from the stage as if the band had
fallen silent and was moving toward the other building, to stand
grouped around it, drinking from the tainted fountain of Bright
magicks.

Judah felt their pull as well. They burned across his senses like acid as their pull strengthened. Give in—submit—*grovel*—

"No!" he shouted.

He grabbed Jakan—who was nearest—by the shoulder and flung him out the door. "Get to the stage!" he shouted. "By the Morrigan, we will whip these dogs to their kennels and leave their bones to rot in the Chaos Lands!"

About the time Eric and the band were halfway through their second number, they had no competition. The band on the stage below had simply stopped to listen—not that TMBG's lyrics made sense at the best of times, really, which was part of the point. As for Lost Angels' erstwhile audience, they'd turned away, toward Ace and the spell she was weaving, and were moving toward the building. They'd simply dropped their banners and signs, as if they were no longer of any real importance. And that, more than anything else, was a good sign the music was working.

Suddenly Eric saw four figures rush out toward the other stage. He saw a flash of blood-red hair. Gabrevys's Bard.

They mounted the stage, dragging the musicians away from their instruments and throwing them bodily from the stage. As they moved within range of the cameras, their images appeared on the two big screens flanking the stage. In the unforgiving close-up Eric could see Jormin's face distorted with hate and pain at the effects of the spell that Ace was weaving.

The Unseleighe Bard wasn't even bothering with the *glamourie* that would give him human seeming. None of them were. Anyone in the audience who noticed would probably just take it for another special effect, though, or some elaborate form of makeup.

Eric saw Jormin's lips move as he shouted something to the band.

And suddenly the opening chords of something oddly familiar to a classically trained musician blasted from the gigantic amplifiers that towered over the Main Stage.

Verdi's *Dies Irae.*

It sounded as if Jormin had opened the gates of Hell. He wasn't even *trying* to disguise the fact that the sounds the four of them

were producing couldn't possibly come from those instruments. A
pure wall of *hate,* carried on the rising tide of the music, swept
over the unsuspecting audience, destroying what Ace had done
and drawing them back toward Pure Blood.

But its true target was Eric and the others.

Inside the casino and cathedral, for once the slot machines
were quiet, there was no sound from the tables, and instead
of recordings of upbeat praise music, the speakers were emit-
ting a muted feed from the concert stage. A lavish buffet and
open bar was laid on for the members of the press who were
more interested in either watching the concert in comfort—all
the screens in the casino were showing the live feed from the
stage—or in interviewing Billy Fairchild and his associates. Billy
was pleased to see they'd had a good turn-out, all more than
willing to listen to what he had to say so long as he was feeding them and supplying free booze. Well, you had to use the
devil's weapons, sometimes. Not that he was entirely averse to
the notion of a drop or two, now and then. For purely medici-
nal purposes, of course. And as soon as those long-hair boys
of Gabe's had finished their caterwauling, he'd go out and lead
God's righteous army of the Faithful gathered here today in a
prayer for the deliverance into their hands of certain knowledge
of their enemies and the strength to cleanse the Lord's house of
sinners. And then Brother Wheatley would say a word or two
about the demons, which would certainly be good for business.
Free-will offerings had been up a solid two percent since Wheatley
had been on the show, and Billy was thinking of having him on
again. Now *there* was someone he understood! Someone with a
goal, and a straight idea of just who the enemy was, someone
who had old-fashioned ideas about what worked and how to
confront your enemies. Reveal the devil's handiwork, wherever
you found it! Go straight for the jugular, that was the way to
do it! None of this pussyfooting around. Why, if he'd done it all
the way he'd wanted, he'd have had his rights as a father, and
had one of the boys just go and *get* Heavenly Grace and haul
her home like the disobedient and contrary Serpent's Tooth she

was, and deprogram her like Gabriel was supposed to be doing and none of this business with lawyers and courts. . . .

The sound from the screens was kept down to a tolerable level, thank the Good Lord, though even with the casino's excellent soundproofing everything seemed to *vibrate* just a bit from the playing of the actual band outside. Try as he might, he could not find it within his heart to like this music, no matter how good it was for the Ministry. It was nothing like his own sweet Gospel choir and his dear Heavenly Grace. Even from in here, the band's playing was like being next to a freeway at rush hour, and according to Gabe, it wasn't the loudest one that was going to play today. At least he could leave after he'd made his speech—and before he lost his hearing.

Oh, how he missed Heavenly Grace's singing! But Gabe had promised him that she would be with him soon. Maybe Gabe had come to his senses about straight talk and straight action. Maybe spending time with the young and impatient had done the trick. Yes, yes, that was surely the answer, for Gabe had sworn that after today, the lawyers and the courts wouldn't matter any more, and that Billy would never have to deal with them again. His lost lamb would soon be back within the fold, and that after today, he wouldn't have to worry about missing her any longer. It could be those long-hair boys had done Gabe some good, set his mind to action instead of dancing around that limb of Satan that called herself a judge. Billy had to give Gabriel Horn this much: only in that one instance had Gabe not been able to deliver what he'd promised. And Gabe had been madder over that than Billy'd been, almost.

Suddenly Billy realized that the God-awful caterwauling had stopped. He glanced up at the screen, and frowned. The musicians were just standing there, holding their instruments, staring off into space.

Just like they were off in a trance or something. Except if this was a Visitation of the Holy Spirit, they'd have been speaking in Tongues, not standing there like a bunch of street-corner hop-heads.

There could only be one explanation. They *were* a bunch of street-corner hop-heads.

His temper flared.

Dammit, he'd told Gabriel no drugs! These were supposed to be good Christian boys witnessing to Jesus through music, not drug-addled Satanic vipers like the kind of rock musicians you saw on television and read about in the papers! He couldn't afford any shadow of scandal—

And where was Gabriel, come to that?

Fuming, Billy Fairchild went off to look for the man responsible for this disaster.

Parker Wheatley stood as far as it was possible to get from the front doors of the casino, but the sound of the guitars was still like the whine of a jet engine; both piercing and exhausting. From the briefing earlier in the day, he knew that they had at least another forty minutes of this to endure before it was time for the Reverend Billy Fairchild to strut and preen.

And for him to do his bit, as well. It had taken every bit of persuasion he had, and ultimately he'd had to point to a miniscule bump in the collection-plate tally that was statistically insignificant, but he'd managed to get Billy to agree to let him have another shot at haranguing the masses.

He didn't much like this business, these neo-Nazi Christians. They were unstable, uncontrolled, dangerous. There was no telling what they might do.

If he'd still been working in Washington—or even had any contacts there that he still cared to cultivate—he would certainly have sent a carefully worded memo or two their way just to consolidate his own position. If Fairchild Ministries wasn't on one of the hatewatch lists yet, it would be very soon, unless the political climate on the Hill had changed out of all recognition. He was going to have to do something about that if he was going to get anything useful out of them at all. Not that he cared about the direction as such—but narrowing the focus to the far-far-far end of the extreme came with a price tag. Pretty soon people like the Anti-Defamation Leagues of both Jewish and Moslem sectors were going to come nipping at Billy's heels, not to mention the Southern Poverty Law Center, and the ACLU and—well, fighting them was going to take away money and resources, and there was no point in pouring both down a hole when simply moderating the tone would keep them away.

However, once they went away—well, that particular far-far-far-out sector and their plans for America were very, very useful indeed, so far as Wheatley was concerned. Moderate the tone in public, that was the key. In private—find a way to control them, then use them, use them for all they were worth.

The close connection between some of the Christian denominations and the White Power sects was a more than open secret. As far back as Reconstruction at least, racism and bigotry had wrapped themselves in the American flag, thumped the Bible, and brandished the Cross . . . when they weren't burning it on somebody's lawn.

And when the times had changed, they'd changed with them. After the end of WWII, certainly racism and anti-Semitism had continued to flourish as ugly blots on the American landscape, but any notions of "Aryan supremacy" had needed to be carefully packaged, as the Nazis had rendered the name—if not the actual concept—unpalatable to the generation that had fought and died to make Europe free.

But nearly six decades had passed since V-E Day; the men that had fought the Nazis were dead, senile, or too old and polite to say anything, and what might seem an unlikely alliance for any student of history—Nazi tenets and far-right Christian fundamentalism—had taken hold in the ideological attics and basements of the Far Right, growing more powerful every year.

And their promoters more savvy. These days the neo-"Aryan" groups recruited at "festivals of European culture" that seemed, on the surface, just as innocuous as the Highland Games and Scottish festivals that had thousands of normal red-blooded American men dressing up in plaid skirts every year. They slicked up their message and set it to a hard-rock beat—just as Gabriel Horn was doing now—and before their listeners quite knew what was happening, they were swept into in the dark, poisonous subculture of "racial purity."

Oh, not many, out of all those who bought the albums or

went to the events. Right now, the recruiters thought that one in a hundred was a good return on their investment. And it was, because for every person who *didn't* get involved on a deeper level, there were a dozen who thought that whatever aspect of European Christianity—to give the movement only one of the hundreds of names it was currently going by—they'd encountered was perfectly harmless. Nothing to make a fuss about. In fact, some of their points were right on, brother! And they'd continue thinking these cheerful, smiling, happy people were all right, a little loud, maybe, but pretty much on the right track. They'd let themselves be lulled, let themselves look past all the warning signs, and if this lot ever found themselves a single charismatic leader, they'd watch and applaud him all the way to the White House.

*Wake up, America. It's 1938,* Wheatley thought sardonically.

Not that he cared much. There was business to be done under any government, and if the power was consolidated at the top without all those checks and balances like the ones that had put an end to his career, that made things a lot easier for guys like him. Parker Wheatley wanted power, and he wasn't at all fastidious about what he had to do to get it—or who he had to work with. Who was in charge at the top wasn't important. What was important was that they helped him get *his* job done. Everything else was superfluous.

In fact, hitching his wagon to Billy Fairchild's star might have been a smart move for more reasons than just the Ria Llewellyn connection.

Oh, he hadn't gotten very far yet hunting Spookies in the Fairchild organization—or demons, as Billy preferred to call them—but there was *something* here to find: he could *smell* it. He couldn't say just what it was, but somebody in Billy Fairchild's happy family had their hand in a damned big cookie-jar somewhere. It took a horse-thief to know one, after all. So far he'd been kept busy making speeches; he'd barely had a chance to interview—and clear—half the staff. His office and his apartment had both been searched, which was interesting in a quiet way. They were after Aerune's equipment, obviously. And that someone was looking for it was very interesting indeed . . . because no one else was supposed to know it existed.

The music stopped—he felt it as much as heard it—and Wheatley sighed in relief. He knew it was only a temporary respite, but they must all give thanks for the gifts they were given, as his current patron would say.

He went over to the bar to get another drink.

Halfway through his Scotch, the band started up again. Wheatley glanced up at the screen in faint annoyance.

His glass dropped from his nerveless fingers.

There were four Spookies up there on the stage. Playing guitars. And, aside from features more angular than he'd remembered, and the pointed ears, looking very damned much like that pet rock band of Gabriel Horn's, the one he'd been so proud of, the one that was the whole reason for this counter-Woodstock. . . .

And it hit him.

*Horn knows. Horn knows what they are.*

The realization filled him with virulent excitement. Gabriel Horn had disliked him from the beginning—Wheatley had put that down to a simple turf-war. But—oh, God—what if there were *more* to it than that? He'd told Fairchild that this was just the sort of operation that the Spookies loved to take over for their own unknowable purposes, and he'd been *right*—

He looked around wildly. Neither Billy Fairchild nor Gabriel Horn were anywhere to be seen.

Cursing under his breath, Parker Wheatley ran to get his equipment.

He'd elected to watch the concert from his office. Better that than subjecting himself to the yammering of the mortal cattle that Billy loved to surround himself with. And on this day of all days, it would have been too great a temptation to simply slay them all.

Personally.

The mere idea of just summoning his royal armor and his blade, and wading through the crowd swinging, was almost too much to resist.

Gabriel Horn paced back and forth across the floor of his office, all but growling aloud. Only the promise of the carnage to come in less than an hour was remotely soothing.

How could everything have gone so desperately awry so very quickly? Only last night he had everything well in hand: the Bright Bard and his brother were his captives, and by now they should have been destroyed and on their way to spend the rest of their truncated lives as toadying serfs. Heavenly Grace had been a small disappointment, but at least there he would have had revenge, if not victory.

And then they had escaped.

And Jormin and the others had not recaptured them.

The humans he had sent in their place had been no more expert huntsmen, even though he had included a Sidhe among their number to trace the fugitives by magick. It had not occurred to him that they would have elvensteeds—impossible to track by magick or huntscraft—and by then the trail was cold.

He'd done what he could to reclaim the victory. He'd set a watch upon the hotel at which Heavenly Grace and Hosea Songmaker had stayed—if Jormin's *geas* held, the apprentice-Bard and the little songbird would return there as soon as they could. But in the wake of so many disappointments, Gabriel had little hope of such luck. Though his hunters were still searching for their quarry—as they would until he recalled them did they know what was good for them—without magick to aid them, the hunt would be long and undoubtedly fruitless.

So Misthold's Bard and his acolytes ran free. And Sieur Eric would undoubtedly go whining to his master—if he was not at Arvin's feet already, licking Bright Court boots—of his ill-usage. And worse. The bedlamite Bard would tell all he knew of Gabriel's plans in the world, and who knew what Gabriel's Bright Court cousins might say to that?

Who knew what they would attempt to do to his son?

And if High King Oberon were brought into it . . .

Gabrevys would not forego his revenge against Eric Banyon, by any means, but it would have to take another form, at another time. For now, he would have to content himself as much as he could with knowing how the fate of the Bright Bard's parents would grieve him—and was it not, after all, a fate truly of Sieur Eric's own making?

He would have Jormin make a song about it.

If he did not feed the wretched Bard to the Shadows instead. At least he could do that, if he chose. Jormin was *his* Bard, *his* liegeman, and Gabrevys had the rights of life and death over him by ancient usage.

How—*how*—could Jormin have underestimated the damage young Songmaker could do? It must have been he who had freed the others: there was no one else. Foolish, the confidence that had left one enemy, however weak and ineffectual, to run free, and only see the disaster it had brought in its wake—!

Slowly a sense of *wrongness* began to penetrate Gabriel's furious anger. It took a long time to gain his attention, but at last he looked—really looked—out the window at the concert venue below.

The audience was moving away from the stage. Turning away from the performers that they had come to see, moving slowly toward the building at the far side of the parking lot, as if there were something there that drew them. But the only thing there should be Gabrevys's own camera setup, placed safely out of harm's way to film the explosion to come.

No.

There were humans on the roof.

The Bard and his companions.

Playing instruments.

Making magick.

Bespelling the audience—*his* audience!—for a purpose Gabriel did not understand, but which must be some plot to further ruin his plans.

And the blend of the girl's Talent with the magick of Misthold's Bard was irresistible.

*But that can be remedied . . .*

Gabriel clenched his fist, summoning a levin-bolt, and took aim at the wretched chit of a girl.

And then, with a growl and an internal wrench, stopped. Even now he did not—quite—dare openly break the Law of the Sidhe that held that there should be no overt usage of magick in the World Above. Besides, there was too much Cold Iron here for him to be sure his bolt would fly true—if it struck Bard Eric instead of Heavenly Grace . . .

Then he would be called to account before the High Court itself, and his enemies would be delighted to see that the accounting fell heavily upon him. Oberon would not be amused. And Oberon was High King, not merely because he was Eldest, which he was, but because he was more powerful than any fifty Magus Majors put together.

There was silence below, and then a sudden upwelling of sound and magick. He recognized the playing of his own Bard, and saw the audience eddy about in confusion, caught between the two Bards.

For a moment Gabriel hesitated. If he went down to the stage, joined his power to Jormin's . . .

But no. Though he was a Magus Major, vast in power, he was no Bard. Even here he felt the weakening effects of the spell Bard Eric was spinning; the lure of Heavenly Grace's singing. Perhaps if it had merely been Bard against Bard, Jormin could have won this battle. But it was not. There was the Bard, who had human creativity as well as magick. There was the Apprentice, who was strong in spirit if not in skill. There was the girl, with something beyond mere magick. And—he sensed—another, who had a Talent that bound them together in a whole that was far, far, greater than the sum of its parts. Much as he honored Jormin's gifts, he did not believe his Bard could prevail.

There was only one thing to do to salvage what little he could of all his hopes and plans.

The bomb must explode *now*.

Wheatley always kept some of his equipment in his office. Not the irreplaceable things, like the parasympathetic energy detectors that detected the reality-manipulating energy that Spookies gave off, or the illusion-filtering lenses that would allow their wearer to see through most Spookie illusions, but the simple things that could be made with Earth technology, like the bolt-guns and the steel capture nets.

Weapons.

It only took him a moment or two to arm himself and stuff some extra equipment into a small bag. If he was lucky, today he'd be able to provide Billy Fairchild with what he'd wanted—a Live Capture of an actual "demon." And all on film! There were cameras all over, trained on that stage. He'd have the capture from as many angles as anyone could want.

And coup of coups, it would be the capture of a "demon" that had been taken into the bosom of the Ministry and cherished there.

As he hurried from his office back toward the casino, he slipped the filter-glasses on. He hated wearing the things: no matter what they'd done with them in R&D, they'd always looked like cheap sun-glasses, and everything the wearer saw looked faintly green.

But wearing them, he'd see the world as it truly was.

And that was vital.


It seemed an eternity as the elevator doors closed and the car began its slow descent toward ground-level, and to Wheatley's intense frustration, it stopped almost immediately.

The doors opened, and Wheatley found himself staring at . . . One of *Them*.

Tall, taller than Wheatley. Features so angular they looked like a cartoon exaggeration of a human. Pointed ears, and the green, cat-pupilled eyes that were the hallmark of every single one of them. There was a frozen moment when they stared at each other, then Wheatley saw understanding in the monster's eyes that he saw it for what it was.

Wheatley raised his gun and fired.

It was something they'd designed themselves, back in the PDI days, based on Aerune's careful descriptions of what would be most effective against his kind. It was a spring-driven gun—a purely mechanical process—that fired inch-long projectiles of pure iron about the diameter of a really fat knitting needle. It didn't have the range or penetrating capability of a conventional weapon, but against Spookies there was nothing on God's Green Earth more effective.

Half-a-dozen of the projectiles buried themselves in the creature's chest with a faint stuttering sound—thank God the guns were relatively silent, because the upper floors were filled with sightseers today. The Spookie staggered backward, falling to its knees, and then to the floor, twitching as if it had been electrocuted. Wheatley noted with faint interest that *smoke* was actually rising from the entry wounds.

He didn't make the mistake of assuming it was helpless. Too many good field agents had died making exactly that mistake. He moved quickly, rolling it over and cuffing its hands behind its back—ordinary handcuffs, but oddly enough, just the thing for a Spookie—and then rolling it up in the capture net. The net had locks, allowing its contents to be body-bagged for easy transportation. Like the cuffs, it was steel, not iron, but steel was nearly as effective against Spookies and a great deal stronger.

It was curious that while the Spookies looked more or less like humans, wherever the net and the handcuffs touched the creature's bare flesh, it actually blistered. It was an odd chemical reaction that they'd never gotten a chance to study thoroughly at the PDI, and now, of course, he lacked the equipment and resources. It was an unfortunate loss to the cause of science.

The creature was bleeding heavily from its wounds and, cuffed and wrapped in steel and with a half-dozen iron bolts in its chest, was no longer able to put up much of a fight. Wheatley dragged it into the elevator and punched the button for one of the still-unoccupied floors. He'd find some place to stash the thing, out of the way, until he could add it to his public captures.

Now that he had time to take a better look at what it was wearing, he was fairly sure that it was—or had been impersonating—Gabriel Horn, and the knowledge both cheered and chilled him. Had there *ever* been a real Gabriel Horn? Or had the Spookie infiltration of Billy Fairchild's organization been at the highest levels all along?

It didn't matter. He could question the Horn-thing later, if it survived. He was reasonably sure it would; Spookies were tough, and he was fairly sure he'd missed the heart. And even if it didn't, he'd have the other four as live captures. It was far more important to neutralize one of *Them* that was so close to the center of power.

*And there won't be any more turf-war going on. Fairchild will be mine, by God!*

The elevator stopped again on the unoccupied floor. Wheatley pressed the button that would hold the doors open and dragged his prisoner into the hall. The Spookie groaned in pain as the steel meshes bit into its flesh, but Wheatley didn't care. Right now he had to get it to a secure place as quickly as possible, and then go after the others.

Fortunately the unoccupied floors hadn't been completely finished. There was vinyl, not carpeting, on the floors. That made dragging his burden considerably easier, for Wheatley was not a young man, and had always left the physical side of the PDI's operations to his carefully handpicked cadre of field agents.

He wondered where they were now, his muscle-squad. They'd been good; smart enough to improvise, smart enough not to ask questions that none of them wanted the answer to, incurious, and closemouthed. After today, he'd certainly have the money to hire at least some of them into the private sector, if they weren't there already.

He opened the first door he found and dragged the Spookie inside. He would have left it in the hallway, except for the fear that it would cry out, and someone might hear, and stop to help it before realizing what it was.

He removed his glasses to check. It was clear that it no longer had the power to maintain the illusion of human form that the creatures so loved to mock humanity with, but its flesh was so burned and swollen by contact with the steel netting that its inhumanity was not instantly recognizable. Only the long pointed ears betrayed it.

"By the Morrigan, you will die a thousand deaths for this," it whispered faintly. It coughed, and spat blood, writhing as it futilely sought some position that would keep its head and body from coming into contact with the mesh of the capture net.

"But not today," Wheatley said, with a satisfaction so deep he wasn't even inclined to gloat. "Today belongs to the human race, 'Mr. Horn.'"

Eric could actually *see* the clashing magicks boiling over each other like oil over water.

And their side was winning. He'd hardly dared believe it at first, but they were. What was it that Dharniel had said?

*"The difference between the Light and the Shadow is that when the Light illuminates what is in the Shadow, there turns out to be nothing there after all but illusion and fear, but even when the Shadow overwhelms the Light, there still exists the rock of courage and the spark of hope. . . ."*

They ripped into their third number with the force of a freight train that had lost its brakes, playing as if they'd gigged together for years. *I just wish Bethie was here to hear this,* Eric thought wistfully.

Pure Blood was giving it everything they had—Eric couldn't hear them, though he could see them on the monitors—but the audience just wasn't buying what they were selling today. The crowd had all moved away from the main stage, clearing the road and the area around the casino and cathedral, and now Eric could see the flashing lights of emergency vehicles moving up the main road. The Bomb Squad had arrived.

He knew he was singing better than he ever had before in his life, his tenor and Hosea's rich baritone automatically finding the harmony to support Ace's soaring bell-clear soprano. It was as if the five of them were one performer now, acting together without thought, without flaw. Even Molly's yips and barks contributed to the music.

Down below people were crying, were hugging each other, were kissing. It might not last, but right here, right now, everything was—was Light. Peace was right. Love was right. No one even thought about hating anyone else right now. This was the way the world should be.

Then he saw Parker Wheatley.

The man was impossible to miss in a bright green suit, his

image twelve feet high on two giant screens. He'd climbed up on the stage, moving toward Judah Galilee, holding something in his hand that Eric couldn't quite make out, even with the magnification the big screen provided.

But Judah didn't react. None of the members of Pure Blood reacted, although Wheatley walked right past the drummer, in plain sight of him. It was as if they couldn't see him at all.

*Green suit—Beth told me—it makes them invisible to Sidhe, or nearly—*

His immediate impulse was to warn Judah, but before he could think of how to do it—never mind whether or not Judah would believe him—Judah recoiled and fell.

All his spells, all his arts, his carefully crafted songs—worthless! The fickle human sheep had chosen another master this day, and no matter how much he raged, Jormin ap Galever could do nothing to change that. He might summon levin-bolts and burn them all to ash, but against the power the Bright Bard had summoned—in the Morrigan's Name, *how?*—he and his minions were helpless to bend the humans' wills.

And that spell, that loathsome tainted groveling *love,* was like a web of Cold Iron laid upon his skin. . . .

Suddenly he howled in stark agony, as a bolt of the metal itself pierced his skin. He fell to the floor—where was his attacker? Who dared?

"Stay back, all of you. I have more of these."

And with a clangor of discordances, the music, *their* music, stuttered to a halt and died.

Judah writhed upon the stage, clawing at his back, but the human's bolt had gone too deep for him to draw it out. He could feel it eating at him from within, boiling his flesh away.

"All of you. Over there. With him."

Abidan and Jakan slowly moved to obey, lifting the straps of their guitars over their necks and beginning to move toward Judah, their postures the picture of dejected defeat. Their instruments dangled from their hands as if they had suddenly forgotten their use. Coz stood up from behind the drums and began to move forward as well.

"Keep your hands where I can see them. And don't bother trying any of your tricks. This suit I'm wearing will protect me from anything you can possibly do."

"Ae, e'en this, maister?" Abidan snarled. Suddenly he straightened, tossing off his pose of subjugation, his guitar spinning in his hands as if it were a battle-axe, not an instrument. He brought it down on the man's arm hard enough to break the bone, then swung it again at the back of his head.

The stranger in the green suit crumpled to the ground with a surprised bleat.

On the rooftop opposite, they saw it all. Ace stopped singing and stared at the scene on the monitor in horror, then looked back at Eric. Behind her, the playing of the others straggled to a stop. First Jormin/Judah went down—then Wheatley, hammered by one of Judah's band!

Now what were they supposed to do?

Eric understood her confusion all too well. Certainly Judah and the others were the enemy by any rubber yardstick you chose to use—but then, so was Wheatley. And no matter what, it wasn't right for them to simply stand by and let two sets of Bad Guys tear each other to shreds. But they shouldn't help Wheatley, not after what he'd done to Kory and Beth, and to all those other people. And they *wouldn't* help Jormin!

What could they do?

But the Unseleighe band weren't pressing their attack against Wheatley. The other three had gathered around their leader, lifting Judah up and carrying him from the stage.

"*Sing*," Eric said urgently to Ace. "We're not done yet, not even close! There's still the bomb. We've still got all those people out there and we can't let them turn back into a mob."

Ace lifted the microphone again.

This time it wasn't a bouncy rock song or a piece of retro bubblegum fluff. She returned to the music she knew best, and the pure soaring strains of her own namesake song, "Amazing

Grace," echoed through the now-silent parking-lot, as the crowd gathered below them in hushed and reverent silence and the emergency vehicles clustered ever-deeper around the Cathedral and Casino of Prayer.

This time her song held sadness.

Sadness for every lost opportunity, every unkind word, every chance at reconciliation turned away through pride or anger. *She* might sing that she had been "lost but now was found," but beneath her words was the aching sorrow for all those who still were lost in the Shadow, who were still blind, who still turned away from love to seek hate, who still could not see the Grace that could save them. Because they'd won now, Eric realized: he could see it and so could she, and that meant they'd both have to face their families, and try to deal with the aftermath of all the terrible things that had happened here.

Things that had happened out of a *kind* of love. Not the sort from Ecclesiastes, the love that was "faithful and kind, does not insist on its own way," but love of the worst and most toxic sort—twisted and wrong-headed and not love by any *reasonable* definition. But it thought of itself as being love; and it was still something that had started out to be—once, long ago—real love.

And so tears glistened in Ace's eyes as she sang, and a lump formed in Eric's throat as he played—for the families, for the parents they both *could* have had, if a thousand things had gone differently.

And down there below—down there, those thousands of listeners looked in the mirror of her song, and saw themselves. Saw that they were cut from the same cloth as Billy Fairchild, as the elder Banyons. Saw, at least in this moment; and at least in this moment, realized all the pain they were creating. Realized that the Grace that had sacrificed itself for them, had done so in vain, because in their hate, their fear, and their rejection of everything that was just a little different from them, they had turned away from that Grace, and into the Shadow.

And they cried. By ones and twos and entire groups, they fell to their knees, or they stood with their faces turned up to the sky, and they wept. Wept as they had probably never wept in their whole lives. Wept for guilt, wept for fear, but most of all, wept for the rest of the message that Ace's song gave them.

*But it's never too late to heal*, the music seemed to say. *Let the anger pass when the time for it is done, and leave the hate behind forever. . . . You have stood in the Shadow, now come to the Light, for the Light will still, ever and always, welcome you, forgive you, want you still. Flawed and ugly as your hearts and souls are, the Light wants you to come home and be made beautiful again.*

And so, most of all, as the Bomb Squad moved in, and they stood beneath the roof, oblivious to everything else around them, they wept for hope.

# CHAPTER 11:
## AFTER THE THUNDER

They played for another half hour, watching the evacuation of the casino and the quiet removal of the crowd they had gathered along the back roads of the business park by the efficient security people that Ria had summoned. An ambulance had come for Wheatley. He was a problem—and probably not Eric's—for another day.

The concert audience hadn't left the business park, of course—it would take hours to move that many people out of here—but they were now at a much safer distance from the explosion—if there was going to be one.

Nobody noticed the five of them—though a rock band playing at full amplification ought to have been hard to miss. But what they were playing wasn't truly meant to be heard, only felt. After that last outpouring of grief-stricken weeping, Ace had sung lullabies, sending the crowd into an exhausted half trance. Old songs.

*"Hush little baby, don't say a word, Papa's gonna buy you a mocking bird. . . . "*

At last Eric saw two figures in Bomb Squad armor come walking out of the casino carrying a large chest between them. They loaded it into a van, which drove slowly away.

He caught Hosea's eye. The big man nodded, looking satisfied.

*Looks like they got it.*

Eric gave the others the high sign, and they wrapped it up in a soft sigh of chords.

It was over.

And it was only now beginning.

Ace lowered her microphone and switched it off.

"It's done, then?" she asked.

She looked tired, but not in a bad way. More as if she'd done a long hard job that had needed doing, and that in setting things right, she'd set things right with herself as well. Something had happened to her, when she'd given herself over to her Talent. As if she'd found just what it was she'd been looking for all her short life.

As for Eric...

He wanted to sleep for a week. No, make that *two* weeks. He couldn't think of the last time he'd been involved in casting a spell this long and involved—and *powerful*. In fact, he thought he'd only heard of things like this being done in the old story-songs he'd studied under Dharniel. Bards working together? Bards and Talents? Perish the thought!

*Magnus!*

Magnus was still sitting slumped over the drumset, his sticks dangling limply from his fingers. Eric walked over to him, and touched him on the shoulder. Magnus looked up, eyes just a little glazed. Not—quite—drunk with exhaustion, but close to it.

"How're you doing?" Eric asked gently. What he really wanted to do was hug his brother—hard—and reassure himself that he was okay, but he doubted that would go down very well.

"So that was magick, huh?" the teenager asked, stretching. His hair was as wet as if he'd just stepped out of a shower; he raked it back from his forehead with both hands and shivered, as if he'd only just noticed it was cold up here.

Eric picked up Magnus's discarded school blazer. The boy's shirt was soaked to the skin as well. After a moment's thought,

Eric took off his own leather jacket and draped it over Magnus's shoulders instead.

"Yeah," Eric said. "That was magick." *And magick the likes of which you'll never see again, if we're all very lucky.*

"I don't like it," Magnus said succinctly. "But the music was okay, I guess."

"Can we get off this roof and maybe go find some coffee?" Kayla said, sounding unconscionably cheerful. "It's freezing up here and it's been *way* too long since breakfast."

Of course they couldn't simply leave. For one thing, they still didn't have a car. And for another, they had a lot of unfinished business here.

Except for Jeanette, they left the instruments where they were. Let someone else wonder what they were doing there. This time, the cleanup could be in someone else's hands.

As quiet as everything had looked from the rooftop, down on the ground, it was well-organized chaos. More emergency vehicles were arriving all the time, and with them, the press. As much as the police might want to keep the area closed to the press, Eric supposed it would probably take the National Guard to actually seal it off. The recently vacated stage made a perfect backdrop for interviews with shocked survivors and anybody who wanted to grab camera time, and the press wasn't shy about using it.

"No . . ." Ace said, and began to run toward the stage.

Eric took a second, closer look at the man currently surrounded by what looked like every reporter in the state: print, radio, and television.

He looked at Hosea.

"That's Billy Fairchild," the big man said grimly.

It was very clear that Billy was in his element. The gist of the story was in his mind of course, but he was able to let the words flow, just as he always had in his sermons, unplanned and impromptu, and so, the more *genuine,* at least in seeming. "—a sorrowful and terrible day for us all here at Fairchild Ministries, but as you all know, I receive hundreds of death threats every week for the message I preach. I'm only sorry that—"

"Did he tell you that he set this one up?" a new voice shouted, carrying clear and high over the murmur of voices around him.

Billy stopped as if he'd been stung; he felt more as if he'd been slapped. Because, in a way, he had been. The newscasters, scenting awards, trained their cameras on the intruder. There were scattered flashes, and the whirring sounds of machinery.

Ace grimly pushed her way through the mob of reporters.

"Did my Daddy tell you that he and Mr. Gabriel Horn planned to set off a bomb here today?" Ace demanded, walking over to her father. She turned and looked straight into the cameras. "I'm Heavenly Grace Fairchild. Maybe my Daddy's talked about me." Her face, instead of going hard and angry, went soft and vulnerable looking, as if she was about to cry. "He's sure been stalking me, right along with talking about me. You can find that out too, if you go look. He set all this up, but then, he's pretty accustomed to using people."

"Now Heavenly Grace—" Billy said. His voice held a stark note of pleading.

"He sure used me," she concluded, her jaw jutting. "That was why I ran away and why I am *never* going back."

There was a sudden frenzied babble as all of the reporters started shouting questions at once, and what had been a carefully orchestrated PR moment for Billy Fairchild degenerated into actual news. Ace looked up and saw two of Daddy's "Helpers"—his polite word for bodyguards—standing a few feet away—Abner and Joshua. She'd known them both for years. They looked confused—they *knew* her, and they didn't know whether they were supposed to hustle her out of the way or not.

She raised her voice, talking fast, knowing the reporters would shut up once somebody was saying something, knowing the cameras and the tapes would get it all. Hadn't she been to enough press conferences in her life to know how these things were managed? She ignored the shouted questions, ignored the microphones shoved in her face, and concentrated on staying out of Daddy's reach and saying her piece.

"They set it up between them," Ace said grimly, but let some of the tears of pain and frustration leak down her face. "Him and a man called Gabriel Horn, who's worked for him for years. The bomb was supposed to be a nice publicity stunt, no matter how many people got hurt, and get him in good with his new bad friends, the ones who think Jesus meant you to shoot your enemies, not love them. It's because of his doing things like that that I ran away from home, and why I'm suing for Emancipated Minor status now, so he can't drag me back to make me do things that are just as bad as setting bombs. I heard them plan the whole thing."

"Heavenly Grace, don't you tell lies like that!" Billy sputtered desperately. "She's lying—she's sick—she don't know what she's saying, poor thing."

But of course, she didn't look or sound out of her mind—only disgusted and ready to cry—and if there was one thing that reporters craved it was the scent of metaphorical blood. She had them. He knew it, and so did she.

By now Hosea and Eric had reached the stage as well and were standing at the back of the mob of reporters. Hosea simply looked at Billy.

When he saw Hosea, Daddy just looked horrified—as if he finally realized he might actually be in trouble, Ace thought sadly.

"I— I— Turn those things off! I have nothing further to say! My office will issue a complete statement tomorrow! Heavenly Grace, you come with me right now!"

Ace shook her head. "No, Daddy. Not now, not ever. You're a bad man, you tried to hurt a lot of people, and Jesus is weeping for you. He may forgive you, but I can't right now, and maybe I won't ever be able to."

Billy turned away, and Abner and Joshua closed around him and helped him from the stage. The looks on their faces as they gazed at her—shock, hurt, disbelief—nearly broke her heart. But not nearly as much as their hearts would be broken when they found out she was telling the truth.

The reporters surged around her, shouting more questions, and she felt a moment of pure panic, but now Eric and Hosea had pushed their way through the crowd and literally picked her up and carried her in the same direction Billy had just gone.

"Don't you worry none," Hosea said in her ear. "We're just goin'
behind the police lines. Ah reckoned you wouldn't want to have
any more truck with reporters than you had to."

"No," Ace said in a trembling voice. "I . . . I guess they're going
to want to interview me now, aren't they?"

She heard Eric give a strangled snort of laughter as he set her
on her feet at the bottom of the steps. "Ace, after that speech you
just gave, I don't think there's *anybody* in the tri-state area who
*isn't* going to want to talk to you, plus several federal agencies
besides."

"I just . . . I couldn't let him get away with it. He was going
to have them all believing him. After that it wouldn't matter
what the courts said, or what the truth was. All anybody would
remember was what they'd seen on the television." That much, she
was sure of, as sick as it made her feel. People were tried and
convicted on television, no matter what courts said. And Billy
Fairchild had learned, and learned well, from every misstep that
every other televangelist had ever made on television. He knew
how to manipulate what went on before the cameras.

Well, so did she. "And in a year, or two," she went on, scrub-
bing at her eyes with her sleeve, "he'd be right back in business
again, just like everybody else who's ever done a bad thing and
gotten away with it. So this time—" she raised her chin, and
looked first Eric, then Hosea, straight in the eyes. "This time, I
made sure I got in my licks first."

Back behind the stage—where they'd slunk around less than
two hours before, stealing instruments to put on their counter-
concert—Eric saw uniforms from at least six different jurisdic-
tions, and the "this is not a uniform" suits that meant the Feds
had arrived. Good thing his conscience was clear.

He'd lost track of Magnus and Kayla when he and Hosea had
made that mad sprint toward the soundstage to follow Ace. He
knew they'd be together, at least, and Kayla wouldn't let anything
happen to Magnus.

And right now he had bigger fish to fry—"fry," literally. Just
as soon as he could get Ace settled somewhere safe, he had

to figure out some way to get into the casino. The wards were off the building—he could see that—and he needed to get in there and see if Gabriel Horn—or Gabrevys ap Ganeliel—or whatever the Prince of Elfhame Bete Noir was calling himself these days—was still in there causing trouble. Gabrevys's Bard had run out on him with one of Wheatley's iron bolts in his back; if Gabrevys was weak enough, Eric ought to be able to call Lady Day and take him Underhill. Or at least, away from here. Maybe he could find a nice deserted steel foundry to dump him into.

Before the three of them had taken more than a few steps they were intercepted by a very courteous, very resolute man in dark glasses, a dark suit, and an expensive coat. He might as well have had the words "Federal Agent" tattooed on his forehead.

"Heavenly Grace Fairchild?" he asked. "Eric Banyon?"

"Yes," Eric said cautiously.

"Could you come with me, please? All three of you?"

*We haven't done anything indictable*, Eric reminded himself. *At least not that anybody knows about.* He glanced at the other two, shrugged, and followed.

Their anonymous minder led them around the side of the Casino and Cathedral. Dozens of official vehicles had arrived by this time—fire engines, ambulances, big black vans with satellite dishes on the top. Eric could see buses being loaded up with people who'd been evacuated from the building, with more waiting to go. The whole area along the side of the building had been cordoned off with sawhorses and crime-scene tape to form a combined command post and holding area—the reporters were clustered at the other side of the barriers—and Eric could see that there was a checkpoint set up down by the road as well. The authorities were doing all that they could to contain the scene, but it was a very big scene.

*And now they're going to ask us what we were doing here, and I haven't got the faintest idea of what we're going to tell them. There's no way I can mess with this many people's heads, even if it was remotely a Good Guy type thing to do.*

He heard a dog barking.

"Well," Hosea drawled, sounding relieved. "The cavalry does seem to have arrived."

"Ria!" Ace said, running forward to where Ria Llewellyn stood, next to a very long—and very black—stretch limousine. Kayla was standing beside her, and Magnus was inspecting the car as if he was expecting to purchase one like it in the very near future.

"Ria, indeed," Ria said, once they'd all gotten close enough not to have to shout. "Thanks, Jasper. I appreciate your finding my lost lambs for me."

"Any time, Ms. Llewellyn," the man in the sunglasses answered, tipping her a little two-fingered half salute. "Try not to let them go wandering off, okay? The scene's still hot."

"I'll do my best."

If there were such a thing as *Fortune 500 Vogue,* Ria looked as if she'd just stepped off the cover, from her white cashmere trenchcoat, to her Emmanuel Ungaro suit, to her Jimmy Choo stilettos. But the perfect ice-queen act was marred when she held out her arms and Ace flung herself into them.

"I got here as soon as I could," Ria said, over Ace's head. "I found Magnus and Kayla—well, they found me—"

"Say hey," Kayla said, offering a two-fingered salute of her own. She held Molly in her arms. The little pug wriggled all over with glee at being reunited with her friends.

"Looks like you'll make the evening news," Magnus said helpfully. "If we don't all get arrested."

"Nobody is getting arrested," Ria said firmly. "Except possibly Billy Fairchild and Gabriel Horn—if they can find Horn. They're still searching the building, but they haven't found him yet."

"Horn's Unseleighe," Eric said, making a long story—a *very* long story—as short as possible. "I don't know if they *will* find him if he doesn't want to be found—or if it would be very good for them if they did. Ria, I've got to get in there and look for him."

"What are you going to do with him if you find him?" Ria snapped. "And more to the point, what is *Magnus* going to do if Gabriel levin-bolts you in the back?"

Eric flinched as if he'd been slapped. He hadn't thought about what would happen if he was hurt or killed in a duel with Gabrevys.

No. He hadn't *thought,* period.

He was a parent now—well, a *kind* of parent. A small-g guardian, anyway. He didn't have the luxury of thinking only of himself anymore, or even of risking his neck just because it was the right thing to do.

He had to take care of Magnus and keep him safe, because that promise came first.

He turned to face Magnus.

"Well, go on, bro. What are you waiting for?" Magnus's voice was perfectly neutral. He could do a good job of hiding his feelings, even from himself. Because there'd been too many disappointments in his life, too many people putting the wrong things first.

"Forgot who I was for a moment," Eric said lightly. "Ria's right: I wouldn't know what to do with Gabrevys if I *did* find him, and I have more important things to do here. I'll need to go Underhill as soon as I can and tell Prince Arvin what he's been doing, though, since Jachiel is staying at Misthold. Gabrevys is Sidhe, and he's broken enough laws of the Sidhe to bring even the High King down on his head. Let *them* take care of him. I've got more important things to do."

Magnus stared at him in the blank way that told Eric that the talk of elves and elven politics had been nothing more than meaningless noise. Finally he said, "So what have you got to do here that's so important?"

Eric managed a wobbly grin. "Well, finding you a leather jacket that fits, for one thing. That one's way too tight."

"Yeah, well, you can't have it back. I'm cold, and I'd rather have a parka or something," Magnus grumbled. But his voice had lost its wary colorlessness.

"After that speech of Ace's, she's going to have more than a few questions to answer," Ria said. "Not that she wouldn't anyway—after today, a lot of people are going to want to take a very close look at the Fairchild Ministries. But I'm pretty sure we can put it off for a day or so—and come up with a reasonable explanation of events that doesn't include elves, goblins, or little green men."

"Ayah," Hosea said gravely. "Best stick to as much of the truth as possible."

Ria smiled. "Now Hosea, you know I always do that. There should be some way to tie Ace's little fact-finding mission into Eric and Magnus's kidnapping if we're creative enough, which will be useful all the way around. But we can worry about that tomorrow. Right now all I want to do is leave before some of those clever little vultures of the press decide to jump the police barricades and head this way, but we'll have to wait here until we're given permission. The traffic out there's a nightmare, anyway; we'll be lucky to get back to Manhattan by dinner time. It's just as well Anita made sure the car was fully stocked before I left."

"Hey, that must mean there's coffee in there," Kayla said with interest, setting Molly down. The pug immediately began to investigate all the fascinating smells in the vicinity, pulling Kayla around in a circle. "Hard to believe they're still finding people in there," Kayla started to say idly. "What were they doing, hiding under the . . . desks?"

Her voice went very flat on the last words, as if she'd suddenly forgotten how to talk. Ria reached out to steady her as she swayed.

"Kayla! What is it?"

"I don't know," Kayla muttered, shaking her head. "Those . . . it's like a hole. . . ."

Eric looked in the direction of the latest group of people being led toward the bus-being-used-as-ambulance. Most of them looked perfectly fine—if a little shocky—but in the middle of the latest group were two people wrapped in blankets being closely shepherded by paramedics.

"No," Eric said, shaking his head. "Oh, no, no, no, no. They weren't supposed to still be in the building. They were supposed to have run like hell. *We* did."

He moved away from the car—not quite running—toward the small group of evacuees.

"Sir? Sir?" A policewoman moved to block his way as Eric approached, her expression impersonally friendly.

"Those are my parents," Eric said flatly, silently daring the woman to try to move him. "Mom? Dad? Hey!"

The two elder Banyons were rumpled and disheveled, but their faces were serene. Far too serene, in fact. Though Fiona's makeup was mostly gone, and the remains were smeared across her eyes and cheeks in a messy blur, she looked uncannily youthful, as innocent and ageless as a nun. Beside her, her husband regarded the world with wide, all-accepting eyes.

They stopped and turned at the sound of Eric's voice, and regarded him attentively, but certainly without anything that could be considered either curiosity or emotion. After a moment, when he didn't say anything more, they turned away again and continued following the others.

Eric swallowed hard, stepping back. It wasn't hard to put together what had happened, though not all of the precise details. Somehow, after he and the others had left, Michael and Fiona Banyon had ended up in the Grey Room, and had met the fate that Prince Gabrevys had intended for him and Magnus.

"Are those your parents?" the officer asked, as if one or the other of them weren't quite sure.

"Yes," Eric said. It felt as if the words were coming from a very great distance. "Their names are Michael and Fiona Banyon. They live in Cambridge, Massachusetts. Michael Banyon teaches at Harvard. My name is Eric Banyon."

The officer made a note. "You're with Ria Llewellyn, aren't you? They're being taken over to the ACMC on Pacific. Why don't you check in there as soon as you get out of here and find out when you can take them home? And ... don't worry too much about they way they're acting. Shock can make people do a lot of funny things." The officer smiled—Eric knew she meant to be reassuring—and moved away, following the others.

Eric stood where he was, watching the evacuees loaded into the makeshift ambulance. He watched it drive off down the road, then turned and walked back to the car.

"They're being taken to the ACMC, whatever that is," he announced simply.

"The Atlantic City Medical Center," Ria said. "It's the largest hospital in the area. Everybody needing medical attention from this little party today is being seen there." She raised an eyebrow. "And if you don't start talking in full complete forthcoming sentences, I might have to do something painful to you."

"You remember I told you that Gabrevys had a bunch of Talent-eating nightmares that he was going to feed me and Magnus to?"

"I remember you promising me the full story about that at some point, yes," Ria said, with a bad imitation of patience.

Just at the moment, he didn't care if she was patient or impatient or waiting to smack him in the head with her Jimmy Choo. He felt as if he'd just been through an earthquake, as if the ground had dropped out from under him. "Well the particularly fun thing about these nightmares is that you didn't have to be a Bard or a Sidhe or a Talent for them to be able to eat you. They could eat anything similar, too. Creativity. Will. Imagination."

"Leaving behind the perfect piece of mindless cannon-fodder," Ria said, nodding. Her face lost that *give me the answers NOW* look, and she touched his shoulder for a moment. "And I take it that when you slipped through his fingers, Gabrevys substituted your nearest available relatives? Eric, my dear, I will not shed one tear for anything that has happened to those monsters. They brought it on themselves in the most literal way possible."

"But," Ace said softly, "nobody deserves to have something like that happen to them."

"Eric and Magnus certainly didn't," Ria agreed coolly. "But the people who tried to do it to them? Could be. Eric, unless you actually locked them up and fed them to the nasties yourself, unless you told them that room was a safe place to hide, or you somehow lured them in there, I'd have to say that this probably isn't something you can reasonably accept credit for—or blame. But that's between you and your shrink, of course."

"Sure," Eric said listlessly. He stared at the ground, but he didn't see it.

She was right. Anybody would say she was right. Oriana—his expensive and highly competent headshrinker—would say she was right.

But, dammit, in his heart he knew he'd been *supposed* to save them. He'd saved—or tried to save—a lot of people he didn't much like—like everybody here at this concert today, for example. It wasn't about picking and choosing who *deserved* saving. It was about saving everyone you could, because the bad guys didn't *deserve* to win.

"Eric," Magnus said, putting a hand on his arm. Magnus rarely touched anyone; Eric knew his brother was making a great effort. "You didn't do it to them. You didn't put them in there. *I* would have. You didn't. You rescued them. They were running the other way the last time any of us saw them. Why does it have to be your fault they're like that now and not the elf-guy's? I mean, *you* know. Bro. Quit making yourself out to be—thinking you've gotta be Spiderman—it's dumb. It's—"

"The concept you're groping for in vain—despite the very expensive education you're currently receiving—is 'hubris.' And for as long as I've known Eric, he's had plenty of that," Ria drawled mockingly, reaching out to ruffle Magnus's still-damp hair. "And now," she said, glancing around, "I think we can finally leave."

The evening news on every station—they watched it gathered together in Ria's apartment—was almost entirely about the cathedral and casino near-bombing. There were clips of Ace's statement—edited down to near-inscrutability—but she wasn't the lead sound-bite after all.

After they'd left the concert-site, a man named LeRoy LaPonte had climbed up onto the stage to deliver—until removed by police—a long disjointed statement about how he was the one who had set the bomb in the first place at the request of Gabriel Horn, who had intended the device to kill Billy Fairchild because Billy had sold out the glories of Christian Race Music to the evil minions of the New World Order as represented by government agent Parker Wheatley.

Gabriel Horn was still being sought for questioning.

Parker Wheatley was still in the hospital. No charges had yet been filed.

Eric Banyon would have found all this very interesting, but Eric wasn't among those watching the evening news. His news for

Misthold wouldn't wait, nor did he think it was anything he could put into an email. As soon as Ria's limousine had arrived in New York—with Lady Day pacing the vehicle with gleeful ease—he'd changed to riding leathers and headed for the Everforest Gate.

It had been less than two weeks—World's Time—since the last time he'd ridden up to the gates of Elfhame Misthold. Then he'd been expected. Then, he'd been facing nothing more than an uncomplicated—if possibly dangerous  diplomatic journey to an Unseleighe Domain.

Now . . . well . . . he wasn't quite sure whether the news he was bringing Prince Arvin would change things, or not.

Though they weren't expecting him this time, they certainly knew he was on his way long before he got there. For all Eric knew, Lady Day had phoned ahead; he was never completely certain of the capabilities of the elvensteeds.

At any rate, Kory was waiting for him at the gate.

"There is bad news, Bard?" Kory asked anxiously.

"There is . . . complicated news," Eric said, dismounting. "But everybody's fine." *Except, of course, for my parents.* He hadn't even begun to think of what he was going to do about them. Hell. He couldn't even begin to think how he was supposed to feel about them.

"Complicated it must be," Kory agreed. "Prince Arvin's news is 'complicated' as well—I have written to you, but perhaps you have not received the letter?"

Eric groaned faintly. "I haven't been home in . . . a couple of days, I think. Except to change clothes. So if it's something you sent recently . . ."

"Very recently. But since you have come in person, Prince Arvin may tell you of this news himself."

Kory led Eric through the Misthold forest to a clearing. Chairs and tables had been set out, and Prince Arvin and the Lady Rionne were playing chess as several members of the court stood and watched.

The chess set was silver and black, and every single figure was unique. Eric didn't *quite* think that the whole scene had been set up for his benefit—though he wouldn't quite put that past the Sidhe—but he had to admit there was something incredibly symbolic about seeing two Sidhe, one of the Bright Court and one of the Dark, sitting in a faery glen playing chess.

Though they were probably just playing chess because they liked playing chess.

*Sometimes a cigar is just a cigar.*

"Sieur Eric," Arvin said, without looking up. "You were not expected, but you are always welcome, of course. . . ."

"But I come bringing trouble," Eric said in a low voice as he knelt. "Or at least, a problem."

"I shall match your problem with mine, then," Arvin said lightly, at last looking up with a smile. "And we shall see whose is more entertaining. Come, sit, and tell us what brings you to Misthold with such unseemly quickness. *Two* visits in a fortnight! We will become quite used to your presence once more."

A chair was brought for Eric and set beside Arvin, and he sat to watch the chess game.

"Prince Korendil told me that he'd written me about new developments here, but I haven't received the letter yet," Eric said cautiously, playing for time.

Arvin glanced toward Rionne. She sighed, shaking her head.

"You know well, Bard Eric, that by law and custom, Prince Gabrevys must be allowed visitation of his son and heir, yet it is equally so that such a visit must be arranged in advance, lest . . . misunderstandings occur. And who else may arrange such things, passing freely from Unseleighe Lands to these, save Prince Gabrevys's Bard, in whom he reposes all faith and surety?"

"Ri-i-i-ght. . . ." Eric said. *Ask a Sidhe the time and learn how to build a wristwatch.* But Rionne had very formal manners—or maybe that was just the way they'd done things in Bete Noir.

"Yet, Prince Gabrevys having no Bard, how can such a visit be arranged?" she finished.

It didn't seem to be a rhetorical question.

"What? Jormin's dead?" Eric looked from Prince Arvin to Lady Rionne in appalled confusion. He'd seen Wheatley shoot Jormin, but he hadn't thought the Bard was that badly hurt. . . .

*And for a Sidhe to die . . .*

"Now why should that venomous serpent be dead?" Rionne asked with interest.

"We have heard—and the Lady Rionne confirms—that Jormin ap Galever has sought Sanctuary at Elfhame Ombrehold," Arvin said. "Renouncing his allegiance to Elfhame Bete Noir and his former master. But it seems you know more."

"I saw him shot," Eric said, very slowly, and choosing his words with care. "With a weapon that fires darts of Cold Iron. By someone who knew him for what he was and wanted to take him prisoner. He and three of his followers managed to escape, but I didn't see where they went."

"Saw him shot?" Dharniel demanded. "In the World Above?"

*No, in the back; it hurts a lot more . . .*

"Yes," Eric said. "It's a long story. . . ."

Arvin raised a hand, and without haste, those watching the chess match discovered business that would take them elsewhere. Within moments, only Dharniel, Kory, and Rionne remained.

Rionne stood to go. Again Arvin raised his hand.

"Stay if you would, Lady. For it is in my mind that what touches upon Prince Gabrevys's Bard is a matter that speaks to your Task, at the end of things. And perhaps there is that which you could add to my Bard's tale, for lately you have had a privy message from Elfhame Bete Noir, have you not?"

"Privy," Eric recalled from his years on the Faire-circuit, meant "private." Apparently Lady Rionne had been conducting a clandestine correspondence with her home Domain.

Rionne smiled, and her smile was like the slash of a sword blade. "You are nearly as careful as I would be in your place, Prince Arvin. Myself, had I detected the messenger, I would have killed him rather than letting him complete his errand."

"To each his own way, Lady," Prince Arvin said easily, inclining his head. "I had hoped by such clemency to induce you to share the message's contents."

Rionne shrugged. "It is of little matter to you—or great. I cannot say. My steward wrote to tell me I am now landless. The wards and seals upon Prince Gabrevys's Domain have been loosed, and all that he has wrested from the Chaos Lands returns to it. Not at once, perhaps, but certainly at last. So he—and certainly all those of Bete Noir-that-was—will go elsewhere, if they have not already. Few of us are strong enough to hold our lands against the Chaos by will alone. Fewer still would care to."

She spoke so calmly, as if she were discussing the weather—assuming there *was* weather Underhill—that it took Eric a moment to make sense of her words.

Elfhame Bete Noir was dissolving back into the Chaos Lands from which it had come.

Every Domain had an anchor, something that allowed it to keep its form against the encroachments of the Chaos Lands. The Seleighe Domains drew their power from the Node Groves, but the Unseleighe Elfhames didn't have the same power to draw on. When he'd first ridden into Elfhame Bete Noir, Eric had wondered what forces gave the place its solidity and form.

He guessed now he knew what it was.

"He's . . . Prince Gabrevys is dead?" Eric asked.

"Or has decided to renounce the rulership of his Domain for some other reason," Prince Arvin said. "It is true that there are some. If he were found unfit to rule. If he were Challenged and lost. If he were maimed—for then, by the Law of Danu, he could not rule. If he lost his magick—"

"'Lost his magick'?" Eric echoed. "Wouldn't he be, uh, *dead*?" A creature of magick without magick was a lot worse off than a day without sunshine.

Dharniel smiled wolfishly. "One can have enough magick to live, but not enough to enforce one's will, young Banyon, and should he be in such wise, he could no longer hold the Borders of his Domain. But come! You were about to tell us all you know of Gabrevys and what he has been doing in the World Above."

Eric took a deep breath and organized his thoughts in light of this new information. Jormin fled. Gabrevys was dead—or at the very least, no longer the Prince of Elfhame Bete Noir. Elfhame Bete Noir was itself dissolving away into Chaos once more. "When I saw Prince Gabrevys last night, he was very much in health. . . ." he began.

The tale took a long time to tell, involving as it did Ria's guesses and Ace's guesses about Gabrevys's activities over the last few years. Some of the details of Gabrevys's activities for the Fairchild Ministry—as well as what he'd actually wanted with it in the first place beyond Ace's Talent—they didn't know and might never know. But on the central part of his tale Eric was quite clear: Gabrevys had done his best to find a legal (in elven terms) way to destroy Eric, and in the process had been willing to kill Magnus, Hosea, and—just incidentally—thousands of innocent people.

Dharniel sighed, shaking his head at Eric's obtuseness. "And does it come as a surprise to ye, young Banyon, that an Unseleighe Prince would bathe in mortal blood to get his own way? Be thankful that some follower of his slipped the silver dagger into his back, or that the Morrigan became displeased with his excesses, or whatever transpired to take him from the field of battle occurred before ye were called upon to face him in truth. Perhaps it was even the High King, moving in secret. Oberon's anger usually burns too hot for that—but his Queen might move him to something more discreet."

"It's sad and disturbing news, certainly," Prince Arvin said carefully, with a glance at his guest. "For the human lives destroyed, for the fact that we do not truly know what has happened to Prince Gabrevys, and for the fact that it makes Prince Jachiel's future so much more uncertain."

This time Rionne actually laughed out loud.

"Uncertain? When a Domain he never wished to rule has been put where it and its folk can trouble him no longer and Gabrevys can no longer compel him as liege as well as father? You have an odd way of seeing the world, Prince Arvin."

*I suppose when you consider it that way....* Eric thought.

"And if Gabrevys no longer has an Elfhame at his beck, that makes everything simple, law or no law," Dharniel said, with what passed—in him—for cheer. "The next time I see him, I'll have the head from his shoulders for what he tried to do to my student. To destroy such a gift is worse than a crime—it is wicked."

"What of you, Eric?" Prince Arvin said. "If anyone has first right of satisfaction against Gabrevys, it is you."

Ria's words came back to him again. *"And what is* Magnus *going to do if Gabriel levin-bolts you in the back?"*

No.

He'd fight Gabrevys if he absolutely had to—for Magnus's life, or the lives of his friends, or to stop some greater evil. But he had dependents now, and that meant he had to choose his battles carefully.

"Let the Sidhe tend to the matters of the Sidhe. I have other things to do," Eric said simply. "And they're a lot more important than revenge."

The next day, Eric stood in a waiting room in the Atlantic City Medical Center. He'd come alone, riding Lady Day.

He'd promised Magnus that he could come next time, but there wasn't much point to his coming this time. Today Eric was just going to play out the charade of pretending he didn't know what had happened to his parents or what was wrong with them. Then, after a battery of tests that would turn up nothing, he could do what any concerned American offspring would do—sue the hell out of Fairchild Ministries, Inc., while making sure that Michael Banyon's expensive disability insurance kicked in, because he was fairly sure that his father would never be able to go back to teaching again.

In fact, he was pretty sure that neither of his parents would be able to be left unsupervised again, for the rest of their lives. He had the impression that watching cartoons was going to be the most exacting task they could manage, and even then, their attention span probably wouldn't hold past the first commercial break.

He supposed he ought to be down the hall, in his parents' room, playing the concerned son, but he couldn't quite manage that. He'd looked in, and what he'd seen had sent him down here to the waiting room.

They'd been lying on their backs in their beds, staring up at the ceiling. Eric was sure they'd continue to lie there, in exactly that position, unmoving, until somebody came and told them to do something.

If the room had been empty in truth, or if there had been two corpses lying in the two hospital beds instead of the two ravaged people, the room would have felt less empty than it did. Whatever had happened to them in the Grey Room, it looked as if it had been far more . . . thorough . . . than what had been done to Devon Mesier.

Perhaps they would recover some of their autonomy with time, but they'd certainly never be able to resume their old lives.

They were not moving in with him, though. In fact, they were not even going to be living in New York State. It had taken Anita Sheldrake about fifteen minutes to discover the perfect place—the perfect *expensive* place—in Massachusetts. Fall River Assisted Living Complex had everything on its grounds from a full-scale sanatorium, to condominiums, to rustic little cottages, and best of all, so Ria told him, it specialized in imaginary diseases of the rich. His parents would be very well cared for there.

He'd have to put the Cambridge house on the market, but of course neither he nor Magnus wanted it. And its sale would defer some of the immediate costs of the move.

But although Eric already knew what the future held, for today, he had to behave as if he didn't. He couldn't exactly tell the attending physician that the reason for his parents' condition was because a Sidhe Lord's personal nightmares had gotten at them and eaten up everything that made them human. . . .

"Mr. Banyon?"

Eric looked up.

A woman in hospital whites was regarding him with faint trepidation, as if he were about to do something overdramatic. "I'm Dr. Turin. I'm the attending physician on your parents' case. I know you'd like to take them home, but we'd really prefer to keep them for a few more days. Now, physically, they're in fairly good shape, considering their ordeal, but we'd just like to run a few more tests. . . ."

One week after the last time they had appeared in Judge Springsteen's courtroom, Ace and her father met there again.

This time, the circumstances were slightly different.

Sound-trucks filled the streets outside the courthouse, with all the major networks wanting an interview, a sound-bite, or even just footage of the players in the current hot story. The corridors of the courthouse were filled with reporters trying to cover what had become—despite all of Ria's attempts to prevent it—a huge media event. While criminal charges had not yet been filed against the Reverend Billy Fairchild for the events at the Pure Blood concert, it was only a matter of time, and the mysterious disappearance of both the members of Pure Blood and of Gabriel Horn did nothing to quiet things down. The few copies of the band's debut CD that had reached the market were selling and re-selling for fabulous prices, and if lawsuits had not kept their videos from being aired, the now-vanished band would have achieved all the prominence its label could have hoped for. As it was, it was fast becoming a legend.

Ace had already made a detailed statement to federal prosecutors about what she'd seen and heard that night in Billy's office. In the end, an explanation for her illicit presence in Billy's office hadn't been that hard to come up with: she'd been looking for something to make him withdraw his opposition to her Emancipated Minor petition. That was even the truth, in a way.

In exchange for her free cooperation, no charges would be filed against her, though technically of course, she hadn't been trespassing at all. She was, after all, Billy's daughter, not yet an Emancipated Minor and so a dependent member of his family still. She had every right to be there.

But despite—or perhaps because of—all the turmoil and publicity of the last several days, neither Billy Fairchild nor anyone else in his organization had quite gotten around to doing anything about the petition and countersuit that was still wending its way along in the Ocean County docket.

Judge Springsteen was a woman of discretion, and had no appreciation for having her courtroom turned into a three-ring circus. She'd managed to bar the press from the courtroom itself, though there was little she could do to keep them out of the building, and nothing she could do to keep them off the street outside.

This time Ria had accompanied Ace and Derek Tilford to the hearing. There was no longer any point to staying away, after all, not with her connection to Billy Fairchild's daughter being front-page news across the tri-state area. The three of them entered the courthouse through the back entrance, moving quickly, and were conducted by a pair of rather harassed-looking bailiffs to a secure waiting room.

"Are you sure you want to go through with this, Ace?" Ria asked again. "After everything that's happened, it's almost certain that the judge will rule in your favor."

"But not a hundred percent," Ace said grimly. "Even with Gabriel Horn—or whatever he called himself—gone. So . . . yes. I want to talk to them before the hearing."

"I'll go speak to opposing counsel," Derek Tilford said, going to the door.

Even now the man was playing to the gallery, Ria thought irritably. As the three of them waited in the empty courtroom—just about the only place in the building where they could be guaranteed a chance for Ace to speak to her parents without either interruption or eavesdropping—Ria could hear Billy Fairchild in the corridor outside, giving an impromptu press conference.

Her hearing was quite good. The subject was, as always, Billy himself: his unjust persecution, his many enemies, his good works, and the certainty the Lord was on his side. For a preacher, he surely spoke the word "I" a lot more than he spoke the word "He."

*The Lord might be with him, but the IRS is a different matter,* Ria thought with grim amusement. Without Gabriel Horn's Unseleighe *glamourie* to smooth the way—and his Underhill wealth to jump-start Billy's various programs—the many weak points in the Fairchild Ministries house of cards would soon be exposed. The civil suits being brought against Fairchild Ministries as a result of the Pure Blood concert were only the tip of the iceberg. Ria had friends in low places, and after she'd gotten the full story from Eric and Magnus about Christian Family Intervention and the Soul-eaters, she'd dropped a few words in the right ears. Once people started checking into the kids who'd come through that program—Devon Mesier for one—and took a really good look at them, there wasn't going to be any pit deep enough for Billy to hide in.

Then there was the question of where all that money had come from and gone to. Ria wasn't the only one to whom it had occurred that the two best places for money-laundering were a church and a casino, and here had been both, under the same roof.

And the IRS was looking into the legality of combining a church and a casino in the first place. Bingo was one thing . . .

All that, *before* the business of setting a bomb on his own property to kill hundreds, if not thousands, of people kicked in.

At last the doors opened, and the senior Fairchilds entered the courtroom. This time Billy Fairchild had an entire legal team with him—not that *that* would do him any good, Ria thought cynically.

And this time Donna Fairchild had accompanied her husband.

Billy's wife looked very much as her fans would have expected her to look, a combination of folksy and very "done." Her hairdo was elaborate, her makeup was emphatic without being vulgar, and her "ladies who lunch" suit managed to combine plaid, ruffles, and tweed and was just—barely—on the side of good taste. It was modest, though, as modest as a Mennonite, high-necked, with a skirt well below the knee. She wore low-heeled "sensible" shoes.

Ria priced the string of demure pearls around her throat at the cost of a new Mercedes.

She gazed around the courtroom, obviously looking for her daughter, and when she finally saw Ace, she looked horrified. She would have run forward then, but Billy's hand on her arm kept her beside him. In her place, like a good Christian wife.

The two of them reached the front of the courtroom.

Ace stepped forward.

"Mama. Daddy."

For once in his life, Billy Fairchild didn't try to bluster.

"I'm in a power of trouble, Heavenly Grace," he said simply.

"I know, Daddy," Ace said. "You did a lot of bad things. And there's not one thing I can do about what's going to happen now. I won't lie for you. And I'm telling you now, when that judge comes in today, you have to tell her that you're withdrawing your objection to my petition. Both of you have to tell her that."

"Honeylamb—" Donna began. Billy silenced her with a look.

"Now Heavenly Grace . . ." Billy began, and now the wheedling note was back in his voice.

"You have to do that," Ace said softly. "Or I promise you, I will be appearing on every talk show that's asked me. *Every. Single. One.* If it takes me every day for the next year to do it. And I will answer all their questions, and I expect the answers won't please you. I'm going back to New York with Ms. Llewellyn, and you're going not going to stop me."

"Billy," Donna said, turning to her husband as if she could no longer bear the sight of her daughter. "Don't you think . . . ? I mean, Grace can take care of herself. She's always been such a *sensible* girl, truly she has. And you know how those report-ers twist things." She looked from Ace to Billy, obviously more distraught over making a scene than over what was actually happening. "It's only temporary," she added meaninglessly. "And maybe when that nice Mr. Horn gets back from that business trip you sent him on we can all sit down together and talk things out."

"You'd rather go off with *strangers*?" her Daddy asked her, as if he were hearing her for the very first time.

The question made Ace want to laugh aloud—or burst into tears—or both. It was he and Mama who were the strangers, and had been for as long as she could remember. And things wouldn't be better now that Gabriel Horn was gone—and he wasn't coming back, no matter what Daddy'd told Mama. From what Ria had pieced together, Fairchild Ministries was in a real mess right now, and things were only going to get worse. Daddy would want her to go right back to using her Gift in that ugly way he'd always made her use it, just to make him money and get him out of his trouble. No matter who it hurt.

"Yes," Ace said evenly. "I'd rather go off with strangers, than live one hour in your house. *'Better a dinner of herbs where love is, than a stalled ox, and hatred therewithin.'*"

Billy's face hardened—as hard as his heart had surely become. And the only reason she didn't cry right there and then was because she had cried up all her tears for him a long time ago. "Then go," Billy Fairchild harshly. "And burn in Hell with the rest of the sinners."

The actual legal proceedings were over quickly once the court convened. Billy and Donna Fairchild withdrew their opposition to the petition for the grant of Emancipated Minor status for Heavenly Grace Fairchild. Judge Andrea Springsteen granted the uncontested petition, which would become final in ninety days.

"I *will* make him regret that," Ria said, as they drove back toward New York. It was almost an hour later; Ria had considered it diplomatic to give the media its pound of flesh, and a carefully tailored sound-bite. It had been scripted and rehearsed in advance, of course; spontaneity was always much better when it was planned.

"Condemning me to Hell? Ria, he does that to most of America five nights a week," Ace said evenly. "Or did. I would rather be in that hell than his heaven."

"And I disapprove of that, too," Ria said, her tone lightening slightly. "But since it looks like he'll be losing his bully pulpit—along with most of his fortune—maybe I won't have to keep him on my 'To Do' list after all."

Ace licked her lips. "Don't think I'm feeling guilty," she said, finally. "'Cause I'm not. Did you ever read *The Last Battle*?"

Ria looked puzzled. "No. History?"

"Fantasy," Ace replied. "Or some people would call it that. It's supposed to be a kid's book. By a friend of Mr. Tolkien—C.S. Lewis. In the end of it—well, there's these folk that are the good people, with the Lion Aslan, that's supposed to be like Jesus, and there are some folk that are the bad people, with this devil-thing called Tash. Except it isn't that simple, and there are some good people who are on the side of Tash because they're ignorant, but they keep doing good, not bad. And in the end of the book, there's this little boy, with the Tash people, and he realizes that the last battle is over and he's being let into Heaven with the Aslan people. And he asks why, since he was with Tash."

She looked expectantly at Ria, who had an eyebrow raised. "So? What was he told?"

"That even if you did something in the name of Tash that was good, you were still doing it for Aslan," she replied, slowly. "And even if you did something in the name of Aslan that was evil, you were still doing it for Tash." Then she shrugged. "I think—I think I know who Daddy was really doing what he did for. Besides himself."

Ria raised an eyebrow. "Rather sophisticated for a children's book. But I would have to say that your father was definitely on the side of—Tash."

"I guess it's all sorted out then," Ace said slowly, still sounding faintly sandbagged by it all. "I got what I wanted. Eric's parents aren't going to try to take Magnus away from him any more. And Jaycie is—I guess—safe."

Ria shrugged. "As safe as things get in Underhill. And even though I doubt anyone would want to suggest such a thing to Eric, I suspect that in their current condition, his parents are happier than they've been in years. God moves in mysterious ways."

"Ria!" Ace said, sounding scandalized.

"Even the devil may quote scripture to her own purposes," Ria Llewellyn answered serenely. "And my happiness would be complete if I knew *exactly* what had happened to Prince Gabrevys. . . ."

# EPILOGUE:
## DON'T LOOK BACK

His prison was by the sea—or what passed for the sea here in Underhill. He knew that much, though he knew little more. There were many Domains, many oceans.

As Gabrevys ap Ganeliel had many enemies.

Death . . . oh, death would have been kinder, but the Unseleighe were not a kindly folk. Not while there was advantage to be gained in keeping a fallen foe alive.

It was Toirealach who had found him—Wheatley knew much about their kind, but not that they could summon aid, mind-to-mind, even when bound with steel and iron—but by then it was too late.

The steel mesh that entrapped him had eaten its way into his face, marring his Unseleighe beauty past the skill of all but the greatest Elven Healer—and worse.

He was blind.

Toirealach—a loyal liegeman, then—had brought him through the Everforest Gate, hoping the power of his own Domain would Heal him. But Gabrevys was marred past all Healing, and none who was maimed in body could rule, by Danu's ancient law. The moment Toirealach had brought him through the Gate to his own Domain, his mutilation had shattered the magicks which held Bete Noir apart from the Chaos Lands.

Had Gabrevys been conscious at the time, he would have prevented Toirealach from doing what he had done. It would have made no difference to the fate of Elfhame Bete Noir in the end, but it would have bought him time. Perhaps that would have made a difference to his own fate.

For the moment the wards had shattered, Toirealach had realized the truth.

Gabrevys was Prince no longer.

And Toirealach was still Unseleighe.

There was profit to be made in delivering Gabrevys—powerless, now—to his enemies. It was a profit Jormin was too proud to share in—the injured Bard had come home as well, and, finding himself masterless, had simply taken his own personal followers and left to seek a new Court.

And so might Toirealach have done. But Toirealach had seen opportunity. He had always been one of the strongest of Gabrevys's vassals. It had taken all his strength, and that of those whose temporary self-interest he could compel, to retain Gabrevys against the others of this now-decaying Domain who sought to claim the prize for themselves.

Gabrevys, conscious by then, had fought as hard as he could against this treason, but the destruction of his Domain had taken much of his power with it, so closely had he bound himself to his Domain. And scarred as he was by Wheatley's bindings, he could no longer summon the spells of a Magus Major.

And so he had been bound again, though this time with silver instead of iron, and carried from his crumbling Domain—his no longer!—into an unknown realm by Toirealach and those who now followed him.

And there, he had been sold.

No one had spoken their names in his presence—for even as he was now, to know the names of his enemy was to hold power of a sort—and so Gabrevys did not know who they were. But they used him as he would have used them, should their situations have been reversed. He would not die, but he would have little cause to enjoy his life, either.

He drew small comfort from the knowledge that Toirealach had not survived to savor the fruits of his treason. The first secret Gabrevys had been forced to surrender at the bidding of those who held him was that of calling the Soul-eaters from their pocket Domain and controlling them when they fed, and Gabrevys had listened as Toirealach and all who had accompanied him were given to them, one by one.

Now only he remained. And all who knew where he was and that he yet lived were dead.

And he would live a very long time. . . .

Eric would not have called it a "small" bright spot in his day—it was certainly bright, but it was *not* small. It was also very, very, pink. Barbie pink. Bubblegum pink.

Pink as only 1950s pink could be.

Ria had not called in help for the problem of finding a way to keep Margot from killing him and Hosea over the destruction of her car.

Kory had.

"Help" had come from Elfhame Fairgrove, and had arrived in the person of a tousle-haired man with a deceptively young face and a pronounced limp. "Deceptively," because when you looked closely, and you saw the crinkling of laugh-lines around his eyes, you realized that he dressed like someone out of the eighties in his "Battlestar Galactica" field-jacket, not because he was being "retro" but because this was his favorite jacket, acquired new, and lovingly cared for. And he was not nearly as young as he first looked.

Eric had first met Tannim Drake a few years before, when Chinthliss the dragon, to whom he had gone for aid in his battle against Aerune, had rescued him and his companions from its aftermath. Chinthliss had called Tannim his son; something Eric had never gotten a real explanation of. He did know that Tannim was a test driver for Elfhame Fairgrove, which was turning out to be more than handy.

"Help" had advised telling Margot that he'd had an accident, but that Big Pink was being restored to pristine perfection at the hands of the automotive wizards of Fairgrove Industries. "Help" had given him a series of photos and a contact phone number for Margot to call to prove it—and the keys to a loaner for Margot, a red-and-white 1967 Corvette, which was a car she had coveted so much the first time she laid eyes on it that she forgot to be mad at either him or Hosea.

And now, almost six weeks later, "help" had turned up again, with—to all intents and purposes—Big Pink. A new, and substantially improved Big Pink.

"All I can say is," said Tannim, "I, for one, am really, really happy that she told us she's a big fan of *Rides*."

Eric blinked. "Who?"

Tannim laughed, and tossed the keys in the air and caught them again. "Show on the Discovery Channel. Doesn't matter, except that it means she won't be mad that this isn't exactly her original car. In fact, she'll probably be all over the improvements and won't notice that the only thing that matches is the VIN number."

Eric could certainly understand that. He'd taken a look inside. The sound system alone must be worth—well, probably more than the original Big Pink. But he was still puzzled. "I thought Kory said you could restore the car. . . ."

Tannim shook his head, and a curl of black hair fell into one eye. He brushed it back, before he began to look *too* much like a Japanese anime hero. "Nuh-uh. Cold Iron, my friend, which Keighvin Silverhair and his merry band cannot touch nor ken, and don't go borrowing this beast again and trusting her to keep you sheltered from Unseleighe. She's all-aluminum now. They weren't going to make her fiberglass, because your Margot would certainly have noticed that, so aluminum is what you got. Even the engine block. All we did with the original was to use her carcass to Far-See into the past to find out what she'd actually looked like, then take her VIN and consign her to the honorable grave of a warrior." He laughed a little. "Of course, your friend Margot will probably notice a substantial improvement in the gas mileage now, given how much lighter she is. But—"

But at just that moment, Margot shot out of the door of Guardian House with a squeal of glee, and whatever else Tannim Drake might have said on the subject was forgotten. And by the time Margot stopped dancing around the car and Eric thought to ask him to continue the sentence, the auto-mage was gone . . . like the Lone Ranger, into the sunset.

Now it was June, and the New York weather had finally become seasonable. Columbia's course year had ended a few weeks before, and this coming fall, Grace Fairchild (Ace intended to change her name legally as soon as possible) would be joining Kayla there as a freshman.

Donna Fairchild had moved back to Tulsa, Oklahoma, leaving her husband to weather the escalating storm of lawsuits, controversy, and criminal charges on his own. The Fairchild Business Park—and the Casino and Cathedral of Prayer—had been shut down, and would undoubtedly be sold to help defray Billy's swiftly mounting debts and legal expenses.

But Ace had decided exactly what *she* wanted to do.

"I," she announced to Ria, "am going to help you run the Llewellyn Foundation."

At Ria's astonished and utterly speechless stare, Ace had blushed and dropped her eyes. "Not *run,* run, or at least not at first," she had stammered, flushing. "But I'm going to get a business degree *and* a minor in psychology, and I'll be the assistant for whoever you put in charge of the school, and I can do it, Ria, I want to! You said yourself even thinking about trying to run it makes you crazy! And if you've got me there, you'll have someone telling you what you need to hear about all the time, and—"

"All right!" Ria said finally, laughing, and holding up her hands to stop the torrent of words. "All right! You win! I was going to ask Inigo Moonlight—but I knew he wouldn't want to do it for very long. Well, 'long' as the Sidhe see it. But if you want to take the whole thing on—"

"Yes." Ace set her chin. "I do."

Ria just shook her head. "All right. I'll put Moonlight in charge, with you as his apprentice. You are hereby in training to become

Professor X, does that suit you? Just do me a favor and don't do anything that puts you in a wheelchair or makes you go bald ... it's a good look on Patrick Stewart, but not on you."

Parker Wheatley's contribution to the entire concert-slash-bomb affair had dropped off the media radar after a few news cycles, but Ria's Washington contacts reported that his former colleagues and employers were extremely unhappy with him. She was fairly certain that this time they would arrange matters so that he led a very quiet life, assuming he managed to escape prison on some charge or other—though as far as she knew, he'd had nothing to do with the bomb plot at all. The rest of his anti-Sidhe technology cache—green suits, sunglasses, fancy wristwatches—had all vanished before anyone else in the government could get their hands on them. Ria had thought that was best.

Without Eric's parents to interfere, his adoption of his brother— now, legally, his son—had gone through without any further hitches, and Michael and Fiona Banyon were comfortably installed at Fall River. The only family-related problem that Eric currently had was what to do with Magnus during the summer vacation. Next year would be Magnus's last year at Coenties & Arundel, and Magnus would have to start looking into colleges. Or else find a permanent drumming gig. . . .

But then Magnus himself came up with an answer.

Magnus would be going back to Boston. To school. But not just any school.

Magnus was going—and he was grimly determined about this—to Berklee College of Music.

"Look at this, bro!" he said, dragging Eric over to the computer, where he had the Berklee site pulled up, pointing to a course called "Making Music With a Garage Band." "These people live in the *real* world! They're into music real people listen to! They've got a network to get gigs, they teach how to be a road-manager, or a session-musician, or a film-score writer, you come out of there knowing what's *what*!"

Looking over the curriculum, Eric had to agree. Berklee certainly sent its graduates out into the world with a much better preparation for life as a commercial musician than did—say—Juilliard. Mind, anyone with a Bard's abilities was never going to starve, but—

But it looked as if, when you walked out of Berklee, you had all the tools you needed to make a living, and if you couldn't, it sure wasn't for lack of instruction.

So, when this last year was over, Magnus would be going to Boston's Back Bay, and Eric would be an empty nester.

Unless, of course, something happened between then and now. . . .

Hosea's article about Fairchild Ministries and the concert had been the cover story for *Rolling Stone.* Suddenly, as a writer, Hosea was very high on the radar. Before the summer was half gone, it was clear that his days as a busker were over.

Not that he minded, though for old-time's sake, he did keep his license current. But it was soon clear to him that writing for a living had a lot of advantages. Air conditioning, for one. Regular hours, for another. A much, much bigger potential audience.

And the fact that, as a Guardian, writing for a living had a lot of advantages too. Because he could drop what he was doing at a moment's notice—and as another Guardian who had once lived in this very building had learned, a writer could do his (or her) job from virtually anywhere and *still* save the universe, one small bit at a time.

So all in all, it was beginning to look as if every member of Eric's immediate circle was going to be able to settle down and actually *plan* their lives with a reasonable expectation that those plans would be carried out.

It was a strange feeling. But one that Eric thought he just might be able to get used to.

"Cake!" Magnus greeted its arrival as if he'd never been fed in his life.

"There's plenty for everyone," Ace said, setting it down in the middle of the table.

The six of them—Eric, Magnus, Hosea, Kayla, Ria, and Ace— were gathered at Ria's townhouse. Tonight was a celebration.

Today Ace's final papers had come. In the eyes of the State of New Jersey, she was legally an adult.

"What's the candle for?" Magnus said.

"It's because today is the first day of the rest of her life," Kayla told him. "Yum. Chocolate."

"I'm just as glad to have put the last few months behind us," Ria said, when the cake had been cut and served. "There's something to be said for a nice, old-fashioned monster. At least that way, you can knock it over the head and know when you're finished dealing with it."

Eric shuddered feelingly. "Monsters—or complicated political plots. I think I'm getting too old for either one of them."

Magnus snickered around a large mouthful of cake.

"They do tend to trouble a body's rest," Hosea agreed. "And get in the way o' the important things in life. How are yore students comin' on?"

For a while the friends spoke of the everyday matters in their lives. Many of Eric's students (most of the paying ones, in fact) were going to be away for the summer, but that left Eric free to concentrate on his *pro bono* clients. Hosea's feature article had attracted a lot of attention, and the *New Yorker* had asked him for a think-piece on "The neighborhood as a village." Kayla was going to be going home in a couple of weeks to spend the summer with Elizabet, and looked forward to visiting old haunts—though with the time-slip, she'd have to be careful that she didn't run into anyone who remembered Elizabet's foster daughter, who should now be much older than Kayla was.

*Just normal life,* Eric thought, looking around the table at his family and closest friends. *As normal as it gets. And it feels good.*

*After all we've been through, I think we deserve this.*

"Well, heck," Hosea said, looking around the table with a smile. "Ain't we the family. Ah reckon we're 'bout due for some peace and quiet. So here's to it."

"You said it, Too-Tall." Kayla grinned, and raised her glass. "To *un*interesting times, and lots of them, and plenty of time for our very own lives!"

"Amen," Ace said with feeling.

"Ditto. As long as there's cake," Magnus added, clinking his glass with the rest.

Eric added his glass to the rest. *Uninteresting times. Peace and quiet. Nothing more stressful than nagging Magnus to clean his room. Time to heal. Maybe*—he glanced at Ria—*time for something else, too. I can get behind that.*

"Works for me," he told them all, and with a pleasant shock, caught Ria looking back at him with a soft expression in her eyes that he almost didn't recognize. "Yeah!" he added, with more enthusiasm, speaking directly to her this time. "I can really get behind that!"

*Things are looking up . . . definitely.*

He let his smile creep into his eyes, and saw, with pleasure, the faintest hint of a flush on Ria's cheeks. So, Ms. Overachiever was finally willing to take a little Her-time, hmm? And maybe they were finally going to sort something out. That would be good. Very good.

*So, maybe the times won't exactly be uninteresting . . . and I can get behind that, too.*

He ate a bite of cake, and smiled.